Found in Corfu

Francesca Catlow

Gaia
Fenrir

Published in 2023 by Gaia & Fenrir Publishing

First edition

ISBN: 978-1-915208-27-9 (paperback)
ISBN 978-1-915208-28-6 (ebook)

British Library Cataloguing in Publication Data A CIP catalogue record
for this book is available from the British Library.

For anyone who has found a family outside of their DNA.

Acknowledgements

I would like to thank everyone who replied to my questions in the Kassiopi Facebook groups!! I really enjoyed visiting this part of Corfu to do my research, but there's always something someone else knows that I don't. The generosity of information was so helpful. Thank you all!

I would like to thank my editor. This manuscript gave us a lot to think about! As always, I'm so grateful for the time and effort you put into fact checking to keep me thinking about what could be possible.

I also want to acknowledge my mum, who got a headache going through all the details of this manuscript and has read it at least four times more than I have! Thank you for always taking the time to talk through every idea.

Finally, thank you to Gemma for taking the time to give your feedback. I'll *try* to be more organised in the future (no promises!!).

Part 1 - 2021

Chapter 1

The bathroom floor chats away to me as I pace, squeaking and moaning in response to my every move. A moment to be alone in this house can be rare, because if Mama was home, she would probably knock on the door asking what all the squeaking was about.

I face the test packet on the sink.

'Get it done.' I exhale the words to silence the floorboards before descending to the test.

Shaking my fingers out first, I pick up the instructions and read them carefully for the third time, desperately trying to consume the information like it's hiding a more tricky truth. It's not exactly advanced maths. In fact, it might be the easiest test to take.

I pick up the cup and do my best to fill it, but I dribble some just as I hear Mama calling up the stairs. Home early. She's never home this early when she's been to see Theía Agatha.

'*Kalimera*! Dora, are you home?'

I stutter a reply and manage to catch my chin, smudging my lip gloss across the back of my hand.

'Calm down,' I quietly chant to the floorboards.

There's no reason not to call back calmly, explaining I'm in the bathroom. There's nothing strange about it. It's not as though she has reason to question why I'm going to the toilet.

I scrub at my hands under the tap, but the gloss is so sticky, and looks like a shimmery slug has been across the back of one.

Come on Dora, you're eighteen, not eight. Calm down!

The sound of Mama's feet trotting up the stairs is enough to make my chest feel tight. In my haste, my fingers fumble over the papers, instructions and such, as I attempt to thrust everything back in the envelope they came out of. I do up lids and wash away evidence as best I can. A sheet of paper tumbles to the floor before I manage to scoop it up and push it back into its packet.

I glance around the room, clutching the packet to my chest, spinning one way then the next. Where the hell am I going to put it?

Mama's tight fist descends on the door. Three sharp knocks. *Thud, thud, thud.*

'Theadora mou, are you in there?'

'Yes, one moment, Mama.'

I tug off the lid to the clothing hamper, hesitating over it before dropping the packet in. There's nowhere else to hide it, not that I can see. There's nothing else that can be done. I close the white wicker lid and make my way to the door.

Exhaling and shaking off my tension, I pull open the door. Mama is right there, yet she looks almost surprised to see me as I exit.

'You're back early, Mama.'

'Yes, well, Theía Agatha wasn't feeling too well. She thinks she's caught something from one of the children. They've been generously passing around a cold. I must pop to the little girl's room. If you're done?'

I lower my chin in a nod before glancing past her towards my bedroom. My palms feel clammy, but I smile and slowly move across the narrow hall to my bedroom at a smooth and regular pace.

Shutting the door behind me, I swiftly settle down onto my childhood bed. Today I feel a little too grown up. I'm making choices that I'll never be able to go back on. Ones that could split my family and shape my future for good. No. We are strong. I've spent so long worrying about this, and every time I come to the same conclusion: Mama and Baba love me. No matter what I do, what I've done or who I am.

Rubbing my damp palms into the pale lime bedding, I begin clawing it like a cat.

As soon as she's out, I'll sneak in and get the packet. The words thud in my head like Mama's fist on the door. They beat along with the hard sound of my pulse in my ears.

Then it sweeps in... her voice, low and cutting like a rumbling thunder caused by electricity splitting the air.

'Theadora. Can I see you in my room?'

'Is everything alright?' My attempt at sounding breezy is destroyed by my vocal cords cracking in the middle.

Just as her voice so often fills our home with both love and discipline, silence now engulfs my room.

She's waiting for me.

If I don't peel myself off my bed and head to her immediately, there will be some prickly consequences.

My knees feel like the oranges Mama freshly squeezes to drink with breakfast, from firm to crushed in an instant. Flimsy and useless, unable to carry my weight.

She loves you, Theadora. She will understand.

With a final snatched breath, I make my way past the busy walls layered with photos of me as a child, and into Mama and Baba's room. Each photo draws forward a miniature flashback, my first day of school, my last day of school, the Christmas I got the stuffed white cat that still sits next to my pillow. It's all written in images on the walls. I acknowledge them as I always do when leaving my room.

All I can do is hope that my parents will forgive me now.

'I see this is why you wanted to collect everyone's post this morning.' Mama's frame is silhouetted by the sun streaming in the window behind her. Triangles of light pour in around her elbows as her fists sit firmly on her hips.

The packet and its contents lie sprawled on her bed between us. Squinting into the sun behind her, I wish I could run, escape out towards the sea for a swim. It must be peacefully rippling under the white glitter of the sun right about now.

Mama's voice cuts back into my dreams of escape. 'And I thought you were trying to be helpful. Instead, I see you were being deceitful.'

Like a fish thrown onto my friend Dinos's little red fishing boat, my mouth stutters as I suck in air, hoping something will come to save me. A small noise escapes my lips but nothing comes close to a fully fledged word, let alone a sentence.

Being half a foot shorter than me doesn't stop Mama from holding the floor. Her dark eyes focus on mine, completely unmoving. She thinks blinking shows weakness. I must blink one hundred times more than she does each day, at least.

'I was just nervous of what you might think. I don't want you to think less of me.'

'Less of you?' Her arms drop from their ridged stance on her hips and flop by her sides. 'Please, don't ever think that. I'm upset you haven't spoken to me sooner. That's what hurts. We'll talk about this when your father is home tonight. I think he needs to be a part of this conversation.'

'Sebastian is taking me out tonight, with his yiayia and pappoús. I can't let him down.'

The fact is, Mama and Baba like me seeing Sebastian maybe even more than I do. He's from a good family, with money and standing. She holds these traditional values close to her heart. They even let him call them Zeta and Marios right away.

Her fists find her hips again and a small *tsk* erupts from her lips. 'Fine. Tomorrow then. After work, a family meal and a meeting about...' She waves her hand across the bed and the test packet that she's put there and looks down in disdain under her glasses. '...this.'

Chapter 2

As soon as I hear his car in the drive, I hop up from the chair and sprint for the door.

Baba isn't home from the shop yet, so Mama and I have been moving around the house like water and oil, trying not to touch. I've spent most of my afternoon squirrelled away in my room, reading and getting myself ready for Sebastian.

'*Kalinikta*!' I call up the stairs and I hear something about staying safe as I whip round the front door and leave.

There he is, already holding the door to his car open for me. The sight of him is enough to catch the breath in my throat. It's that broad smile of his that gets me. Like it only exists when he's looking at me. For everyone else it's more subtle, reserved, but for me there's always something more, an extra depth.

I bound towards him almost tripping into his arms. He's there to catch me, his lips ready and waiting for a kiss.

The elation of having a night to forget everything else and just be consumed by Sebastian is like being shot with a cosmic pulse straight from the sun. It lights me up. It consumes me. Being whisked away to fancy restaurants is a treat I'd never had until meeting him.

This time of year, when the sun is so high in the sky it's easy to forget what shadows look like, and the streets of Kassiopi fill with people from all over, it's hard to get the time together. Harder for him particularly, for Sebastian. He's got an important role in his family. He's the only boy, the one to take over the family business. Not just *any* family business, but a chain of luxury hotels and restaurants across Corfu. But his responsibilities never stop him from messaging me every morning to ask about my dreams.

'You look perfect,' he coos as I step away from his lips and slide into his car. Not *good*, not *beautiful*, not *pretty*... Perfect. To him, I'm perfect. I'm sure no one else has ever said something like that to me, or even about me.

He lets out a satisfied exhale as he stands over me and closes the door. I watch him move around the car, his energy rolling over my spine with a delicious tingle like fresh lemonade on my tongue.

I offer a well-placed smile as I fasten my seat belt.

It took me half my afternoon to decide on my dress. I have to have a stock of simple and beautiful clothes for the times he shows me off in the restaurants he is soon to own. Today's dress is the colour of sand, made of linen and wraps around me in layers.

We make small talk; he asks about my parents, I ask about his and his grandparents too. They're very close. He already knows not to ask after my grandparents as they passed before I was born. We were meant to be meeting with his tonight, something we regularly do, but he messaged earlier with a change of plans. I kept the information to myself. I didn't want there to be a reason for Mama to demand I cancel my date with him.

As he drives through the curves of Corfu, with its lustrous greens that would make emeralds feel self-conscious, I like to watch him. The way his hands grip the wheel or the smile he sends me out of the corner of his eye.

He tells me about how he's been practising drifting in his car, how he wants to show me sometime soon. It worries me, but he reassures me, 'I wouldn't want to do anything to hurt my princess,' he says.

He treats me like I never imagined anyone could or would, showering me at any opportunity with jewellery, flowers and champagne.

Stretching across the car, I move my hand over his neatly cropped dark hair and curve my finger around his ear then jaw as he tells me about what he's been up to. His lips twist to kiss my fingers as they move over his freshly shaven cheek.

There's no way I'll spoil the evening by telling him about the test. What would be the point? It's not as though I have test results to relay anyway. That's a bridge I'll have to cross later. Not tonight. Tonight, I can fall into the warmth of his conversation, some crisp champagne and the deconstructed Greek salad that I love.

Chapter 3

After our date last night, Sebastian went driving with his best friend Konstantinos only to crash his car, leaving it to become scrap metal. Luckily, he's fine. This is the second time in as many months that it's happened while he was practising drifting and handbrake turns. Each time I beg him to be careful he tells me how much it means to him that I care so much. Whenever he says he is going driving with Konstantinos the air in my lungs seems to disappear.

His parents have already organised a new car for him to collect today. He messaged, desperate to meet later and show me. I've told him I can't. I can't avoid my parents and this insane test forever. There's no way Mama will let me out of dinner twice, however much I would like to hide.

I still haven't told anyone about the test. Not Phoebe or Xristina. We usually share all aspects of our lives — we have done all through school. I didn't really want anyone to know. In two hours Baba will be home, and we will all have dinner together and talk about the future, or perhaps the past. Who knows how it'll go.

In the meantime, I'm hiding out. Well, sort of. I'm not hidden from the sea. This is often the spot for lovers of an evening, but right now, it's mine. Sometimes Sebastian brings me here and we watch the ripples of the sea.

Usually, I would sit on the outcrop of rocks much closer to the edge, feet dangling over into the cool water, absorbing the warmth of the sun given to me through the wide flat boulders that angle down into the water. It's too hot for that at this time in the afternoon, though. People visiting the island can often be found hanging about in the midday sun in July and all through the afternoon too. This is not normal for a local like me, in particular a local that looks like me. One with bright blonde hair and blue eyes. I've not been blessed with my parents' olive skin. I do tan of course. This time of year, my skin's the colour of caramel, but if my mama gets her way, I'm still ushered out of the house with a layer of sun lotion, which is unheard of by all of my friends.

A pine tree hangs over the jutting rocks offering me shade to shelter under. It gives me the camouflage I need to hide from the world. Occasionally someone new to the harbour will wander down from the wall above, manoeuvring down the worn and precarious steps to glance in a rock pool or take a photo, and then they're back on their way. Most haven't even noticed I'm here. I keep my eyes on the sea as it turns from a clear and pale green to the most vibrant blue. Mama always says that's the blue of my eyes. She calls it Theadora-Blue.

I never feel alone, even sitting here watching the little boats bobbing about in the harbour further to my right. I can hear the snippets of conversations as they go on above my head. My English is very strong, it's something my parents invested in when I was young. With English I'll always find work. It's what I wanted to study at university. Not that I'm leaving for university now. Not with the pandemic still looming. I also know some German and French too. Not enough for a full conversation, but enough to understand a basic request or to offer a welcoming pleasantry. Mostly I listen to the English as people walk past above my head. They sigh and gasp over the view across the water, or point and talk about the buildings they can see across the way, buildings that are mostly the colour of lemons, with their terracotta roofs slanting this way and that, their windows like big rectangular eyes looking back at us all as if questioning, *Why are you staring at us?*

I breathe it all in while I can. The soft scent of seaweed from the rock pools and the taste of salt in the air from the occasional sea spray. This is my home. The only home I've ever known. Corfu, Kassiopi. It's mine. Except, it's not really mine. Not at all.

I turn and lie down on my back. The pine tree is strong and still over my head, letting in only the smallest flecks of dappled light, keeping me cool on this scorching day.

If the pandemic has taught me anything, it's that having freedom and time outside by the sea should be enjoyed and consumed at every possible moment. The past year left me with too much time to think at home in my room. I should be going to university in September, instead I cancelled my travels, delaying them until a time comes when I feel safe away from my beautiful island. Instead of leaving, and finding myself in the same way most people my age do, staying at home is the thing that's put everything else into motion. It's led me here to a pine tree on a rock, wondering what my parents are going to say about a simple life-changing test. Will they cry? Will they tell me that it can't go ahead? I feel as though Mama wanted me out of her sight for the past day, and I've been more than happy to oblige.

'I saw you from my boat. Thought you might need company.' Dinos's voice rumbles across the waves, physically shaking me out of my reverie, leaving my heart pounding and spots in front of my eyes.

'Holy–, Dinos, you frightened the life out of me.' Sitting up, I take a deep breath to calm myself.

'Sorry, I can go.' He points back the way he came.

'No, it's fine.' Then I add a hello. '*Yassou.*'

Dinos smoothly climbs up on the sharp silvery edges of the rock where I'm sitting. He's tall, taller than me, taller than Sebastian. I tower over all the girls I know and many of the boys. Dinos towers over most people. He looks a little smarter than usual in a pale blue linen shirt with boardshorts. Usually, he's topless and jumping on and off his little red fishing boat with his pa.

'I saw you from the boat.' He inclines his head towards the harbour before running his fingers through his crop of black curls.

We've known each other since our first days of school. Dinos has always been there in the background, quietly growing alongside me. Once upon a time I thought he might *like me-like me*, but he never asked me out or was even particularly flirtatious. It was just based on the extra attention he gave me, favouring talking to me rather than to Phoebe or Xristina.

It was only when I was having a stupid argument with a boy in our class, I can't even remember what it was about now, and Dinos jumped in to tell him to shut up that it was confirmed that Dinos doesn't *like me-like me*. The only thing about that day I remember clearly is the irritating Spiros Sakkos – one of three Spiros in our class – said, 'You *would* defend her, because you fancy her!' Laughter spread like fire and Dinos denied having any feelings for me whatsoever.

I've since realised we're just good friends and nothing more. For a time it left me with sadness the way the sea leaves lines of salt to dry on the sand, a residue that would sting in a childish wound. One that Sebastian has made me forget with his wide smile and never-ending romance. He's never ambiguous. He tells me I'm perfect, a pure princess, and takes me where I want to go. Anything for me.

'You look a bit smart to be fishing.' I gather in my knees and edge round to see him better.

'Some people offered me a handful of cash to take them out for a ride and some fishing this morning. Didn't want to be impolite and not accept.'

'Ah, that's why you have a shirt on. I'm not used to seeing you in clothes.' As soon as the words fall off my tongue heat skims my cheeks and I turn my face to look back out to sea.

Dinos doesn't rise to it. If that'd been Sebastian, he would've been all over it, ribbing me or offering to take his clothes off. He does find it funny to tease me.

Dinos lets out a little snort of acknowledgement. 'Don't worry, I know what you mean.' In that moment the world carries on, but we pause. Birds still chatter overhead and the sea still rolls, covering our silence. He says, 'You look like you're looking but not seeing.'

Turning, I look at him square on again, making sure I really *see* him, looking down my nose at him and narrowing my eyes for effect. There's a playful lift of his cheek bones as he licks his full lips. His short curls are wild from being out at sea and his pale hazel eyes glimmer. His eyes aren't as pale as mine, but paler than everyone else I know, and his skin is dark like burnt caramel. How he hasn't picked a girl yet, I can never understand. I know many who have tried but none that have caught his eye.

'What do you mean?' The expression on my face hasn't been enough for him to explain his comment.

'You're doing that face, the one where you're in a dream and you're not really seeing what's there in front of you. A unicorn could be steering that boat over there and you wouldn't bat an eye, because you're not really seeing what's out there in front of you. You may as well have your eyes closed.'

I furrow my brows and don't reply. I guess he's right. I hadn't even noticed there was a boat at all. Perhaps I was aware of it on some level, but my brain has fogged up in thought and I'm not taking anything in.

'What have you been dreaming about?' He leans a little closer. His voice teasing.

I hesitate. Of all the people I *should* tell about the test, Dinos is someone I *could* tell. I know he would hold the information locked up tight to his dying day if I asked him to. Once, when we were about six or seven years old, I found a ring in amongst the rock pools. I showed him and no one else. I made him promise to never tell anyone, just in case they told me to hand it to the police. I so wanted to keep it. It was the first promise of many he's kept over the years. If I'd told Xristina, she would've blabbed for sure, and Phoebe would have gone on and on telling me to do the right thing. Dinos told me it was lost treasure and that one day I should wear it as a wedding ring. We even pretended to get married. I had to hold my hand in a fist to keep it in place. I still have the ring at home, hidden in a box of secrets. It's got a gold band and three big clear stones. To this day I have no idea whether it's worth anything or not. But as far as I know, Dinos is the only other person who knows about it.

'No need to tell me. If you want some peace, I can go. Pa would've liked some help cleaning up the boat, but I ducked away using you as an excuse.'

'How much cleaning does it need?'

Dinos tilts his head and bites his full bottom lip. 'The woman threw up on the way back. Too much sun, not enough water. We told her, she wouldn't listen.'

I nod along, knowing it's the same thing week in week out during the summer. Someone else didn't wear a hat and went out in the midday heat, wanting as much sun as possible on their week away, nearly killing themselves off in the process. Now they get to waste a day of their hard-earned holiday feeling sick in the shade. I still envy them, knowing what I have to come home to tonight.

'I still think that poor woman will have a better evening than me. I've... upset Mama and we all have to sit down tonight and discuss the consequence of my actions.'

'What have you done?'

'Nothing... yet.'

'Yet?'

'I bought this test... and Mama found it in the bathroom.'

'Wait... What sort of test?' Dinos crosses his arms and screws up his face.

I lick my lips and begin to explain everything that's happened. He's the only person I can tell. The only one who will keep it to himself and be completely impartial in all this mess.

Chapter 4

It's all out in the open now.

Mama made slow-roasted chicken with feta salad, and now I'm sliding a creamy lump of cheese around my plate. It was all perfectly salty, tender and delicious. The perfect distraction to the painfully stale air around the table. Perhaps stale isn't right. Cold. The air is oddly cold; even though my parents' words have only been warm towards me, something isn't right. They were giving each other shifty looks while we talked about the test.

They quizzed me about why I had hidden it from them, what I was looking to find out. The answer is so obvious. I want to take a DNA test to know where I come from. They've never tried to hide the fact I'm adopted — how could they? My white-blonde hair has flowed down my back since I could walk, and now I'm grown, I'm as tall as my baba, maybe taller. I look like a cuckoo that's invaded the nest.

I wish I'd told them about the test before buying it, but I didn't want to upset them. Which I must have done because they're both so quiet. I knew it wasn't simple, not emotionally, but at least spitting into a small cup seemed simple enough that I could forget for a moment what it might mean to my parents and focus on what it meant to me.

'Theodora, are you going to eat that, or do you intend for it to do the *choreia* all night?' Baba is smiling at me from across the table, but his finger is tapping rapidly next to his glass. I stop circling my food around my plate.

I guess I must be back to "not seeing what's in front of me". I smile at the thought of Dinos and his example of a unicorn boat earlier.

'I know you think this DNA test won't show anything up,' I exhale hard at this thought, 'and you're probably right. If it doesn't, can we go to where the orphanage used to be? The one you got me from? In Romania? Maybe someone could tell me something. What if I have brothers and sisters who were adopted too? Or my mother was forced to give me up? I think if I was forced to give up a child, I'd want to know they were happy and safe. Wouldn't you? And if I have siblings,' I shake my head and slump back in my chair at the thought, 'I need to know them.' It's one of the biggest reasons I want to take the test. To see whether I'm alone or not.

I pop the last forkful of chicken and feta into my mouth and neatly place my cutlery back on the plate.

Mama coughs, making Baba glance at her again with a narrow look, like a hawk scanning the land. Carefully she pushes her plate away from her. Her hands come to rest elegantly on the table as she begins, 'Theadora, there is something more we need to tell you. Something about your past that we didn't want to have to tell you. But now...' She glances at Baba again, only briefly. Only her eyes move and nothing more.

I swallow the chicken without chewing it properly and the lump slowly travels down like a stone, hard and painful in my throat. There's something about Mama's face, the creases between her brows and the tension in her neck. I've never seen this expression before and I don't know how to prepare myself.

'What is it?' I rasp. Quickly I pick up my water glass, only it's empty. I put it back down on the table.

My father hurriedly picks up the ceramic jug and glugs water into the glass for me.

Picking it up, I begin to sip. Mama continues. 'We have always been vague about your adoption, saying we knew very few details. Which isn't completely true,' she nods a little too enthusiastically. 'You're old enough to know a little more. To know what we know.' Mama nods towards Baba. He pushes his chair back and leaves the room. I track his every step until he's out of sight and I can hear him jogging up the stairs.

'When you were a baby, you were found here in Corfu. Theía Agatha got a phone call about an abandoned enfant. She went and picked you up and brought you to her house outside of the Children's Community Home, the farm. You had been left outside a church with a note scrawled in English. The priest called the authorities, and the authorities called your Theía Agatha at the Children's Community Home.'

'What? No. I'm from Romania.'

'We had to tell you that, had to tell everyone that. But you were born here.'

Mama extends her hand over the table towards me, but I don't take it. I stare at it as my stomach feels like it's been kicked. All this time... my whole life I've believed I'm not from here, and now...

'So, I was an orphan here? Looked after by Theía Agatha and Ria?' Both women are my godmothers. They work at the Children's Community Home charity. They are some of the live-in staff with cottages on site, and sometimes staying in the main accommodation to be on hand at night.

Mama nods. Her hand slides back along the table and holds her other hand instead of mine. She begins wringing them together with her elbows resting on the table.

'Why have none of you told me this sooner? You said you adopted me in Romania. Why would you say that if it's not true? You told me the orphanage closed years ago, that's why you couldn't find anything else out.'

Baba's feet bang down the stairs and he reappears with a newspaper in his hand. 'Here.' He passes it over, already open.

'Is that me?' There's a picture and a caption about a foundling child. I glance up from the paper but my fingers stay stuck to the picture of the baby.

Mama and Baba nod in unison, their faces so tense they look as though they've formed new lines around their noses and in the hollows of their cheeks. They are in their sixties, but they suddenly look twenty years older. This is a house of glowing smiles and laughter. Not one filled with the fear of ghosts, or so I have always thought. Their faces tell a different tale now.

My eyes drop back to the paper and away from the haunting image of my parents now clutching each other's hands across the table.

The picture isn't very clear, just a baby in a blanket. It's close up, but small enough that it could be any child at all. But it's not any child, it's me.

I try to focus on the words one by one. It's so hard to take in. The article is plain and simple, but it's about me. I read and reread sentences but nothing is going in. I move along the words and all the hearsay. It's a short article, but I guess someone dumping a baby isn't something that happens here, so it still made the local news. I reach the words, *Tell God, at least I didn't kill it. Call it Keres.* The words are in English then translated into Greek. Keres. I know that word. Keres... they're the Greek goddesses of violent death. A burning sensation hits me in the back of my throat.

I look up to see the pain in my parents' eyes at what I've just read. I repeat the English words, the words likely spoken by my mother before she left me: '*At least I didn't kill it. Call it Keres.* Why would anyone say that, or choose that name?'

There's another question behind that one. A question begging Mama and Baba to tell me this isn't true, that no child could ever be so unloved at birth. I know, of course, it's true. Children across the world go unloved, and apparently, I really was one of them. Over the past year of lockdowns, I've been dreaming of a lost family that didn't want to give me up. One that loved me but knew I could find a better life elsewhere, with a full belly and an education. It turns out they wanted me dead. This whole time I've been dreaming, when the reality is a nightmare.

My eyes begin to feel hot and it's as though the tears gathering under my lashes are more salt than water, because they sting terribly. It's one thing to know you were unwanted by the two people who put you on the planet, but a whole other feeling to see the complete disregard for your life there in black and white. From this article, I was lucky they let me live at all.

I turn my face away, wishing I was anywhere else.

'Is there anything else I should know? Anything else you haven't told me about *my* life?' The word *my* falls from my lips in almost a growl. How could they hide this truth from me for all these years?

'Please don't say it like that.' Mama's voice loses all its gravitas. The bottom has fallen completely out of it, and she's left with only a wisp of volume. With an exhale her shoulders curve. 'There's nothing more we can really tell you.'

I look from one to the other. Mama's brightly patterned chiffon top in lime and pink now seems garish instead of modern. It makes her skin look a little too green. Baba looks as bad, carefully pulling the neck of his t shirt as though it's suddenly strangling him. They've known this all my life, yet they look as uncomfortable saying it as I feel hearing it. I can't bear to look at them.

'May I leave the table?' My breath catches in my chest as a tear runs cold along the flush of my cheek. My skin burns and I'm not sure whether in outrage or upset. 'Please.'

'Please don't run away. We love you.' Mama stands, and I do the same. We're so close, but the expanse between us over the table now feels like a kilometre long void.

'I know. I love you too. I love you both so much, I just... Please, may I leave?'

Mama nods her head. She seems smaller than she did earlier, like any fight has long gone with the change of the tide and now she's only able to hold herself up, nothing more. I make for the door, but then realise I've left my phone on the counter in the kitchen. We don't bring our phones to the dining table, even if it is all the same room. As I scoop it up, I glimpse Baba, still sitting, and Mama standing. He is gripping her hand so hard their fingers look withered and pale. Their knuckles almost glow in the dim light of the evening.

'I'll be back late. Love you.' The words burn as much as the tears.

'Before you go, Theadora...' Mama's voice is strong and determined but higher than normal as she struggles to contain her emotions. 'Please don't tell anyone of this. We have spent your whole life protecting you from this ugliness, and from those interested in your story. This truth will shine a light on your life from all the wrong people. I know you want to think about this. You need space, we know you well enough, but please, please keep this part of your story as only yours,' she presses her hands together like a prayer. 'Only a small handful of people know the truth, and we must keep it that way to keep you safe. Who knows what the people that left you are capable of.'

I nod my head, but it feels like it's spinning instead.

'We can talk more when you are ready,' Baba adds.

I back out of the room, into the living room and towards my trainers and the front door.

With the call of their voices telling me to be safe, and to keep secrets, I'm gone.

Chapter 5

Sweat trickles over my skin and my heart pounds so hard I can see white spots like fireworks in my eyes.

What just happened? I was born here? Here in Corfu? Really?

My heart races as I march along the road. Cars pass me on their way into Kassiopi for the evening. The people inside are probably happy, laughing, and ready for a wonderful night out at one of the many restaurants we have to offer. Maybe Petrino for Grandma's lamb or Sousouro for *stifado*. Or maybe Old School with its harbour view. The view I need right now.

My world caves in under the weight of confusion. Running away to hide is easier than staying and finding out more. It's all I can do to keep tears from rolling down my face and dripping onto the hot pavement. Every now and then I run my fingers under my eyes to scoop up any that manage to escape.

I was born here, found here, somewhere among olive trees or the wildflowers perhaps. Maybe born on a street like this with low stone walls and metal gates, with houses painted lemon or terracotta, with well-kept front lawns and flowers for each season bursting into colour like the changing of the tides. Did they put me in that blanket? The one in the picture? Or was I discarded like a cigarette? Where was the church? Perhaps I was placed in the dirt. If I was lucky, a basket, if not, a hard concrete floor. Or worse... maybe a bin.

My chest squeezes like my ribs are trying to crush my lungs. I exhale hard and snatch minuscule breaths. I think the article said who found me. Who I need to thank for saving my life. I need to find them. Tell them thank you. How could my parents hide this from me? Stop me from telling this person I'm grateful?

My pain is replaced by an anger as boiling as the crimson sun as it lowers on the day.

I think about messaging Phoebe and Xristina to see what they are up to. It might do me good to find some distraction right now. I hover over my phone as I march towards the harbour. It's a short maybe fifteen-minute walk from our house, past the shops and restaurants lined with people I've known all my life.

No. I need space, not friendly faces. I don't want to cry at them and not be able to explain why. I'm close to my friends, but I know I can't share this with them. Not now. Not with all that information sprawling around my head. I don't even understand, so how could I explain it to them? They might be in for dinner anyway. Maybe not Xristina — her family owns an ice cream parlour in the village, making it hard to know when she's needed there. At this time of year, it starts to feel like all day every day, particularly since everywhere had to stay closed until recently because of the pandemic. Now that businesses are open, they stay open. Not that the supermarket my family owns was closed. We were able to make some income when others couldn't.

Xristina does have breaks, of course, but this isn't what any of us thought we would be doing. We all thought we would be getting ready to say goodbye and head off on a new adventure, studying away from the island. But the pandemic tipped all of us off course. Phoebe wants to be a singer and dancer and to study performing arts in Italy, where her grandfather is from, but that course won't go ahead this year. Above all, her parents wouldn't allow it. Xristina wanted to study business at university. Then there's me and my distant and somehow pointless dreams. I've always been creative. I love music, and used to sing with Phoebe and play the saxophone too. Everyone thought I would study music. In the end, knowing I never wanted to perform, I decided I wanted to study English to learn more about the culture and the history of the language too.

All I do right now is work in Mama and Baba's shop, but not too often. They want me to have a good work ethic, but to also give me the freedom to find my own path. Mama has said many times she only wants me to work in the shop long-term if that's what *I* want to do. She is adamant I should find my calling. I've tried to point out that's not what she did, but she always says I was her calling, and that all she ever wanted was me.

All she wanted was me. Why did that come with lies about where I come from? If I was born here, why don't I look Greek? Am I Greek? Half Greek maybe?

I can't stop gently sniffing like I've caught a summer cold. If only. I pass Cleo's house, a friend from school, and the smell of a particularly musky climbing jasmine hits me in the back of my nose, sticking like glue, making me splutter as I pass.

It's enough to reset my brain back to what I don't want to think about. The words in that note split my brain in two. *Tell God, at least I didn't kill it.*

A shudder makes my knees feel liquid like sticky honey. All of me feels weak and uneasy.

As I get close to shops lined with brightly coloured T-shirts with evil eyes swirling in their centre, and traditional dresses for baby girls, I pick up my pace. My trainers eat up the road now the pavement has disappeared for a short time. I continue on toward the harbour and the freeing view of the sea. It's the place where I grew up, the place that is mine, the place that's always brought me comfort, watching the boats carefully tied up and secure. Everything else changes but the sea doesn't. It's calming shades of blue are always there.

As it comes into sight, I check the road before running across it to be closer to the still surface of the sea. I stop to cling to a tall black lamp post. It still holds the warmth of the sun even though the sun is now setting in brilliant lilacs and pinks, with dashes of scarlet.

'Back so soon?' Dinos's disembodied voice doesn't have the same bone-chilling effect as it did earlier in the day. Here, at the edge of the harbour, it's busy and people's voices sway in the warm breeze. One more voice being pushed in my direction is no surprise at all. Or maybe I've been shocked enough for one evening. Maybe I've hit a limit. 'How did it go?'

I look up at him and do my best to smile. 'It was... better than I expected, I suppose.'

'That bad, huh?'

'What's with you reading my mind today?'

'What do you mean *today*?'

He's right, I suppose. He's always been able to look at me and know how I'm feeling.

'One look at your face and I can tell you've been crying. Were they angry about the DNA test?'

'No, it's just... There's more to it. I don't think I'm going to send it off now anyway.'

A car horn sounds with three hard punches and brakes abruptly squeal. The pungent smell of rubber on hot tarmac leaves the air ripe, and I turn towards the commotion. There's a car I don't recognise, bright blue with white stripes along the side. I do recognise the driver as he exits the car, leaving the door wide open, and marches up towards us.

'Sebastian.' I snatch a breath even though I'm not sure what to say. I know how fiery he can be when he gets jealous. We've already had to have one conversation about Dinos only being a friend, and I thought he was going to hit a German boy who asked for my number right there in front of him.

'My princess, what are you doing here? You told me you had a meal with your parents.' The tone of his voice leaves me with the impression he thinks I've been lying to him.

'I'll go. See you around, Dora.' Dinos turns away from us.

Sebastian wraps his arm around my neck, and the weight of his bicep tugs on my hair.

'*Kalinikta*, Dinos,' I wheeze.

Sebastian sarcastically waves him off. He waits until Dinos is out of earshot before he looks me over. 'How come you're out here with him and not me? You said you were with your parents.'

'I was. It was just...' I don't really want to finish the sentence with any detail that might open up questions. 'It was just over sooner than I imagined. I should've messaged you. It's good to see you in person, not just facetime. You look alright after last night's accident.'

I twist under his arm to check over his face, stroking my hand over his bronzed forehead.

'I'm fine, I told you. That's what seatbelts are for. If you're so worried about me, why are you out here with him?'

'I wasn't out with him. We just bumped into each other–'

'Fine, fine. If you say so. What do you think of the new car?'

I look past him. There it is, stopped almost in the middle of the road, door still open. These things mean something to Sebastian. He's used to having whatever he likes. He does work hard, and he deserves nice things for it. He deserves the right sort of car, the right sort of watch, the right sort of clothes because it's as important to the people who stay in these hotels as it is to him. He tells me it's about creating the right atmosphere in every detail. I suppose having a rusting old truck sitting out the front wouldn't have the same appeal as his sports car.

'We're off to 54 Dreamy Nights tonight, after driving around the island. You coming with?' The place where we met. A nightclub. There's no way I could face drinking, dancing and people right now.

'I told Mama I would be back soon. I lost something earlier, and I just came out to look for it.' The lie sticks to my mouth like cottonwool. But mama did say not to tell anyone the truth. I owe her that much. At least until I know more.

'Fine. But you owe me a date, okay? I want to take you around in this beauty,' he lifts a finger towards his new car. It's much better than the last one. I need a beautiful girl to go with my beautiful car.' Sebastian curls his index finger around my chin and tilts it up before landing a deep kiss on my lips. '*Kalinikta*, princess.' With that he jogs back to his car and doesn't look back.

Chapter 6

After an hour of circling and tail-spinning, I realise it's impossible to hide in a place I've lived in my whole life, and I don't have a mask or money with me, so I can't go inside anywhere to hide. I go home.

It's more walking, but I like it. I like walking. Sometimes I take the moped my parents got me for my eighteenth birthday when I need to be somewhere. It's nothing like Sebastian's car, new and sparkling in the sun a deep midnight blue. My moped isn't brand new, but it's in good shape, plain black with no added extras or fun paintwork. All I care about is that it goes along. Our whole situation is different though. Sebastian is older than me, but that's quite usual here. I think men like to establish themselves before finding a suitable partner. And I guess I'm suitable. Although sometimes I wonder how.

I hover at our front door. The sunshine-yellow door isn't so bright now that it's only illuminated by the automatic lamp that comes on when it senses movement.

Swatting away a mosquito, I wonder about taking myself through the back garden instead, perhaps hiding out under a tree in the dark might work for the night.

The door swings open and Baba leans on the door frame.

'Are you coming in, or are you scouting to rob us?'

This isn't the first time I've heard this joke of his.

'You don't have anything I want.' My mouth curls into a hidden smile because I know exactly what's coming next.

Baba clutches his chest like he's been shot in the heart. 'You wound me,' he moans, before we both silently laugh behind small smiles. It's a silly exchange, but it thaws me enough to move towards the open door and the glow within the house.

As soon as I'm within his reach, he pulls me into a warm hug and kisses my forehead. He smells like mama's baking; she must be at it again.

'I know you like space, but I hate when you leave.'

'Sorry, Baba.'

'Come on, let's try this again.'

We step into the living room and Baba calls Mama to let her know I'm home.

She bustles in, whipping off an apron as though she's been making dinner all over again while I was out. She's probably been stress-cooking. This is something Mama likes to do, being the feeder that she is. When anything outside of her control happens, she begins to cook meals and sweet treats, some to be consumed right away and some to be frozen in batches to feed us all up on another occasion.

'Thank goodness.' Mama presses her cold damp hands on my cheeks. She must have just washed them with cold water. She tilts my head to look me over. 'Why do you always have to leave like this?'

I shrug and whisper, 'I'm sorry', because I don't really have an answer. It's what I've always done. When I was very small, I would hide in the olive tree outside. The first time it happened my parents thought I'd run away and had half the village looking for me. By the time they found me, Mama was distraught. She hugged me so tight I thought my head might pop right off, before she told me to never hide from her ever again because she couldn't live without me safe.

Mama's eyes crease in the same way they did when she found me in that tree. It makes me want to pull out my own insides as a punishment for making all this happen. Clearly my biological parents don't deserve to be found, so why on earth should I take a DNA test?

'I've decided I'm not going to send it off. The test.'

'Thank goodness.' Mama exhales a breath so hard, you'd have thought it had been waiting to jump out for days. 'I'm so happy.' She crosses herself in relief. It's not that she's hugely religious, but sometimes, on the odd occasion, this action occurs in our house.

'Are you sure, Theadora mou? If you want to send it off, we understand.' Baba's voice is steady as he takes his seat on the sofa, leaning on the arm in the way he always does.

I study his face for a moment, taking in his grey hair and weathered skin. He's serious. Very serious. I glance back at Mama whose mouth is clenched as tightly shut as her hands by her sides. The colour is back in her cheeks now. She doesn't look as green as when I left her.

I hate this. Everything about it pulls me in every direction like a plastic bag discarded in the sea, being tossed from place to place.

'We understand you want to know about who made you,' Baba continues, 'but you might not find anything worth having, or anything at all. As long as you understand that.'

'Or worse,' Mama adds, 'you could find people who want you dead.' She says *dead* like it's a dirty word and she doesn't really want me to hear her say it.

'Who knows about me being found here in Corfu? Theía Agatha, of course.'

'Only a small number of people at the Children's Community Home. They know that you were adopted to keep you safe from anyone who might want to hurt you,' Mama rushes over her words so quickly she trips over them. 'It's how we managed to adopt without the red tape. It was thought your life was at risk. It's why, why, we had to lie to everyone else,' she stutters, 'including you, of course. If they knew who you were, who you are, and word got out, who knows the problems it could cause you. What parent sends a death threat to a baby? It's unhinged.' Mama's eyebrows shoot up and she aggressively shakes her head in utter disgust, making her curly, shadow-grey hair move from side to side.

'And they have no idea who left me? Why they left me? Were they English or just writing a note in English?'

There's no answer my parents can give. They've given me all the puzzle pieces they have and it's up to me to decide what to do with them; find more or discard them completely. I didn't think by ordering a DNA test online I would be opening up this can of worms. I thought it would just tell me a little bit about my history, that's all. And maybe find me a distant cousin, maybe a brother or sister if I was really lucky. Seems so ridiculous now. Childish.

'We love you. We are here for you no matter what you decide. You're still young, there's no rush to these things. Take your time to think about it all.' Baba's warm hand reaches for mine, and I move to sit next to him and hold his hand.

'We only ask that you never tell anyone you were found here. We don't want to invite questions about lying to our friends for all these years. They'll all be offended we didn't trust them. We don't want that, and we don't want to bring harm to our doorstep.' Mama's dark chocolate eyes narrow on me. She looks genuinely afraid. She must really be worried someone would still take it upon themselves to hurt me after all these years.

Up until today, I thought this was a house of honesty, and now I don't know. My lie, that is, my hiding this test, has opened up a floodgate of half-truths shrouded in darkness. I guess at least light has been brought to it now.

'Okay. I won't tell anyone else. I'm going to try to sleep now. Today has been—'

'Exhausting,' Mama finishes for me. She dusts her hands over her hips.

We all kiss cheeks and hold each other for a moment longer than normal. I take in the smell of Mama's baking that lingers in her clothes before she says, '*Kalinikta*', and turns back to the kitchen.

The first step creaks as I go to walk up the stairs, and then I pause. 'If I change my mind, and take this test, and find my birth parents and other relatives, what then? What if the lie comes out?'

My mother turns in the kitchen doorway, casting her eyes around the room as though searching for the answer. Instead of looking at me, her eyes settle on my father who's still sitting on the opposite side of the room.

'We'll deal with that if it happens.' It's my mother's voice, but they sound like my father's words through her. A chill blasting down on me from the air con makes me shudder as I creak up another step.

It hits me, something so simple, so obvious I don't know how it's taken me so long in the line of thoughts to get to this one.

'What about my ID card?' I turn and stomp back down the steps, my hands gravitating to rest above my hips. My fingers dig into my narrow waist to the point of painful as the vision of my ID card flashes in front of my eyes. Romania is listed as my place of birth.

Papa's face falls flat into his hands and Mama hasn't moved from her place half in the kitchen half in the living room.

'Please remember, everything we do is to protect you.' My mother has never been a mouse. She's always been a lion, unafraid of anything. Not now. Now she is shrivelled and her voice is weak. 'It's fraudulent,' she moves towards me. I dig my fingers harder into my skin to stop the tears threatening somewhere deep in my core. I must stay strong. 'We couldn't risk anyone knowing the truth and hurting you for it. You were so young. You *are* so young.'

'Did you have it made?'

Mama nods her head, suddenly a mute again.

'And what if I got stopped and asked for my ID and someone found out it was fake? How safe would I be then, Zeta?' I want to be calm, but my voice is shrill. I shouldn't have used her name like that but anger is swelling and darting inside me like a crazed murmuration. It was spiteful and I instantly regret it.

Tears overflow and tumble over her cheeks as she pulls my hands from my hips and brings them to her chest.

'You must believe me, Theadora mou, everything we have done is to keep this family safe and because we love you more than anything. Please, forgive us for holding these secrets to our hearts all these years. None of this should be the burden of a child.'

Baba appears at Mama's elbow cooing, 'Zeta, shh.'

He pulls us both into his broad chest with ease.

'You're old enough now, Theadora mou, to hold these burdens with us,' Baba's voice sounds distorted with my ear pressed to the shoulder of his shirt. 'But before you judge our lies, remember the words in that article. Would you tell a child that's what they were born to? Or would you do your very best to protect them for as long as you could? How long before you tell a child Agios Vasilis isn't the one leaving them gifts on New Years?'

'You've been lying about Agios Vasilis too?' I pull away from the group embrace enough to share my laughter through my tears. It's enough to break the tension in the room. Enough to let them know that I understand. Even if I don't like it.

Chapter 7

The air in my room is still. There's no aircon unit in here. Sweat seeps into my sheet as I thrash around unable to rest. I pick up my phone, scan social media and the deluge of photos and videos of beautiful people with beautiful lives all being lived again in these glorious summer months.

I click on the lamp on my bedside table so I can study it again, my new ID. Although it's not new. It was issued when I was twelve and my parents squirrelled it away, replacing it with a very good fake. Something made by a friend of a friend of a friend, so they said anyway.

It looks the same as my other one, only this one says I was born in Corfu. My parents have asked me to keep this one hidden and only produce it if I could get in serious trouble showing the fake.

This morning when I woke up, my biggest worry was Sebastian after his accident, then telling my parents more about the DNA test and my dreams of finding cousins or siblings. Now I feel like someone's knocked over all my dominos and it took me eighteen years to get them in a row.

I get up and move over to my practice keyboard under my window. There's a proper piano downstairs, but I also have a small keyboard in my room that I've had since I was a child. Without switching it on, I silently play Concerto in D minor, BWV 974 by Bach. I could put headphones on, but I don't. Sometimes I like to imagine the sound. It's what I used to do as a child desperately wanting to practice. Before I had headphones to listen to myself play late at night when my parents thought I was sleeping. It's a long lived habit even now.

My head drops to my shoulder as I imagine the sound of each note as they build and flow out of my fingers. There's only the click of the keys as I press down on them, nothing more. But in my mind the emotion of this piece feels like electricity in my fingertips until I have to stop.

I can't sit here suffering in this bizarre silence of the night. I need the great outdoors.

That's what I want. What I need. Fresh cool air on my face.

Anything would be better than trying to visualise the parents that left me behind while silently playing Bach.

I'm glad they left me, so why do I need to know who they were? Why do I still so desperately want to take this test and find out something about myself?

Spending the past months stuck indoors and in masks led me to this DNA test. It gave me space to think about who might be out there looking for me. Maybe not my parents, but maybe someone else. The idea of not sending the test away fills my heart with lead. In the hands of my birth parents, or perhaps just my mother, I was lucky to be left alive, and now more than ever I want to know why. I want to know why she left me for dead. How she could be so dreadful. Was it postnatal depression? Has she spent the rest of her life in regret? If there's a chance I could find out, I have to take it.

I move around my room, tugging on denim shorts and an oversized white shirt. I don't even give myself time to run a brush through my long wild hair. It must look crazy from the sleepless turning and twisting.

Mama left the DNA test on my bedside cabinet for me to decide my own fate. I check everything is inside that's needed, and seal it all up ready to post it off. There's a postbox in the centre of Kassiopi. I've passed it twice today already. It's a long straight line from my house. Ten minutes at most. I'm going to do it. I'm going to post it.

Creeping towards the stairs, I briefly pause to smile at the photos on the wall. Only the screen of my phone lights the way but I can still see the glint of smiles as they watch my every move.

Mama and Baba are still awake — there's a light on downstairs. Carefully I tiptoe on each step, avoiding the places that make the most noise.

When I eventually make it to the bottom, I realise they must be in the garden, because I can't hear voices. As I move into the living room, I look across at the kitchen. I can see that Mama's phone is charging on the kitchen counter.

I send her a message, knowing she'll only get it when they come in. I tell her I couldn't sleep, and I've gone to have a drink with some friends. With that I escape out the front door, creep across the drive, through the iron gates as silently as I can, and across the road onto the sidewalk towards the centre of the village. All that gives my escape away is the light outside the front of the house that flicked on as I left.

The heat of the day has left an oppressive humidity in the air. Even though the temperature has dropped, moisture still clings in the atmosphere. Where the sky had been streaked with lilac, now a thick, dark purple rests above me, punctured with bright stars and the curve of a crescent moon.

Everyone here knows their family line. They can tell me where they came from, the strength of their ancestry. All of it. Their roots are as attached to the island as those of the great cypress trees that reach for the ancient Greek gods, or the Christian god, that watch over us and laugh at our mistakes. I'm more into the old Greek gods and myths than the Christian ones, although I do love the festivities and traditions of Easter and Christmas. I wonder what traditions my parents had, my biological parents. Was I an accident? I suppose I had to be. If they wanted me, they wouldn't have given me up and be proud of the fact they stopped themselves from killing me.

I pass by shops filled with people in masks. As long as I'm outside I don't have to worry about wearing a mask, and if I keep my head down, hopefully I won't invite conversations from everyone's friendly faces.

I've never been made to feel like an outsider, even though I stand out as one. Although, I remember once when I was small, standing in the playground at school and Spiros Sakkos loudly asking why I had white hair, and adding insult by questioning my age. He thought I was actually as old as his yiayia because she had white hair too, only I didn't have wrinkles. Some of the boys laughed, but not Dinos. Dinos pushed Spiros over and got told off by the teacher. I remember going home and asking Mama why I had to be different, why my real parents hadn't loved me.

41

That was the first time I must have used that phrase, *real parents*, because Mama sat me down on my bed and held me so tight my cheek was squashed to her chest. I remember so clearly what she said to me. 'I am your real mother. I dreamt of you before you arrived in my life. You were born to be mine, no one else's. It doesn't matter who birthed you, it's about who loves you.'

Remembering her words and how much they meant to me stops me in my tracks. It's not the only time she's said it. She's confirmed her love for me many times since.

I'm not far from the postbox now. If there weren't a rusty white car parked in front of it, I'd be able to see it from where I am, outside Jasmine, one of the ice cream parlours. I'm a matter of metres from the central square in the village where cars waltz past each other. It's always a miracle when a tourist bus turns the blind corner without taking out oncoming traffic in the summer months.

I know who my real parents are, and they are the ones who have loved me and sheltered me, but something inside keeps telling me that sending this test *has* to be done. I need to at least find out where my heritage is. England? Greece? Somewhere entirely different? This test will show me that, even if it doesn't find a single person I'm related to. A chart will show me my genetic map, and where my ancestors are likely to have come from — the reeling past of all of those who brought me to this moment. The website says it will tell me that. It demonstrates it with fascinating examples with shades of colour over maps to show the places each individual's ancestors would've lived.

I glance both ways and jog across the road before stepping up onto the stone path and heading for the bright yellow postbox.

Around me there are people coming out of the bars and restaurants that light up the evenings here. It's getting late, and the throb of people talking and laughing swells in my head.

My clammy hands stick to the shiny silver plastic envelope as I present it to the postbox. My chest heaves, and the air seems thicker than ever as I slide the envelope into the slot, knowing it's too late to change my mind now as I hear the dull thud of it landing on everyone else's post. Whatever happens now, happens. I've put something into motion and there's nothing I can do to stop it. Nothing.

Chapter 8

It's two Sundays since sending off my DNA test, and Theía Agatha and Ria are coming round for dinner. Mama spent a week mildly sulking about the whole revelation and so did I. Most people wouldn't have even noticed she was being off. She still went about the house and the shop getting things done with enthusiasm, but she kept baking more food than normal and I knew if I wasn't careful, I'd soon gain a kilo on my thighs if I let her feed me up between shifts. I've kept out of the way, spent more time out than normal. Even when my friends are busy, I've been happier looking at my new ID card in a quiet corner of one of the bays instead of sitting at home surrounded by the smell of freshly cooked cakes.

Mama has told Theía Agatha and Ria that they told me I was born in Corfu. I got a phone call from Agatha to make sure I knew I could always talk to her and Ria if I ever had any questions. It meant a lot to me. She even apologised for keeping it secret for so long, but said I needed to trust their judgement on this. I do. It's her job to protect the children in her care. The more time I've had to sit thinking about it all, the more I've come to terms with that simple truth. I do trust these people with my life, and if they say they were trying to keep me safe, I truly believe that to be the case.

Baba has arranged cover at the shop, but we aren't far if there's an emergency. Baba has said that part many times, he always does when he leaves someone in charge who he isn't related to.

Leaving my room, I stop to study the pictures on the wall. The bright and beaming faces of the past. I hone in on one where I'm on Ria's shoulders and Theía Agatha is stretching up to hold my hand. They're best friends, and Ria is as my much my *theía* as Agatha in my heart. They've both always been in my life, cheering me on.

Moving away from the photos I stomp down the stairs and into the smell of slow cooked lamb in the oven. I hope it's in feta. Maybe cooked with some spinach too. My stomach rumbles at the thought of it.

Our guests will arrive soon, but with Mama and Baba happily waltzing around each other in the kitchen, I take the opportunity to sit at the piano in the living room. It's a polished ebony upright piano. I run my fingers over the keys and begin to play them before I've even pulled out the seat that's tucked away underneath. I don't play a song, I improvise. Something lyrical with a dreamlike quality fills the air. I close my eyes and play without thinking, falling deeper and deeper into my own world.

When the doorbell rings I physically jump round to see Mama and Baba grinning behind me, my adoring audience. They praise me before opening the door to our guests and I leave the keys behind to join in with the hugs and kisses doing the rounds.

I think now is the time to talk about the test and being found here in Corfu. We've all devoured our lamb in feta. Now, with full bellies and the right amount of wine circulating between us, I make my move. After all, it's been two weeks since I told everyone about the test. They've had time to think about it, time to realise it might just be okay for me to go ahead and send it. That's what I hope anyway, seeing as I've already sent it off.

'How are the kids at the Community Home?' It's a start. A way to bringing the conversation to my adoption. We've all been avoiding bringing it up. Or at least, that's how it's felt to my mind. Bigger than any elephant in the room. Maybe everyone has been waiting for me to talk about it, not wanting to put pressure on me to talk if I didn't want to.

Ria places down her glass and says, 'They're all doing really well right now. They'll probably be feeding some of the animals on the farm in the next half an hour.' She looks at her watch.

'I still can't believe I lived there with the other children once.'

I imagine the big house in the centre of a farm. Buzzing with animals and the children helping to look after them, learning life skills under the watchful eye of the team of mentors. They also have social workers and a school teacher there. But in my head, it's an idyllic place where children run free among horses and goats.

'That's not quite right,' Agatha interjects. 'You were a newborn baby, we couldn't exactly have you in the main house keeping all the other children awake at night. You came to live with me in my cottage down the road from the farmhouse where most of the children live. You didn't interact with the other children, they didn't even know you were there. Then you were soon adopted. You weren't with us for long at all.'

I've asked questions over the past week, here and there. Mostly I've been quiet on the subject because I'm frightened I'll have to admit sending off the DNA test. But now I want to know more. I want all the details from start to finish.

Mama begins to clear the table.

'Thanks, Zeta,' Ria balls up her napkin and places it on the plate. Mama takes it to the other side of the room and into the kitchen half of our kitchen-diner.

'How long's not long?'

They all start to stutter over words and rub their chins, all except Mama who scrapes the plates into the bin.

'Not long, a month or two before we really started transitioning maybe,' Ria shrugs. 'Your mama came to live with Agatha, didn't you Zeta?'

'Yes. Luckily Theadora was worth the trauma of staying with Agatha and her dreadful habits.'

'Cheek! You'll eat wood if you carry on!' Theía Agatha makes this threat with laughter spilling over and creasing her eyes. She doesn't look much like mama, more cousin's than sisters. Mama always says Agatha got the good looks of their mother, and Mama got the looks of their Baba. I can't imagine this is right, as Mama is beautiful and elegant, nothing like a man in the least.

'And do you think I'm in danger now? Have any of you ever had threats about me? Surely everyone would assume I was taken to the Community Home?'

'Not necessarily. We have cared for children from different parts of Greece for different reasons. There's nothing to say you weren't taken far away from the island.'

'So you don't think the DNA test might work out? I mean, what are the chances of the person who left me there, taking their DNA too? *And* finding me now? I'm sure it'd be safe.'

Their collective silence leaves me thinking I've said too much. All the blood looks as though it's drained from Agatha's olive skin leaving it blotchy and sallow. Her hazel eyes bulge wide and she pulls at her neck of her blouse. She looks from Mama to me so many times she looks like a windup toy. Ria squeezes her arm.

'It's good that she knows the truth of being in our care, Theadora can help protect her own secrets now.' Ria has that magical way with people. Like she can sense problems and pinpoint them. When she turns her soothing voice on, everything seems a little better.

'Still, the DNA test is not worth the risk. We have all worked so hard to protect you, why would you want to risk that now?'

'I wouldn't, I was just saying–'

'Good. Good you wouldn't risk it,' Theía Agatha breathes and stretches over the table to squeeze my hand. 'Good you're a sensible girl. Good.'

Silence lingers so I fill in with another, more simple question.

'Mama did say you might know what happened to the person who found me? I wanted to thank them'

'Sorry, little one,' Agatha uses her usual term of endearment for me, 'they died a long time ago. They were in their eighties when you were born.'

So that's that then. I won't be thanking the person who found me, or asking them the questions I thought they might be able to answer, and I won't be telling my family I've sent the DNA test already. It's too late for everything.

All I can do now is wait. Wait and see how things play out. That, and hope that I don't find the wrong person in all this.

Chapter 9

I searched the internet and triple-checked the website to find out how long it would take to receive my results. At least I won't have to get half the village's post from the post office — the DNA place will email me the results after five to ten weeks. Five to ten weeks of not knowing. So far, I've suffered through eight of them.

My parents haven't pushed the matter, and neither have I. It hasn't been mentioned again since I was testing the water when Agatha and Ria were over. There was no way they would react well to it being sent off, so I'm keeping it to myself. I keep getting the feeling my mama somehow knows. It's stupid really, she hasn't said that. It's more that she always seems to know or find out when I'm up to something. I'll keep it to myself until there's more to report. I'm sure when I get the results, we'll all be able to exhale a sigh of relief, and I'll be able to learn something about where I really came from. I'll be able to find a small sense of history and identity.

Tonight, it's a rare summer night out with Sebastian. He's been working so hard with the hotel chain that we don't always get to see each other as much as we would like. He's taking me for a romantic meal at one of the hotels his parents own. The hotels all have luxurious views across different parts of Corfu. None of them are near the sea; they're hidden away in the mountains with infinity pools and award-winning restaurants.

There's a rap on my door. 'Theadora, Sebastian is here.' I hear Mama's feet move away from my door and back down the stairs. I take one last look in the mirror. Unlike my parents, I don't have hair that is beautifully curly, but it does have a natural wave to it, and tonight I've taken time to curl it. I'm wearing a sleek, lilac dress. I thought about high heels, but they would make me taller than Sebastian, and I don't know how he'd feel about that. I've never asked. I slip on some clean pumps and head out of my room towards the stairs, nodding at the photos as I pass.

As I skip down the steps, I can hear polite chatting and laughter coming from the living room and the sound of my baba's palm connecting with Sebastian's shoulder in approval.

As I appear near the bottom step, Sebastian looks over at me.

'Perfect as always.' He sighs.

'Have fun you two.' Baba kisses my cheek and Mama does the same. The only difference is, she then runs through a check list of things that I should have with me before we escape out the door and into Sebastian's car.

'I thought we could push dinner back a bit. I've been practising more of my drifting. I'd like to show you what I can do.' He glances at me then back to the road. 'What do you say?'

I can't deny the squirming sensation in my stomach, knowing how many times he's destroyed cars. I've spent months avoiding going with him when he's been out driving with Konstantinos, dreading this moment — the unavoidable moment when I am in the car with him while he does something dangerous. I knew it would happen, and here it is.

'You'll be careful, won't you?'

'Don't worry, I know I've got fragile cargo.' His hand reaches across to squeeze my left knee. 'I'll keep you safe.'

I'm confident he wouldn't do anything intentional to hurt me. He just wants to show off a little. I can understand that. I like to show my language skills or tell him about a new song I've learnt to play on the piano. During lockdown I learnt so many songs on the piano and the saxophone, I likely doubled my repertoire.

My phone beeps from my handbag. Picking up the bag from Sebastian's immaculate car floor, I dig the phone out.

It's Xristina and Phoebe checking we're all still on for drinks tomorrow night. We've all been working so hard, it feels like ages since we've been out together. I confirm before checking my emails. Every time I open my phone, I check my email. Since hitting the eight-week milestone of waiting for the DNA test, I check my emails so often the battery on my phone is almost dead before dinner. I had to charge it today before coming out. I refresh and wait for it to load. Nothing.

'Anyone interesting?'

'Just the girls.' I close the screen and put the phone back in my bag.

The sun sets at our back and shadows from the cypress trees below the road streak over the trees around them in long pointed lines like arrows guiding the way.

Usually our time in the car is filled with music and chatting, but today it's quiet and charged with a new energy. The car is still filled with music. Sebastian turns it up and his thumbs hit the steering wheel to the hard dance beat and his woofers pound boom, boom, boom, vibrating in my chest.

'I can't wait for this. When we get to the right place, I'll show you how it feels to go sideways. Have you even been in a car going sideways before?'

'No.' My voice is delicate under the music as the thought of going sideways makes my stomach turn. I don't tell him that the one time I went sideways at speed was at a waterpark when I was a kid. I threw up within thirty seconds of getting to the bottom of the flume. Although, that also spun me round a few times, not just sideways. They had to close the pool while they cleaned it. Another secret of mine kept by Dinos.

'What?'

'No,' I call louder over the music. The muscles in my face tense, doing my best to press my face into a supportive smile.

I'm not a kid anymore, I'm sure it'll be different in a car. It's not like I get travel sickness on the ferry to the mainland or in cars or ever. It was just one time. I'll be fine. I want to join in with what Sebastian loves to do. He's been so supportive of my decisions about university, talking me through all the options. He even offered me a job at one of his hotels and said it's always there if I want it.

Sebastian starts talking about Corfu Race Club and things they do and sponsorships. My hands turn clammy.

'Can I watch from the sidelines?' I interrupt.

'At the club? With the races and the drifting? Yeah, sometimes.'

'What about tonight?'

'It's just us in the car tonight, practising. Oh shit, I should check the Smurf app.'

'The what?' A laugh eases the knot in my stomach.

Sebastian turns the music down enough that we don't need to shout over it.

'Oh, I'm sure I've told you before. It's that app that tells you where the cops are. If anyone's seen them, they upload it to the app saying they've seen a Smurf. Wish I'd thought of it. Best app I have.'

'Sounds cool.'

I'm not sure it sounds cool. I guess it is if you're off breaking the laws of the road like we're about to.

It's late and my stomach is churning with hunger and anxiety. As we make our way down a narrow road, the world around us glows scarlet in the setting sun.

'This olive grove isn't used any more,' Sebastian says. 'The whole place is dead. My mate's pappoús owns it and he won't let anyone else farm it even though he can't anymore. He'd rather wait until he's dead for anything useful to happen to it.' He shakes his head as we progress towards a dusty expanse. 'Glad my pappoús isn't such an arrogant fool.' The tumbling olive groves undulate around us.

There's a stone building in the distance. Everything on the lead-up looks unkempt with tufts of yellow grass pointing up like spikes warning us off.

As we come into the clearing near the farm building, Sebastian turns the wheel hard and we glide sideways into the open space before he rights the car, then drives forwards and stops.

'Good, right?' His hands smack down on the wheel. 'I've got it perfect now. Reckon I could get this car around a track and not even clip a cone.'

The drift manoeuvre was impressive, I have to agree with that much. Sadly, it made my insides feel like they were sliding up into my ribcage, and I'm not sure when they'll come down again.

Before I can answer him with more than a fleeting smile, he excitedly booms, 'Watch this.' He turns the music back up and spins the car in circles.

This is what a doughnut feels like. I'm sure there are millions of people the world over who would love this sensation. Sebastian clearly does. He's grinning and biting his bottom lip hard as he grips the wheel, making his knuckles almost match the car's white interior.

I can feel my stomach lurch and my mouth tingle from dry to filling with saliva as I try to suppress my gag reflex.

'Sebastian, stop!' My head bounces against my window with the G-force. 'Please.'

'What?'

The music's too loud and I don't have the strength to shout. My blood drains to my feet and my stomach lifts further towards my mouth.

I heave, pressing my hand to my mouth. Tears stream down my face. I heave again.

'Whoah! Whoah! Not in the car!' He abruptly stops the car, jolting me one way then the other. In the dying light we nestle in a cloud of dust that glitters as the headlights burst into life. 'Not in the car!'

I heave again, but hold it all in. My whole body still feels as though it's going round in circles. I throw open the door and vomit into the cloud of dust.

Sebastian rubs my back.

'Thank fuck you didn't vomit in the car. I've just had her cleaned. If you felt ill, you should've told me.'

Chapter 10

After last night's humiliation, Sebastian kindly took me home instead of out for a meal. My stomach didn't recover right away, but he looked after me and reassured me at least.

If I'm honest with myself, I've spent most of the summer being okay with not seeing as much of Sebastian as I might have. There were times I could've pushed to see him, but I didn't. I hate hiding my thoughts from everyone around me. I'm sure I love him. He's attractive, most of the girls have openly complimented him, he's smart too, and protective. And of course, he has good prospects working in his family business. The problem is, I feel pressured when I'm around him like I need to be a better version of myself. Vomiting outside of his car last night made me feel so inadequate, but it reassured me too, because he was so kind and caring. He may have been worried about his car, but he had just had it cleaned. After that, he just wanted to know I was okay. That was all that mattered to him.

I haven't told Phoebe or Xristina about the embarrassing events of last night. That's something I'll be keeping to myself. It's nice to sit in a bar, a little bit dressy with my girls, sipping cocktails. It's not something we do much. Not in our own town. There's something about going further along the coast and away from the prying eyes of our tight-knit community. But sometimes it's nice to know all the faces around you, to feel not only the warmth of the final days of summer, but the love shared by community. Like tonight, in our beautiful Kassiopi.

'You're not checking your emails again, are you? What on earth are you waiting for?' Phoebe's voice knocks me out of my daydreaming. It's riddled with accusation and when I look at her across the table, she's quizzically assessing me, her eyes searching mine for answers. She's nosy at the best of times. I've been doing my best not to check my email too much to save my battery today, knowing that we're going to be out a bit later tonight.

'Maybe she has a secret boyfriend that isn't Sebastian,' Xristina joins in, although the chances are she hadn't even noticed what I was doing on my phone. She's probably more worried about the selfie we took two minutes ago, and the position of our glasses on the table.

'Why would you say that?' I drop my phone on the table.

Her shoulders rise and fall before she pushes her thick black curls off her bare shoulders and says, 'Just thought it was funny to say.'

'Well, it's not. I'm waiting for an email, that's all.'

'What for?' Phoebe watches me, unblinking, as she picks up her glass and sips from the thin black straw.

'I applied for a piano gig, that's all. It's nothing. I won't get it, but they said they'd email me.' The lie makes me feel cold in the warm night air.

'Why are you lying?' Phoebe's glass smacks down on the table.

'I'm not!'

'Yes, you are. You wrinkled your nose. You always do that when you lie.'

'Shut up, I do not.' I pick up my drink and use it as a buffer between me and Phoebe's hard stare under her fluffy eyebrows. They normally look delightful and playful, the way she puffs them up, now they look menacing over her narrowed eyes.

Phoebe's elbow finds Xristina's bare ribs under her white crop top.

'Ow! What was that for?'

'Don't you think she is?'

'I think your elbow bruised my rib.' She rubs at it and sticks out her bottom lip.

I sip hard on sticky, sweet strawberry ice until I've drained the contents of my glass. 'I'm not feeling great. I think I'm going to go.'

'Dora, are you kidding? What on earth is going on? Tell us.'

'I'm fine. I just need to get some air.'

Phoebe spits out an incredulous laugh. 'We are outside already, or pretty much anyway.'

'I'll see you both tomorrow.'

Scooping up my bag and my phone, I scoot off my chair, and kiss both their cheeks while Phoebe stutters questions. Xristina shrugs it all off, giving me space, and I leave to the sound of Phoebe muttering, 'I only asked why she was checking her emails so much.' Xristina tells her to leave me be.

I keep my head down as I make for the exit, trying to avoid brushing past people as they come in.

'Leaving so soon?' It's Zander, Dinos's friend. My friend too, but more Dinos's.

'Yeah, I wasn't feeling so great.'

Dinos appears behind him like a large shadow sneaking in.

'What are the symptoms? Should we get you tested?' Zander steps back and pulls his T-shirt up over his mouth in lieu of a mask.

'No! I drank my drink way too fast. I need to clear my head, that's all. See ya.'

I squeeze past them, but instead of heading home, I turn towards the sea. It has its own gravity and it pulls me towards it. My feet eat up the pavement. I need to find some peace, some breathing space. I'll go back in half an hour when the bee in Phoebe's bonnet has flown away.

'Dora, wait! Theadora!' I turn to see Dinos jogging towards me.

'Hey. What's wrong?'

Dinos lifts his right hand towards me, his fingers pinching something between his fingers.

'Phoebe was coming after you to give this to you, but she seemed like she was on some mission so I said I'd do it. Gave her some money to get drinks instead.'

I put out my hand and Dinos drops a small golden hoop into it. Automatically I pinch each earlobe. Sure enough, there's one that's lonely without its decoration.

'Thanks, Dinos.' I turn back towards my mission of getting to the harbour so that I can walk along next to the sea and clear my thoughts. Waiting on these test results has left me permanently thinking about where I'm from. After years of imagining myself as a baby in Romania, being swaddled in the arms of my new parents, Zeta and Marios, and being brought back to Greece with them, only to find out that I was born here in Corfu. I've spent the past eight weeks wondering how Greek I am. I've started to think I must be. I really hope I am.

'Hey, Dora, did you ever get the results of the test?'

'Huh?' I stop so suddenly that my body jars forwards, as though my feet knew to stop but no one told my body about the idea. 'How do you...?'

'I've known you since we were kids. It's obvious. There's no way you *wouldn't* have posted the test. Is that why you're feeling off? Have you heard something back?'

In the last eight weeks he hasn't mentioned the subject at all, as though our conversation all that time ago never even happened. That's Dinos though; when he wants to, he can hold everything in like a locked treasure chest that's fallen to the dark depths of the ocean floor. I guess we haven't been alone together recently, so how could he have asked?

I shake my head and slump in disappointment, trudging along, now with Dinos in tow. 'No. Nothing. They'll email me the results, but it can take up to ten weeks. Probably longer because of the pandemic delaying everything.'

'How long's it been?'

'Eight weeks, three days and... I don't know how many hours. I guess it depends when they picked the post up, and then is it ten weeks from posting or ten weeks from them getting it?' My words race and I look up to see a smile in the corners of Dinos's eyes.

'You'll find out one way or the other. Is it one of those places that update with more people the more people that test?'

'What do you mean?'

'Today it might say you have two estranged cousins and next week another one takes the test so you have three...'

'Oh, yeah, I see what you mean. Yeah, it is. I don't really expect my birth parents to be on there. Surely they wouldn't want to take a DNA test for this very reason — so that I can't easily track them down.'

'You don't know that. Maybe they couldn't afford a kid and wanted the best for you. Who knows why they had to give you up.'

Heat rises up from my chest, pulsing along my veins. Dinos doesn't know the whole truth. I keep my eyes focused on the water as we make our way towards it. The boats lining the harbour are so still it's hard to imagine they aren't on solid ground. Focusing on that is easier than doing the equation of truth in my head. Who are they? Who were they? What were their motives? It doesn't really make sense, not with the note they left with me. But I hope it was some sort of temporary psychosis. I looked it up, and it can happen. But Dinos doesn't know any of that. He doesn't know what I know. He still thinks I was born in Romania.

'What is it?' Dinos's voice is low and his question hits with more gravity than the words would have from anyone else.

'I can't say. But I know they won't be looking for me. This test is only to help me learn where I'm *really* from. What part of the world and maybe, if I'm really lucky, I'll find I have some distant cousins or something. I just want a slice of my identity. But you're right about one thing, I couldn't even leave the test a whole night before I sent it away. It was like an itch that I had to scratch.'

Dinos chuckles to himself, 'Why am I not surprised?'

I feel him look me over as we amble along.

'You don't ever have to tell me a thing, Dora. But you know that if you did want to tell me the result, it would never pass my lips, not for anything.'

As we make to cross the road, looking right and left, I glance up at him. His often wild curls are neatly coiled on top of his head this evening, although his chin has more than his normal stubble.

'How are you, Dinos?' I keep my eyes on the side of his face as he thrusts his hands into his denim shorts and we carry on toward the edge of the harbour.

'Good. Busy. Pa wants me to take on more responsibilities. Maybe save up and get another boat so that one would be mine.' He points at the red boat that I've watched him climb in and out of for as long as I can remember. I can still see them piling out the catch of the day. 'There's more money in the tourist fishing trips than in catching the bloody fish sometimes, and even if it's a bad haul, we still get paid. But if we had two boats, we would maybe do both. I did well with the people the other day. Pa says I just need to use a little more charm.'

Dinos isn't one to actively charm people. In that way he really is the complete opposite of Sebastian, who could charm his way out of almost any situation he found himself in. 'What do you say on these trips then? Is it all men fishing and women throwing up? Or do you try to charm the women into not vomiting?'

We pause, both looking over the boat in front of us. It's cleaned down each night after a day at sea to make sure it isn't left with a lingering smell of old fish in the sun. It's not a big boat. It can't fit many people for these trips, maybe four or five people with Dinos and his pa. Maybe more, but it would soon be a squish.

Dinos wipes the beads of sweat off the stubble on his lip.

'Even if there was a girl on these trips worth looking twice at, I couldn't manage charming her with my pa looking over my shoulder telling me what to do and to pass everyone bottles of water every five minutes.'

'I bet you could,' I tease, leaning towards him a little, angling my head and fluttering my lashes.

'Do you want to come on the boat now? I can show you just how it is at sea with me.'

I snatch a look at the peaceful water. I'm tempted. The sun hangs low in the sky in the west and bruises the sea with its reflection. Deep purple and orange colours move and swirl around with the onset of late evening. 'Yeah. It's better than having Phoebe nag me for checking my emails too much or sitting alone in my room at home silently playing the keyboard.'

'Glad to know it's only a yes because the competition is so low.' Dinos steps onto the boat, then turns around with an outstretched hand. 'Come on, you know you can hide anywhere with me.'

Chapter 11

When we are away from the coastline, able to look back at the glittering lights of Kassiopi like they're fairy lights at Christmas, and the haze of Albania is closer than before, Dinos cuts the engine, and drops the anchor. I scoot onto the front of the boat. I've never paid much attention to the names and parts of boats, which I suppose is strange for someone living in a harbour village, but boats aren't our family trade, and they're not something I've needed to know about or ever been interested in. I've always been all about music and languages.

Dinos sits by my side, and for a moment the only sound is that of the waves gently knocking against the boat.

My brain is so full, it's hard to empty it. Even now, looking out at the expanse of our coastline, I can't help but wonder if my "real" parents live here still. Have I ever seen them? Are they English? Part Greek? If I met them, would I know they were my parents? Would my face match one of theirs or parts of both?

'I can hear your brain from here,' Dinos whispers close to my ear.

'Shh, no you can't.'

'I can. You're worrying.'

'No. I'm not.' As I watch him over my shoulder, he shrugs and moves a centimetre further from me. 'Okay, I am,' I admit.

'Is it just the waiting, or is it the stuff you can't say?'

I look back across to Corfu, searching the lights. They become brighter as the sun disappears for the night.

'Both.' At least that's something honest I can say.

'Do you want to talk about it, or do you want distraction?'

'Both.' I grin, shifting to turn away from Corfu and towards Dinos.

He lets out a puff of laughter. 'Well, you're always easy to please, aren't you?'

'You wouldn't want me any other way.'

'Correct.'

'You were going to tell me about how you flirt with girls on the boat.' I tuck my feet to one side of me, careful to keep my modesty in my white dress.

'Pretty sure that is not what I said. I think I said something like, I can show you how it is out at sea.'

'With me... *I can show you how it is out at sea with me*. That's what you said.'

We sit in eye contact for a moment longer than normal before Dinos turns his head and moves to stand up.

'Yeah, I guess I did say that, didn't I. Well, this is what it's like to be out at sea with me. And luckily without Pa watching over me.' The boat sways as he leans on the bit in the middle, the bit where the steering wheel is.

'So why aren't you flirting with these rich girls? Half the boys from school have already slept with at least ten girls each this season.' I can't help but roll my eyes at some of the things I've heard at school. It makes me feel lucky to have Sebastian who is that much older. It's one of the many reasons a lot of girls in school have older boyfriends. The ones our age are more interested in one-night stands with girls they'll never see again than the fear of using one of us and being hung by their balls by our fathers. I remember Spiros Sakkos loudly announcing that girls on holiday drink and do things they would never do at home, and he was going to let them do what they liked to him. Zander laughed so hard and told him he'd be lucky to find one girl stupid enough to sleep with him. I don't even want to recall his facial expression and hand gestures even if they are imprinted on my frontal lobe forever.

'Not everyone is like that.'

'You must've had girls offer.'

'Oh yeah,' Dinos's lips curl in the dimming light in a smug sort of way, 'I've had girls offer all right.'

'But you're seriously not interested?'

He folds his arms and shakes his head. 'Nah. I like someone else.'

'What? Really?' Coming bolt upright at this news, I shift to sitting on my knees. 'Who? You have to tell me who!'

'Nope. No way.' Dinos folds his arms over his broad chest.

'Why not?'

'Because... because you'd tell her.' His voice sinks so low it hovers over the water barely audible.

'So, you can keep a secret, but I'm not trustworthy?' I narrow my voice to a pinpoint, hoping it will needle him into telling me.

'I didn't say that. And anyway, you didn't tell me the big secret earlier. I thought we always told each other our secrets.' A shadow falls over Dinos's face. The bones, so well sculpted under his skin, seem harsher than a moment ago.

'We do,' I say softly. 'We did. I guess some things are more complicated.'

He's right. We always told each other our secrets. A wash of awkwardness sits on my skin like the delicate film of sweat between my breasts and at the back of my neck.

The moment is too weighted. I move out of it by checking my email again, pulling the screen to refresh the page.

'Checking again?' Dinos turns on a bright light in the centre of the boat, then comes to sit by my side.

I nod, transfixed by the blueish light of my phone, dazed by the wonder of what might be there, but at this time of the evening likely won't be.

'Out of interest, have you checked your junk mail?'

'What? No.' This pulls my attention from the sickly blue light and back onto him. 'No, no, I didn't even think of that.'

I click on the junk mail. As I wait for it to load my tongue feels as though it's swelled to a thousand times its size and goosebumps ravage my skin in spite of the warmth of the evening.

There, nestled amongst emails telling me I've won a million euros or I have an impossible delivery on the way from Amazon, are two sensible emails. One to say my results are in, and another to say:

We've found a match!

Chapter 12

My breathing becomes ragged. Short shallow breaths nip in and out of my lungs and spots of light dance in front of my eyes. I slide my phone away and lie down, covering my face with my hands. Dinos is by my side, telling me to breathe slowly. He counts to make me take longer breaths in and out, but it's not helping. Wheezing sounds rattle in my lungs and tears stream along my temples. Not floods, but thin rivers into my hairline.

I have a match.

Someone out there has DNA like mine, and they could be anyone.

'Listen to my voice. Hey, Dora, listen to me. Focus on my voice and not what's in your head. Do you remember your first day of school?'

School? I shake my head. I suppose I do, but not really. Not in this moment that's for sure. In this moment all I can see is the baby – me – in the newspaper, left behind. If I open the email, what will I find? A parent? A distant relative? I need to open it, but my throat is closing up. My dress suddenly feels too tight and my skin crawls in a cold sweat.

'Listen, I still remember your first day at school. You had your hair in plaits on the side of your head. You were skipping towards me, well, I thought you were, but I was standing by the teacher, so you were skipping to her. Your mama was in floods of tears, and you turned to her and gave her a big hug and some reassuring words. I opened my mouth to tell you my name, but you sweetly smiled and ran past me. I still remember it so clearly. I thought you were an angel with your long blonde hair and clear blue eyes. Even with all the people who visit the island, I'd never seen a girl who looked like you. Still never have.'

Dinos slips his hand into mine, removing its grip from my dress. Although my chest is still rattling under the weight of the emails, listening to the mellow tones of his voice is comforting enough to get air back into my lungs.

'You c–can't tell anyone,' I stutter between gasps. I need to tell him everything. I can't deal with this alone and I have to open the email before we hit dry land again. It's hours before anyone will wonder where we are. Or at least anyone who would go looking for us. Other than Dinos leaving Phoebe buying drinks, no one would think twice about the fact he didn't go back right away. But she'll have soon worked out that he wasn't coming back, and other than wondering and being nosy, she won't care all that much.

'Just focus on me for now. Not on your phone or anything else.' Dinos flops down next to me, our arms pressing together and his warm hand still gripping mine. 'Open your eyes, look at the stars coming out. Can you see them?'

Now that the sun is barely visible, stars are starting to appear.

Dinos continues, 'Sometimes, when the sun is raging and sweat is pouring out of me, I think of those stars hiding behind our pale blue sky. They're always there, living their own life or whatever. They exist and we can't see them. It's the same with whatever's in that email, Dora. It only changes things if you want it to, like looking at those stars can make us feel something when we see them. They haven't changed, they didn't do anything new. It's only our reaction to what was there all along.'

My breathing begins to steady itself enough, just enough.

'I was born here,' I wheeze.

'What? On this boat?'

A laugh makes fresh tears stream from my eyes and into my hairline.

'No, you idiot.' Hysteria bubbles up in laughter. 'In Corfu. I–, I was born in Corfu.'

'I thought you were from Romania.'

'So did I.'

Instinctively I roll towards him. He pulls me in as I squeeze my eyes shut, doing my best not to let out the deluge of emotions that want to pour from me. I inhale his masculine scent with its hint of motor oil and sage. I think of the stars. He's right. Nothing changes, only my sight and my insight.

He silently holds me for the longest time and it's impossible not to wonder what it would be like if things were different, if he loved me differently and not just as a friend. The thought makes me pull away from him as guilt about Sebastian, loyal Sebastian, ripples over my bones. And anyway, he likes someone else. He's said as much.

'How do you know you were born here?'

I sit up, removing myself from Dinos and taking my hand out of his. I'd almost forgotten it was there; mine fitted so neatly inside his. Gently rubbing my face, I question how much I should say; I shouldn't have said as much as I have. But I suppose it's too late now.

'Mama and Baba told me. It all came out with this stupid DNA test. They didn't want people to know about me, about how I'd been found here. Thought I might be hounded, or my real parents might do something to harm me.'

'Harm you?'

I take a breath and work out how to start from the beginning and where the beginning even is. It takes me time to get my words out, to tell him how I was found with a note as a newborn baby, and being a special case, I could get adopted quicker than most. The words from the note haunt me and it's hard for me to relay them to him. I know Dinos is good with his English, it's one of the reasons his pa wants him to have a boat and take people fishing when they're here on holiday. His pa's English isn't as good. It's slow and cautious. Dinos excelled at English at school; we used to study and practise together.

I recite the words, slowly and carefully, 'The note left with me said, *Tell God, at least I didn't kill it. Call it Keres.*'

'Hell, Dora, that's dreadful,' he growls. 'Isn't that the name of those weird death creatures we learnt about in Greek History?' I nod. 'You sure you want to look at those DNA results?'

I know he's trying to lighten the mood, but he's right. It's one of the reasons I'm terrified.

I turn to assess him over my shoulder now that he's sitting with his legs tucked up against his torso, his arms holding them in place. The light on the boat illuminates his forehead and cheekbones but leaves his eyes in shadow. The movement of the boat had been soothing when Dinos was holding me, rocking us, now it jostles against the waves and it feels like it's trying to push emotions out of me. Shaking me until words fall out.

'This is why I'm afraid, *and* have to know. What if I'm walking around and they recognise me, because I look like them, and they know it's me, and they regret letting me live? Then what? Every possible outcome has crossed my mind over and over in the past eight weeks.'

'Slow down, slow down.' His voice remains steady in spite of mine running wild. 'I think you need to look at the email. While we are here, alone, you can scream and cry or look them up and process it all, and there's no one to question you, no one to hide from.'

'Only you.'

'You can't hide from me, even when you try.'

'Hmm, I guess not.'

Dinos pushes my phone towards me. It has to be now or never. He's right, I won't get this level of solitude anywhere else, even though I'm not actually alone. I have support, impartial support. Support with no agenda other than kindness. Not that Mama and Baba have an agenda, but they do wish to press this all into the ground and bury it for no one to find. Although I want to do the same, I guess, I know Dinos won't need me to hide anything from him.

Sucking in a deep breath, I hold it in my lungs, letting it burn a little with pressure. I pick up the phone, keeping the breath in, I press on the email that says there's a match. I'll come back to my DNA profile after. I need to see this first. The email takes an age to load, making the air in my lungs feel like it's expanding, ready to burst, burning like I've swallowed the sun. I'm just about ready to vomit the breath out when the email loads and there in black and white is a list of names of people who match. The air spills from my lungs as I read the top one.

There's a rectangle where a profile photo can be uploaded, only there's no image other than the standard outline of a head and shoulders where they haven't uploaded one, and it says, Mother: LP

Chapter 13

There are no words, there's only numbness. I slide my phone over to Dinos and he reads what I've just read.

'Gamoto, your mother is on here? "LP"? Is that it — there's nothing more? Now what? What happens next?'

'I can message her.' My voice is almost consumed by the soft churning of the waves under the boat.

What now? The ultimate question I have no desire to answer. *What now?* Perhaps we could stay on the boat forever, or move to a remote part of Corfu where no one else lives. Or maybe we can leave the boat and live on a mountain. Only there's no part of me that would truly wish for that. I could never wish to be away from this place I love and the people I love. This is my home, with the boats in the harbour, restaurants renowned for one delicious dish or another, and smiling faces that greet me in every shop. I don't want to run from it all. Not that Dinos would agree anyway, even if I did want to go. Which, of course I don't.

At least I gave him the sensible answer that jumped into my head; I can message my biological mother now through the DNA website. Why be on here if she isn't looking for me?

Dinos slides the phone back towards me. I snatch it up and scroll the other names. The others are all distant cousins a thousand times removed. No one who would likely even know my parents. Some are paternal and some maternal. Thirty four other names in total, that's all. With surnames like Jones and West and Pelletier among others. Most live in England from what I can see. My mother doesn't list any information other than her initials.

Dinos leans over the edge of the boat and lets the sea lap his fingers, giving me time to roll the facts around in my mind. He has strong instincts, his silence is to give me space, which part of me wants and the other part of me wants to pour out thoughts and words in no sensible order. So much so that they've all lodged in my throat at once.

If she did want me dead, she now knows I'm alive. Unless I'm not the only child she dumped. My breathing still feels laboured in a way I've never felt before, making me lightheaded.

'Would you like some water?' Dinos wipes his fingers over his shorts. 'I think there should be some going in the emergency pack. Might be a packet of crisps too if you want them.'

'Water would be good. Thank you.'

Dinos manoeuvres around the boat making it sway as he turns and dips down into the hatch, rummaging around god knows where.

I take a deep breath and hold it in like I did before opening the email. It already seems like an age ago, even though it can't really be all that long at all. Thirty minutes? Three hours? The minutes have folded together and I can't tell how much time has passed.

I look back at my beloved Corfu, my home of Kassiopi glittering as brightly as ever, with streaks of light dashing across the gentle waves. The warped reflection of life there in the sea. The imperfect mirror that has a beauty of its own. That's how I feel, like I've stepped into a new world that's full of uncertain lines and I have no clue what the rules are or how to progress. It looks like my life, only it's not. It's a strange reflection of it.

Dinos passes me a bottle of lukewarm water, open ready for me. I gulp it down, realising how thirsty all the upset has made me. I pass the bottle back to him, and he takes a gulp too.

'What am I going to tell Mama and Baba? Should I message this person first? If I do, what should I say?'

Dinos wipes his mouth on the back of his arm and settles down next to me.

'I wish I could help. But you're going to have to work that out by yourself.' He tilts his head up to the sky. 'Just remember, they're always there, the stars, the email. You do what you want to do about it. You can talk about the stars, or forget they're there. It won't change their existence.'

'But what I do next, what I've already done, it has consequences. What if my parents hate me now?'

Dinos spits out laughter. 'Your parents could never hate you. I don't know anyone who hates you, Dora.'

'Not even Alexia Gataki? Doesn't she hate everyone?'

'Nah, she's just stuck up. Everyone adores you'

Dinos jostles into my shoulder slightly and we're left with our arms pressed together.

I look up into his eyes, the lights of Kassiopi making them glimmer. My heart hammers in my chest and a hot flush of lust makes me dizzier than the shock of the finding my biological mother. We look at each other for a moment more than we should. It's enough to make me question everything. What would I do if Dinos told me I was the girl he liked? Right now with the look in his eyes...

My breathing accelerates more than before.

'I best get you home. It's getting late.' Dinos stands and moves towards the centre of the boat.

The tension must have all been in my head.

I'm confused, that's all.

Confused and drowning in all the raw emotion that's been brought about and I'm projecting it all on to him, that's all. A way of distracting myself from the shock of finding my mother.

This time I look back out to sea, away from my island. Away from the island that found me, with the people who took me in and looked after me, kept me alive and helped me to flourish. They haven't just fed me and kept me warm, they've loved me. Played games with me when I was small, taught me to read and write. Given me a real name and peace. And for the sake of knowledge, I may have ruined that peace.

The boat engine whirs and stops. This happens enough times to draw my attention. Dinos shuffles and swears under his breath.

'What's going on?'

'It won't start. It might be low on fuel. Pa was meant to fill her up. On a rare occasion when he's being lazy, he does it in the morning.'

'What do you mean, *might*? Can't you tell? Why wouldn't you check before we left?'

Dinos emerges into the overhead light, scrubbing his forehead with the back of his hand.

'The fuel gauge hasn't worked for years. I just thought he would've topped it up. It's no big deal. There's always a small canister of fuel for this reason.'

A breeze sweeps over the water, although it's not in the least bit cold. Not yet. The weather won't really start to turn for a good few weeks, but at this time of year, things can change in a moment.

I can hear Dinos swearing under his breath.

'What now?'

'There's no fuel. He must've taken it to refill. We're stuck here.'

Chapter 14

Dinos calls around for help. At first, it's nothing but dead ends. People are out, people can't get here for a while, people don't answer their phones or they're working a second job in a family restaurant. Eventually, he calls Konstantinos. Sebastian spends a lot of time with him driving around, but Dinos has known him forever. We both have. His baba also owns a boat that's moored in the harbour.

It shouldn't, but this call makes me nervous. However much I know I've done nothing wrong, I also know how Sebastian will react when he finds out I've been alone at sea with Dinos.

If I'm being honest with myself, it's more than just the fact Sebastian might try to punch Dinos for spending any time alone with me. It's the way my skin tingled when Dinos was close to me, the same way it does when I stay out in the sun too long. I'd give anything not to feel this way towards Dinos. When I'm with him, he seems to read my thoughts and pre-empt my needs. It's more than that, but I can't explain it.

No. Stop it. I'm with Sebastian. Things have been so magical with him. He spoils me, he's grown up and ready to start a life together. That feeling between Dinos and me probably comes down to our shared history and nothing more. I need to tuck it away again, into a drawer in the back of my mind. I'm glad to have him as a friend, at least I have that. I might've thought I loved him that way many years ago, but not now. Not anymore. We're just friends.

'Konstantinos will be here soon. Sebastian is giving him a lift over.'

We share a look.

Dinos's face, I'm sure, mirrors my own. Lips pressed together, we both nod. We both know he won't like that we're alone on a boat together. The muscles in my neck feel tight. Everything feels tight. Drawn out. Pulled to its limits.

'I take it he doesn't know about the DNA test.'

I shake my head and reach for my bag to check my face in the little compact that resides there. Luckily, lying on my back to cry has stopped my mascara from turning me into a circus clown. Only a few flecks of mascara are misplaced and only a few fine streaks of black. I dig in my bag and pull out a raspberry balm for my lips and cheeks to freshen my face and hide my feelings ready for Sebastian.

Dinos snorts and turns away. I don't ask what he's thinking, I don't want to know. We sit in silence. It's the first time there's been any awkwardness between us. Dinos keeps himself behind the wheel, and I stay on the front of the boat. Keeping the windscreen between us. The boat's blinding light stretches over our heads as a beacon showing our location. It's as though we are hiding from each other in plain sight. It's more than I can bear, with the inward turmoil of what to do next about my biological mother, and Dinos now hiding from me, and the imminent arrival of Sebastian. I can't take it.

'You won't tell anyone will you?' My voice cuts through the tension, much harsher than I intended.

'I'm not going to answer that. It's a stupid question.' His arms are folded solidly across his chest. I can't see his face but the tone of his voice suggests the deepest sneer imaginable.

I know he's right. I knew it before I spoke. But it broke a silence that even the gentle pounding of the waves couldn't cut through.

'I guess you're not going to want to come out on the boat with me again.' Dinos gets up and skulks towards me. He sits down next to me hard enough to make the boat sway. 'But I'm always here.'

His open palm rests between us. My fingertips tingle at the thought of tucking themselves up in his hand. It's impossible to resist. I slip my hand into his and he gently squeezes. I know he will always be here for me, no matter what. He's the best friend I've ever had.

Boat lights draw closer to us from the distance.

'Look, do you think that's him?' I snatch my hand from Dinos's and extend my arm to point at the bright dot drawing closer. Standing, I shade my eyes against the harsh light of our boat to focus in on it. As the bright dot gets closer, I can see the outline of a boat, and three shadows standing on its deck.

My palms turn clammy. I do my best to look calm in case one of the shadows belongs to Sebastian. I know how bad this looks and how it could tarnish my reputation, which is something that means so much to my parents. It's okay to turn a blind eye at what all the boys get up to, but there's still some pressure on girls to be seen to be doing the right thing.

An engine hums along the water towards us. My legs begin to buckle and I sit back down. I watch the light speeding towards us until my eyes ache from its glare on the black waves.

It's hard to figure out who's who. I hear Konstantinos's booming laughter, calling Dinos a *malaka*, a jerk. There's a tone that suggests it's more than banter. Zander's there with them too, he stays back in the shadows, directing a sympathetic nod towards Dinos. He doesn't look at me at all.

Sebastian comes into focus. As his boat comes level with ours, he studies my face. With some careful manoeuvring, Konstantinos's bulk steadies the boat, then Sebastian somehow manages to launch himself with one big stride onto our boat, making it rock, and nearly projecting himself, and us, off the other side. Quickly he rights himself, looks at me, then before I can speak, he turns to Dinos. 'Think I'll be coming back with you. Think we have some catching up to do.'

A few words are muttered from one boat to the next; none come from me. Dinos is quickly passed the fuel, and the other boat with Sebastian's friends on board only hangs around long enough to check that our boat can start up. Then they're off at a great speed that makes us rock and sway. They seem to leave at a much faster pace than they came to find us.

'Are you cheating on me, or did this *malaka* kidnap you?' Sebastian sits next to me and crosses his arms over his chest. In the harsh light of the boat, with his features pulled tight, he reminds me of a dragon. I'd never really seen that in his features before. But he isn't in the wrong. I am. I'm in the wrong to spend time with another man. I've been hiding a part of me from him and sharing it with Dinos instead. I guess that's sort of cheating. Not in the normal sense, but right now I'm riddled with guilt.

The anchor creaks as Dinos winds it back up ready for us to leave. We've moved to the side to be out of his way.

Under the gentle punches of the sea on the bow, Sebastian hisses into my ear, 'What have I done to deserve this humiliation? This disgrace? I thought we had something here, perhaps a life, and here you are alone with this... this...' As he struggles to find a word, my eyes flick up towards Dinos's back as he works. He only deserves good and kind words. I'm the one letting everyone down.

'Nothing happened. Dinos was, is, a gentleman. I wasn't feeling very well, and he suggested I could clear my mind at sea. He was telling a funny story about chatting up the girls he takes fishing.' I call over the last of the clattering sounds, 'Weren't you, Dinos? Telling me about chatting up girls on the boat?' I turn back to Sebastian. 'We're friends, we have been from our first day at school.'

'So, he takes you to be one of the girls on his fishing boat?'

The muscles in Sebastian's jaw contract and the pulse in his temple visibly throbs. I don't want to lose him. Throwing everything we have away for Dinos, who is only a friend and has never said he feels anything more for me, would be the definition of insanity. I'm too all over the place with everything that's going on, that's the problem. I've confused my raw emotion for everything I've found out tonight with depth of feeling for Dinos, because I can talk to him. That's all it is. I'm overly emotional about everything and I'm projecting it onto him. I couldn't tell Sebastian because I wouldn't want his parents or grandparents to find out. That's all. I don't want to drag his family into my mess. I don't think they would understand, and my parents would be devastated at me sharing information of my adoption. Dinos doesn't want to get involved. Instead, he turns the boat and guides us at a measured pace back towards shore. Gently we bump along over the black silk that is the sea.

'You have humiliated me.' It's a growl close to my ear. Sebastian keeps his voice low to avoid it reaching Dinos behind the wheel.

'I haven't. Nothing happened. Nothing.'

'My family could ruin you, you know that, don't you?'

Words fall short. They all drop off the boat and into the sea to be swept away with the jelly fish. *My family could ruin you, you know that, don't you*? What the hell does that mean? And no, I didn't know that. Well, I suppose I know they hold influence of sort but to *ruin me*? What does that mean? What does it entail? Fear swells like a punched eye and I'm too afraid to ask.

'Not just you,' he adds, 'your family. All of you.'

'Please, Sebastian, how can I make it up to you?' I clutch his hand. It's burning hot and clammy. I do my best to pull it toward me. I can't let him hurt my family in any way. I'm doing enough of that myself.

His eyes drop to our hands wrapped up together.

'I like you, Theadora. I think I could marry you. I can see you being my wife and bringing up our beautiful children. But this—' He looks out to sea and shakes his head. For a while I think this is it, but then he turns back to face me. 'You cut him out. He is dead to you, or your family business will be dead to Corfu along with your reputation.'

Chapter 15

Back on dry land, I still feel as though I'm swaying on the sea. Sebastian wants me to whisper in people's ears that Dinos tried it on with me, that I obviously turned him down and now I no longer want to speak to him.

Sebastian herds me away with his arm slung over my neck. We leave Dinos sorting his boat with barely a goodbye. The look in his eyes cuts me as he watches us leave. They've sunk back and there's a shake to his head before I force myself to look away. If Sebastian sees that I've let my attention fall on him, it will equate to more problems, and I'm already accumulating enough of those to last me a lifetime.

'Can you walk me home, please?'

'One drink, then you can go home.' Sebastian turns and greets someone who says hello in our direction.

I bite my cheek. This isn't the Sebastian I know. Yes, he's always been passionate and fiercely jealous, but in a way that made me feel protected, looked after. This is something else. It reminds me of a time I was early to meet him from work. I heard two members of the staff talking about him, although I denied to him that I had heard what they said. I was scrolling my phone and not obviously eavesdropping. Sebastian had rounded the corner unseen and heard them. He blew up and there was something about his tone and the way he pointed his finger at the two young girls that was actually a little frightening. He was harsh with his words, threatening the girls, but then they were very clearly in the wrong. They'd openly called him lazy. In my head I'd defended him, sure that they deserved this because they were being so rude about him. But now I know I was right to have been left with this strange niggling sensation. Something has been lurking under the surface and now it's being turned on me.

'Can you please take me home? Now I'm off the boat, I don't feel very well again.'

'I thought people usually suffered with *sea* sickness. Besides, I thought you wanted to make it up to me to show you're mine, not *his*. It was bad enough with last night's performance from you in the car.'

'I don't belong to anyone.' I'm not sure whether he has heard my soft tone or if he's choosing to ignore me as he winds me past a group of older people, freshly on holiday judging by their pale skin. They laugh and smile in our direction. I even overhear a blonde lady saying *young love*. If only she knew how confusing this *young love* was, maybe she would have a different expression on her face. Yesterday, I thought I was in love. I had it all mapped out. Everything was simple and even this DNA test was just going to be something interesting, not... whatever it turns out it is.

I end up back where I started.

Back sitting at a table with Phoebe and Xristina. Only now there's a few more people, including Konstantinos and Zander from the boat. The conversation pauses as Sebastian sits me down then disappears to the bar to get us drinks.

'So where have you been? As if we haven't heard.' Xristina looks almost giddy. Her eyes are wide and she's biting her bottom lip, holding back the cascade of words that she wants to burst out with.

This is normally Phoebe's area of expertise, asking all the questions, getting all the gossip, but she's being oddly reserved. Maybe because of my earlier sharp exit over my stupid emails. All of this has at least snatched my attention away from my biological mother, but I would really have preferred something positive to draw my attention, instead of squelching around in all this painful awkwardness. It's like being sucked into the wet sand where the sea meets the beach. If you stand there long enough it's easy to sink and disappear millimetre by millimetre. I'm afraid that if I stay here with everyone looking at me, the same could happen right now. I might disappear forever.

Sebastian puts two Mythos beers on the table, scrapes up a chair and places it next to me before settling into it.

All eyes are on us. Both of my friends are silent for a change; Konstantinos is sniggering.

Xristina nudges Phoebe a little too hard in the ribs, making her suck in air through her teeth.

'Xristina!' Phoebe rubs at her side.

'Getting you back for earlier,' she hisses.

'So, what really happened? These idiots seem to think you were having a little too much fun with Dinos on his baba's boat.

We've both said that's insane. You two have been friends forever. If you liked each other like that, why wait till now to show it?'

Sebastian, who has been taking deep gulps of his beer, slams it back on the table.

'Well, Theadora was telling me that the *malaka* made a move. Obviously, she told him where to go. I'd bet my hotel chain that he knew his boat didn't have enough fuel. He was trying to keep her there as long as he could.'

Everyone around the table shifts, looking from one to the other, mouths gaping and flapping with nothing but the warm night's breeze to pass between their teeth.

'Is that what you think?' Dinos's voice sounds from behind me. 'That I orchestrated this and hit on your girlfriend?' He begins to laugh.

Sebastian stands with another scrape of his chair. 'Yeah, it is actually. But the woman has class. She knows a good thing when she has it.'

Dinos lowers his brows and curls his lips. His words are unspoken but I can hear his voice in my head anyway, asking me to correct Sebastian about what happened, asking me to defend him. I want to, but all I hear is the sound of Sebastian shouting at those two young girls and then the same voice deep in my ear threatening my family. I want to come up with words that will please everyone, but the truth isn't something I can blurt out without causing more damage and confusion to my family. Sounds stutter out but no words follow.

'Guess that's how it was then.' Dinos's eyes narrow on me and a shadow descends. Then it's like he's seeing through me. He shakes his head, turns and walks out of the bar.

Sebastian sits back down and shuffles his chair in as though nothing has happened.

Phoebe lets out a hard exhale. 'Bloody hell. I'd never have expected that from Dinos.'

'Funny. I can't believe it either,' Zander's voice is completely monotone. His black eyes are fixed on me. I can feel his glare pressing down on me, but no one reacts to him. Everyone's talking at once. Everyone except me and Zander.

I monitor my breathing and grip the cold Mythos in my fingers until the frozen touch is almost painful. I count in my head the minutes until I can get home and cry.

Zander finishes his drink and leaves without another word.

'I feel like I'm going to be sick with shock,' Phoebe announces above all the noise and the music from the bar.

'Please no!' Sebastian starts. 'I had enough of that from this one. Twice round in a circle in my car and she vomits everywhere. You're just a delicate flower, aren't you? Easy to damage.' Sebastian shoots me a look from the corner of his eye as he swigs from his drink. It's a sly and narrow look, albeit brief.

I never thought he would humiliate me like this. Konstantinos can't stop laughing at me. They all are.

'You should take me out sometime,' Xristina says. 'I love fast cars.'

'Maybe I will.' Sebastian puts down his empty bottle on the table.

Konstantinos manages to stop laughing enough to interject, 'I could take you.' It's the first time I've been relieved by his presence all night. At least now he can supply a diversion by trying to flirt with Xristina while I work out how I can get out of here as fast as humanly possible.

Chapter 16

I cry silently so as not to wake my parents. It's only when my eyes burn and my lungs feel as though they're about to collapse that I manage to stop. It feels like hours until I'm calm. Eventually I pick up my phone and message Dinos.

I'm sorry.

That's all I have to say. It won't be that long until I need to be at work in the family shop. I need to look human – and be human – although I feel like a gelatinous mess. It all feels so impossible. Where the dead of night meets dawn, I meet a shadow in my mind, one that's riddled with guilt. Light gently seeps in the cracks in my shutters. I need to focus on sorting one problem at a time — like deciding what to say to my biological mother. But not now. Now I need to find some rest. Some impossible peace of mind.

After a short bout of sleep, Mama bangs on my door startling me before barging in.

'Theadora, you must get up. You'll be late to help with the deliveries. Baba is already there getting everything ready. The baker will be dropping off early today, remember?' She throws open my curtains and I throw my sheet over my head in the full knowledge that she'll come and tug it off. Usually, I'm up and ready early. It's only on the rare occasion we go through these motions, like I'm still a child. She often reminds me that I'll always be *her* child, no matter how old I am and how many children I may one day have. I'm still *her* baby.

Before she gets to me, I yank the sheet off myself.

'Mama?'

'Come on, Theadora. Up! Up!' Mama bustles about, picking up last night's clothes from the floor and pacing the room full of intention and looking at things I don't even see. Invisible dirt perhaps. It's like when a dog stops and stares into space. I'm sure I'm not the only person to believe they are looking at ghosts.

'Mama, you know the story you told me about the time you first saw me. How much of it was true?'

She almost stumbles as her feet stutter to a stop. All the fast pace from a moment before is gone, her momentum interrupted by my words, and she's like a car that's stalled and won't start again. Frozen in time.

'I shouldn't have asked. We're in a rush.' I swing my legs out of the bed, sit up and rub my face. Even the question was enough to unnerve her. I'm not sure she'll answer.

She used to tell me about the day she first saw me. That she had been dreaming about me for months, then she and Baba were at the orphanage in Romania, and as soon as she saw me, she knew that everything had been leading to me. It was her job to look after me. She held me to her heart and that was that. My parents did everything to make me theirs. She always tells it better than I do of course, with tears in her eyes and usually combined with a lovely – but finger-numbing – hand squeeze.

Mama comes to sit next to me, her arms still cradling the dirty clothes she's collected from around my room like they're a baby in her arms.

'It's much more complicated than you can know, or that I would want to tell you. Not now, not this morning. You have to get to work. But perhaps we could go for a walk together this evening and I'll tell you how it was when I first saw you. How it really happened.'

'I'd like that.'

We share a wistful smile before she tilts her head, as though seeing me for the first time.

'Your eyes are as puffy as marshmallows. Have you been crying? What happened last night?'

I turn away, shaking my head. 'No time now. I guess I'll tell you tonight.' And with that I pick up my phone and slip out of the room to get ready for work.

As I make my way past the all-seeing photos outside my room, I nod a good morning to them. No happy smiles for them today. Instead, I look down at the phone in my hand. There's a message from Dinos.

I know.

That's all it says. *I know.* Of course, he knows. He sees me and knows I'm a fool. A bubble of emotion swells in my chest, wanting to burst, but I don't have time to focus on it. I need to get ready. I can't let anyone else down today. And besides, what can I say? I'm sure he'll never forgive me now. I trust him enough to keep my truth *and* take the blame for us being out there together too. He would never come forward and call me out as a liar, nor Sebastian either, if it might hurt me. He's much too kind for that. There's no way he could hurt anyone, I'm sure.

'Theadora, don't just stand about! Get ready!' Mama sighs, and I do my best to focus my mind with one step at a time.

Chapter 17

After the deliveries are done, it's my morning to sit at the till. Baba is out the back doing the accounts and orders today. All the boring stuff that has to be done. Stuff that I have no interest in at all. I often sit here and wonder what I *really* have an interest in, and whether that even matters. I'm good at things, I used to think they were my interests... music, languages. All I really want is to have a happy life in my beautiful village with family and friends around me. I could work here forever; I don't suppose it would really matter. It might be nice to have an adventure, but it doesn't feel possible anymore.

The shop's quiet today, which is perfect. Normally I would read a book or doomscroll on my phone, but today, although I am spending time staring at my phone, it's mostly to study the information about my heritage.

I'm English. Eighty-four per cent English according to the DNA test. Mostly East Anglia, some Northumberland and some other places too. There's a bit of Scottish and Norwegian, with a dash of Swedish for good measure. I guess it's no wonder I'm so blonde. But mostly, I'm English. Not Greek. Not even a little bit Greek.

Based on this, both of my parents were likely from England, which means the letter that was written in English was also probably a first language. These are assumptions still, but at least they're ones with some merit behind them now. Maybe my mother came here, had her baby, dumped me and then went home like nothing happened. Maybe she hid her bump under layers of clothing and always intended on leaving me here.

I move on to looking at all the distant cousins from around the world. They are so far removed they only hold a distant relative in common with me, and each one seems to be different. On one of the profiles there's a small photo of a middle-aged man with a round face and a balding head. He looks jolly but I can't see even the tiniest speck of myself in the image. I guess when I took this test, I thought I might find a connection to the past or to someone else that felt real, but all of these seem like a story on a screen that belongs to someone else. Not me. This isn't my family. My family are Mama, Baba, Theía Agatha, Ria, my friends and those around me. No one else. I can't believe it took all this to make me see there's nothing else out there worth having.

I swipe away the information on my phone and open up my notes to begin picking out words to say to my biological mother.

Dear LP

I am your daughter. The one you tossed aside and left for dead.

I proceed to type out six similar messages only to delete them as a customer comes in, an old lady who looks like a holidaymaker in her wide brimmed hat.

'*Kalimera*,' I call.

The customer shoots me a coy smile as though she's unsure whether I'm talking to her. She then busies herself in the crisps aisle. She must think I don't speak anything other than Greek. Likely it's her first time here in Corfu and she's afraid I'll talk to her and she won't understand me. Funny how some people can be so painfully shy.

As soon as she's out of sight I write another message.

Dear biological mother,

How do you sleep at night? Did you write the note or was it you and my biological father? I need to know!

No. Too harsh. Too honest.

What if my father had taken me away from her? I know nothing at all about the circumstances. What if she had psychosis and has no memory of what happened to me and has been looking for her lost child ever since? Although, surely, she would have been able to see the newspaper report. Except they were in Greek, and if she only speaks English, she wouldn't have been able to read them. But there was the photo in the newspaper...

Too much speculation. I take a long steady breath and fill myself with the sweet smell of fresh peppers from today's deliveries.

Dear LP

I am your daughter. I was hoping you could give me some answers. I do not want or need anything else from you. I'm not sure you would be interested to know, but I have loving parents and they have brought me up well. I'm not looking to replace them. I would just like to know why you left, and if you have ever spent time regretting the action.

If you could possibly tell me where you are from, where you grew up in childhood, I would be interested to know.

Thank you,

Theadora (Keres)

This letter is better. It has promise. It's to the point, yet soft enough. It's been the best part of twenty years since she gave birth to me and time can change how people feel about almost anything.

Hearing shuffled footsteps, I quickly tuck my phone under some papers to my left and ready myself to serve the shy old lady who's been hiding with the crisps. But when I look up, I catch my breath at the sight of the person standing there.

'Dinos?'

'Theadora.'

Something about the way he says my name feels like a paper cut deep in my chest. It's not a mortal wound, but it's enough to niggle and upset. He almost never calls me Theadora.

'Why are you–?'

'My father is outside. I was told to come in to apologise to you.'

The elderly lady, tall but slightly bent-over, waits behind him.

'Let me just...' I gesture to the customer. 'Hello, please come forwards.'

Dinos steps back and waits. From the woman's accent in English, I think she's German. As she leaves, I call, '*Bis später*', and she beams at me, nodding before she exits.

'Sorry about that.'

'About the customer or the fact everyone thinks I'm a *malaka*?'

Dinos stands tall and looks over me in my seat. His crossed arms in his sleeveless shirt present the kind of closed body language I'm not used to seeing on him. It's not as harsh as squaring up to me, but I've hurt him and I don't know how to fix it.

'I didn't say any of that stuff, it was Sebastian.' I keep my voice low, and lean in, clutching the counter. 'He threatened my family.'

Dinos furrows his brows and his top lip curls into a snarl. 'What?'

'He said... What were his words?' I snap my fingers, trying to recall the exact wording. 'Something like, if I humiliate him, he will destroy me, the business and our reputation. I don't even know if it's possible, but I can't risk it, Dinos. I–'

'Dinos, have you apologised? I'm sorry, my girl, if Dinos came on too strong. He's still practising. No harm intended. Now, do you forgive him? Can we get on with our day?'

Manolis, Dinos's father, looms in the doorway with his tatty sleeveless top that very much matches Dinos's. Not that it's a uniform, or a style choice. It's the most practical outfit for the labour they undertake each day.

'Of course.'

'Good. Come on, boy. We have work to do. Good day, Theadora. Send my regards to your parents.'

I watch them leave, Dinos turning back to glance at me with his eyebrows still knitted tightly together.

Silence descends on the shop again, apart from the gentle hum of the freezers and the chillers. The air is dense with the fragrance of fresh fruit.

'What was Dinos apologising for, Theadora?'

Air rushes into my lungs and I clutch my chest at the low rumble of my father's disembodied voice.

'Baba?'

His silent feet step out from the shadows of the furthest aisle.

'I heard what Manolis said. I wasn't trying to hear, I was coming to tell you I'm going out for a short time. Is there something I need to know about?'

My hands fold into my lap and for the hundredth time in the past twenty-four hours I feel trapped and know a lie is about to vomit itself out of my mouth.

'Nothing. It was silly. A misunderstanding.'

'Silly enough that his father brought him here to apologise.'

'Honestly, Baba, it was a misunderstanding. Nothing more. I can't believe he made him apologise. Dinos has always been a good friend to me.' That's close enough to the truth that I can feel good about it and my lungs don't feel too tight, even if my clothes suddenly do.

'You've forgotten your mask. You know to put it on when customers are in here.'

The mask hangs from one ear. When I'm alone I leave it dangling for comfort, but I totally forgot it.

'Sorry, Baba.'

'If you want to talk to me, or your mama, you know you always can.'

'I know.'

Baba gives a sharp nod and catches a hooked finger on the tip of his nose. 'I'll be back before lunch.' He removes the distance between us and kisses the top of my head. 'Remember to put your mask on when people are in the shop.'

Then I'm alone, and I feel more alone than ever before in my life.

Chapter 18

Our chatter disturbs a small lizard that's basking in the last of the day's heat. It keeps pace with us along the wall then disappears into a crevice so small it seems impossible for it to fit, yet it does. A lot of things that once felt impossible are happening lately. I'm starting to wonder whether anything would shock me anymore.

So far, other than disturbing a lizard, our chat hasn't been too exciting. The cicadas sound more enthusiastic than we do, filling the air with a noise that I always think sounds like a million tiny maracas being shaken in perfect rhythm.

Mama and I have always been close, which I'm grateful for, but today, knowing there is more to be said, we are skirting around, talking of nothing and everything. In the same way we are skirting our way up to the twelfth-century castle above Kassiopi.

Mama had suggested walking next to the clarity of the sea and perhaps even down to one of the bays, but instead we decided to climb up across the rough stone slabs to the castle. Sometimes we walk side by side, then Mama walks ahead of me, only slightly disrupting the conversation as the path winds and narrows.

At this time in the evening most people visiting Kassiopi are settling down with a menu and choosing between the catch of the day, salad or souvlaki skewers, while gazing at the glittering sea.

As we make our way past the dappled shade of a large old olive tree, we carry on towards the wooden doors of the big stone building. We drop into silence, knowing that when we get where we are going, questions will be asked and answered.

Even with our vastly different heights, we keep in step with each other as we continue to climb, now encased by the stone walls as we walk through the remains of the castle and back out the other side.

I wonder when I first came here. How old I must've been. A baby? A toddler? I remember playing here when I was very small, and Baba calling to me to slow down, but I didn't listen. I'd seen a lizard that day too, bigger though, and scurrying away from me as fast as it could. I tripped and managed to graze my hands, knees and chin. I wailed, big tears falling faster than the blood on my knees. It pales in comparison to how much I cried last night, though. What I'd give to go back to worrying about the surface wounds of childhood instead of those that scar my insides when they tear me up.

We turn right and right again, then up six neat stone steps to our view across Kassiopi. A bird's-eye view, one that should never be skipped or overlooked. We've walked to this spot without verbal planning, letting our instincts guide us.

A couple nearby are gazing out to sea. We stand a short way from them, both of us leaning on the high wall. The beige stones are still warm.

After a pause long enough to give the couple time to move away, Mama exhales through her teeth. 'I don't know where to begin. I don't know how much to say.'

Leaning my forearms on the wall, instead of my hands, brings our faces more in line. I look over at the woman I call my mother. The woman who will always be my mother. The one who has sworn to love me no matter what. The one who has put everything on the line to protect me.

'Start wherever you need to.'

She studies my face in turn. Sometimes I wonder what she really sees. It's not as though she can look in my eyes and see a reflection of hers or Baba's. There is no vanity in her love for me, no reflected love because of her love for Baba. Her love for me, their love for me, is unique. Special. They brought me into their lives just for the love of me and nothing else. In that way I think being adopted is much purer than children born from the parents' flesh and blood.

A smile grazes my lips, but Mama doesn't return it. Instead, she looks out to sea. The sky is a hazy pink and all the terracotta roofs look as though they've been washed with warm-pink paint. It's another beautifully calm night.

'I was pregnant. We've told you it was hard for us to have a child of our own and you've never questioned that. I had been pregnant many, many times and lost them all. This baby was different. She had hung on longer than any other. Long enough to confirm we were having the girl I'd always dreamed of.' She stays focused on the sea, looking as far away from me as she possibly can. With her grey hair neatly tied in a bun, I can see her swallow before she continues. 'Baba thought I should stay with your Theía Agatha in Agios Stefanos. He thought it might help me to keep the baby, without all the reminders of loss scattered in each and every room at home. At first, I thought he was right. Things were progressing nicely with the baby but fear was always there in the back of my mind. It was so hard to escape.' She swallows again and licks her lips. 'It's true that I was dreaming of you, of a blonde child. Of course, then I thought I was dreaming of the child in my belly, wondering how on earth she'd got such bright blonde hair.' This brings light to her face, and a brief moment of elation dances over her eyes and her cheeks, but it quickly fades. Sweat touches the skin under my hair. It's another warm night, but this is something else. 'Then I had the most dreadful dream that I was drowning in a thick liquid. I remember that the most. A lot of what happened next is unclear. Very unclear. I know that I woke up and, and I had lost the baby. I called out for Agatha, but she wasn't there. I didn't know it then, but she was out looking after you. When she came home with a baby, and I saw you, I knew you were mine, but at the time it was more than that. I believed you were mine, I believed that I had birthed you. I took you and I wouldn't let you go.'

Confused images roll around my head. I'm sure none of them bear any resemblance to the truth of what really happened. It was probably uglier than anything I can conjure.

'This isn't a truth you can tell a child, Theadora. I hope you understand that, now you are a woman yourself. One day I hope you will give me many grandchildren to adore, and you will have a new understanding of the losses I suffered and the joy I had bringing you into my heart.'

'I'm sorry you went through that, Mama. You're so brave, and I'm lucky to have you as my mama.'

'I'm lucky to have such a kind and beautiful daughter.'

Mama wraps her small hand over mine and squeezes. I join her in looking out over the water and the little boats moored in the harbour.

I want to tell Mama that the woman who left me has been found. Although, that's all I know. She could be anywhere, here in Kassiopi, back in England... anywhere. But Mama has been through enough.

Down at the harbour, I can see Dinos walking along with a gas canister in hand to put on to the faded red boat. I can't take my eyes off him. He knows the secret I promised I would never tell anyone and he knows about my DNA test too. He is the only person I've been able to talk to and now he is mad at me. I would be mad at me, if I were him.

'Baba tells me something happened with Dinos.'

I whip round to look at Mama who's watching Dinos as he pulls in his boat closer to the dock before launching himself onto it with one big step.

'It was a misunderstanding. Nothing more. Nothing important.'

'He's been a good friend to you. At one time I thought Baba would be walking you down the aisle and he would be at the end of it.'

My lips vibrate in dismissal.

'No, Dinos has never seen me that way.'

'But you've seen him that way?'

'No! No. We are friends. Well, we were. I think we still are. But I'm with Sebastian. There's no changing that.'

A lump forms in my throat. A while ago I wouldn't have wanted to change that. Now I'm not so sure. Mama always seems to cut right to the bone and sees everything that's there in my core. I wonder if she believes me now.

'I like Dinos, of course I do, but Sebastian is a good and polite boy too, and he can give you a security that Dinos can't.'

'Is that what you thought about when you married Baba?'

Mama lets go of my hand and places it over her heart as she laughs. Her curls shimmy as a warm breeze touches our skin. She looks as though she's blushing, but it's hard to tell in the pinkish hue of the light.

'No, no. I knew we would never be millionaires. He had good prospects, of course, all of which will one day be yours to do what you want with. But no, I fell in love with him and it would not have mattered if he couldn't provide clothes for my back. As long as we were together, we had everything...' Her voice trails off and her eyeline dips towards the thick stones of the fortress that we're leaning on. 'Almost everything. You made our family complete.'

The lump in my throat swells. I can't work out why. Is it because of Mama's loving words, my lie about not seeing Dinos as more than a friend, or the fact that I don't think I love Sebastian? I'm wondering whether I ever really did, or whether I liked the idea of him more than the reality. Or perhaps it's that I haven't told her about the DNA test.

'Was there anything else making your eyes puffy this morning? Or was it just this misunderstanding with Dinos?'

'Just Dinos.'

The things I'm not telling my mother are beginning to pile on top of me, but I still can't manage to tell her about the test and the mother who left me behind.

In the dead of night, I'm still awake and staring at my phone. My message to my biological mother is written and lined up ready to send. There's no one to help me decide what to do. This is it. I send it, or I don't.

My hands are so clammy I'm in danger of dropping my phone as I read the words over one last time.

Dear LP

After taking a DNA test, I've been notified that I am your daughter. You have likely had the same notification by now. I do not want or need anything from you. I have loving parents and I'm not looking to replace them. But, if you would be willing to answer some questions, that would be very kind.

Thank you,

Theadora (Keres)

I hover for a moment longer before my thumb moves, almost in a spasm, and hits the SEND icon. Then it's gone.

The stars are always the same, but I'm changing my view of them, and I'm changing the future. For the good or the bad? I guess I'm about to find out.

Part 2 - 2022

Chapter 19

Our mouths collide and his hand slips its way across my back making me shiver. The sun is hanging low in the sky to our side, casting its glitter over the sea's blanket.

'Theadora,' he breathes into my mouth as he pulls me in.

Nervous energy trickles down my spine with the droplets of sweat from the heat of summer. At least here, out on the rocks that jut out into sea, we have shade from the olive trees and the sea breeze to cool us off after a hard day at work.

Sebastian pulls away. 'We've been together for over a year now, Theadora.'

His statement fills me with confusion. It's not that it's untrue, it is. But this sounds like the lead-up to something. Borderline an accusation.

Things have been okay for the past year. After I took on the acceptance that Sebastian and I are in this for the long haul, because I can't risk my parents being ruined in any way, we've been back to enjoying passing our time together. He takes me out for a nice meal now and then at one of his many restaurants and we see each other once a week, sometimes more, sometimes less. Sebastian is the perfect charming gentlemen as long as he isn't jealous. What more could a girl really want? I get to spend time with my friends, I get to go for delicious meals, and he even buys me gifts that make Phoebe and Xristina almost drool with envy. He bought me a sapphire necklace for our one-year anniversary.

Sebastian scrambles a little to stand, then steps unceremoniously over me and jumps down from the rocks with a slap of his feet. He begins to march away as I slide carefully off the rocky slope down to the next one.

'Why aren't our names on there?' He points aggressively to a cactus. Not just any cactus of course, one whose leathery-looking flesh has been carved with declarations of love. This is a romantic hotspot overlooking the sea and a place we like to sit, a place I've always liked to sit and dream.

I shrug as I move in closer, looking at all the scars on the cactus. Hearts with L + M, D + J and many more all over like tattoos.

'We are the hottest couple on the island, we need to be on here.'

I abide by what he wants. Fluttering my eyelashes and giving a coy smile, I agree.

Sometimes I wonder if many relationships are full of detachment instead of deep and meaningful love. I guess I do love Sebastian in some way. He was furious that I'd spent time alone with Dinos, and after a lot of thought I wondered how I might've felt about him being on a boat with some good-looking girl all alone. I'd have trusted him, but I'd have been jealous too. He loves me so much he was willing to do anything to keep me in his life, and with time I've realised that's a good quality not a bad one.

Sebastian pulls a flick knife from the back pocket of his chinos and opens it with a snap.

'It has to be done, and there's no better time.'

I watch as he scratches away at the flesh of the cactus, aggressively tearing at it to tattoo it with our initials. It takes longer than I'd imagined. Not that I've spent time imagining this moment. Or even wanted it. But it's here, and it's a sweet gesture.

Sebastian begins to curve the knife to form a heart. Carefully he moves to grip the plant as best he can, to steady it as the knife struggles with this shape. The curve looks tricky, impossible in fact. I look around at the others only to notice their angular lines. As Sebastian digs and twists with the knife, it slips down.

The knife clatters onto the rock under our feet and Sebastian doubles over, gripping his hand. A tornado of swearwords swirls from his lips.

I rub his back, asking, 'Are you okay? Is it bad? Sebastian, should I call someone? Are you okay?'

He straightens up so abruptly, it's all I can do to get myself out of his way.

'No, I'm not *okay*.' He snarls through gritted teeth, 'I've just cut my thumb doing that *shit* for you!'

He begins to move off towards the dirt track that leads back up to the street. Quickly, I snatch up the knife and chase after him. I stumble before I even get to the first step. Running with a knife is a stupid idea; it's one of the first things children are taught.

Carefully, I flick the blade back into place before continuing, calling after Sebastian.

He's storming away and I have to skip steps to keep up.

'Where are you going?'

'To find someone useful. You can't even drive to get this looked at. Go home, Theadora.'

I stop and watch as he disappears into a taverna owned by the parents of one of our friends. I guess at least they can drive him to a clinic.

I open my palm and study the offending object in my hand. This little knife tipped our lovely summer evening into a disaster so easily. From romance to ridiculous with ease. I squeeze my eyes tightly shut. My bag. In chasing Sebastian, I forgot I'd left it where we had been sitting. Now we've vacated it, another couple will soon snap up the beautiful spot.

Clutching the closed knife in my hand I whip round just in time to see Dinos turn and walk in the opposite direction. He must have realised it was me and gone the other way. Sebastian banned me from talking to him unless it was in a group, and even then he doesn't like us saying more than hello. In the past year we have barely said two words to each other.

A few months ago, maybe six or more now, he texted me asking if I'd ever got a response from my birth mother. The answer then and now is no. She never replied. Maybe one day she will. I still check my junk mail regularly since our boat trip, just in case.

I miss Dinos's kindness. It's like I've been left with a wound much like the cut to Sebastian's hand, one that bleeds and scabs and scars. I'm still waiting for mine to scab over.

'I see you walking away from me.' I shouldn't have said it. But it's too late now.

Chapter 20

Dinos slowly turns to face me. Some people step off the pavement to walk around him then around me. We wait in silence looking at each other.

'I didn't want to get you in trouble.'

'Sebastian's just cut himself carving our initials into that old cactus, so I don't think us talking on a busy road will be high on his list of problems today.'

This information causes Dinos to break his unwavering face of silence. The face that gives nothing away. Almost frozen but not quite. One eyebrow lowers over his eye as the other lifts.

'Guess that's why you're walking around with a knife then. I thought you were just trying to frighten passersby.' A twitch of his lips is enough to know he wants to laugh.

I glance down at my hand and realise that although the knife's not open, I'm holding it in such a way that I might be ready to flick it open and threaten someone with it. I release a noise like a satisfied huff.

'Anyway, it's nice seeing you. Well, nice to see a little expression on your face anyway. I've left my bag down there, I best go and grab it before someone else finds it down there.' I point back over towards the staircase that leads down to the rocks and the sea.

'Do you want me to go with you?'

I shake my head, 'No, I think I'll be fine. Thanks though. See you around.'

I make my way past him. He still smells as good as ever. Masculine but not overpowering. He doesn't walk around in a cloud of cologne the way Sebastian often does.

I trot down the steps, and carefully pick my way along the sandy dirt track.

On the ground I do a double take as there's red petals on the pale grey slab of rock. It takes me a moment to realise they aren't petals at all; it's big globs of Sebastian's blood in front of the cactus.

Luckily no one else has turned up to take our place yet and watch the glittering blue sea as it falls into its deeper shades for the night. I skip over to my bag, and stretch to reach it.

Something unexplainable makes me hesitate, something I can only explain as a feeling, or a knowing. I look up towards the street above to find that Dinos is watching me over the railing. As I catch sight of him, he steps back.

It's too late. I caught him watching me.

Thrusting the knife into my bag, I make my way up to find him still there, leaning on the barrier.

'How come you were watching me?'

His hands are in his pockets and his posture is slumped, unlike his normal way of standing tall. Dinos shrugs me off. 'I just... It's getting dark and you're running around with a knife in your hand. I thought someone should keep an eye on you.'

The street lamps have come on now, as though confirming how dark it's getting.

'I'm a grown woman–'

'So? Sebastian is a grown man. More grown than you, and he still cut himself.'

'The blade isn't even out.'

'I get it. Sorry I cared. See you around, Dora.'

'Wait, I'm sorry. Hold on, weren't you walking this way anyway?'

'Changed my mind.'

I watch as Dinos walks away towards the bay, and I turn to head back toward the harbour and home.

I look up at the sky to see the gentle twinkling of the stars as they begin to emerge one by one. It's hard to see them without thinking about what Dinos said. His words always rattle around in my head even though I so wish they wouldn't. Sometimes I think I would be happier if we had never met. Life with Sebastian would be so much easier, and I might even still see him through the rose-tinted glasses I did at the start.

Taking my phone out of my bag, I check my emails. I still do it much more often than I used to before the DNA test. It's a habit now, one I can't seem to stop. A compulsion in case one day I do get a message back.

Sometimes I do get emails from the DNA place when another far-off relative has taken a test and they're added to the people

I'm sort of related to. But there's never anything from her, from LP, and never anyone else interesting.

A new email sits there from them telling me I have another match. I wonder how distant they will be this time. I open it and the words make me falter.

Melodie Greenwood: Sister

My breathing quickens and I see spots instead of my phone. I press the phone to my chest, shutting my eyes for a moment. I've stopped walking in the middle of the narrow pavement, meaning people have to manoeuvre around me. I'm a stone and the river has to flow around me. I feel as heavy as a stone, and as still.

I pull the phone back off my chest and check what it says. Sister. I have a sister. A full sister. Not a half-sister. A full-blood sister.

I begin to walk again without taking my eyes off the screen. There's no image of her on the site, but I have her full name. That's something at least. It's huge in fact. Before, all I had was LP, with nothing more to go on. Nothing. Now I have the name of my sister.

Melodie.

My sister's name is Melodie.

Chapter 21

I don't remember how I got to this bench. It looks out over the harbour, but it's not a place I like to sit. It's too exposed and usually busy with over-heated old ladies or parents organising their children as they walk about looking at the cannons or the boats.

I tuck my dress around my legs so as not to expose myself as I bring my knees to my chin. I feel exposed either way. Cut open once more after only just recovering from finding out that my birth mother had taken a DNA test and proved for the second time in my life that she still has no interest in me. Now this. What I *really* wanted. A sibling. I don't know why, but I've always felt like there was someone else out there who was part of me. It's silly, but I thought perhaps there might be someone else like me. Someone else who had been left behind.

I squeeze my eyes tightly shut against the throbbing emotions as they ride up with every breath. They're all a muddle of excitement, fear, rejection…

It's hard not to swing my head from side to side and let the dam I've been building inside burst, pouring my tears into the sea. No. This isn't LP. This is a girl, a woman, someone who also might not know our parents, who might also have been left. She might need me as much as I need her.

This evening started off so normal, so peaceful, another night with Sebastian, a delicious meal of fresh sea bass dripping in lemon and butter at one of his parents' hotels. But life can change without any warning. I thrust my feet to the ground and slide my shoes off, edging the heel off with the opposite foot and a wiggle. Scooping them off the floor, I turn towards Kanoni Beach. I might be able to find some peace there. A brisk walk in search of clarity is exactly what I need. It's good to move. Anyway, if I stay here any longer, the attention I'll draw from people I know will be all too much and soon I'll have someone asking whether or not I'm alright.

I walk with the sea on my right, my right-hand man, always consistent and quietly listening to my troubles. It's a glittering navy blanket with lights beginning to stretch across it. This is a small island and I know all the owners and families in every taverna, every bar. I feel as though I know everyone here. Someone will have noticed me sitting on the bench, someone else will notice me marching along with no shoes on my feet, hoping the connection with the earth will somehow ground me. Someone else will ask my parents whether everything is okay with me, and if they saw the state of Sebastian earlier. They'll likely be asking if everything is okay with us. At least if I keep walking, they won't ask me right now. Or hopefully they won't.

Oh god, Sebastian. I'd almost forgotten to check on him. I call his phone. He went off in such a huff, then there was my bag, Dinos... Melodie.

I must be the worst girlfriend in Corfu. I'm lucky he bothers with me. I barely understand why sometimes.

I wave at staff as I skirt around the chairs belonging to the taverna whose tables line the path. The ringtone sounds in my ear over and over until it drops off with no reply and no voicemail. I try again as I pass a couple reading over a menu stand, deciding which taverna to stop in. I could tell them to pick any, because they're all going to be good, and here, right along the road, the view across the sea, even in the darkness, is beautiful. The stars punctuate the clear skies and tonight the moon is high and as silver as a shiny coin, reflecting onto the sea.

I plough on, eating up the pavement as I go, bare feet silently weaving. It's not the best place to walk barefoot, and I can see people glance at my feet with narrowed eyes and raised brows. I'm okay with that. I just want to move quickly and feel some connection to the ground to keep myself steady as I go.

A family marches towards me. I recognise them. They've been in the shop getting lunch a few times and they're always smiley. The mother clings to her daughter on her hip and the son and husband trail behind. They're all wearing matching navy and pale pink in different combinations. I grin up at them.

'Kalinikta.'

The mother double takes and then relaxes at my smile. 'Kalinikta!' the little daughter joins in as I skip past.

The walk is helping me. Walking is good, walking was the right idea. I'm forced to smile and be normal. The buzz of Kassiopi warms me like a reassuring ray of sun even though it's night.

It's enough to find my balance. These are my people. It doesn't matter whether or not this person on the screen rejects me. I can handle it. I can handle anything.

I come to the dusty path that leads down to the sea. During the day it's a place that's often packed with people rotating in the sun like chickens on a barbecue. There are two bays either side of the spit of land. People even crowd onto the smooth rocks that go out to sea when they want to relax and tan. With their colourful towels, many could be mistaken for lazy mermaids in the fuzzy hot lines of a summer's day.

The street lights illuminate parts of the bays and the water's edge, but soon I'm moving forwards into the dim moonlight. Reflections of the village streak across the sea. I use my phone to keep my eyes sharp on the uneven surfaces of grit, grass, sand and stone. Without shoes to hold me back, I feel my way along, my feet guided by the earth.

Moving away from the throng of people going about their evening, it's nice to step into a slice of real solitude. I find my way past rows of neatly closed parasols and empty sun loungers. In the dim light they are all shades of grey until I shine my phone torch onto them and bring back their vibrant blues and whites.

I push ahead, past the soft sand and shingle, climbing along to a more distant bay, and further solitude. I make my way along the sloping rocks and down towards the edge of the world. That's how it feels anyway. This is the edge of my earth, where my home meets the abyss. A world I've never seen lives far beyond.

At the point where land falls away into the inky sea, I slide my toes along the slippery mossy surface that hides in the dark, splitting the water with my toes. It graciously makes space for my feet to cool off. My feet and my mind.

I discard my shoes behind me, tuck my dress around my legs and squat down to stare into the water. I switch off the torch mode and put the phone near my shoes, out of reach of the rhythmical sea.

Another family member to wonder about. Another message I need to carve out and pore over until the words don't make sense anymore. Only this time I have a name. Melodie. I roll it around over and over in my mind, as rhythmically as the sway of the sea. *Melodie, Melodie, Melodie.* What should I say to my sister? Unless she beats me to the punchline and messages me first. I've never been one for waiting about to see what will happen. When I decide on something that's it. I wonder whether she's the same. Or maybe she's cautious and thinks everything out. Or maybe she lives with our mother and they're both laughing at me. Toying with me. For all I know they watch me every day and I'm some sort of strange experiment to them.

I wish I could know.

My heart leaps with a thought, a sensible and clear thought. I have this woman's name. First and last! She might be on social media. Just because there is no way to hunt down someone who only puts LP on their profile, doesn't mean I won't find Melodie Greenwood. I can at least try.

Stretching for my phone, I fall back onto my bottom, soaking the edges of my dress. It doesn't matter, it'll dry. I open the search engine and type out her name: Melodie Greenwood. A handful of women come up. Then there's a link for a business based in Corfu, one that helps people with social media and advertising. Something like that. I click on it and a website comes up that's all sleek lines and beautiful images of the island.

Surely this can't be her website? She can't be here on the island with our DNA being mostly from the UK and no Greek whatsoever... but then I'm here. Maybe she was born here too? A cool breeze rolls of the sea make my skin breakout into goosebumps.

I click "About Me", and there she is. My sister, Melodie. I know she's my sister because she has my face. It's a little more mature than mine, and she has light brown hair with a wave to it. I can't tear my eyes from her face, the narrow chin and the shape of her eyes. Tears roll down my cheeks before I'm even aware I'm crying. She's the reason I took this test. This is who I've been waiting for. I know it. I don't know how I know it, I just do.

Chapter 22

'Dora? Dora?' A disembodied voice drifts along over the gentle throb of the water. I look over my shoulder to see a light whizzing from side to side. 'Dora!' It's the last shout, louder and slightly more manic than the rest, that gives me a click of recognition. Plus, no one else calls me Dora.

'Dinos?'

The light stops dead, then aims in my direction. Dinos is a hazy shadow behind it, following like a dog on its lead.

He marches to within a few metres of me, slipping a little on the slabs of rock.

'You're not here to drown yourself, are you?'

'What?' I don't mean to laugh, but one comes out anyway. Almost a snort and a wobbly giggle. I push my long hair from my shoulder to get a better look at him as I twist round. 'No! Can you get that light out of my eyes?' Squinting isn't enough, even raising my hand to protect my eyes doesn't make him think to lower it. He does now though. Now he's illuminating his trainers instead.

'And, you're okay?'

'Yes, I'm fine. Is that why you followed me down here? Some sort of suicide check?'

He scuffs one foot on the smooth surface under us. With the dizzying spots still scattering my vision from his harsh phone light, all I can make out are his well-lit white trainers.

'Yeah, I–' Dinos interrupts himself. 'This was stupid. I saw you looking all sad. I didn't want to come up to you and get you in more trouble with Sebastian.' He says *Sebastian* in the same way he might talk about finding out he's stepped in gum with his new trainers. Like it's dirty and sticky and he's afraid it might soil him if he touches it. 'Then I saw you coming up here alone, and you didn't come back–'

'Are you stalking me?'

With a flick of his wrist, he brings the torch back up to my face. I don't squint quick enough and the light feels hotter than the sun as it digs into my eyes.

'Please lower that thing, Dinos.'

He doesn't. Then comes his voice as deep as the sea. 'Is that really what you think of me? After all these years?'

I fold my left hand over my eyes, because it's all too much.

'No. Of course not. I know you're just looking out for me. I just wanted to be alone. That's all. Please stop blinding me.'

I've had enough of this interrogation, at least that's how it feels with the light on my face. I hold my phone up, scrambling with the screen to try to retaliate. Aiming the screen up at him instead.

'Then I'll leave you alone.' Dinos takes a step back and tilts his head before lowering his light. 'Didn't know you were the type to mess about with those shit filters. You look better as a blonde. *Kalinikta*, Dora.'

When I remove my hands from my eyes, the light's no longer on my face. It's going swiftly away from the sea, away from me.

Filters? What was that all about?

I fill my lungs with the bitter smell of seaweed and salt before puffing it out again. I hate where we are, Dinos and I. But Sebastian is my future. That's all there is to it. There's no point in dwelling on the space between us. I may have lost a friend, but I've gained a future.

I find my head gently shaking from side to side as I look back at my phone and the girl on the screen. I had been waving my screen at him and he must have seen her and thought she was me with some kind of filter. I guess that confirms it's not just me who thinks we look so alike, at least at a glance.

I scroll down to read the website wording.

Hi, I'm Melodie Greenwood! Thank you for visiting my website. I've been managing social media accounts and analysing statistics for almost a decade now. If you are interested in working with me on your next campaign or the day-to-day upkeep of your business accounts, then please drop me an email. I've recently relocated to Corfu, Greece, but I'm happy to work remotely with clients around the world.

She goes on to list some of her bigger-name clients, some I know of and some I don't. I could so easily email her or pretend to be a client to suss her out. My sister is there at my fingertips. My thumb skims over her face.

Instead of going about this the wrong way, I need to try again. Do it the proper way, through the proper channels so she knows I am who I say I am. I'm her sister. I don't want to come across as a strange stalker.

I type out the first thing that comes to my head before reading it back twice and hitting send.

Hello!

I am your sister. Did you know you have a sister? I didn't know this. I hoped to find my birth family and I have. I also sent a message to our mother, but she hasn't contacted me, or returned my message at all. Perhaps she wasn't looking for me or even wanting to find me. Were you? I would love to know.

Theadora

The message has gone in a flash of adrenaline and excitement. I read it again. I should've sent it in English. As she lives here in Corfu, it was my reaction to send it in my first language. But her website is in English; she might not speak Greek at all. I console myself with the fact it should be easy to translate online.

The air around me begins to whip up and the sea shifts from its inky navy to black. A shiver scurries along my spine like a mouse. This quiet September evening is changing.

I look up at the sky. The stars have been swallowed by clouds rolling towards the shore. Even the moon is being threatened by their teeth. A large spot of rain hits my cheek and the sea begins to groan. I push myself away from the edge. It's muggy, hot, with a feeling of saturation even before the rain begins to pour. I grab my shoes and begin to manoeuvre along the rocks and onto the path.

As I skip and dance my way along, the rain begins to hit my skin in an unruly downpour. It's like a baptism into a new family. Guilt floods me with this thought. I want my real family too, the parents who have brought me up and given me my life, but I know in my heart my sister is important. I don't know how yet, but I'm sure she is. I can feel it in my bones.

As I reach the main road, a laugh touches my lips and vibrates in my chest at the sight of so many people hiding from the rain. During the day they all gather next to the sea, but when water pours from the sky, threatening to dowse them, they all vanish like rabbits hiding from owls.

Eyes are on me. Unsurprising as I'm quickly being soaked and still happy to saunter through the rain with my dress clinging to me. I'm the strange blonde Greek girl. It's who I've always been. I've always stood out and at times I've leaned into it. What other choice is there? I can't hide my adoption and my differences.

In amongst the eyes, I see Konstantinos. He runs towards me from under the shelter of a taverna. He ducks his head like he's walking in a tunnel and this will somehow shelter him from the warm downpour. His round face is dripping when he reaches me.

'Thought you were with Sebastian tonight. All okay?'

'He cut his hand.' I project my voice over the hammering of the rain. 'It's raining chair legs! I didn't know it was meant to rain today.'

Konstantinos almost jogs along and I have to skip steps to keep up with him until we are under the parasols at the edge of the road where he stops.

'Where've you come from? Were you coming from the bay?'

I nod. 'Sebastian left and I went for a walk. Until it started to rain of course.'

I grin up at him, but he doesn't return it.

'I just remembered, I've left something behind. See you around.' He turns back into the rain, making his white shirt as clear as glass. There is something off about Konstantinos, but I can't put my finger on it. It doesn't matter anyway. I've got my own thoughts to deal with, and that begins with how I tell my parents about finding my sister. I guess that means I'll have to mention the email to my biological mother too... and the DNA test. I've got some explaining to do.

Chapter 23

It's three nights since I saw my sister's face on a screen for the first time. That means two days of stalking. Finding her on Instagram and looking at her daughter and husband. She hasn't posted for a while. She doesn't caption images much or tag locations. There's a couple of pictures from her wedding day with her husband and daughter. She thanks somewhere she calls Waves for providing them with the most beautiful beach reception. It doesn't take long to work out where they were from the name and the images. Agios Stefanos, north-west Corfu. Either they live there, or people there know who she is. How could they not? Dinos might've said he prefers me blonde, but I'm sure she's the beautiful version of me. She's refined and her husband is gorgeous, their daughter too. The pictures look like something out of Vogue, only more accessible with none of the pretension and all of the pretty. It's a cultivated account though, with only the most stylish of images. No mention of her parents. Only the loss of grandparents. I've never had grandparents. They all passed before I was born or when I was too little to remember.

I haven't been able to tell anyone about Melodie yet. I don't want to burst out with it over breakfast. I'd have Mama and Baba choking on their yoghurt and honey if I'm not careful. I want to get the words right when I tell them about what I've found. Melodie hasn't replied yet, but it's only been a few days, and she might not check her emails every day, or maybe, like mine, it's gone to junk and it could be ages until she sees it. I don't think I can wait forever though. I'm already on the brink of taking matters into my own hands. It's one thing to be conflicted about the person who left me, my supposed mother, but this is different. Something in my bones says I'm meant to know Melodie.

I plan to tell Mama and Baba in a couple of days. We have a nice family meal planned with a barbecue. No matter what, we always carve out quality time at least once a month to be together. Right now, life is a ticking time bomb down to that moment. Soon everything will change. I can't help but think back to Dinos and the stars. All these people are here in the world, it's just about how much we see and what we see and what we look at. The situation doesn't change, only how we feel.

I don't think I'll be telling Sebastian anytime soon. He didn't reply when I tried to check on his hand the night I found out about Melodie, and apart from a phone call the next day apologising for not returning my call and telling me how sorry he was to leave me worrying about him, we've only had time to message in the mornings the way we always do in-between seeing each other.

But that's not today. Today is one of my days off and I've had one simple plan for weeks, and that is to see Theía Agatha. She's always very busy with the children she looks after. I've wanted to go to the Children's Community Home for ages and see where Theía Agatha and Ria work, I've never been there, but I can't because I don't have the right paperwork to hang about up there to make sure the children are kept safe. That's what they've always told me. Some of the children have complex issues and all of them must be protected.

It's hard to think that I was one of those children once, when I was a baby. This thought still consumes me every time it comes into my head. I was born here, and Theía Agatha brought me to the Children's Community Home to live and that's where Mama and Baba adopted me. I was lucky, being a special case. I don't know how they got around all the paperwork, but they did. I've wanted to see it all for myself since finding out that's where I was taken to be adopted. Last year I asked Theía Agatha if I could get the paperwork so I could go there and help out, but she said I should wait for things to settle. Ria, who is almost like another theía to me, agreed. She's Theía Agatha's best friend. They're almost always together, both working and living at the Children's Community Home. Well, part time living there. They both have cottages on site and stay in the main community home on a rota with the other mentors and carers. Maybe I can ask Theía Agatha today about getting the right paperwork so I can volunteer or something. It's been a year now since I found out. It's a charity, so surely there must be some way for me to have a look around or get involved as a volunteer. Maybe I could teach the kids piano. Surely some of them would like that.

I exhale at the thought of Melodie's face as I slide onto my moped and start it up. I wonder whether she was adopted. Whether her grandparents were my grandparents too. I'm meeting Agatha in Agios Stefanos. When she asked what I wanted to do today, I suggested the beach, and said I fancied a little ride on my moped, and wondered about Waves for lunch. There was the inevitable lie of telling her a friend of mine had been that way and said it was nice. She agreed. Why wouldn't she? It's nearer where she is on the island than coming into Kassiopi. Plus, it comes with the added possibility of a chance meeting with Melodie. Or of someone telling me they know a girl who has my face. My skin tingles at the idea of coming face to face with my sister. I'd have to act shocked. My acting skills aren't very good, but I'm sure coming face to face with her would still feel shocking enough to pull it off.

Depending on how the conversation goes, I might confide in Theía Agatha. She's my godmother as well as my theía, she and Ria. They've both always been very invested in my upbringing, and I understood that better when Mama and Baba told me I was taken to the Children's Community Home, of course. Theía Agatha and Ria did everything to help my parents adopt me, and kept the secret for all these years so that I would be safe.

Weaving around cars, I glide on my moped through Kassiopi. With the longer journey ahead, I've opted for some more sensible shorts instead of a dress today. The whole morning it's been in my head that I must look smart in case we bump into Melodie.

The nervous tickle in my tummy reminds me of when I first met Sebastian and he took an interest in me. We'd all been looking in his direction. He had befriended Konstantinos from our school because they both liked the same cars and went to the same events. I'd never met him before, although his reputation lingered anywhere he went. Wealth has a way of doing that, plus his charming nature. We were out at 54 Dreamy Nights and he was with the VIPs, but he was watching us. Watching me. He invited us over and focused all his attention on me. Each time his hand glanced mine, or there was a lingering look, it felt like someone was drawing a line up from my belly button with a feather. I wish I could get back that feeling about him, that intense interest. Now it's a settled pace of life and the knowledge that this is it. We are together and that's that.

The sea is to one side now, with scattered buildings the colour of the sand on my left. A breeze flings my plait over my shoulder. Unlike many people here, I always wear a helmet. The one time I didn't, my mama caught me, and it wasn't worth the days of dramatic nagging on the subject. That cost me more of a headache than if I had fallen off the moped and bumped my head.

I whiz along and I'm soon into the flood of green of Corfu's interior. A range of greens from the colour of sugar snaps and limes through sage and, of course, olive, all spread across the landscape, vibrant with the sudden downpours we've had lately as if the leaves have been cleaned ready for their winter break. It's coming into that time of year when the weather can change on a pin. It's probably my favourite time. I love the in-between, the unpredictable.

Being on my bike gives me the perfect opportunity to daydream. The fresh salt air coming in from the sea cleanses my skin as I continue weaving around the edges of the sea on my way to answers. Well, I hope for answers, but I'm no fool. I'll have to come clean to Theía Agatha about it before I get anything close to an answer as to what to do about Melodie. When I told her and Ria about the DNA, I'd never seen them so white. I didn't dare tell them I'd sent the thing. She might feel differently knowing I have a sister out there.

I spent so much time thinking about it all. Running it over in my head. I know they wanted to protect me as a child, from some unknown family danger, but how much danger am I in now? I've come to the conclusion it's more about saving face now. It's easier to maintain the lie. My birth mother could easily see I'm here, alive on the island. It's there on the internet in black and white. She doesn't care. No one cares. Maybe Melodie will. I hope Melodie will. I still think they must have left her too. She's older than me; maybe they left her in England then came out here?

I have questions. So many questions that seep out of every pore so ferociously that I'm surprised the whole island can't read my secrets there on my skin. So many questions roll around my head, that sometimes it's hard to even formulate one, because they seem to get stuck. I do my best to iron them out, to calm my thoughts and think it all over. It's not always so easy. It used to be that I could talk to Mama about things, or my friends, and always Dinos. This past year things have shifted. I've felt a zip close over a gap that I wish wasn't there. The zip holds it all together though. If it came open, and words shaped like hooks seeped out, each one could catch on the fabric of our relationship and rip it a little more and a little more. I'm terrified of that. Keeping my mouth zipped is a much safer option. It means I can still look at the beauty of the stars and they're basically unchanged. Even if I sort of see them differently. Bloody Dinos and his stars. Sometimes I wish that thought would leave me, instead of lingering on. All it's done is make me think of him, every time I look up at the stars, and remember the night our arms were pressed together on his little boat. How he soothed me.

It's not like I can exactly tell Sebastian any of this. He could use it against me if I did decide I couldn't take it anymore and tried to break up with him for any reason. His words last year were so vicious. There's no way to share anything in my head with anyone, apart from maybe Agatha.

With my piles of thoughts for company, it doesn't feel long until I'm making a left in Sidari and driving past trees laden with olives that are on their way to being ripe. Not long to Agios Stefanos now.

A shot of adrenaline burns warm in my chest and radiates. She could be there. Melodie could be there. How long now? Ten, fifteen minutes? I could ride right past her there on the street. Maybe even now. I should've paid more attention in Sidari. I don't actually know where she lives. I'm assuming in or near Agios Stefanos because it's where she had her wedding reception. I could be wrong. I could be very wrong. She could be here, or in the car behind me. I use my mirrors and squint to see into the little white Mercedes behind me. No. Two young men. Not her.

As I go along now, I watch everyone I encounter, just in case it's Melodie.

By the time I arrive at the beachside parking in Agios Stefanos, all the squinting at people in their cars and by the side of the road has made my face so tense a headache looms behind my eyes. Yanking off my helmet I begin to rub at my forehead.

A voice calls from over my shoulder, 'Hey! Beautiful girl! What are you doing here?'

Chapter 24

Theía Agatha squeezes my shoulders before I spin round to embrace her. Like Mama, she's much shorter than me. I have to hunch forwards to wrap my arms around her neck.

'It's been too long, little one.' Theía Agatha stretches up and cups my cheeks in her hands. It doesn't matter how tall I am, I know she'll always insist on calling me *little one*.

Agatha doesn't look all that much like my mum. From the photos of my grandparents that I've seen, Mama always points out how Agatha looks more like their mama, with a full bottom lip and hazel eyes.

We kick up the warm sand as we walk towards the beachside restaurant. The long stretch of sand is dotted with beachside tavernas, many boasting not only stunning views of the turquoise sea, but many sunbeds with thick, soft-looking mattresses and parasols overhead. The smell of the salt air rolling in collides with the mouth-watering scent of garlic and roasting meat coming from some of the tavernas. Of course, I always think my mama's cooking is the best, but it's also nice to go out for a meal.

I don't often get to see Theía Agatha when it's just the two of us. Usually, we spend the time as a family unit. Theía Agatha, Ria, Mama, Baba and I sit outside in the garden at home swelling our bellies with Mama's homemade lamb with spinach and feta or her rich, spicy *bourdeto* pie; the first is Agatha's favourite dish, and the second is Ria's. There's always mountains of food, though, including cheeses, honey and roasted vegetables. I often help Mama bake it all beforehand. Whenever we have guests, it's as though she's misread the instructions for every dish; she always quadruples the quantities.

I'll never complain about being overfed by Mama, though. I love it. I adore my parents and everything they've done for me in life. Agatha too, and Ria.

As we come to the perimeter of Waves, it looks nothing like I expected from Melodie's wedding photos. But then why would it be awash in white lace and ribbons now? I can see why she picked it though, as the covered terrace is only one step down onto the soft golden sand. It's perfect.

A waiter shows us to a table and gives us menus. He's put us right at the front looking out at the rows of sun loungers and the sea glittering beyond.

She might have sat here. On this very chair.

She will have certainly looked out at this view on her wedding day, and many times before, surely, given all the planning these things take.

'You alright, Theadora?'

Air rushes into my lungs as I try to find words. I've been gripping my closed menu and staring out at the sea without realising. I'm too bogged down with my own thoughts.

I manage to squeeze out, 'Yes, you?'

Agatha nods, but her raised eyebrow and curl of a smile says something else.

'How's Ria?' I open my menu only to realise it was upside down the whole time. No wonder Agatha had her eye on me. I'm much too easy to read.

'She's well. We've been very busy with the children lately. They have got some new ostriches on the farm and it's causing mayhem. They all love it of course, but they all want me to go outside with them when they need to be at school learning. Plus, we have a new girl and she's only four. She's very shy, but luckily she's taken to clinging onto Ria's leg, so she'll get there.'

It's always comfortable being with Theía Agatha. It always has been. When I had too much time to think during lockdown, I started questioning everything much too much. I missed so many people I love and she was top of that list. I was lucky to still live with Mama and Baba of course. But that isolation made me think about family and friends and that's what got me into this sticky mess: waiting for my biological sister to stumble across me while I'm out with my adoptive theía. If meeting Melodie were to happen that way, as if accidentally, it's like I'm not responsible for it, even though I am. I can't really believe she lives on my little island. If I can really call it mine. I was born here, and it feels like mine, but my parents feel like mine and biologically at least, they're not.

I do my best to stay focused on Agatha and her story about the escaping ostrich and how a man who works on the farm around the Children's Community Home had to sneak up on it, and how they're lucky to have someone so patient both with the animals and the children.

'Can I take your drinks order?' Cautiously, I look up at the waiter, wondering whether he'll tell me that I look just like this woman who got married here. He doesn't, of course; instead he's listening to Agatha as she orders a cola. I order the same and look back at my menu as the waiter moves away.

Theía Agatha narrows her eyes on her menu and her lips draw into a tight line. She's almost sixty now, I guess, although she looks younger. Pulling this face, sort of tense and dissatisfied, ages her. It brings out her true years.

'It's funny to think I was a baby at the Children's Community Home once.'

'You never went in the home with the other children,' she quickly corrects. 'Like I told you before, I brought you to my cottage on the outskirts of the farmland around the home. You were a tiny baby and needed to be looked after at all hours of the day and night. The children's home was the only place willing to take on such a responsibility. A newborn baby is like nothing else on this planet.' A softness snuggles back into her cheeks, bringing the light of the sun on to her face.

'Did you ever want kids?'

'Wow,' she says, 'you're pulling out all the bold questions today, aren't you?'

'Sorry.' I clench my teeth into a grimace and try to shrug it off. She's right though. I can't help it anymore. I have a desire to understand as much as I can about what has been.

'No, it's alright. This was all bound to come out one way or another, and you aren't the first person I've taken into my arms to eventually ask me that question. It's a simple answer. All I ever wanted was children, and I have had many of them. I've been very, very privileged.' Agatha tucks her chin towards her chest, discarding her menu fully now and placing her hands over it on the table. 'If Zeta and Marios, your mama and baba, hadn't taken you in, I think I would have done everything I could to keep you for myself. But it's better this way. They needed you as much as you needed them. You saved each other.'

Our drinks are placed down carefully on the paper tablecloth, which has a map of Corfu printed on it. A smile lingers in the corners of Agatha's eyes and I'm sure it's there in mine too.

'Are you ready to order?'

We both nod and Agatha orders a salad. It only took one small glance at the menu for me to know exactly what to have, *kolokithokeftedes*, courgette and feta balls, one of my favourites. I just hope they're as good as the ones Mama makes.

As soon as the waiter is out of earshot, Agatha looks out at the sea. Perhaps at the people far out on their boats, or those with their children splashing and laughing in the shallows.

'I often wonder about what could've been,' she exhales. A silver strand of hair glides across her face in the breeze, glittering in the midday sun. 'But there's no point dwelling on all the past mistakes we've made, or what could've been. I don't regret anything. How could I? If I hadn't taken the role as team leader and manager at the community home, then I would never have been there to pick you up when you were found, and Zeta would never have seen you... then what? Then what would've happened to you? I only wish there wasn't the red tape with adoption back then. I wish things had been... simpler.'

'How do you mean? My adoption went through easy enough, from what you've all said.'

'Yes, yes. I suppose it all worked out for you. I just wish I could say the same for the other children across Greece born at the same time,' she licks her bare lips. 'We home and help so many children who need our support. I'm grateful to be a part of that. To be a part of all of your lives.'

Agatha reaches over and holds my hand. It's the same size and shape as my mama's hand in mine, but rougher around the edges.

'I'm proud of you, little one. You have handled all the secrets with grace. No matter what things have been hidden from you by us, you know it's because we love you.'

I remove my hand and pick up my cola to take a sip before carefully replacing it to the table.

'There aren't other secrets I should know about, are there?'

She then mimics me, picking up her glass and finishing the last mouthful she finds there.

'What can I say? The only details you don't know now, are the dull ones about paperwork. Things you don't need to know, things no one wants to know. The only thing you need to know, little one, is you are adored. What could be more important than that?' She's right. Nothing is more important than having that stability. I'm lucky to have them support me. I have a swelling urge to tell Agatha about Melodie right away. But I need to get this right.

Chapter 25

I slip the last mouthful of crispy courgette ball into my mouth and savour the creamy feta inside. These ones might actually be better than Mama's. I thought it was impossible, but here they are. Placing my cutlery down on my plate, I watch Agatha take her last mouthful. This is my last chance.

After my initial outburst and driving things in the direction of my past, it still takes me time to blurt out the news about Melodie and the DNA test results.

Each time I try to broach the subject my mouth dries up, and I gulp back cola, leaving Agatha space to strike up a new topic of conversation.

'I need to tell you something, and I need for you not to be mad.'

Agatha begins to chew more slowly on her last slice of pepper, as though I've thrown her into slow motion.

I clear my throat and inhale a clarifying breath to ready myself.

'I sent away the DNA test last year. I didn't tell anyone.' Untrue, but I figure Dinos doesn't count. I try to keep my nose from wrinkling. Ever since Phoebe pointed it out, I've done my best to stop myself.

'And what have you found? You must have found something otherwise you wouldn't be here with this face of yours.' Agatha places her fork down and waves her hand at my face before sharply smoothing her hair.

'I have a sister. Here in Corfu. A full sister. Her name is–'

'No, Theadora, please don't tell me. I don't want to hear anymore. You're playing with fire, and you will hurt your parents if you carry on down this path.'

A trickle of sweat runs down the back of my neck and I scratch it so hard that it hurts.

'They've been so supportive so far.'

'So, you've told them?' Her eyebrows lift sarcastically, knowing the answer before it's said. 'Told them about these results?' I've never heard Agatha's voice so staccato before. Every beat is sharp and off.

'No, but–'

'Then I beg you to forget about it. Forget about this sister. You have so much to live for. Have you not had a good life? Are your Mama and Baba somehow not good enough?'

'No that's not it, it's just–'

'Then don't be spiteful. You'll all get hurt. Surely? How can there be another outcome? You were left for dead. To keep you safe we had to...' Theía Agatha closes her eyes and visibly swallows, reminding me of when Mama recounted the story of when she first saw me. 'We had to move a lot of goalposts to keep you safe.' She opens her eyes, but she doesn't look at me. She turns her head towards the sky. There's not a single cloud today and it's as warm as any summer's day could be. 'I know Ria said it's good you know the truth now. God, I wish she was next to me right now. She would know what to say. You must be curious, I know that. I'm being too harsh, I'm sorry. It's only because I love you so very much, and I'm worried for you. For all of us. This is a path you can't easily come back from. Once you walk this line there may be no going back for any of us.'

This isn't how I thought Agatha would react. I knew she wasn't that happy about the DNA test idea, but she's always been on my side. When I was little and Mama was being overprotective, never wanting me to play outside with my friends, she was the one who told her I'd be safe. She was the one who always backed me up. I really believed that she would do the same here and tell me it was okay to talk to Mama and Baba and meet this sister of mine.

'I didn't mean to upset you,' she says more softly now, but the damage has been done.

'I know. You've surprised me, that's all.'

Agatha looks back across at me and squeezes out a tense smile. It's a forced expression with tight lips, another one I've never seen before on a face that usually fills me with light. 'Just, please don't do anything rash. Maybe don't tell your parents right away and give it all some space. You don't want to bring someone into your life who isn't worth having around.'

I nod and smile, but I can feel my throat restrict and heat nip at the back of my eyes as though I've accidently looked directly into the summer sun.

Now I really do have no one to talk to. I have found new family and yet I couldn't feel more alone.

Theía Agatha's phone blares, and as she picks up her bag from the floor and scrambles to answer it, I look across the taverna only to catch sight of a couple at a table behind us whispering and looking directly at me. I smile and they smile in return. There's something shifty there though. They both look away and busy their hands.

'Is everything alright... No, no, it's okay... Yeah... I'll come back now... No, honestly, it's alright. I'll be there soon.' Theía Agatha pushes her phone back into her bag. 'Sorry, little one, I need to go.' She pulls out her purse and lays money on the table. 'Leave a tip and keep anything left over.' She moves around the tables and holds my face before kissing my cheeks. 'Have your eyes fourteen. I love you.'

I can't help but return the smile she gives me. *Have your eyes fourteen* is the way mothers and theías tell us all to keep safe, to keep a look out. This oddly comforting phrase takes the edge off somehow.

'Love you too.'

With that she's gone, and I'm left to sort the bill.

When I turn to gesture to the waiter, I see that the couple behind are watching me again, and I think I know why. I can't help it. I lean over towards them.

Guessing that they're English, I say, 'Excuse me, do you know my cousin, Melodie?'

'Oh yes, you're her cousin, you say? We knew her grandparents well. Watched her growing up here one summer to the next. She never spoke of a cousin, but I thought you were related to her, didn't I say?' The woman continues without waiting for her husband to answer. 'You look so alike. Could almost be twins. Where are you from?' The woman has short moon-grey hair in curls around her face and a pointed nose than I'm sure likes to find itself in everyone's business.

'I've been looking for her.'

'Oh yes, I'm sure. Are you here because of everything going on with that husband of hers? I hear he's doing a lot better now. I expect you know.'

I nod my head even though I haven't the slightest clue what she's on about. I put on my best empathetic face to mirror hers. 'I had her address written down, but I can't find it. I was at the wedding. Were you here for the wedding?' It's a gamble, but I'm already lost in this act. My whole body is so alive in the lie that I feel like I'm glowing golden in the sun, with electricity pulsing, making me itch. What the hell am I playing at?

'Oh no, we couldn't make it. Could we? No. Beautiful photos though, weren't they, Bill? Beautiful.' The old man next to her mumbles agreement before she continues. 'They live in Karousades, don't they, Bill? Seen photos of that too, with its pretty pink shutters. Lovely it is. Just lovely.'

'That's all I can remember too. I think I might be able to find my way there again. Let's hope so, yes?' I cross my fingers and shrug. 'Thank you so much. It was so lovely to meet you.'

The waiter places down the bill and I turn back to my table to sort the money. My hands are shaking and my feet itch, wanting to run away from my insane behaviour.

Pushing my chair back to stand, I turn and smile at the couple behind me.

'Have a nice day.' I use my shop voice. I say this phrase all the time at work. *Have a nice day.*

'Send our love to her won't you, dear? It's Jade and Bill!'

Swinging back round I put a thumb up, which as soon as my thumb slices through the air I know looks dumb, but it's too late now. I've just squeezed Melodie's information out of a stranger and now I need to run as far away from Agios Stefanos as I can, because I feel like I've stolen something and it's time to escape.

Chapter 26

Today we're celebrating that Phoebe is going to live her dreams in a matter of days. She's off to study music this year at university, a year later than it should have been, but at least she's going. It might not be Italy, as she had planned before the pandemic, but at least she's making her dreams happen. I'm a little envious that I've sort of given up on even finding out what my dreams are. I have the stability of Sebastian and the distraction of working out who I am and who I was born to. The fixation takes up a lot of my brainpower. But now on this Monday lunch, I can forget everything outside of fun with my friends. I can be a normal nineteen-year-old for a change. I need this.

We're starting off by going out for a lunch at one of Sebastian's hotels, at his suggestion. He even booked the table for us weeks ago. It was a really sweet gesture. He's always thoughtful about these things. After lunch we'll be spending the whole day together.

I'm always impressed when I come into one of the boutique hotels owned by Sebastian's family. Each hotel is all-inclusive, but they also have a separate exclusive dining area for special meals, special guests and where people not staying in the hotel can dine on food from their award-winning chefs. They all have multiple dining areas, but only one is open to the public.

This one has an entrance with floor-to-ceiling marble and gold pillars either side of the welcome desk. The decor was done maybe twenty years ago, I'm sure before I was born. It still looks good though even if it leans a little heavily into the ancient Greek vibe. When the hotel was shut for the pandemic, they pulled down a few paintings that were too on-the-nose, and everything had a refresh. It's all clean and plain lines now. Simple – except for those gold pillars.

Our feet make a cloud of noise that follows us along as we step into the hotel's foyer, with its atmospheric muzak. It's a bit like getting into a very large American elevator, or how I imagine one anyway from the films I've seen – that calm lounge music.

The girl at the welcome desk has an immaculate manicure and tidy gelled bun. She recognises me immediately, and as she shows us to our table we politely chat, more than when Sebastian is with me. Usually, she directs her conversation at him. She takes us through archways of plastic vines –they'd be too much hassle to look after if they were real.

I've opted for navy sandals and a simple strappy navy dress with tiny white flowers dotted across the fabric. My feet slap along, echoing, although no worse than Phoebe and Xristina, both in their heels ticking like clocks with each and every step.

I feel like both girls look much fancier than me. Maybe I've become too used to coming out to these beautiful places and being spoilt. I've been here so many times now, it's lost its sparkle.

'Wow,' Xristina breathes as she takes it all in. The tables are spread far apart giving diners space to have quiet conversations. This isn't the place to ram people together like farm animals. This is a place for private conversations, marriage proposals and champagne.

Each table has fresh white roses in a glass vase. They're cut short and almost look like loads of English brides walked in and placed their wedding bouquets in the vases.

Our table is in the corner and already has a bottle of champagne in a bucket on a stand next to the table. The girl with the neat hair and sharp fake nails indicates a note on the table as we all make ourselves comfortable on the golden, cushioned chairs. We're the only ones in here, but we are rather early. The girl, I wish I knew her name, opens the champagne and starts to pour us all glasses of the bubbly wine.

As soon as I'm seated, I reach across for the note.

'It must be from Sebastian. He's probably telling us to have a good time with the champagne he bought. He's so sweet.' I press it to my chest before looking at the envelope. There's no name on it, but I know it's from him to me. My heart swells with his kindness. I can't believe I ever doubted him sometimes. As long as I don't make him jealous, he really is a wonderful and generous boyfriend.

I prise open the white envelope, pull out a card and read it out loud.

'Theadora, please thank Xristina for her kindness. I wish Phoebe well. Sebastian.'

My stomach knots and I regret reading it out for all to hear. Even the always-polite, beautifully turned-out girl pouring the champagne shoots me a look under her thick fake lashes before wishing us a lovely afternoon and moving away.

'Why is Sebastian thanking you?' I narrow my eyes at Xristina.

With a cough and a shuffle of her chair, she begins to speak, but she's looking at her glass, not at me. 'Surely you know why. He's *your* boyfriend.'

I glance from Phoebe to Xristina. Phoebe's looking from me to Xristina, and from the lowering of her brows and the way she's leaning in like she's waiting for the punchline, I don't think she knows anything either.

'Xristina?' I squeak out her name.

'I thought he would've told you by now. It was last week after all.' She huffs out a shallow breath and smooths her hair. It's as gelled as that of the girl who works here, but pulled into a tight ponytail on the side of her head, with a mass of wild curls falling almost to her shoulder. 'Well, he had cut himself, and he needed to get some help. He came into the taverna, Old School, and I was just walking through from the church with my yiayia. I said I would drive him. So, I did. Same as any friend would. As even a stranger would.'

She's right. Such kindness is easily given here in the community that I love. A gift of time is easily passed from person to person. What more beautiful gift could be given?

I want to snap and ask why no one told me, why he didn't say, but I know it's irrational. As irrational as he was with me and Dinos, and I don't want to lose more friends for no reason.

'Thank you, Xristina. I don't know why he didn't tell me. It must have slipped his mind. I'm so grateful you were there to help him.'

'Yeah!' Phoebe chimes in. 'Thanks for earning us some, hopefully, *free* champagne!'

We all relax, scooping up our glasses and raising them. *'Yammas.'*

After over an hour of laughing, food, and enjoying even more fizz on our tongues, the man in question arrives. I haven't seen him in the flesh since he cut his hand. Our messages have been sporadic, but that's not unusual at busy times like these. His texts have been loving and thoughtful in the way they so often are. I thought at first that he was a bit upset about cutting himself, but he's clearly over it. Why else send champagne? His hand is still bandaged, but it hasn't stopped him from working. The cut wasn't deep, but it needed to be cleaned.

I push my chair back to stand as Sebastian glides between the tables. Perhaps he is working here today; he didn't mention it, but we didn't get to speak much this morning, only brief messages to wish each other a lovely day.

He looks fresh from a magazine with his neatly cropped hair, oversized white linen shirt coolly moving around him with one too many buttons undone and fitted black jeans to smarten the look. Something about today's look almost seems old-time romantic, as if he's an artist ready to paint his muse. My cheeks warm at the thought of it. *I'm* the muse.

As he reaches the table, he moves towards me. I lean to kiss him. Our lips briefly meet before he turns to the table.

'How's the champagne, ladies? All to your taste I hope?'

We speak over each other to see who can agree the most, and thank him the most.

'Good, good. I'm glad you're enjoying yourselves. It would be my pleasure to pay for everything you wish for today, to thank Xristina for her kindness and making sure I feel,' he exhales a hard, thoughtful breath, 'as good as I possibly can.'

My girls both gasp and I curl myself into Sebastian's body and kiss his neck.

'It's too much,' I whisper into his ear.

'You're more than welcome, Sebastian,' Xristina gushes. 'I'm always happy to help.'

'I only ask one simple favour.' I step back to assess his expression, but he isn't giving anything away. We all wait, suddenly still after our giddy outburst. 'I'd like to borrow my beautiful girlfriend for a moment.'

'I think we can spare her, can't we Xristina? More champagne for us.' Phoebe raises her glass as Xristina empties the contents of hers.

'I'll send another bottle to make up for her absence.'

I pick up my bag from the back of my chair before slipping my fingers into his and weaving us together like vines.

Following on half a step behind him, we pass the girl at her desk who politely nods then taps her sharp nail repeatedly on her desk as she looks over the books for the day. Sebastian leads me along a corridor left then right, our footsteps echoing around us.

'How's your hand? Is it healing?'

'Much better.' He briefly opens his palm to glance down at the bandage.

'Where are we going?'

Sebastian doesn't answer. He pulls out a key card and opens the door to one of the ground-floor rooms, usually reserved for those on the nightshift from what I've been told by Sebastian in the past.

He holds open the door and I walk in. It's a simply furnished room; everything's white. There's a black-and-white painting on the wall, a black old-fashioned phone beside the bed and not much else to speak of. Still, it manages to be more elegant than anywhere I've stayed before now. I've never seen the inside of any room here before. Even if this room is for people who work here, it's still kind of interesting to be nosy.

Slowly I spin around, taking in every inch of the blank space until I'm facing Sebastian.

'So, what's up? What do you need me for? You're not asking me to work here, are you?' I grin at him as he moves towards me.

His face stays serious. So much so, a trickle of anticipation drips over my spine.

Sebastian's dark eyes track my skin, moving over my face, my neck, my décolletage, before his index finger runs along my cheek and rests on my jawline. He moves in so close to me, I can feel his breath warm on my skin. His cheek touches mine, light stubble scratching my skin, and a shiver turns my flesh into waves of tiny bumps.

'Someone saw you with Dinos. Is that true?' The sound of Dinos's name on Sebastian's lips feels like I've punctured a lung. His voice resonates in my ear. 'Theadora?'

The acid from the mouthfuls of champagne I've had burns at the back of my throat and leaves me lightheaded. I know exactly who saw me. Exactly who has stirred this up for me. Konstantinos.

'No, well, yes. He came to check on me–'

Sebastian is so close to me that he's out of focus. He's a blur, my mind is a blur.

'I thought we said he didn't exist anymore. After the last time.'

'I can't control him coming after me.'

'Bit strange to be wandering about in the dark on your own. Seems more likely you were meeting someone.'

His finger digs into my jaw. It doesn't hurt, but I don't like it. I step back and he catches my arm and tugs me back like a dog on a lead.

'Do we have a problem, Theadora?'

'No. No problem.'

His eyes flick between mine, and the vein in his forehead runs like a river about to burst in his face.

'I want to be able to trust you, to protect you, but don't make it so hard. We have something good here. My grandparents, they adore you. I don't want to break their hearts, or hurt your parents.' His tone drops at the mention of my parents.

Blood rushes to my ears and spots flash across my vision like late-night strobes.

'I haven't done anything wrong.'

'It's not wrong to continually humiliate me and my family, after all we do for you?' Sebastian shoves me towards the bed. I stumble backwards and land sitting on it. My handbag slips off my shoulder and the contents spew out. He paces the room muttering to himself as I collect my phone, purse, mirror and lip balm and put them back into my bag.

After a moment or two, he stops in his tracks and takes in a deep breath before turning to face me. 'I don't know why you want to hurt me when I do so much for you, when I love you so deeply. Go, be with your friends. I can't even look at you.' I open my mouth but quickly close it again. All I want to do is leave anyway.

I press myself as close to the wall without looking ridiculous as I pass him, and at the door, I turn and say, 'Sorry', before leaving. I don't know why, I haven't even done anything wrong. My head hammers like I downed the whole bottle of champagne to myself, and hot tears sting my eyes. I can't go back to the table like this. I need to get out of here.

Chapter 27

I walk on tiptoes so my shoes don't make any sound as I return the way we came in. My stomach is squeezing hard to hold back the tears and the emotion that's building up inside me. Everything is drawn out like a painful line of torture.

Did Sebastian just push me? Did he threaten me again?

Surely, I must be confused. He said he loves me. He's just too passionate. He loves me too deeply. Even as the words swell in my head, I don't believe them. My hands curl into balls and my chest burns. I'm trying to convince myself and defend him when I shouldn't. But what choice do I have? He has money and power. I have to put up with it. I have to take his threats seriously. I've heard rumours about his father and the things he's done. Setting fire to a competitor's restaurant. It was never proven, but that's what people say. I believe that Sebastian could follow through and ruin my family.

It's a different person at the desk. Luckily, they don't look up as I carefully skip my way outside. I can't go back into the restaurant now. I'll explode into a dreadful blubbering mess if anyone asks if I'm okay.

I make my way into the blinding light of the sun and duck towards the service entrance at the side. At least that way I can hide while I compose myself. I march under the sweet-smelling arches of bougainvillea and olive trees, head down just in case.

'Hey, Dora, are you okay? Is that you?' It's the worst possible voice to be here.

Tears begin to choke me. I bite down on my lip to hold it all in and clench my fist so hard I think I might split the skin on my knuckles as I quickly turn to run the other way. In two strides I walk back the way I came. There's laughter from people moving towards the entrance of the hotel. I'm trapped. Trapped in a world of my own stupidity. If I carry on, I'll be seen and make a scene; if I stay here, I'm left with the person whose very existence and caring nature got me into this mess — Dinos.

'Dora, wait up.'

All I want to do is escape. I want to run home like a child and curl up on my mother's lap the way I used to. She used to joke that having me as a daughter was like having a cat as a pet. When I was frightened or sad, I'd coil myself around her for security.

The spots in my eyes come back and begin to pulse. This is the side entrance; what if Sebastian appears and sees Dinos coming towards me? What happens then? What then?

My chest heaves in painful gulps of air that wheeze as my throat begins to close. The gap for air becomes smaller and smaller. I push myself against the wall of the building. My eyes tightly shut as I press my forehead into the wall, its surface as rough and as golden as the sand. It spitefully grates me as I tremble.

The weight of Dinos's hands land on my shoulders. Surely, he isn't *really* here? Why is he everywhere I don't want him to be? Why is he always making my life more complicated? How can one human seem to be so linked to another that he always turns up when she's in the most pain?

'Breathe, come on now, breathe.'

Each breath I do manage is like a swelled hiccup bursting air into my lungs. Each muscle in my body is taut. Please don't let Sebastian find us like this. *Please.*

'Listen to my voice, focus on my voice.' His lips are so close to my ear, it's like the night on the boat all over again, the night Sebastian first threatened me, using the excuse that it's only because he loves me so very much.

'Dora, I need you to focus on me, nothing else. Just the sound of my voice.' This is worse than last time. Cold sweat drips down my neck. We're out in the heat of the midday sun, yet my hands and toes feel numb with cold. Taking a breath is getting harder and harder.

'Remember the stars? They're still there, still with you now. Watching over us. Nothing ever changes, only how we see it changes. Sometimes it's important to see the truth, even if it hurts. You need to take a slow breath no matter what's happened. Slowly in, slowly out.'

I manage to sniff in a deeper breath, only to smell the hint of fish on Dinos's clothes. My stomach twists and my gag reflex sets in; I begin to retch. Pushing myself back from the wall, I double over, leaning my weight on my knees. My legs tremble underneath me, as I gag on empty lungs and a full stomach. Something about the gagging makes me suck in a deeper breath.

My eyes blur in strained tears as my stomach twists harder until I vomit, there next to the wall.

Dinos *shhes* me and rubs my back; he holds my hair back as best he can. I've got myself in such a state. I feel like I've been balancing on the edge of a boat with a bag of rocks tied to my back. On the edge, waiting to fall into the darkest of doom.

'No matter how dark the sky is, even when you can't see the stars, even if they disappear, they're there. And so am I. I'm here. I'm still your friend, even if you hate me, even if I don't understand why.' The last part is added under his breath, and I can't figure out whether I should cry harder or attempt a laugh. 'If you need me, you know I'm always here for you. Focus on the good in the world. Focus on my voice, on light, on good. You are good, you are light. When you walk in a room, you're more golden than the sun setting over the sea, and all the other girls at best stand in your reflection hoping to be seen. I understand why Sebastian wouldn't want to let you out of his sight. I understand why he would hold on tight. As long as he doesn't crush you by holding on too tightly.'

I wipe my mouth on the back of my hand and drag myself up to standing and look over Dinos's face. His heavy eyebrows are pulled together and a shadow from the arch behind me is casting a dark line across his face. If I didn't know better, I'd think he liked me the way Sebastian does.

The image of Sebastian pushing me down on the bed, and the tension running over him like the spikes of a porcupine, slaps me in the face.

'Get,' I snatch a breath, 'me,' I snatch another, 'out of here.'

Chapter 28

Dinos weaves me across the grass instead of along the path we were on. We move between hedges with me clawing at his arm. Everything muddles again. How does Dinos have this way of confusing everything? His words shatter everything and leave me broken and confused about life.

Between the manicured garden of sweet flowers and shaped hedges, with water jets keeping them pristine in the heat, I spot Dinos's blue Seat Ibiza parked on the edge of the grass. He helps me to hop over the short, neat hedge and before I know it, I'm in the back of his car and he's driving out of the car park with only the rumbling of his engine filling the air.

I don't bother with the seat belt. Instead, I lie across the back seat with my legs bent up. Tilting my chin, I can see the sky out of the window, and the occasional bird of prey circling high above. I imagine the stars behind the blue sky and wonder why the hell it's blue anyway. I think it's refracted light or something. I don't know, I can't remember. Considering these questions is enough to calm my breathing, because I'm no longer focusing on all the other stuff in my life. Dinos told me to focus on the stars, on anything else, and it turns out that it does help.

The car bumps along the road. There's no real speed to it. Maybe Dinos doesn't know where we are going either. I don't care. Take me off the edge of a cliff and put me out of this dreadful misery. That would be what's for the best. Drive me out to sea and this time leave me there. Sebastian wouldn't have a reason to hurt my family then. He would mourn me and move on to someone else. Easier all round.

The car slows to a stop and Dinos cuts the engine.

'What happened?' He undoes his seat belt and twists in his seat to look down at me. There's no light in his eyes, only lines of sadness.

I shake my head, not knowing where to begin. I run over the scene in my head with Sebastian shoving me back. Which started with going out for the meal before—

'Oh Christ!' I sit up and scramble for my phone. 'I just left them there. I wasn't thinking. I just left them there! What do I say to them? They're there, waiting for me to come back. Sitting waiting for me!'

'Who is?'

'Phoebe and Xristina. They'll hate me.'

I press my face into my other hand, my blonde hair forms a curtain around me and I wish I could hide in it forever.

'Tell them the truth. Tell them you were sick outside and had to get a ride. They're your friends, they'll understand.'

I do as he suggests and tell the truth. I was sick after all. My stomach churns and gurgles at the memory of it.

There's a message in our group chat from Phoebe:

Where are you?

It's from five minutes ago. I type out my simple message and hit send.

'Shall I take you home?'

'No. Can we drive round?' I glance out of the window at the cluster of olive trees and the old dirt track. 'Where are we?'

'They make soap here. I know them. They won't mind us stopping.'

'Do you mind driving? I don't like the idea of sitting around.' I want to add *waiting to get caught again*. But we weren't caught, because we weren't doing anything wrong. If Dinos was a girl, Sebastian wouldn't care. I exhale the thought. I'd promised not to interact with Dinos, and I did. That's on me, I guess. I could've told him straight away, and I chose not to. I knew how he would react, so I decided to hide it from him. That's also on me. Perhaps if I'd just said, and beat Konstantinos to the punchline, then none of this would be an issue. Now it's such a big issue I have no idea where to go from here.

When Sebastian threatened me last year, I could write it off as a one-off. He was upset, and I knew he had reason to feel that way. Maybe he could smell it on me, the guilt rising from my skin like mist over the sea in the early morning. Now I'm in a car with Dinos, the worst person to sweep me away from Sebastian. I don't know how I'll come back from this one.

'Why were you at the hotel?' I study Dinos's profile as he tries to twist toward me a little bit more.

'They'd run out of fresh sea bass. Sebastian called my dad to see what he'd caught today. I took a tray over in the boot because dad had some other rounds to make. It's not my usual drop-off.'

'Sebastian called? Does he normally call?'

'Nope. Never. Must be the first time.'

Why would he call them? Why would he bring Dinos to where he knew I'd be? Was this a test and I failed? But he called Dinos's dad, so how could he possibly know it would be Dinos who dropped off the fish? He couldn't know. He must've just been desperate, that's all.

'Please drive.'

Dinos shifts in his seat and does up his belt again, clicking it into place. All I can see in the mirror are his bright hazel eyes. 'Only if you do up your belt this time.'

I sit in the middle and pull across the lap belt. This way I can look at the world as it passes and comes towards me. The sweeping curves of Corfu. My island. The island I share with those I love. I wish I could talk to someone other than Dinos about this. Anyone.

I can't talk to Mama or Baba. I'm not sure how they would react if I told them Sebastian shoved me. I can only imagine Baba would explode in a hammering of fists on Sebastian's face. I can't have that. It would end badly for everyone. Even Dinos might do something regrettable if I tell him. I need someone who might care enough to listen, but is far enough away that they wouldn't be able to do anything stupid.

Melodie.

'Dinos, I need you to go to Karousades. Do you know how to get there?'

'Yeah, it's easy enough. Where in Karousades?'

'I'm not sure. A house with bright pink window frames. Can't be too hard to find, right?'

Dinos watches me in his mirror. I wish I could see what he was thinking. He always so easily reads me, although maybe less so now I know about the nose-wrinkling thing. Dinos isn't that easy to read, and it's even harder when all I can see is the mirror-shaped slice of his face.

'I'll take you and help you find this place if you tell me two things.'

I fold my arms over my chest and slouch back into the seat.

'One,' Dinos says. 'What happened that made you so upset you left your friends without even remembering they were there? And two: who lives at the house with the pink window frames?'

I knew I wasn't going to like the questions, but I'm going to hate lying a whole lot more.

Chapter 29

Once, many years ago, my baba said to me that he read something someone shared on Facebook, someone who visited the island regularly and had a second home here. The post said something like: *If you think something, it becomes real, because you are real, so your thoughts are real. If your thoughts are real, then everything you think is real.*

I remember talking to Baba about this idea at great length. He quite liked the idea, and so did I. Every book we read, every dream we have, it's all real because it happens in our mind and our minds are real. It also means those who have passed are still real, still alive in our minds. They're real because we're real.

I'm not so sure. It might be real in my head, but a dream about a flying unicorn was never going to be real to the outside world. It made for a good debate though.

I think about this concept now, as I try to come up with answers for Dinos. If I think it, and say it, then to many it would be real. Real enough perhaps. At least. Maybe?

I can't meet his eyes in the mirror. Instead, I watch as we meander away from the olive groves, up and down on the bumps of the dry dirt road.

A more useful thought strikes me. It's not lying to hold back part of a story. It's just poor storytelling. It might just need a small amount of twisting then.

'Someone told Sebastian they saw us together that night you followed me to the sea. He was really upset, and I thought he was going to break up with me. I went outside for some air, then I saw you and... Well, seeing you set me off. And now what will he think?' Something about wording it this way soothes me. I'm rewriting my present history. It removes all the hard lines of the full fat truth.

We pass land that couldn't be more opposed to the manicured gardens of Sebastian's grand hotels. Here it's every colour fighting for attention as plants weave around each other pushing up towards the light. Everything looks like a mass of luxuriant undergrowth. A different kind of beautiful. Nature with its soft edges, instead of the cool lines found in luxury hotels.

'I'm sorry to have caused you so much pain.' Dinos's voice is flat. When I look back at the mirror, he isn't looking back at me. 'And the house?'

I might as well tell the full truth with this one. I have nothing to lose, other than him trying to talk me out of it. Which he won't be able to do. It feels as though everything has been leading to this. Meeting my big sister and her telling me it's all going to be okay. Sitting down with her and getting her to meet my family. No more hiding, no more negativity. Then she'll tell me the truth about our mother. If she knows it. I don't think she speaks to her either. There's no obvious mother figure in her instagram photos. Nothing to suggest they're close. I'll know soon enough.

'I have a sister. That's where she lives. In Karousades, with big pink shutters and doors.' I assume shutters, did the woman say shutters or frames? They must be shutters. Who doesn't have shutters?

'Frames or shutters? You said frames before? Now shutters.'

Why has Dinos got to be so picky? Why does he have to notice every little thing about me and what I say? Most guys barely even listen, and here he is paying attention to every last word.

'How is that your question, and not *"You have a sister?!"* No. Just, *"Shutters or frames?"* Shutters,' I say, taking a guess. 'I meant shutters.' I stare him down as he looks back at me in the mirror.

It takes a lot of effort to keep my nose still. I sort of want to rub it too, but I leave it alone. Based on today, I think if anyone else has noticed my strange nose behaviours when it comes to lying, it would be Dinos.

'I take it this sister you've found, she knows about you? You're okay to turn up at her house?'

'Why not? She's my sister.'

I shift and pull my dress over my legs a little more.

Dinos doesn't answer. Instead, he keeps looking at me in the mirror. Inspecting me. That's how it feels anyway. He's inspecting me for flaws. For cracks in my stories. Holes in the plot. I'm riddled with holes nowadays. As a younger teen, it was all pretty simple. I've always wondered a bit about where I came from, but finding all this out has nibbled and gnawed away at my very being until all that's left is holes. I'm confident though about Melodie. I know she'll be worth finding. I can feel it.

Dinos and I stay silently observing each other for another twenty minutes before we snag a problem.

'So, what's her address? I'll put it in my phone. We're only a few minutes out now.'

My nose wrinkles. I feel it go and hope to God he hasn't noticed in the mirror. I don't have the address because I got the information from some nosy women in Agios Stefanos. I can't say that. Another lie is beginning to bubble up.

'She's told me about her place. Said I could come over when I've told my parents about her. But I can't wait. I need to meet her now. I need to talk to her, see her face in the flesh. Look, there's a man and a child over there, going into that gate. Stop there and ask them if they know.'

'What?'

'Just do it!'

Dinos pulls the car close to the rusty white gate and the older gentleman, likely the boy's grandfather rather than baba, comes back towards us.

'Ask him if he knows where Melodie Greenwood lives, okay? Greenwood. The house with the pink door.'

'And shutters.' Dinos adds in a gruff tone. I don't confirm this part of the hearsay I'm basing all of this on.

Dinos casually asks the man, who squints down at us both, stretching his head almost into the open window to look me over before deciding he can tell us where to go.

Now we have directions, and I'm going to meet my sister. I'm going to meet Melodie. Melodie Greenwood.

Chapter 30

The woman wasn't wrong about the door, and I wasn't wrong about the shutters. They're all the same pink as bright bougainvillea. It's easy to tell, too, as there's an archway of the stuff to the side of the house that I assume leads to the back garden. The colour matches perfectly.

There are a few parked cars to one side of the house and a large gravelly driveway at the front.

Dinos makes a sliding whistling noise as he looks the house up and down. 'Nice place. Your sister obviously has money.'

If she doesn't then her husband certainly must. This place could swallow up my house in two easy mouthfuls, I'm sure.

'Will you wait for me?' I look in the mirror, but this time to check myself. I'm pale for me, but I've cleaned up my face a little in the last five minutes with crumpled tissues I found in my bag. I just look a little off colour, that's all. But she doesn't know what my normal colour is, or my normal anything.

'Are you sure about this? I can still take you home to your real family.'

I stop my fidgeting and look at Dinos square on as he turns in his seat to face me.

'I'm sure. I've got nothing left to lose. Will you wait?'

'For you, Dora, I'd wait forever.'

I hold his gaze and see the sadness that's lingering in the back of his eyes. Hazel eyes paler than ever with the sun streaming over his bronze face catching the light in such a way to make him look ethereal. His skin looks like satin with the way the light's hitting it. Why would he say that? That he'd wait for me? It's left me a little lost for words as my heart crakes as easily as thinly blown glass. I manage to squeeze out a strained, 'Thank you', before scooting out of the car.

After today, I need to find a way to avoid Dinos completely. It hurts too much to be around him.

The gravel crunches under my feet, but nothing could be louder than the beating of my heart in my ears. I feel like it's swapped places with my brain. That's exactly how it feels in fact. My heart has jumped to where my brain should be and it's taken over and led me to the door of a stranger who has my face.

I wish I could get Dinos's voice out of my head, *I'd wait forever.* I've waited forever for this moment, and all I can think about is Dinos waiting for me in the car and that he can never be mine.

As I lift my arm to knock, it's like it isn't my arm anymore. I'm seeing everything in some distant out-of-body floating sort of way. My hand curls into a fist and taps on the door. If it even is my hand at all.

There's a pause. I can hear voices on the other side of the door and footsteps closing in. I have the urge to run, but fear and my heart banging against the sides of my skull root me to the spot.

The door swings open and it's like looking into a strange phone filter just like Dinos said when he saw that photo of her.

'*Yassas.*' My disembodied voice begins with a mind of its own. In my native tongue I tell her my name and that I'm her *adelfi*, her sister.

She hasn't moved at all. She's like a mannequin in a shop, frozen in the window display.

'Sister?' she responds in English. At least she must have understood my Greek as I suspected. Her full lips move but the rest of her continues to be as still as a corpse. She has my lips and my pointed chin but eyes and hair the colour of a soft pale bark.

'I'm sorry. No. No, I'm so sorry.' The door slams in my face. Its jolly pink paint adds insult to the action somehow.

It's my turn to freeze now. No? Doesn't she see that I'm her sister? Can't she tell with one simple look? Her face said she could tell.

There are a lot of voices the other side of the door. Laughter and chatting. The normal sounds for a family home in Corfu.

I knock again. Gently this time. Perhaps it was just the initial shock, or the fact she has a house full of people and I've picked a bad time.

A voice begins to talk loudly behind the door. I can't make out what's being said exactly. I take a step back as it opens again.

This lady is more like my mama, short with curls, and in her manner alone is unmistakeably Greek. She curses at me and crosses herself.

'Is this her? *Kalese tin astynomia*! Call the police!' The woman's voice is piercing, almost hitting the notes of a scream.

The police? Why would they call the police? I begin to shake my head as a gaggle of giant men claw their way to the door to take a look at me.

'*Sygnómi, sygnómi,*' a man continues in Greek. 'There has been a misunderstanding.'

I can feel the tears welling up again and the bright spots in my vision begin to glimmer as I back away from them all. With one last look at Melodie, I run back to Dinos.

I hear the door shut behind me again as I jump in the car and tell Dinos to drive.

Chapter 31

I flop into the front of the car and Dino drives away.

This pain is different to any other I've experienced so far. I don't feel like my chest is going to cave in this time. I don't feel like I'm about to explode or that my heart is still in my head. In fact, I feel as though my heart has dropped back into place with a hard thump in my chest. Hard enough to rip it free from my body, leaving it floating and strangely absent.

She didn't do that test to find me. She had no intention of finding a sister at all. I'm a complete idiot. Silent tears roll down my cheeks this time, instead of the trapped anxiety that's been balled in my chest since doing this stupid DNA test. The stars have fallen from the sky now. I saw them for what they really are. Explosions that are beautiful and life-giving from a distance, but will burn you quicker than you can run away on closer inspection.

Dinos drives without a word. He doesn't rush or speed and he doesn't attempt to ask what happened.

After maybe five minutes of gliding along past the spikes of cypress trees bobbing up out of the swaths of icy-green olive groves, he shuffles in his seat. I know he wants to talk now. He doesn't need to open his mouth for me to know. Something about the twitch of his fingers in thought and the awkward movement in his seat tells me.

'Do you want to go for a walk? Today was meant to be my day off and... It'd be nice to get out of the car. Maybe get something to eat?'

I've been completely selfish and haven't even thought about what Dinos might have planned for today. I can't even begin to think why he helps me all the time. Why he even bothers with me. Why he likes me at all.

'That'd be nice. My treat. I think I owe you some food at least.'

Dinos chuckles to himself and strums the steering wheel. 'Sidari?'

'No. Can we go somewhere quiet, please?'

He glances at me before turning his attention back to the road. 'Of course.' He strums some more, harder with his thumbs. 'We went past a place, Taste Me.' I turn in my seat to face him, and he laughs. The name is in English and his accent saying it is heavy but still sort of amusing. 'Looked nice enough.'

'Okay. Let's give it a try.'

Dinos finds a driveway to turn around in, and we head back towards Taste Me.

With everything that's happened today, I've been left feeling numb. Most of the time lately, I've been thinking. Thinking,

thinking, always thinking. Wondering about who these people are, what they might mean to me. The conversations we might have. As it turns out, I've been wasting the past couple of years on dreams and ghosts. At least now I know for sure. Something about knowing that nothing will come of this search for my birth family has calmed my nerves at last. At least that's one good thing to come out of it all. The downside is, it's given me space to fill with worries about Sebastian. I look at my phone. Missed calls from Xristina and Phoebe alongside a message from Sebastian:

Where did you go?

They must have asked him what happened and, of course, he would have no answers for them. Nothing he could share without hurting his reputation anyway.

Outside the window cypress trees look like miniature conifers where the land slopes down from the road. Only small tips poke out at this height. Like the tip of icebergs, the rest unseen under the surface.

I wonder what the rest of the world is really like. Next year, I want to find out. I want to travel. Really travel, outside of Greece. I vow to explore beyond this beautiful island and into the unknown. Maybe somewhere cold. Something different. Even if it's just to confirm how lucky I am to live on an island buzzing with cicadas, butterflies the colours of rainbows and lizards spying on my every move. Sometimes I wonder what it must be like to go somewhere that doesn't hum all summer long. That doesn't just fall silent when the cicadas stop their song at the end of the sizzling heat of summer. I need to know what it's like to be somewhere else.

Dinos pulls up outside Taste Me. Next to the main building that boasts *Coffees 'n' More*, there's a terrace, or veranda, with vines hanging down from above creating a shady area to sit and have a drink. It's quiet and we have a choice of seats. There are even two swings next to each other looking out over the trees. It's the perfect Instagram opportunity —if I wasn't here to not be seen that is.

'That view–' I begin.

'I know.' Dinos takes in a deep breath and lets it out hard. 'We're lucky really. To call this our home,' he nods towards the view. 'Worse places to live in the world.'

We smile at each other as we pull out black metal chairs in synchronicity and sit down to look over the menu.

'Looks like it'll be desserts and coffee if you're okay with that?' I glance up at Dinos from my menu, realising there's not much in the way of lunch on offer.

'Coffee and cake's good with me. Anything.'

It's not long before we've ordered what we want and we're looking out at the view again. Well, I am. Dinos, on the other hand, is watching me.

'Theadora–'

'Oh no, he's using my whole name.' I lift my hands up sarcastically and try to plaster a smile on my face as I turn to face him. But I'm sure he can see right through it. He doesn't return the smile. Instead, he leans his forearms on the table in front of him to bring himself closer to me. In turn, I sit back in my chair to maintain our distance. I want to slip off my sandals and hide behind my knees, but I resist the urge.

He says, 'You don't owe me anything.'

'Apart from coffee and cake.' This gets a smile out of him. My playful dodging softens him enough that the ache in my chest lessens.

'Apart from coffee and cake,' he agrees. 'What I mean is, something else happened today. There's a feeling, like a burning low in my chest and I know you're holding stuff back from me. I know it. It's not just that sister of yours. I knew you hadn't spoken to her before. It was obvious. But... it's more than that. I know I'm speaking out of turn, but since you've been with Sebastian...' Dinos shakes his head and licks his tense lips. 'It's like you've put on a face, a mask. Even a damn wall to hide behind. I know he doesn't want us to be friends, I can't blame him for that, and yeah, I miss you. I know, I know... I get to see you when we're there in groups but it's not the same. You don't even laugh the same when he's there. Be honest with me. What really happened with him today? Did he, did he hurt you?'

'Here are your drinks. Who ordered the baklava?' the waitress says.

I raise my hand to my shoulder like I'm back at school then quietly thank her as she slides the plate in front of me.

The waitress isn't even one step away from the table when Dinos is urging me to tell him.

'He didn't hurt me.' My nose wrinkles, I feel it go. But it's not really a lie. I wasn't *hurt*. Other than maybe emotionally, I suppose, and that's not what Dinos is implying at all.

Dinos's jaw clenches and his eyes narrow on me.

'Theadora...'

'Don't call me that. I've had a really, really shitty day. The blood climbed up in my head today.' My finger stabs at my temple. 'More than that. What is it the English say? My *blood boiled* today with everything that's happened. I don't think we should talk about Sebastian. He isn't here to defend himself.'

'Does he need defending?'

'No, it's just... Eat your cake. Food makes everything better.'

'Theadora–'

'Dinos, stop *eating my ears* over this. Going on and on... I don't want to talk about it.'

I pick up my sticky honey-covered baklava and thrust it into my mouth so that I can't talk. Dinos puffs air through his nostrils but does as he's told and begins to eat his cake and sip his coffee.

The tension evaporates in the heat of the sun, and I look out at the sea in the distance. Between us and it, there's a different sea, a green one below us; there's even the top of a lemon tree not far from our feet. From our vantage point everything seems possible. Maybe even telling Dinos the whole truth. I need to talk to someone. I wanted it to be my big sister. But I've spent much too much time dreaming about her and building her up in my head. That was a foolish thing to do. She's a person, not a picture. Not the nicest of people either from the way she put a door in my face.

I snatch a breath and dust off my fingers. 'He pushed me. He didn't hurt me.' I hold up my index finger because I know Dinos wants to interrupt. 'But he has threatened me before, and again today. I don't know why I'm telling you this.' Every muscle in Dinos's narrow face turns to harsh lines like a face made of daggers. His chest visibly rises and falls, the pace quickening like a train tipping on a downhill trajectory. I carry on before he can interrupt me. 'I know he didn't want to hurt me. He's just very protective of me.' Dinos almost spits and mutters *protective!* as he shakes his head. I don't let him cut over me. 'I can't leave him. He threatened my family, so don't ask me to. Don't even tell me to. I'm happy enough and I don't want you to push me on the matter. I'd much rather you changed the subject, in fact. How's your family? How're your parents? Your sister?'

Dinos closes his eyes. His face contorts out of its usual handsome shape. His mouth opens, but his eyes stay closed, 'My sister, she's not well. She's going for some tests in a week or so. We'll know more then. I'm sure she'll be fine.'

Sometimes when I'm wrapped up in my own pain and drama, it's easy to forget that others have problems too. My problems are mostly of my own making. I'm at the centre of the drama and I'm the one to blame. Poor Dinos, he's only good. I'm trouble and he doesn't deserve such a dreadful friend. When did I become so self-absorbed?

Dinos rests his hands on the edge of the table. Instinctively I reach across and rest my hand over his. He opens his eyes and looks down at our hands. Slowly, gently, he twists his round, and his open palm lets me in.

'I hope she's okay.'

'Me too.'

'Do they have any ideas?'

He shakes his head. 'If they do, no one has told me about it. Now it's my turn to change the subject.' Dinos runs his thumb over the back of my hand making a shiver roll from my hand across my arm and all the way down my spine. 'What the hell was going on with *your* sister?'

I roll my eyes at my own stupidity.

'You're right, we'd never spoken before. I just built her up in my head and felt sure in my gut that if I turned up at her door it would all work out. She could somehow help me with Sebastian, and I'd gain a sibling.'

'So, you *do* need help with Sebastian.'

'Please don't.'

Dinos bobs his head, and a coy smile slips from his lips. He continues looking at our hands and soothing me with his thumb.

In a low gravelly voice he slowly and methodically says, 'If he touches you again, Dora, I'll kill him.'

Chapter 32

Another night staring into the darkness. At least the nights aren't so blisteringly hot now. With my fan whirling above my head, I can comfortably exist under my sheets. It hums over me as loud as cicadas during the day. I always find its rhythm strange. *Voom... voom... voom.* It's a circle, continuous. How does it sound like such a gentle beat — a rhythm? Maybe it's my imagination. Maybe it *is* continuous and I'm trying to find a pulse where there isn't one.

I close my eyes. It's not that much different to when they're open. Only, now I can see Dinos's face. *I'll kill him* echoes like he's there in the room with me. His pupils, normally round and full, were pinpoints.

I believe he would kill Sebastian. I have no doubt about the truth of his words. It's what happened next that plays over and over.

I open my eyes again. I don't want to see him say it again. It's played a hundred times already.

'Why him?' Dinos had said, his voice breaking, before snatching his hand from mine and scrubbing his face with it. 'I thought you were better than being influenced by all that shit.'

I argued back. Said I had no idea what he was talking about, that he didn't understand. That it was my family in danger. What would he do if it was his family? I told him I love Sebastian, that we're together and that's what's important. Even thinking back on what Dinos said next makes me want to choke.

He started a sentence that will be open forever. 'Why wasn't it...? Never mind.'

Never mind.

I paid and we drove back with only small talk passing our lips. What was he about to say? *Why wasn't it him?* I'm sure that's what he was going to say. I could scream now at the thought of it. I wanted to scream then too, scream, *You never asked! You never told me you were interested!* Too late now. Too late. Sebastian was right to be jealous. We've brought this on. It's Sebastian who's caught up in it all, and it's all our fault for hiding what we've felt for so long.

With each exhale I hope it'll all get easier.

It doesn't.

I did manage one cathartic and grown-up thing when I got home from today's disaster. I messaged my sister on the DNA website. In English this time, as she only replied to me in English on the doorstep.

Melodie, I am sorry I came to see you without asking. It must have been a shock. I should have waited for you to respond. I now realise that you and our mother were not looking for me. I am sorry to have troubled you. Theadora

I didn't have to message her. I owe her nothing. She owes me nothing. I just hope this closes the door for me. I'm saying goodbye to the idea of finding a sister and understanding what happened to me, and how I ended up in this place.

There's no time to think about her, or my past. It's the future that's important now. My future. Everything was simple a week ago. Sebastian and I were plodding along fine. Everything was fine. Manageable. I'd convinced myself of the life that was perfectly planned out. I could see it. He'd propose, I'd have beautiful children and they would have the best in life. I'd give them everything my parents gave me and more. Everything my birth parents didn't want for me. I'd thrive and make sure they did too. Was it going to be a heart-wrenching deep love match? No. But it would be comfortable. Sustainable. I could see that life simply mapped out.

With Dinos I see *what if* and a man who hasn't even told me how he feels. At least with Sebastian it's easy and obvious. He tells me all the time that he makes himself bleed trying to show the world how he feels about me. What does Dinos do?

What *does* Dinos do?

Turn up when I need him most.

Listen when I need it most.

Care when I need it most.

Doesn't care if anyone sees him do it.

Chapter 33

The summer season is all but over now. Back to the peace of winter. I'm ready for long walks wrapped up in layers. That's still a way off. At least I'm back in jeans.

A youngish man with round glasses comes through the door of the shop. I look up from my phone to give him a proper greeting. I can tell by his accent he's Scottish. As soon as he turns down one of the aisles, I go back to my phone, doomscrolling to keep myself sane.

Sebastian wants to see me tonight and talk about what happened yesterday. I have no idea what to tell him. Dinos said he wouldn't tell anyone if that's how I wanted it. He also made it clear that he would be there for me if I wanted that too. I roll my eyes away from my phone thinking about it all. I haven't decided what to do yet. I'm back to where I was last year, wishing I could walk away and be alone for a while. I don't want to feel frightened to do what I want.

At least I can tell Sebastian a part truth about yesterday — about vomiting and leaving. The question will be *how* did I leave?

The man with the glasses reappears. He's holding some fridge magnets with Corfu and Kassiopi written on them, and houses with little blue doors — the picture-perfect idea of life here. He also has one glass on the same theme and a packet of Kumquat Greek Delight.

'Did you find everything you were looking for?'

'Yes. Thank you.'

'I only have newspaper to wrap. Is that okay?'

'Oh aye, fine. Thanks.'

We ran out of the good paper a week ago and I don't think Baba wants to buy more until next season. We won't be selling many nick-nacks for a while now. I pull a sheet of last week's newspaper up and tuck it all around the glass in the same way I have since I was fourteen and started working in the shop after school.

I pull another sheet up and freeze at the sight of it. I recognise the handsome face looking back at me in the newspaper photo. Melodie's husband. I'm sure it is. Sure.

'Everything alright?' The sound of the man's voice makes me jump. Only minutely, but still. He didn't move, my brain did.

I stuff the sheet of paper back under the counter.

'Yes. Thank you.' I scoop up another sheet and wrap the souvenirs before putting them in a bag and passing it to him.

'Thank you. Have a good day.'

Grasping the blue-and-white striped plastic bag, he gazes at me. I want to tell him to leave because I'm itching to read the article about Melodie's husband, but he says, 'I think I owe you some money.'

I slap my hands on my knees and apologise in a complete tizz. I turn and look at the amount on the till. 'Fourteen euros thirty.'

He pulls out two notes and tells me to keep the change. I turn to the till, adamant that he needs his change, but when I look up with a handful of ten-cent coins, he has gone.

'Thank you,' I call towards the empty doorway, and slide the coins back into the till.

Taking a surreptitious glance around the shop, I reach down towards my feet and pull up the newspaper article.

Local Father Found in Old Perithia

Anton Greenwood, 39, was recently discovered dehydrated in Old Perithia after being missing for days. He has many injuries, including a snakebite, but is recovering well in Corfu Hospital. His wife, Melodie Greenwood, thanked

everyone who put up posters and tried to help her find him.

I read the short announcement over and over again. The photo is from their wedding day. I think so anyway. There in black and white he's smiling with straight white teeth and neatly swept-back hair, and cheekbones that could almost get in the way of his vision if they were any higher on his face.

Now I really don't know how to feel. Did I see him there? At the house? I close my eyes and think back. No. The man who spoke resembled him, but with longer hair in a knot on top of his head. There was a gaggle of them. It's hard to remember. There was the short bustly woman, Melodie, and a sea of bulky men.

I wonder if my timing was dreadful. She still wouldn't have shut the door in my face if she were a good person. She can't be. I wouldn't do that to a sister of mine if she showed up at my door. I'd welcome her in, open my heart to her, let her have anything she needed. I'm Greek, even if not by blood, and I know the importance of family and putting them first. If I didn't care about family, I'd have left Sebastian a year ago. That's the truth of it. I don't want to find out what could happen if I hurt his ego — not what might happen to me, but to my family.

'Alright, Theodora mou?' Baba's voice in the doorway makes adrenaline run through me like electricity and I quickly lower the paper like I've been caught doing something I shouldn't. 'Anything interesting in yesterday's news?'

As soon as I look at his warm face, my heart relaxes enough to smile. I'm safe when he is near me. Everything else melts away.

'Did you know about this man? He was missing, but they found him.' Just asking him this makes me feel like I'm playing with fire. It's a dangerous game, walking this line and putting my sister's husband right in front of him like this.

Baba leans over to see what I'm looking at on the counter where I dropped the paper.

'Oh yes, it was all over Facebook. Haven't you seen posters around the village?'

'No? Where?'

Baba shrugs as he leans his hip into the counter. 'Some of the tavernas. One of his brothers came round handing them out until he ran out of them.'

A distant memory of someone's Instagram story rings in my ears. *If you see this man call this number,* sort of thing. I've been so distracted I hadn't noticed any posters anywhere. Not that I've really been anywhere other than here and home most of the time.

'I heard he had been abducted by a sister-in-law. Who knows the truth though, eh?' Baba pouts his lips in a jovial manner and folds his arms about his chest. 'Strange world, Theodora.'

'Wait, sister-in-law?' I feel like at some point every day something insane happens that sends my pulse racing around like it's in a sprint against time. This is another one of those crazy moments. A sister-in-law would be *my* sister! Another sister of *mine?*

A scream swells in my lungs, but I bite it back.

No, stop. Those men could've been his brothers. It's much more likely that the sister-in-law is one of their wives. I'm getting myself in a tangled mess now, thinking strange thoughts out of turn.

'It's only a rumour. I don't even know if he has a sister-in-law. Are you okay? You look pale. You're not ill, are you?' Baba presses the back of his hand to my forehead. 'Are you hungry? You look hungry.'

'How can someone look hungry?'

'Too thin.'

I roll my eyes and stand up to stretch my legs. Moving out from behind the counter, I lean on it next to Baba.

'Baba, what do you do when you don't know what to do for the best?'

'Eat. Food makes everything better.'

A miniature snort of laughter jumps out of me. Of course this would be the answer.

'Seriously. I don't know what I'm doing with my life. How do I know what's right?'

'Are you sure this isn't a problem for your mama?'

I press my lips together as I look at him and fold my arms mirroring his, only I put a little more emphasis into it to make sure he's paying attention to the action.

'Alright, alright.' He drops his arms and tilts his head back to look at the ceiling. Baba's hair is quite grey now; in this light it seems more obvious. Each thread glints in the synthetic light.

He's gained a thicker waistline in the past few years too. Probably from solving problems with food. 'What's the real problem?'

I drop my chin to look at the scuffed flooring while I think what to say. I have layers of problems and they're all my fault. I don't want Baba to be disappointed in me, but I really need someone to talk to, and Baba was always there to make things better when I was younger. He could solve any problem with ease.

Baba hooks his finger under my chin and carefully lifts my head to meet his eyeline.

'Theodora mou, what's troubling you? I know I joke, but you can always tell me anything you like.'

Maybe I could, but it's too much of a risk. Could I really come out with *Oh, by the way, I lied and took that DNA test? I found my biological mum and sister on there and turned up on my sister's doorstep. Also, I'm a little bit frightened of Sebastian and he keeps threatening the family if I'm found talking to Dinos, who I might actually be in love with.*

No. I can't say any of that. Not without hurting everyone involved.

'It's nothing, Baba. Maybe you're right. I think I'm hungry.' I lean forwards and kiss his cheek.

I'm going to have to figure all of this out alone.

Chapter 34

I didn't know Sebastian would be picking me up with his yiayia and pappoús in the back of the car. I'm so taken aback as Sebastian hops out to open my door that all I do is give them an awkward wave through the window.

'What's going on?' I ask through a gritted-teeth smile.

'Yiayia and Pappoús want to take us for a meal. They heard you hadn't been feeling well and wanted to check on you. They're too kind. Are you better now?'

'Much, thanks.'

With that I'm sliding into the passenger seat and being whisked off to another one of the hotels in the chain for us all to have dinner together. I hope it's not the same hotel as yesterday.

Although, they all look much the same to me, so flashbacks are inevitable either way.

His grandparents are the people who *really* own it all. One day, it'll be Sebastian, but these are the people who built the business from the ground up.

Our short journey is filled with polite small talk about the changing of the seasons and how business is doing. They've lived a much more luxurious life than anyone else I know for generations. They're landowners, proprietors, people of wealth and status from birth and for generations to come. The hotels might be newer, but the money isn't. I'm the adopted kid from god knows where who's caught the eye of their perfect grandson. They're always good to me, but I can't help feeling awkward when I have to do anything with Sebastian and his family. They're very kind, but I feel the vast difference between us.

Sebastian takes his grandparents out almost as much as he takes me. They're very close and he adores them both. He's particularly close to his grandfather, whom he sees as a mentor.

It doesn't help that I thought we would be having a conversation maybe in a bar. I'm in my tight black jeans and a backless silk top. Not what I'd have worn had I known we were going out with the grandparents. For some reason I would have preferred to keep my shoulders covered as if we were going to church. I have been to church with them more than I have with my parents. Maybe that's why.

Sebastian's grandmother, Kalista, has a haughty air, not that I feel like she's directing it at me, but she has a way about her. They've only ever been kind to me. Sebastian talks to them almost every day and must've shared that I'd been unwell. It's so thoughtful to want to take me out and check on me. But at times I catch the lowering of Kalista's eyes at people. That hint of condescension comes more from the expression on her face than the things she says.

Both of them are dripping in ostentatious gold jewellery with Rolex watches and Kalista with her Chanel chain. More than a statement of wealth, it's a statement of wealth I could never imagine.

We arrive at the very same hotel I ran out of yesterday. Why here? A sicky feeling pricks up inside me at the memory.

Sebastian pulls on the handbrake and cuts the engine before reaching over and moving my hair from my shoulder, exposing my bare skin.

'You look beautiful. Doesn't she look beautiful?' He turns to his adoring audience who promptly agree. 'I should have warned you we were going out though.' He looks down at my jeans and my naked shoulder and back. 'My fault, I suppose.'

Sebastian slips out of the car to open the door for Kalista. After a measured breath, I slip out of the car and take his other arm. Philippos lights one of his fat cigars and puffs out a few clouds.

'You take in the ladies. I'll follow on.' He nods behind the pungent tobacco smoke.

Sebastian leads us along, making our way into the restaurant.

It's hard to fault how attentive he is with his grandparents, pulling out his yiayia's chair for her. It's like he's a different person to yesterday. He's a kind and loving grandson, always ready to pour a drink and ask the right question. It must be nice to have grandparents. I'm lucky I have parents though, seeing as I was left for dead at birth, so I can't really complain.

Kalista often taps Sebastian on his cheek and pinches it now and then too. I know she'll order extra food for him to make sure he is well fed and well looked after the way she always does. They're kind and generous with me too. I'm always overfed when we're with them. I can't escape their overwhelming generosity.

'So, Sebastian, when will you be putting a ring on this girl's finger? Her hands look rather underdressed, wouldn't you agree, Philippos?'

I look behind me to see Philippos arriving at the table. He laughs from his round belly in return. He might be smartly dressed but laughter tugs the buttons across his belly.

We are a finished product with my life mapped out. Nothing's changed, and as long as I spend the rest of my life avoiding Dinos I can be just about happy enough. These are good people, a good family. They've welcomed me from day one, and if Sebastian is as attentive with children as he is with his grandparents then he would make a good father.

If only the thought of never seeing Dinos again wasn't completely crushing.

I keep the serene sweet smile on my face and watch Sebastian. He's ready with his standard answer, I'm sure.

'Maybe soon. Who knows?'

He reaches over and squeezes my hand. That's not the answer I was hoping to hear. I was hoping to hear that he had big plans, and I was in them, but he was still working on the best way to make it all happen, the best way to propose and the perfect life for us all.

Now I have visions of him throwing his chair out of the way and falling down on one knee to claim me as his in the here and now.

I don't speak. Heat rushes over me in a wild, frenzied panic that I hope comes across as a coy blush.

'Look at her, she can't wait. I do hope it's soon. I love a wedding.' Kalista reaches across and pats her grandson's hand.

Philippos sits down next to me. 'Don't worry, my dear. We know girls seem to get married later and later. I married Kalista when she was your age. I hear many leave it until their twenties now.'

'Maybe those who can't afford it,' Kalista says, without flinching, from behind her menu.

I hate the idea that marriage is just ticking another status box. The big wedding to impress everyone. Sebastian thinks I look good on his arm, his family seem agreeable to the match, and that's it. My life has been signed away and he keeps me as his pure princess waiting for marriage. My teeth nip at my cheeks. I regret the day I met him.

Bile threatens to burn the back of my throat. I hold it in. I hold everything in.

Chapter 35

After the meal, as Kalista and Philippos walk ahead of us in the car park, Sebastian squeezes my hand and leans in close at my ear. 'Up for a drive once we've dropped them off?' His teeth gleam and I'm reminded of a tiger looking for prey.

'Sure.'

'No throwing up, though.' He lets go of my hand to pat my bottom before we reach the car, and he opens the door.

One time I threw up. Once. I've been in the car with him hundreds of times in the past year and held it in, although admittedly he has never gone in circles again. He'll never let me live it down though. Openly laughing at me at any possible chance he can find.

As I sit down, the intense synthetic sweetness of the car's air freshener hits me in the back of my throat and makes me want to choke before we've even started.

After a short drive, and an even shorter goodbye to his grandparents, Sebastian is already on at me to check the Smurf app.

'I deleted it.'

'Then download it again, Theodora. We're going to race with Konstantinos. He's brought Xristina to impress. He's been trying to get her to come along for months and she's finally agreed. I'm going to drive him into the ground.' Sebastian bursts into a manic laugh and slaps the steering wheel.

'She didn't mention it to me.'

His laughter fizzles out. 'Maybe she would have if you'd bothered to stick around for five minutes yesterday.'

He's probably right. I think she and Phoebe are both upset at me for running away without even a goodbye. Phoebe at least was kind about me feeling unwell; Xristina on the other hand was pretty quiet about it all, at least in the group chat.

Sebastian speeds round each hairpin, and there are times I'm sure he's going to slide us off the edge and into the trees below. It's like being in the car with a completely different person to the one I was sitting next to ten minutes earlier. If he was always the man I first fell for, the one he is when he is around his grandparents, then I think I could be in this and still be happy enough. If only.

'I think I want to go home.'

'Too late. It's in the wrong direction. Anyway, I'm bringing you to show you off.'

Good to know my new purpose in life continues. I really should look into studying abroad again. I know Mama and Baba were pleased when it didn't happen, but at least then I'd be able to escape *him* even if it would mean giving up the island that I love. It would hopefully only be for a short while.

I'd quite happily leave for a time to gain perspective. It would have the added bonus of being further away from my sister too. I hope I never see her again after humiliating myself. At least she would probably walk in the opposite direction if she ever saw me.

'Have you downloaded the app yet?'

'No, I don't have enough signal.'

A growl resonates through the car. 'Come on, be useful for a change.'

'Are you seriously talking to me like that?'

Sebastian laughs. Not the same manic outburst. It's low and dark.

'Does it matter? We both know you'll stay with me, and I'll get to show you off like I do my jewellery and my cars because if you don't, I'll shame you and I'll drive your family's business into the ground. Now stop being a bitch and download the Smurf app. All I need right now is having to pay a fine and pissing off my parents. They've said if it happens again, they'll cut my privileges for a month. A fucking month, Theadora! I don't want to have to go to my grandparents begging.' Then he changes his tone and says, 'Be a good princess and download the app. Now.'

Anger bites like bile burning my throat. How dare he talk to me like that? I'm so taken aback that I have no words. Nothing sharp or smart to say. I'm done. Finished. It doesn't matter whether I'm angry. It doesn't matter if I'm upset. This is it.

No, this can't be it. I can't give up and let this be it. I need to find a way to keep my family safe and to get away from *him*.

I'll study abroad and stay there if I have to. I'm not being treated like this my whole life. I need to protect my family, but I can't stand being treated dreadfully just because I spoke to another man. Hopefully he'll get bored without me here to look at his app for him, and move on to someone who dotes on his every word the way he wants. I just need to play the long game.

The car skids and swivels into a hard handbrake turn. I wasn't at all ready for it, and my neck whips to the side. In a smouldering cloud full of dust, we come to a stop. When I look up, I see Konstantinos's car lights. As the dust settles, I can see Xristina grinning beside an irritated-looking Konstantinos. I swallow hard. She looks giddy to be involved in all of this. If only she knew.

As soon as I'm out of the car, Xristina is asking me how I am and what the hell happened the day before.

I try to download the Smurf app as Xristina chats at me about how cool the cars are, how much fun the whole night's going to be. She's got a miniskirt on and a tight T-shirt.

'I thought you weren't interested in Konstantinos,' I mumble as I watch my phone trying to download the app as slowly as it possibly can.

I remember him looking at her at school, and the way he does everything to sit near her when we're all out together. She's openly said to Phoebe and me that she's not interested, implying he's beneath her. Saying he's too chubby and boring. At the end of last year, she was seeing a man she met when she was out, but we never met him. With Covid restrictions back in over the winter it wasn't a top priority. It seemed to fizzle out, but she has never shown any interest in Konstantinos before.

'A girl can change her mind.' She leans in closer and adds, 'I just thought it would be fun to hang out and see the cars. You know I like fast cars and he's been begging to take me out forever. Free food, free fun.'

The boys pace around their cars, talking about recent changes they've made and what's on their list of improvements. This must be half of what they talk about. Maybe more. It's so dull

I think I'd rather spend my evening timing how long I can hold my breath than be here.

From the corner of my eye, I see Xristina shrug. 'I like him well enough at least.'

'Wow, that much, hey?'

She gently giggles and shrugs again. 'Yeah... Well... his car. When are we racing?' She steps away from me and speaks in her loud look-at-me-voice. 'Theodora was saying you're the king of drifting, Sebastian. Maybe you could show me.' She steps away from me more and towards the boys.

I resist the urge to say, *No I didn't*. But then maybe she means in the past, back when I was under his spell and he treated me like a queen. Seems like a lifetime ago now.

'Oh, did she? Thanks, babe.' Sebastian steps past her, pulls me in, crushing my hand and phone between us and kisses me hard on the mouth. He drops me just as quickly and turns to Xristina. 'Want me to show you? You don't mind me showing Xristina my moves, do you, princess?'

'Nope. It's fine.'

Sebastian shoots me a look from the corner of his eye. I suppose I was meant to gush or have some other response that wasn't nonchalance. Maybe I should've protested, saying his moves should only be for me. Oh well, this is the only rebellion I have now. Maybe if I don't behave well in public, he'll break up with me naturally and I can be free. That or I'll get told off again.

Xristina practically skips to his car, her black curls swinging from one side to the other. They both get in and accelerate away from me and Konstantinos, leaving us choking in smoke and dust. We watch the lights disappear as they look for the nearest spot good for drifting.

'I know it was you.' I almost choke on my words. I don't bother looking to my right at Konstantinos. He doesn't care anyway, I'm sure.

'What was me?'

'Telling Sebastian about Dinos looking for me.'

At last, the app finishes its upload and I can put my phone in the back pocket of my jeans. The battery is getting low as it is.

I turn to assess Konstantinos head on. I tilt my chin up to meet his eyes. He doesn't deny my claim. His bulky shoulders rise and fall under his baggy sports shirt. He looks so smug about it I could slap him. I used to think he was okay. Sometimes too defensive and a little sarcastic. I never realised how badly he needed validation. Enough to do anything to be in with Sebastian as far as I can see. I don't give him the attention he so desperately wants. Instead, I walk away from him and lean against an olive tree where I can hide in the sound of insects and the fresh smell of earth instead of kicked-up dust and smoke. The world around me is lit only by the white stars overhead and the shit car at my back.

I wonder what my parents are up to right now. What Dinos is doing. Phoebe will be packing now, I'm sure. I'm going to see her tomorrow to say goodbye. But that's it. A simple goodbye. Sebastian ruined our day together. I've lost that forever because of him. Then she gets to go on an adventure. I would rather be anywhere but here.

Konstantinos gets in his car and speeds away, plunging me into darkness. It takes a moment for my eyes to adjust. I don't even really know where I am. I saw some rundown houses maybe a kilometre back. I look out across the sky. With Konstantinos's car now moving away in the same direction as Sebastian's, I can see the stars clearly. The constellations all pop out from the darkness and the full moon shows me its craters with pride.

I swat away a mosquito then slap one on my arm before stepping out onto the empty road.

I've never been so alone before.

The background noise of humming insects around the trees is like a familiar blanket held in the hands of a child, but other than that, I'm alone. It's beyond rare, and even more rare not to have someone within screaming distance. Maybe the last time I was this far from people was when I was left as a baby. The church I was left at isn't exactly close to much else.

I don't know. Maybe not even then.

I've never been more alone. I've never been more at peace. I hope they never come back for me.

Chapter 36

When they come back from their drive without me, Sebastian doesn't even apologise for leaving me stranded in the middle of nowhere in the dark. He has a smug look on his face, like he's being strangled by silent laughter.

Konstantinos, on the other hand, gets out of his car and paces, his feet slapping the ground with every step. Xristina has swapped cars at some point. She's pouting, her face lit by the blue glow of her phone screen in Konstantinos's passenger seat. She doesn't get out to check on me either. If things were the other way around, I'd get out and ask her how she felt being left behind.

Eventually, Konstantinos slams the door that he left open.

Sebastian stands next to me and lights up a joint. I don't enjoy anyone smoking anything near me. I was glad when we got to walk away from his pappoús's cigar earlier. Now I'm stuck next to this choking smell unlike anything else, sickly and earthy. It hangs over me forcing me to turn away from Sebastian. I hate how the smell clings to my clothes and my hair and generally makes me feel icky from the inside out. He knows that too. I've told him before.

'What's wrong with the snitch?' I nod towards Konstantinos.

Sebastian explodes with smoke and rippling laughter, looking like a hysterical dragon.

'That *snitch* is pissed off because I'm better than him, and everyone knows it. That's all. We'll be going after this.' He dips his head at the joint. 'You got the app sorted? Ready to be my spotter?'

'Yep.'

With the hand still holding his joint, he rubs his thumb over my cheek. I have the deepest urge to retch. 'I'm glad I've decided to forgive you. I know things can be good again.'

He turns and jibes at Konstantinos, informing him that soon we'll be off to race. I take this opportunity to move away from the safety of the olive trees and towards Xristina, who is still in Konstantinos's car. Seeing me coming towards her, she gets out.

'What happened?' I break the distance between us.

Xristina says, 'Nothing, nothing. Honestly, don't even worry about it. Sorry we left you here on your own.'

My shoulders lift before sagging back down.

Then she shuffles, squeezes her hands onto her hips, and says, 'Do you... Do you ever think of breaking up with Sebastian?'

'Why would you ask me that?'

She glances from the boys to me. 'The more I know him, the more I can't see you two together.'

If only she knew. It's not like I can confide in her, most certainly not here. Not at all. She's not known for being the best at keeping secrets. Phoebe's good at finding out gossip and Xristina is good at passing it along from one person to the next. If I told her I didn't want to be with him and that he threatened my family, everyone would know. I can't even imagine the anger that would unleash from Sebastian, given that my simply passing the time of day with Dinos is enough for him to get so aggressive.

'You don't know half the things you think you know.' I skulk off towards Sebastian's car.

'What the hell does that mean?' Xristina calls towards me.

'Nothing.'

Konstantinos's car door slams as Xristina gets back inside. I'm left in Sebastian's passenger seat stewing in the synthetic cherry air freshener and the smoke from Sebastian's fingers that feels like a stain on my cheek.

What happened to make Xristina question Sebastian like that? Maybe his childish nature on show is enough for her to think we wouldn't work out. She's always been jealous of our relationship, openly saying she liked him before we were together and obviously wanting the lifestyle that being with someone like Sebastian brings. She wants to be a princess. If only she knew the curse that came along with it.

It's not long before we are racing around the island and I'm in high demand to keep an eye on the Smurf app, and where police have been spotted. We drag-race and the boys practise drifting around bends in a way that makes my toes curl and my eyes lock shut. They practise manoeuvre after manoeuvre and drive like maniacs on the hairpins of Corfu.

'My battery's getting low.' Sebastian doesn't acknowledge me, so I say it again. 'My battery's getting low.'

'There's a charger in the glovebox.'

I open it up and the contents spew out. I move around an array of items, from more weed to manuals. No charger.

'It's not in here.' I look back at my phone. There's a Smurf, a police car, maybe a kilometre or two away. 'There's–'

'For fuck's sake, Theadora, it's in there. Just look!' He turns the radio up so loud it makes my insides tingle.

He glares forwards, tension over his whole body that I'm irritating him. He didn't hear me. He wasn't listening to what I said. I don't care if he gets caught. I switch off my phone and carry on looking for a charger I know isn't there.

My palms begin to sweat knowing that soon, around one of these bends, there might be a police car waiting to pounce. My heart beats in time with the music pulsing through my fingers and my chest. I keep my head down as I rifle through the glovebox, with my eyes on the floor. I count the seconds. How fast are we going? Is this going to be one of the places Sebastian might do a handbrake turn where he shouldn't, dipping his lights to check there aren't any lights on the other side of a bend before he does something crazy? He hasn't had an accident with me in the car, but the number of cars he's got through... I don't like my odds of not crashing in his car. His money problems are nothing like most people's. His money problems have left him spoilt and a junkie for pushing boundaries.

He curses under the music then punches the brakes and turns the music off at the same time. The tyres screech and my head smacks the open glovebox before my seatbelt catches me. The car is filled with blue flashing lights.

Sebastian rolls out a line of curses under his breath, but he continues driving. I sit up and do my best what-the-hell's-going-on act. Rubbing the sore parch on the top of my head.

'Smurfs. That's what. Didn't you see them on the app?' He snarls through gritted teeth.

'I told you. My phone died and there's no charger.'

Sebastian hits the steering wheel with the heel of his hand.

'We got lucky this time. They're too busy to bother with us.'

He's right. They're already talking to a group of guys in front of a row of cars with spoilers and modifications just like the one we're in.

'Time to go.' Sebastian drives away sensibly now, as an officer stares us down through the window. They might have known we were going a bit too fast, but whatever the others had been seen doing was obviously more important, or at least more interesting.

I've managed to put an end to this dreadful night. At least now I can go home. It's worth the painful patch on my head.

Chapter 37

Mama is there when I get in, reading next to a lamp. As soon as she looks up at me from under her glasses, a warm and comforting smile lights her face brighter than any lamp could.

I can't help myself; I gulp back air like I'm drowning in it. Like air is too thick for my lungs and I can't cope with the feeling of it.

She slams down her book and rushes towards me, wrapping me up in the warmth of her bare arms.

Tears stream down my face and my nose begins to run away with itself. In a matter of moments Mama's shoulder is a wet sticky mess and I'm barely a foot into the room.

She pats my back and begs me to tell her what's wrong. Why is it, I can't tell anyone what I want to tell them? I tell Dinos about one thing not the other, and now that's all I have to tell Mama too... one thing and not the other.

'I've been hiding something...'

'Your DNA results.' Not only does she take the words from my mouth, but her level tone manages to both calm me into knowing she's going to be kind about it, and frighten me into knowing she's not happy I didn't say anything sooner. Maybe I'm reading too much into it, but I don't think I am. When it's your mother, and you're close, you can read the little signals and the subtle changes in tone. Each and every day we tell each other things between our words, and if we are smart, and if we care, we learn each other's nuances. I'm confident this is one of hers.

She releases me from her vice-like grip and fetches me a tissue. When she comes back, I've placed myself down on the terracotta-coloured sofa next to the coffee table.

'Tell me. You've been storing this all up for some time now. You must have found something, or someone, interesting.'

I begin by telling her about the mother who never replied. LP. Two letters with no meaning whatsoever. That part seems so easy now. Something that a year ago was impossible to say, now pours out of me as though there's nothing really to tell, nothing really to say about it. It's easy. A nameless, faceless woman never responded to a message sent. My sister on the other hand, that has a story now. A stupidity. My stupidity. Like a maggot my stupidity bites at my flesh and soon all I'll have left are the bones of who I was. It's not just Melodie though, it's the thought of Sebastian. But my mama likes him and wants him to bring stability into my life. I sometimes think being older parents has made them worry more. Knowing what they went through to have me, it's no wonder Mama sometimes holds on so tightly.

When I finish my short explanation about my birth mother, Mama pulls her shoulders up and smiles, 'That's not so bad. Anyone who could leave you isn't worth knowing anyway. I'm sure there's nothing to worry about.'

'I also have a sister, Melodie. She lives in Corfu and...' Mama leans in closer to me, her face crumpling into concern like a falling house of cards. 'I turned up at her house uninvited. She looks just like me, Mama, like a mirror, but older than me and with light brown hair.' I try to carry on, but I'm hit by the rejection all over again. Rejected at birth and rejected now. Wheezing sobs rattle through me again as I press the sodden tissue into my face.

Mama frantically rubs my back. 'What happened? What did she say?'

'Nothing. Not really anyway. She didn't want to know.'

The only sound in the room is my staggered breaths and Mama rubbing at my back. I thought she would hit me with a deluge of words, but she doesn't. She doesn't say anything for the longest moment. It's enough time for a moth to dart around us on its journey to the lamp.

Her hand stops in the centre of my back then comes to rest with her other hand on her lap. 'Theadora, my beautiful, smart and kind daughter, no matter what happens, as long as there is air in my lungs to breathe, I am here for you. *We* are here for you. I'm trying to think how this girl, Melodie, must feel. Did she know about you? Did she want to find you, or to hide from you? We don't know what she might have been thinking about or what she herself has been through. But it's not your problem. You have a life ahead of you, one filled with promise, and a handsome man too.' Mama's elbow finds my ribs.

I wipe the now useless tissue over my nose. 'About that. I think I want to travel. I want to apply for a passport. I didn't get a chance to apply for one before because of lockdown.'

'Is this to do with Melodie?'

I lower my chin to my chest.

'No. Although, sort of, I guess. It's given me a chance to think about what I want to do with my life. I want to see the world. Whenever we travel, we only travel to Athens or one of the other islands. I want to take my driving test too. I need to get out of this bubble. I love Kassiopi, I know I want to be here in my heart, but I also need to spread my wings.'

Mama nods her head in agreement. 'I have lived on this island my whole life. Not always here in Kassiopi, but never far. When your father and I were first married we went away and travelled far and wide in the winter months, but nothing filled my soul with more joy than my beloved Corfu, from the tops of the cypress trees to the fish nibbling your toes in the shallows. I love it here. I'll live here and I'll die here. You are at the right age to go on new adventures. You'll be a married woman giving me grandchildren in the blink of an eye.' She looks up at the ceiling. 'So, for now, I'll do all I can to get you where you want to be.'

I wrap my arms around Mama's neck, and she struggles with a choked laugh.

Now I have hope, and hope is all I need.

Part 3 - 2023

Chapter 38

I passed my driving test a few weeks ago. I hadn't bothered getting one for my moped, lots of people ride around without a licence for something so small. But this is something I wanted to achieve. I passed first time, and Baba bought me a little car last week. It's a start, the beginning of achieving my goals for this year. The year I turn twenty.

The driving school asked for a photocopy of my ID, they normally take it themselves, but their copier was broken. Mama took the ID to get it copied and I haven't seen it since. She has said she will look for it but hasn't taken it very seriously. Now I have a driving licence I have some form of ID to carry around, and I still have my fake ID, but that won't get me a passport. I suppose to her, I've carried around a fake on its own for years without knowing, but difference does it make now. I still have real ID, in the way of my driving licence, if required.

If it's lost, I need my birth certificate and my adoption papers so I can apply for a new ID card. Mama has told me not to worry and that it'll show up, but I can't keep waiting around when I need to grab life in my hands.

I don't want to bother Theía Agatha with it again. I've already asked her for my adoption papers. She said she would ask the charity that owns the Children's Community Home and farm if they have the papers on file from back then. Apparently, a lot has changed. More things have been digitalised and other things haven't. Something like that. Theía Agatha might be in charge of the day-to-day lives of the children, but everyone answers to someone. That's what she said anyway. She said Mama and Baba were the best bet.

As Mama and Baba aren't helping, and Theía Agatha can't help, I've decided to skip her out and call the charity on a number I found on their website. I need to get a passport. With Mama and Baba visiting friends, I've decided to take matters into my own hands.

I pace the living room as the phone rings. It purrs in my ear over and over.

There's no answer.

I leave a message with my name, explaining that I was adopted almost nineteen years ago, and I wondered if I could have access to my adoption file. Hanging up, I slide my phone onto the coffee table and fall back onto the sofa making a fine layer of dust spring up. Mama would be mortified. We would have to take every cushion out and beat it. Another reason it's good they're away.

I rub my temples and close my eyes.

Mama must've brought the ID card back here and put it somewhere. She's too worried about the wrong person seeing it to leave it outside of the house. If I don't hear back from the charity soon, I'll hunt around the house to find it. It has to be here somewhere.

I keep wondering whether Mama and Baba are stalling to keep me here. I've decided I want to study English in England. I can't imagine there's a better place to study it. I haven't told Sebastian my full plans yet. When I told him I was looking to study abroad, he sulked for a week, telling me it would be pointless as I won't need to work once we're married. I already know the day I marry him is the day my life ends and that's why I'll do anything to delay it or avoid it completely. Sometimes I feel like a toy that he keeps around so no one else can have me. But I've been playing ball. At least he treats me like a pure angel on the most part. His pure princess. When he calls me that it turns my stomach, but at least saving me for marriage keeps him at arm's length.

Dinos has stopped speaking to me when we are in a group. I catch him looking at me sometimes though. If our eyes meet, I smile. It's automatic. On the rare occasion it's happened, we both turn away. Disappointment seeps out of him and into me. I can almost smell it on him even at a distance. I want to tell him I'm disappointed in me too. It's impossible to think about him or look at him without the hollow pain of numbness seeping in. That strange ache. Numbness can only occur when you know you've lost something, and when that something is as gaping as the loss of Dinos, that sort of numbness hurts. It causes blisters around the open wound.

This is exactly why I don't look at him.

Exactly why I don't think about him.

As soon as I do, numbness becomes overwhelmed and raw pain takes over as feelings rush back in. It becomes unbearable.

Before, even though I knew I could never have him as mine, at least I could talk to him and enjoy being around him. To have his light resting on my face and warming my soul was enough to sustain me. Now the thought of the light is enough to leave more blisters than I could count.

I shake my head and a shudder rolls down my back. Stop thinking about him. I now have time to kill as that phone call amounted to nothing.

I'm meeting Xristina later. I'm sure it'll be stilted as it has been for a while. Since Phoebe went away, there's been a hole left in my friendship with Xristina. We spend less time together and when we do, I always get the feeling she doesn't really want to be around me anymore. I'm not sure what I've done, or whether the whole time it was Phoebe holding us together and I hadn't realised it.

I kick my feet up onto the coffee table and slump lower into the seat. This is the year I turn twenty. I'm a grown woman, and I'm quickly learning that relationships change as we grow. The difference is, it's harder to forge new friendships outside of the bonds formed at school particularly when you haven't changed location or job. I have other friends, pockets of friends who all socialise at the same places, but the three of us were so close for so many years. Inseparable, or so I thought.

Phoebe didn't even come back for Christmas. Instead, she got a job singing in the chorus of a theatre production. I'm proud of her. She's come a long way since singing with me in tavernas. I do miss it. Agatha had agreed that I could come along and teach some piano once I'd got some safeguarding paperwork sorted, but she conveniently forgets to bring it and I've stopped asking. Clearly, they don't want me at the Children's Community Home. I'm starting to feel displaced everywhere.

A message comes through on my phone. I'm meant to meet Xristina in two hours, but she's probably cancelling on me. It wouldn't be the first time.

Picking my phone up off the coffee table I glance at the screen. Seeing what's there is enough for my heart to stop in my chest. I'm sure of it. It starts again almost as fast, but I'm quite sure it literally stopped.

Dinos: Can we talk?

Chapter 39

I'm up and pacing the room again, only now my feet move faster. If Baba were in the room, he'd tell me to stop making a draught with all my pacing.

Why is Dinos messaging me now? It's been so long since we even held eye contact for more than a nanosecond.

Can we talk? Yes.

Should we talk? Probably not.

Another message comes through from him under the first.

I'm happy to drive and meet you somewhere. Somewhere you won't get in trouble with Sebastian.

My heart pounds in my chest as I hesitate over my phone, my thumb poised and ready to say something, anything. I push the message away and a thin squeal echoes in my throat.

Where?

As I drive out of the village, I note every single person I see. Anyone who waves and nods. Anyone who might tell Sebastian of my meeting.

Having secrets feels the same as having sand stuck in your shoes. The grit wears away at your skin. If it's left there it can slowly gnawing you down to the bone. It's like that if I lie to Mama or Baba. It feels that way with most lies and half-truths. Not really when I lie to Sebastian, though. Not anymore. With him it's becoming easy and cold. I tell him I'm busy helping my parents when I'm not. I'm not even sure he cares anyway.

The car weaves along narrower and narrower roads until it's just a single-track lane to a church on a hill. There's a small car park. It's empty except for Dinos's car. He's leaning on his car, his fingers tapping on his jeans.

I park my car next to his and before I'm even out of it, he's there with a burst of words and a nervous energy.

'I don't know why I needed to see you,' he blurts out.

I'm so startled by his presence next to my car door that it takes me a moment to register what he's said. The sun shoots blinding rays across his face, catching on the tips of his eyelashes. They glow red instead of black in this light. There's something behind his beautiful mask, lurking under those lashes. His eyebrows are pulled tightly together, and his eyes are bloodshot.

I climb out of the car. 'What's happened?'

Dinos tilts his head back, as though he's seen an interesting cloud. There's no point looking up at it with him. It's a bright blue sky and I know there won't be any clouds there. He's head flops forwards and he swivels on his heels before walking away. If I didn't know him better, I'd think he was sulking, with his hands deep in the pockets of his jeans and his curved shoulders.

My feet skitter to keep up with him. 'Dinos, what's happened? You didn't drag me up here to stay silent.'

'Drag?' he repeats.

Guilt flushes my cheeks as Dinos turns and pushes through the tall rusted gate under a bell tower. He screeches the gate closed behind me, and we pass under the thick walls and away from the road. The church might be up a narrow track in the middle of nowhere, but it's best to be away from any possibility of prying eyes. Not that there is any real possibility, not here. I don't think I've ever been up here myself before. It's only a short drive from home, but it somehow feels as far away as the other end of the island.

Dinos takes a few big strides then slumps down on a low stone wall that runs along behind the bell tower. His body is still curled as he rests his elbows on his knees and his head on his hands. I can't be sure, but he might be crying. I sit down next to him and stretch my arm around his back.

'Please, talk to me.'

'It's my sister,' he chokes. 'She's been doing it to herself. She's not ill at all. My parents won't listen and the doctors just think she needs to eat more. You know I said about the tests last year? And that they didn't find anything? She had fainted a couple of times and that's why my parents sent her for tests.' His voice trails off, and I feel like each time I swallow it's like drinking lava. I begin to rub his back in the same way that Mama does to me.

'She's so weak and all my parents do is stuff her with food. The doctors wouldn't believe it. Then I heard her, making herself... throw up.' Dinos looks out across the folds of our land and the dark greens of the thousands of trees spread out in front of us, carpeting the way to the sea.

I can see her in my mind so clearly, his sister, Anna. She's always been bouncy and her curls have always been wild. She's never been overweight a day in her life. The idea she'd want to make herself ill to be thin is baffling.

'I don't know what to do. I tried to talk to her about it and she called me a liar.'

'Did you tell your parents?'

'I had to, but she said it was just one time, because she was eating so much to keep up with the doctor's demands, but I know she was lying. She wears all these baggy clothes to hide her frame and I don't know what to do. You're the only girl I'm close with... *was* close with. I was hoping you could help.'

I roll my tongue under my lips, over my teeth, as a lazy blue butterfly moves in front of us. What can I say to him? I have no idea about these things. I don't know anyone who has an eating disorder. Then something hits me. 'There's a girl, an Italian girl, who works at one of Sebastian's hotels. She's so thin I've often wondered whether she eats at all. Then I saw her come in with her boyfriend once when we were there. I think it was for a special occasion. She got up to use the bathroom three times during the meal. It made me wonder if she was hiding food in her bag, and yet she seemed to be eating everything on her plate.'

'Anna does that. Stops halfway through to use the bathroom. I hadn't thought about it, but now... I wouldn't have remembered if Pa hadn't made some joke about her being worse than an old man. Always needing the toilet.' Dinos exhales and attempts a smile. 'I looked it all up on my phone and it freaked me out.

People kill themselves trying to be thin. Why would she want to do that?'

'I don't know.' It's true. I have no clue why anyone would do that to themselves. Are there times I'm critical of my body? Sure. I'm not perfect, but I can recognise that no one is, and any imperfections I might see aren't going to get in the way of me eating one of Mama's cheese pies or wearing a bikini on the beach.

'What do I do?'

We sit for a time muddling together ideas, weighing up the options that might actually work to help her. Anna's a fourteen-year-old girl and she clearly needs some help that we can't give. We aren't her parents. As a plan, of sorts, emerges, I can see the lift in Dinos's shoulders again. He stands up, shoulders pulled back, and paces along the path in front of the wall as he relays it back to me.

'I need to try to get my parents to catch her out and I need to somehow stop her being able to get into the bathroom during and after at least one mealtime a day.'

I shrug. 'It's a start.'

'It's a start,' he repeats back. 'Dora...' He stops walking and faces me. 'Would you meet me here again, same time next week? If this doesn't work, we might need a new plan.' I shift my weight on the hard wall and Dinos quickly adds, 'You're the only person I can trust with this.'

I've burdened him with my secrets, and made people doubt his chivalry, it's the least I can do. Besides, I want to see him and I want to know how Anna is. The idea of her ending up with tubes in her in hospital is all too much. I know I should tell him no, it's too dangerous for my family. Sneaking around, even though it's innocent. It's the lie that makes it wrong. A breeze rolls over us, making light golden strands of hair stream across my face like lightning strikes. I tuck the lock of hair firmly behind my ears and stand to face Dinos head on, to tell him what I know I need to say.

'I'll be here.'

Chapter 40

I'm meeting Dinos in half an hour to find out how he's got on with the plan of action. I hope he managed to catch his sister out, or stop her altogether.

I study myself in the mirror. What does poor Anna see? She's always been slim. I grew hips and a bust at quite an early age. I've never been shy about them. They're part of me. Perhaps the fact I've always been different has helped me deal with these things.

I change again, settling on jeans after trying on three skirts, only to decide that a skirt is a bad idea. It's no less innocent to wear a skirt, but it makes me feel like I'm trying. I don't want to be trying to look nice, even though I know that's exactly what I'm doing.

I've had messages from Sebastian asking to see me later. He wants me to be on Smurf watch for him, I think. It's not the day of our usual date night, the arbitrary day that he takes me into the rotation of his restaurants and shows me off. I enjoy the food and the people-watching. It's impossible not to like having a reason to get dressed up, but our date nights remind me of a conveyor belt at an airport and I'm the lonely suitcase going round and round and bored of seeing the same thing over and over. My phone rings from my bedside cabinet where it's on charge. It's probably Sebastian so I don't rush to answer it. After two rings I meander over to look at the screen.

Unknown number.

I don't bother to answer. It's probably someone selling something.

I pull the cable out, leave my room and greet all the photos on the wall in the same way they greet me, with loyal smiles.

A voicemail pings on my phone as I reach the bottom of the stairs. I press the phone to my ear. Mama asks who I'm calling as she moves towards the kitchen.

'No one, there's a message,' I call after her.

It's a lady's voice. Sharp yet softly spoken. 'Theadora, this is Maria Karagiannis from the Children's Community Home. I'm sorry, I can't find a record of you on my system. I'm wondering whether you called the right number.' She goes on to leave her personal email for me to contact her with more information as to who I am. Maybe it would've been easier to speak to Theía Agatha about it. Maybe the people in the charity that runs the Children's Community Home can't see who's done what.

I drop my phone in the back pocket of my fitted black jeans and slip on my trainers, tugging at the clean white laces.

Wait, what if I was adopted under the name of Keres?

'Mama, have you seen my ID card?' I shout towards the kitchen.

'No. I'll have a look for it. You still have the other one though, yes?'

She said that last week. Checking I still have my fake one.

'Yeah.'

She's been busy. There've been some problems with getting some of the usual products in the store. It's been taking up her time, making phone calls and organising things. There's always something to be done.

'I'm going out now. Love you.'

'Theadora!' Mama's slippers slap along the kitchen tiles towards the living room. 'One moment!' She appears with hands covered in flour and her glasses on the very tip of her nose. 'We're going out this afternoon. I know I said we could all have dinner together, but Theía Agatha called and wanted to meet.'

'Can I come?'

Mama pushes her glasses up with her wrist, 'Not this time. We have some business to discuss. Next time.'

Business? Since when do they have *business* to discuss? Automatically my chin tucks in and my eyebrows lower.

'Don't be like that,' she adds. 'We all have different relationships that need to be tended to.'

I can't deny that; I have one that needs tending right now. 'Fine. See you later.' I turn with the squeak of a trainer and escape out the door.

I hope Agatha isn't calling a meeting about me and the DNA test. They all know now. It's all in the open. It's been talked about at length, and I still spend most nights thinking about it when I go to sleep or in the dull moments in the shop. A few times I've had dreams about Melodie shutting the door in my face. Nightmares really — those ones where you wake up sweating and panting. The door is always huge, and it isn't a playful pink, it's blood-red. Her face is contorted with anger at my presence and when I tell her all I've ever wanted was a sister, she cackles in a vile high-pitched voice. Just thinking about it sends a shiver creeping from my head to my toes and every hair on my arms stands on end.

I push it to the back of my mind and think about how Dinos must be feeling. I saw him in passing the other day after work. It was all I could do not to say something to him. He saw me too from across the road. He gave me the smallest glimpse of a smile, so tiny that no one but me would've recognised that's what it was. A flicker of movement from one side of his mouth, then he looked away. It was enough. Enough to sustain me like the wait for winter rain that is needed to get beautiful fat olives.

**

His car is already here, but he isn't anywhere to be seen. I slip out of my car and shut the door as quietly as I can. 'Dinos?' I hiss over the buzz of the insects. It's so quiet up here that it's gone full circle to loud. A deafening, haunting peace.

I edge out of the car park and around towards the bell tower. It's a traditional stone tower with two bells at the top, the larger on the right. It's not as well kept as some I've seen. Even there at the top, just under the bells, tall tufts of grass have sprouted along with the moss. The stones, surely once white, are grey and dull. I like it though. I think clean can be dull. This has age and character. Who knows the things it's seen from all the way up there, looking down at Kassiopi?

Dinos is already on the other side of the gate, sitting on the wall waiting for me. I can see him staring into space like a statue. In fact, he's doing a beautiful impression of Rodin's Thinker, with his chin resting on his hand. He's nicer to look at though, and his hair doesn't resemble a helmet the way that statue's does. Dinos's curls are neatly sculpted on top of his head today with the sides perfectly cut and trimmed. Even while he's this pensive, and in baggy jeans and a plain grey long-sleeve top, he's still his very own work of art. Dinos doesn't need anything to be authentically perfect.

I creak through the rough, rusty gate. Dinos whips round, and his mouth and eyes hang open as though he's surprised to see me. As though we didn't have plans at all.

'I'd got lost in thought. I've been here ages.' He automatically wraps his arms around me as soon as I'm close enough. He smells like Dinos. That's stupid, of course he does. I hadn't realised how much I'd missed that smell of him. Now that he's pressed to my face, warmth spreads over my entire body, lighting me up. That dark rugged smell like sage, honey and a tiny bit of something else. Maybe fuel? I'm not sure. Occasionally there's a hint of fish depending on what he's been doing, but this is the sweet smell that makes me see his face even if he's nowhere in sight, a smell my memory has attached to him. If I could bottle it up, I would.

'How's Anna?'

We pull away from each other.

'Not good. Walk?'

'Okay.'

We move around towards the cemetery at the pace of a tortoise, the sort of pace where it's easy to trip over your own feet.

'I haven't managed to get my parents to believe me or to catch her out. I did manage to fake a stomach issue to keep her out of the bathroom for a whole dinner time. So at least something will have stayed in, I guess.'

'That's something. It's a start.'

'It's hard because we don't always eat together, and now she knows I know, she's avoiding me. Avoiding eating with me at all.

It's worse since I managed to force her to keep stuff in *one* time.'
Dinos scratches his head.

'You need to persuade your parents to believe you.'

'I'm trying.' Dinos's shoulders slump as we skirt our way
around the gravestones. 'I don't want one of these for her yet.'
He nods at one of the older stones in front of us. 'She's a kid.
And that bloody kid has to outlive me.'

'She will. Just try to live to an old age first to really make it
worth it, okay?'

'Why? You going to miss me? We haven't spoken in months.'

'I saw you last week.' I lightly bump my arm against his as we
walk, and bite my lip.

Dinos groans in the back of his throat, 'Yeah, apart from that.
You've found it pretty easy to cut me out. If I'd died a month ago
it could've been years until you noticed if no one bothered to tell
you.'

I stop, and Dinos takes another step before turning back to
face me.

'That's not fair. This isn't my choice. It's not what I want.' My
words are as light as the clouds and just as thin and pathetic.

'What the–?' Dinos splutters and I turn to look where he is
looking.

A wild tortoise has poked its head out from behind a
gravestone. I jump back, knocking right into Dinos, taken aback
by the pair of beady eyes watching us. Dinos crumples into fits
of laughter and I can't help but join in.

As we recover, our eyes lock together as our chests heave to
catch our breath.

'How are you, Dora? Really?'

Really?

Really, I don't even know the answer. I bury everything as
much as I can, hiding it under hope for the future far from

the one place I love. Between Melodie-based nightmares and Sebastian-based day-mares... None of this will kill me though. These problems are like paper cuts, superficial wounds that hurt, but I'm sure won't take me down. It's nothing compared to the fear Dinos must be facing with Anna.

'Fine.' My nose wrinkles before I can stop it, and Dinos folds his arms across his chest.

I've told countless half-truths to Sebastian lately and he hasn't questioned whether my nose wrinkles or not. Dinos clocks it right away. He doesn't say as much, but I equally clock the twitch of his eyebrow, the minute rise and fall of disbelief.

'Anything new with that sister you looked up?'

I shake my head.

'And Sebastian?' I keep watch for the tortoise that's making its way around the graveyard. I don't need to look directly at Dinos to imagine that he has the same expression on his face as the last time that Sebastian's name passed between us. It was months ago now, but it almost feels like another lifetime ago. Lately the world is a grey wash of activities I'm not invested in. Only here next to Dinos do I see in colour.

'Has he hurt you again?'

From the corner of my eye I see his fists clench.

'No. Nothing like that. Nothing physical. He's just used to being the boss. He's the spoilt baby boy in a house full of women. He's the man of the house and he's a kid.'

'He's a man, not a kid. He's older than I am by a long shot and I'm a man.'

I grin up at Dinos as he pulls his shoulders back. I meander past him and leave the tortoise behind to its business.

I can't hear him following me, but I don't look back. I don't let myself. I hate the way I feel when I'm around him — the tickle of excitement like tomorrow's Easter and I know I'll be getting all of my favourite food and seeing all my favourite people. But the feeling is more than that. It's closer to how it felt when I was a small child and everything was a mixture of new and familiar. This feeling digs into my heart like a trailing vine wrapping around it and crushing it. I've never felt this way about anyone. I used to feel excited to see Sebastian, but I can see how shallow that was now. I was more excited about where he was going to take me than I was to spend time with him. That's not love. It's a poor man's replica, and even with all the money in Corfu, Sebastian could never buy my love with his fancy meals and sparkling jewels. It will never work. With Sebastian, it's as though a sculptor were trying to carve out love to show others what it is. To the outside world it's the real thing, but it's no more real than the reflection in a mirror. A backwards version of reality. You could give Sebastian a list of romantic things to do, and he could tick them all off one by one, but that still wouldn't capture my heart.

Dinos's feet pad along the ground behind me to catch up.

'Since when did you walk so fast?' His arm pushes against mine playfully as he falls into step next to me. We've both always walked slowly together. We used to be the same at school. Now and then walking back from the bus Mama used to say we took just as long walking back together as the bus took bringing us from school.

'As long as I'm here helping you with Anna, can we not talk about Sebastian? My life is mapped out for me now, and meeting you here is putting my family at risk. The least you could do is let me have half an hour of pretending everything is different.'

Dinos clears his throat. 'I agree to your terms under one additional condition.'

'What?'

'If he does hurt you, or you feel afraid, you have to tell me.'

233

'Fine. But that doesn't mean you get to go and hurt him in return.'

Dinos makes a low groaning noise in the back of his throat.

'Dinos,' I extend his name as long as it'll go.

'Alright, I agree.'

'Anyway, it's not all mapped out. Hopefully, anyway. I've decided to travel, to take a course in London in English.'

'You should front bands with your voice, like you used to do with Phoebe.'

'I used to throw up before every gig. I can't live like that.'

Realising what I've said, and how insensitive it is to talk about vomiting with everything Anna is going through, my face crumples and I press the palm of my hand to my forehead.

'Sorry Dinos. We'll help her.'

'Don't worry, I knew what you meant. It's not the same.'

We walk in silence for a moment in the dappled light of the tall trees dotted around us.

'I'm glad I can talk to you. Even if it's a secret, it's good to have you back in my life.'

I feel the same. I have to bite my lip to stop myself from asking him what he wanted to say to me back at Taste Me. I want to know how he *really* feels about me. Only I don't. Because that would make life even harder. To hear the words I'm sure he wants to say, would only make life uglier than it already is.

My heart has shooting pains like a headache, and there's nothing I can do to change it.

Chapter 41

Mama still hasn't looked for my ID card and I haven't had a chance to call the woman back from the charity that funds the Children's Community Home or see Agatha about it. But if I can't find my ID card, I will have to use my birth certificate to apply for the ID card and passport. I must have a birth certificate, surely. Today as I say good morning to the rows of photos outside my room, I'm determined to pin Mama or Baba down.

The problem is, when I ask Baba where the certificate is, he says that Mama is *in charge of that sort of thing. She knows where these things are kept.* But when I ask her, she says she'll have to look later.

'Why are you stalling?' I whisper to her image on the wall. It's a photo from when I was maybe three or four. Baba is flinging me up in the air and Mama's laughing as much as me. We look so happy. Not just because it's funny for a three year old, but because our souls are free from baggage.

It's a snapshot, of course. I don't really know the true pain they went through to end up with me instead of their much longed-for baby. One that was part him, part her. They got me, part nothing, part no one.

I turn away from the past sprawled out on the wall and make my way into the future.

Last night I agreed to help make some vegetarian stew for us to freeze. We always do that for Lent, even though Mama and Baba aren't really religious, we still follow many Christian traditions.

I skip down the stairs, avoiding the places that squeak the most. These are the day-to-day things we learn without even realising. One day I'll learn the nuances of a new home, some new stairs. Probably with Sebastian. My pace slows and I hit a harsh squeak.

It doesn't matter, it might not be that way. Things change from day to day. I'm making changes. I can be in control. I stride with purpose towards the kitchen.

'Mama?' As soon as I see her, I know something's not right. She's scrubbing at the same clean-looking patch over and over. 'Mama?' This time my voice is soft as I move to place my hand on her shoulder. She physically jumps.

'Theadora, how long have you been standing there?'

Her eyes are bloodshot and she has no makeup on her usually well-made-up face.

'What's happened?'

She rips the gloves from her hands and presses her fingers to her eyelids. Her shoulders shake as I envelop her in my arms. It's easy to do, being so much taller than her. I feel like the parent in size.

'My mother passed away.'

Her *mother*? I thought she was already dead! Long dead too.

'Your *mother*? I thought she was already dead.'

'No, well, only metaphorically. We fell out about Theía Agatha many years ago. We haven't spoken since.'

Over the past year, I've really started to wonder if I know anything about my parents, or even my life. Everything I thought I knew is wrong. I've been living in a bubble, and the curve of it has been warping my vision, my reality, since arriving in this house.

'I thought she had died before I was born?'

She pulls away from the embrace, puts her gloves back on and begins to scrub without saying more.

'Why did you fall out about Theía Agatha?'

She stops moving like someone has hit pause for a good few seconds before looking at me thoughtfully from behind her damp lashes.

'It's time you knew, although perhaps you do. I've always thought of you as a perceptive girl, Theodora, although, perhaps not always. Theía Agatha and Ria, they're a couple.'

For a split second I nearly ask, *A couple of what?* before it hits me, and heat rushes to my cheeks. How had I not realised it before? This is yet another thing throwing everything into question. Why is it only now I'm allowed to know? Now I understand why Theía Agatha loves the children like they're hers, why she has never married. I'm happy she's happy, that they're both happy. But apparently, I'm only now adult enough to be let in on these family secrets. I'm just hurt that I wasn't allowed to know sooner. It's bound to be a huge part of who they are, and I wasn't allowed to be a part of it.

'When she told our parents, they weren't as... accepting as us.' Mama takes her gloves off again, slower this time, placing them carefully on top of one another. She moves towards the sink to wash her hands. 'They were very religious old-fashioned people. They thought Agatha needed help. A priest or some nonsense. They couldn't see the love. We wouldn't have had you if it wasn't for Agatha and Ria. I will always stand by them. It hurt to take their side, to never see my parents again, but I know it hurt Agatha just as much. Perhaps more, as they rejected her so horribly. It's also when we stopped going to church.' She adds the last part almost to herself.

'Why wasn't I told any of this before?'

'You're a child.'

'I haven't been a child for years.'

'You'll always be my child, no matter how old you get. This is Agatha's truth, and even now I shouldn't be the one to tell you. It should've been her.'

She's still methodically washing her hands like she's forgotten what she's up to. She catches my line of sight and turns the tap off.

'But I'm not a child.' I begin to point out each item on one finger then the next. 'I had grandparents I never met, I was adopted here not in Romania, Theía Agatha and Ria are a couple. How many other secrets of the past am I not old enough to know? Do you even count me as part of this family?'

'Don't talk to me like that. This isn't about you! This is about my pain, my loss.' She thrusts her hand at her chest. 'My parents did meet you when you were a baby. They sent you cards too.' Her voice cracks and tears stream down her face, but her body is pulled as tight as a violin string. The shift in her changes the air in the room. She can command any space she wants. 'They wanted to love you, and I know you would've loved them, but it was them or Theía Agatha. That was the choice! My sister or my parents!' Each sentence is like having knives thrown at me. 'What would you pick?' She now points to her fingers as she lists her choices. 'The parents who easily cut out their daughter because of her sexuality? Or the sister who gave you a child, risking everything?' She wipes her hand over her mouth. 'I'm going to go for a lie-down. This conversation is done.'

She storms past me, her slippers slapping on the tiles.

Guilt ripples over me. She's lost something, and I'm only just finding it out. She's always told me stories about her parents in the past tense, never hinting about any breakdown in the parent-child relationship. I could never have guessed.

I replay her words. *Parents who easily cut out their daughter* or the *sister who gave a child, risking everything. Risking everything?* In what way was Agatha risking everything, or even anything?

Chapter 42

After an hour of lying down, Mama tells me she is going to the shop to help Baba and she never wants to speak of her mother's passing again. She says it in a way that makes me know she means it. That's not to say I won't ask a sensible question in the future, but I'll have to play it right or I'll never find out anything more.

With Easter round the corner things are getting busier in the shop again. It's what she uses as an excuse to leave, but really, she's escaping the cloud in the house. I tell her I'm sorry. I *am* sorry.

With one foot out of the door she turns back to me.

'I'm sorry too, Theadora. I am. But I've lost my parents twice. Once when they let Agatha go, and once in death. No matter your choices in life, know I'll always be doing my best for you.

But just like them, know I won't always get it right.' With tears swelling in her eyes, she slips away.

She lost her mother. Nothing in life is simple. The past few years have been teaching me that. Adulthood is like diving into ice-cold water and trying to swim with weights on my feet. School seemed so simple. Learning, chatting with friends, singing at the weekends. Simple.

I move across the room and slump down on the sofa, pressing my fingertips together above my nose and letting my hands curve around my face. The house is empty; it'll likely stay that way for some time now. The riddles and lies slosh around in my brain.

Is there anything I can be sure of?

I'm sure Mama and Baba love me, and I'm sure that she really would do anything that she thinks is right for me. The problem is, that's exactly how my grandparents probably felt about Agatha. They wanted to help her. Do I think they were completely misguided? Yes. Do I think they should've accepted her no matter what? Yes. But does that mean they stopped loving her and wanting the best for her? I don't know, but I doubt it.

I know what I'm going to do, and I know it's something that could get me in trouble. Big trouble. But what if Mama is making decisions for me, or hiding more things from me for reasons I don't understand all in the name of love? Shouldn't I be able to know everything? I'm nineteen, and it's my life.

I'm going to go into my parents' room without permission and search for my ID, and if I can't find that, then maybe my adoption papers of anything that might be useful. My hands drop down to the sofa ready to push myself up, but I don't move. Every muscle is ready to go, I just need my brain to catch up. I have to do anything to get my passport and get out of here. To get my own perspective on the world. To get some distance and find my own way home. I feel like I'm drowning in secrets and lies. It's time to break free.

With a surge of energy, like a switch flicking on a light, I bounce up from the sofa and lightly skip up the stairs.

Even though I know the house is empty, other than the eyes watching me from the photos on the wall, as I reach the top of the stairs, I creep along on tiptoe like I'm about to rob the place. In some way, I sort of am. I'm robbing information — if I find any, which I might not. I hope I don't. I hope they haven't been hiding anything else. But in the same breath, I know something feels off. It's all gone on too long.

As soon as I'm in their room, I dash towards the bed and pull out the box of papers Mama keeps under there. The big grey fabric box is so stuffed with papers, it's hard to pull it out. I sit in front of it and begin to tug. The toe-curling sound of material ripping splits the air and I slip onto my back with a thud as the handle breaks off.

'No, no, no, no, no!' I look at my hand with the flimsy handle still in my palm. 'No!'

I look up to the ceiling and curses roll off my tongue as easily as breathing.

I'm going to have to get it out and turn it around — it's the only way — to have the other handle showing, and hide this one. It might be ages until she notices. It'll at least give me time to sew it back on another time when she's out. Sweat gathers around my hair as I push it off my face and try to grip the box from underneath. My fingers ache and scrap along the floor as I edge it out. With each small motion towards me more sweat gathers.

Please, don't let her change her mind and come home now.

Once the box is completely on show, it's easier to spin it as I can stand over it. It's halfway round when I check the other side.

No, no! The other handle has already been ripped away! Presumably Mama did the same thing and turned it the other way. I squeeze my fingers into my palms and a shriek gushes out of me like some sort of hysterical witch.

Glue.

I'll glue it on. That'll be enough. For now, at least.

I glide through the house, not caring about any of the squeaks on the floor. Crashing and bounding, jumping and leaping to get to the kitchen and rake through that unorganised drawer that every house has.

'Please be glue, please be glue.'

'Theadora? I'm back. Are you still here?'

My body turns cold at the sound of Mama's voice as I lay my hand on some superglue.

I leave it behind, quietly closing the door.

'I thought you were going to help Baba.'

Mama appears like a shadow behind me.

'Agatha called me back. I left a message about our mother. She's heartbroken. I'm going to see her. I need to get changed.'

'You look fine how you are.'

'The colours, they're all too bright. It's inappropriate.'

I suppose her fuchsia scarf and vibrant orange and fuchsia floral top are perhaps a bit too "happy".

'But surely you want to get to her as soon as possible? Won't you have to be back in the afternoon for your coffee with next door?'

'No, no. I was thinking of cancelling.'

She turns out of the kitchen and moves towards the stairs.

'Let me help you pick something out. It's the least I can do. I was much too hard on you earlier. Now I've had time to think.' I rush towards the stairs and get there with enough time to nip in front of her without looking too rude. 'I know,' I call over my shoulder.

I burst into her room and run to the other side of the bed, her side, the far side near the window. I crouch and push as hard as I can. I can hear her trotting up the stairs. There's no time. None.

Darting towards her wardrobe I swing open the door and begin to sift.

'Here, this. Try this.'

I pass her a hanger with a smart navy dress draped on it. She takes it and looks it over with a sceptical eye under her glasses. If I can just keep her on that side of the room, I might be able to get away with this.

'Theadora, this is much too formal. Thank you for your help, but–'

'I realised,' I stick my head back into the wardrobe and begin to sift again, 'I was making it all about me, but you and Theía Agatha… you've lost your mother. It doesn't really change anything for me. To me she's always been dead. There's just so much I've been finding out about the past over the past two years…' My hands fall still. 'When did your baba die?'

'Not long after Agatha told them about her. Maybe six or more months. I think she has always blamed herself for his passing. As long as Mama has been alive, there has been some hope for reconciliation. Now… that is lost.' Her voice crumples.

I turn away from the wardrobe as she pushes her glasses on top of her head, drops the navy dress on the bed and presses her fingers over her eyes.

'Mama, I'm so sorry.'

I move to sit next to her on the bed, laying my head on her shoulder and wrapping her up in my arms. Her soft hands grip my forearm around her middle.

'You don't need to be sorry. I know it's a lot of information to take in. What you must remember is, once you were a child, a vulnerable child. There's no right time to decide someone is an adult and that they can handle all the facts of the world they were born to. Babies don't come with an instruction manual. This has been a hard road. Strange in ways I could never have expected. You have been worth it though. I know I've made mistakes, but they're all impossible to regret.' She briefly squeezes my arms tighter than before.

'Come on, let me help you get ready.' I stand up, sniffing back tears. 'Theía Agatha needs you.'

I march over to the wardrobe. Maybe I should admit what I was doing. She said herself mistakes have been made. Honesty is the best policy.

'Mama, I–'

'Pass me my navy scarf. Time's getting on, and you're right. She needs me.'

Her hand reaches towards me. I nod my head and turn to the neat row of scarves, and carefully tug off the navy cotton.

'Here.'

'Thank you, my beautiful daughter. I'm sorry I snapped. I thought I was prepared for this, but it turns out I was wrong.'

I lift the stiff fabric lid, ready to search through the papers underneath. At least now I have time to look properly and keep everything in the same order knowing both my parents will be out for some time.

My hands still feel shaky from Mama's reappearance and the guilt of not being honest. Maybe I should put this all back and just ask her to look again, maybe offer a time where we can look together.

Quickly I scan the first document... Then again... and again. My hands tremble and acid sticks in the back of my throat.

It's a birth certificate. *My* birth certificate, there at the very top. It says my parents are my *real* parents. Theadora Makris, daughter of Zeta and Marios Makris. Underneath that is my real ID card. What the hell is going on?

Chapter 43

It's not the case, but I feel like I haven't spoken for weeks. I've kept myself out of the house, busy with anyone but my parents. I've spent time staring at the Smurf app for Sebastian as he spins us round in ever-decreasing circles. The dust he kicks up is the perfect blanket to hide in. He's been pleased, or he seems to have been pleased, that I've been asking to see him. He brought me flowers and said how he never wanted anyone but me. Even thinking about it now makes my mouth dry and my toes curl with unease.

Today I get what I really need. The one person I can talk to. It's my day to see Dinos — our short escape to discuss his sister and catch up on two weeks' worth of happenings. We had to cancel last week. I got a message late in the night and he told me he would explain everything when I saw him next.

I've been frozen in inaction ever since I read my own birth certificate over one hundred times. After seeing it, and reading it over and over, I carefully shut the lid on it and put the whole thing away wishing I'd never seen it. Wondering if this is the dull paperwork Agatha spoke of when we were at The Waves Taverna together. It seems like much more than that to me. So much more.

Each day I spend hours turning everything over in my mind. I wake up in the room I grew up in, the only bedroom I've ever had. Or, at least, the only one I remember. The one filled with bedtime stories and dreams. Shelves with textbooks and ornaments collected on childhood holidays. The place where my parents have comforted me, taught me about life. The room I've spent hours dreaming about what it would be like to be grown up. To be an adult and make a family of my own. To make my own mind up about my life and to have a purpose. I've been such a fool.

When I pull my sheets up at night now, I don't feel the comforting embrace I once did. I feel the loss of something I'm not sure I ever had. The loss of truth and trust. I'm frozen because I know I *can't* be my parents' real daughter. How can I be their child? The DNA test proves I'm not. But that's what the birth certificate says. That I'm theirs. How can that be? If I own up to having found it, my parents are going to give me some sort of story, but whatever answer I get surely will come with a bunch more questions. I worry it'll come with a bunch more lies too. Have they even told the truth about anything?

Easter is on the horizon and everyone's distracted by the build-up of it all. Not me. I can't think of anything but this puzzle that's been laid out in front of me. I'm always half in the moment and half trying to figure it all out. I want to ask for the truth, but I really don't know whether I trust my family to give it to me. I need to find things out for myself, to discover the truth with my own eyes instead of their slant on everything.

Is this something to do with what Mama said about "*Risking so much?*" or whatever it was she said about Agatha. All the people I trusted have been hiding things from me my whole life, and just as I think I can trust them and that I've got all the facts, something else slaps me in the face.

Dinos is the only person I can trust. The only person who has never hurt me. I've hurt him, because of Sebastian, yet he still talks to me.

Last night was the worst, when a dreadful thought came back in full pelt, like the way the water falls at Nymfes after a downpour. It's a thought I've been pushing down and pushing down, constantly running from it. What if Mama and Baba stole me and registered me as theirs? What if they stole me straight from my mother, who has been looking for me? Or maybe they purchased me from her and demanded she never contact me. Maybe she was poor, and didn't want to give me up. Then they came up with this dreadful "*Keres*" unwanted child story for me. Maybe Melodie closed the door on me, because she knows we aren't allowed to see each other. The idea they could be stopping me from making meaningful connections with my real family makes me nauseous.

I pray every night I'm wrong and this is all innocent, that the birth certificate is part of the adoption papers. I know it's not. The internet told me it wasn't, but I hope that the internet and my gut are wrong. Ever since Mama found the DNA test in the bathroom, I've felt like there has been tension in the house. That's almost two years of everything feeling puffy and swollen. We all happily get by ignoring it, but it's there. They know the secrets and with me knowing some it must make them worry I'll find the rest and piece together the whole picture.

Dinos has to help me find clarity. He has to. I need him to. There will be a big family dinner at Easter, with Agatha and Ria coming to stay. I've already decided that's the day to confront them. To find out the truth about it all.

I just need to see what Dinos thinks. He might be able to reassure me somehow — although, I can't begin to imagine how he could.

Chapter 44

Before I can open my mouth to say hello, Dinos bounds towards me, lifts me up and swings me around saying, 'We did it!'

His excitement is the first thing that's lifted me from my misery in so long.

I stumble, suddenly unsteady on my feet as they hit the ground with a thud. Dinos grips my hands to keep me steady. His face glows; he's all teeth and wide eyes.

'She's getting help. At last, she's getting help! I tried to talk to her, the way we said, but she shut me out. Then I managed to break the lock on the door, to the bathroom I mean, which made it so much easier to get my mama walking in on her. She had to admit it and the doctors had to listen.' He stops bounding like a puppy for a moment and swipes his nose with the back of his hand. 'There's still a long way to go. But it's out of our hands now. They're getting her help.'

Dinos goes on to tell me there was crying and shouting and plates of food were thrown to the floor in anger, his parents furious at the waste and the idea of what his sister had been doing. They couldn't understand at all. Still can't. It's the reason he couldn't make it to see me last week, because it had all kicked off and he was the referee. Dinos had done his homework on the disorder and talked it over with me, which meant he was in a strong position to keep everyone in line. Anorexia and bulimia are disorders, and the person needs care and help to get better. They need to move away from whatever is triggering the problem. That's what we think, anyway. We're not experts, but we've both tried our best to club together any information we can.

'She's going to get help from a specialist. We've really made a difference. I couldn't have got through this without you, you know.'

'You don't need me anymore.' I'm smiling, and I am so happy Dinos has propelled his sister onto a positive path, but part of me has just been cut out and discarded, the part that had a little hope left. When I'm around him I don't want to leave. I know I have to. It's just the way it has to be. Now we have no reason to meet at all. No important scheming left to do.

He stops so abruptly a puff of dirt comes up around his trainers.

'No, no. What if she manages to start hiding it again, or I need some girl advice? I still need you. I wouldn't have got this far without you.'

My head tilts and my eyes sting as I look up at him.

He says, 'Don't look at me like that.'

'Like what?'

'That. With those blue eyes of yours.'

'I can't help their colour, you know.'

The corner of Dinos's mouth lifts and I can't help but erupt in a tear-blurred smile.

'Hey, hey, what's happened?'

Dinos pulls me in. I hang off him like a limpet as I calm myself on the smell of his crumpled beige T-shirt — that delightfully soothing sweet sage that lingers.

It doesn't take long before it starts flooding out of me. It doesn't make sense to him at first. My storytelling is jumbled and jarring. I'm skipping from one thing I know to the next in no sensible fashion. It's not made easier by the fact none of it make sense to me either. None of it. From Mama cutting out my grandparents because of Agatha's sexual preference to finding a birth certificate saying I am born to my parents even though I know I can't be. It's as though I'm making it up, or telling a strange tale about someone else's life, because how can my little family be so full of secrets?

By the time I'm finished we're sitting on the wall in silence looking out at the green folds of Corfu and inhaling lungfuls of eucalyptus that's drifting on the air from a nearby tree.

'Why didn't you ask them about it straight away?'

'Because I don't know if they'll tell me the truth. I get this dreadful feeling that they're always patching things up with lies. And Mama had just found out about the death of her mama. Even though I've always thought she was dead anyway... She was so distant and sad, I don't think I could've found the right moment even if I'd wanted to. She stayed at Theía Agatha's for three days. So no way to tell her then. I didn't expect it to be this complicated. I thought I could find the ID card, or my birth certificate to get a passport or a replacement Identity Card and it would be done before anyone could get mad. Now... It's like, I froze up, and now it's gone on too long. The only time they'll all be together – Agatha, Mama, Baba, Ria – will be at Easter. If I ask for answers then, they can't go behind my back and come up with more lies about me and my past. What do you think? Should I wait and corner them together? Say it now? Or leave it? And say nothing? Or, or... what?'

'I mean...' Dinos's head sways from side to side as he blows air through his lips. 'Yeah. Wait, didn't you say someone from the kid's community home place left you a message a few weeks back? What was her name?'

'Maria Karagiannis.'

'Why not contact her? She has no agenda, right? Might be the only way to get real answers. Or at least something.'

'She said they have no record of me.'

'Then get them to look again. Or for the Keres name, like you said. I think it's worth a shot. It's like our plans for Anna, we didn't have *one* plan and that was it. With only one plan there's less chance of success. It's the same as fishing with one line or two, or casting a net. I think you have a lot of fish to haul in. You should email her now.'

'Now?'

'Yeah. If you do it now, she might get back to you before Easter. I'll help you write it, if you like.' Dinos gently nudges me with his arm. The action pushes a smile out of me the way it always does.

My knee begins to jitter at the thought, then I stand up and pace as though my feet have a mind of their own and I'm no longer in control of anything. Everything up here is wild and overgrown, untouched and unkempt. My pacing disturbs some butterflies that have landed in the grass not far from us and they spring up and flutter away in looping circles.

I'm on this crazy ride hurtling through space and time without a seatbelt. I feel like I'm taking more loops than the butterflies.

'Yeah. Okay.' I pull my phone from my pocket and hold it in front of me, poised almost like it's a pen and paper. 'What do we say?'

We spend almost half an hour carving out what is actually a very short email, with all the relevant questions and details about who I am. My thumb hovers over the send button.

'You've got this,' Dinos reassures me.

I hit the send button, swipe my emails away and close the screen of my phone, taking a deep lungful of the sweet fresh air around me.

I rest my head on Dinos's shoulder and watch as a pair of white butterflies dance around each other again.

What would I do without Dinos? He calms my spinning. He's the only person who makes me feel like me. The real me. The true me. Not the me who is trying to be something she thinks people want to see. Just... me.

'It's all going to work out.' His voice is low and strangely distant. 'No matter what, I'm here for you.'

I lock my mouth shut, because my heart says I love you, and I'm afraid if I open my mouth, he might hear the echo of my words.

Chapter 45

Holy Saturday. Easter eve. Theía Agatha and Ria will be with the children today, doing Easter activities. Some years they take them to see the *botides* pot smashing in Corfu town. Some years we all go together, but not this year. This year I'm going with Sebastian while my parents ready themselves for our family get-together tomorrow.

I have no time to welcome the photos outside of my bedroom door this morning. It's been hard to face them lately. So many of the eyes looking over me have known things and kept them from me. Some were alive when I thought they were long dead. I can't look at them anymore. I wonder if I'll ever be able to look at them the same way again.

I avoid the squeaks of the stairs and pick up my keys slowly so that they don't clink with metal on metal. Every movement is considered. I don't want to get caught out. Not that it matters, not really. I'm going to catch my family out one way or the other. If they catch me out, it wouldn't mean much. Anyway, I can tell them some slice of truth if they ask, that I want to get up early for a drive. There's no harm in that.

Today, as I leave the house, it's under an early morning mist that has rolled in from the sea. It's as though all the ghosts from the past have arrived in the village and are walking around to chill us to the bone, even if this can often mean that a very warm day looms.

I pull away from the house as smoothly as I can. I know this should be the last time I do this, the last time that we meet up, Dinos and I. Part of me knows every time we meet up that it should be the last. The other part of me is stronger, though, the part that feels safe alone on a hill with Dinos, sitting next to the church and the bells, and hiding amongst the trees, the gravestones and the wild tufts of grass that sprout everywhere around us up there.

I haven't had time to make an effort and look anything but dressed. I have to save that for Sebastian. When I get back, I'll need time to get done up, or I'll have him looking down at me all day with a *tut-tut* in his eyes. It doesn't matter. Dinos takes me as I am — my friend no matter what.

I drive towards the church and away from what I've lived with my whole life. Soon I'm climbing higher and looking down on the mist. Trees peek out as it settles around them. Everywhere is peaceful; the hint of a golden glow lightens the earth and gives the misty white a golden lining.

In no time I'm turning up the side road, up to the fork in the road where I veer right and drive up until I'm there. I park the car, ready to find the one person in this world of billions I actually want to spend my time with.

Disappointment hits like the pinpoint of an arrow. His car isn't there waiting for me as usual. It's my turn to wait for him.

Getting out of the car, I walk to find the best view down across trees that are tall enough to be seen above the mist or high enough up to have missed the touch of the ghosts. The mist is already beginning to roll away. The sun's touch is enough to make it cower in fear, like me, hiding here with Dinos away from the world, running away. I can't blame it, hiding and running back to the sea. Showing everything in the light of day can be hard.

I wiggle and lift the gate's latch, still stiff this time of the morning, and move to our spot. The stone wall is particularly cold and hard. I think perhaps Dinos's warmth has usually spread across it before I'm here.

I hear a car engine, but don't bother looking round at the gate. I know it'll be him. We've never seen anyone else here; why would today be any different? This is our place. As though it was made to shelter and protect only us.

There he is, creaking through the gate. He emerges from the shadows to find me.

'I'm so sorry I'm late. I wasn't the only one up early and I had Mama asking what I've been up to. She's noticed my comings and goings. Nothing escapes that woman! With everything that's happening, she doesn't trust us anymore. Even though it was me who pointed out everything with Anna, apparently, I'm not trustworthy. I don't think she sleeps any more.'

We briefly embrace, a favoured greeting. I don't want to let go, but I must.

'Have you had a reply to the email?'

Shaking my head, I pull my phone from the back pocket of my favourite black jeans and go to my emails to refresh them.

'And you've been checking the junk this time?'

I quietly snort, 'Yes. Every day. I won't make that mistake twice. Still nothing. Not that I'd expect an email early on Holy Saturday.'

'No. Have you planned how you'll do it? What you'll say to your family, I mean?'

We both sit on the wall, Dinos angling himself to face me as best he can. Our knees touching is enough to quicken my pulse and confuse my mind.

'I'm going to wait until after the main meal.' I swallow hard trying not to look at our knees, where we are connected with a dance of electricity. 'I've thought about it, and I want to live in a bubble a little bit longer. I do love them all so much, but...'

'You can't trust them.'

'I really want to. I'm frightened to trust them now.' I bow my head and rub my forehead. A breeze rolls between us and my hair flicks across Dinos's chest. He doesn't move away from this new connection.

'There's something I am sure of, that's more important than anything else.' His fingers nip at the tips of my hair, but he still doesn't move it away.

'What's that?'

Dinos tilts his head as he looks me over. I sweep my hair to the other side, removing it from his chest. There's something playful in the back of his eyes, but the rest of his face is serious.

'Your parents love you. I know they do. Whatever they might have done to get you here, right or wrong, I know they love you. I'm glad they did too, otherwise we wouldn't know each other.'

In a desperate attempt to hold my tears in, and swallow them back, my entire throat shuts down and closes up. I stand and walk to get a clearer view of Kassiopi, where my parents are sleeping. I can't see the village fully. It's still fogged up like my mind. The sun's beginning to appear on our side of the hill though, forcing the mist away. Shards of light cast new shadows on everything as the sun brings life back to our corner of the world. I guess this is where I've got used to living now, somewhere in the dark, while everyone else can see the light. I've just been imagining it was sunlight this whole time, thinking I could feel the warmth on my skin, when really it was the cold lying rays reflected by the moon.

Dinos is right though; I guess no matter what my family has done, how bad it might be, they brought me to Dinos, and I can't feel anything but gratitude for that. Some people search their whole lives for a friend like him, for someone who will stay by their side no matter what life deals out.

I wish the mixture of hurt and gratitude I feel towards my parents wasn't so unbearable. It curdles deep in my stomach.

'Can we change the subject?' I turn away from the looming sea cloud as it edges away. The thick morning air is making me feel claustrophobic, as though I can't escape its heavy wet cloak.

'Yeah, course we can.' Dinos takes two big strides to catch up with me. 'How's Sebastian?'

It's hard not to feel a blade twisting in my side whenever I hear Sebastian's name on Dinos's lips. I can't work out whether it's the guilt of spending time with Dinos, or that I don't want to be reminded of the dutiful life that everyone has laid out for me.

'Why is it that whenever I want the subject changed you pick him?'

'Because I need to know you're alright. I don't trust him. Why would I?' Dinos can't contain the contempt from slipping into his voice.

'You don't need to trust him. You don't spend any time with him.'

'But you do, and I care about you. I don't understand why you stay with him. He's too much of a *malaka* to be brave enough to really do anything. He's a coward who tries to act brave by driving fast cars. That's not brave. It's having a small prick and hoping a car can make up for it.'

'Don't talk like that.' I up my pace, and Dinos lags behind me by a step.

'It's true though. He's a coward!'

'Don't.'

'I have to.'

'No. You don't!' I twist to face him, stamping my foot in the dirt. I enunciate my words and fold my arms. 'It's none of your business.' I turn back to the path and walk faster, without a clue where I'm going next.

Dinos audibly sucks in air through his teeth, and his presence fades a little as I hurry on. I glance to the side, trying not to make it obvious I'm checking where he is. He's stopped a few paces back and looks like he's about to scream at the sky. His whole body is tense, and his hands are squeezing into tight fists by his sides.

'Do you love him?' Dinos's voice carries long past me over the trees rolling below us.

I come to a jarring stop.

My head drops to my chest and my stomach squeezes like someone has hooked my insides and started tugging them towards the dirt path.

I fling myself round to look at him once more. 'Why? Do you *love* me?' The words bark out of me and my hand slaps against my chest so hard it hurts.

The colour drains from Dinos's face, and his slate eyes burn my skin more than the sun ever could. Behind him, the sun is kissing the world and casting his face into a shadow making it even harder for me to know what the hell will be said next.

Why did he have to ask me that? But even worse, why did I have to turn it on him?

An eternity passes in a second. Birds stop their morning song, the insects quieten and the only movement I see is the dark shell of a wild tortoise in the undergrowth. It's moving like a living stone.

'You know I can't answer that,' Dinos growls.

'And you have the gall to say Sebastian is a coward,' I call through bared teeth.

'Fine! I do love you! Is that better? You going to leave him now? No? So, what's the point? Saying it doesn't make it better. It'd feel better to have my guts pulled out my nose.' He turns and marches in the opposite direction, leaving me in despair.

My voice chokes out of me. 'We could run away!'

Tears begin to stream down my face uncontrollably. If he agrees, I'll go. I'll go anywhere and never look back.

Dinos stops dead. The tension across his back is visible under his T-shirt, and his broad shoulders collapse under the weight of my words. He lets out a roar worthy of any caged animal before turning to face me. As soon as he looks me in the eye, he runs over to me, and pressing me into the warmth of his chest, he says, 'I wish we could. But... We can't...' The words catch in his throat.

'Why not?' I tremble under his arms, gripping my fingers into the soft fabric of his top.

'You don't even have a passport. We have no money—'

'We have each other.'

This can't be real. I should be allowed to be with the man I love. I grip him tighter than before, so tight it hurt my cheek to be pressed to him so hard.

'Neither of us can leave our families–'

'I could.'

'No, you couldn't.' He kisses the top of my head and takes a deep breath, pressing me harder into him. 'Or you would have by now. And I can't...' He pulls away from me, but grips my arms. His eyes are full, but the tears don't pour like mine. He is holding his emotions together by a thread. 'If you can be brave, I can be brave too. If you want me, and you leave him, I will protect you and your family with my life.' He pulls me in again and presses another hard kiss onto the top of my head, then says into my hair. 'I love you, Theadora. Good luck tomorrow.'

With that, he turns and leaves with no mention of when we will meet here again. No arranged time. Nothing. Not even a goodbye.

I hate when he calls me Theadora.

I would give anything to be brave. Instead, I wish I'd kept my mouth shut so I could go on living a lie and spend a few hours a week with the man I love. Now I don't know what I've done. Tears fall from my eyes and drip off my chin to water the ground in big round drops, because I know I'm too afraid of what Sebastian might do, and not just to my family, but to Dinos if he finds out about us.

Chapter 46

It took me two hours to get ready after my meeting with Dinos. I had to hide my tear-stained cheeks and my broken heart.

Mama was up and cooking when I got in, and she could see my puffy face and quizzed me about it until I managed to physically lock her out by getting in the bathroom and having a shower. I had the water uncomfortably hot in the hope it would burn off the layer of pain from the morning. It didn't work. Nothing from then until now has worked.

It even took me over an hour to put on a plain burgundy top to go with my jeans, and to plaster enough makeup over my face to cover any traces of my heartache. Plastering on lipstick to match the colour of my top helped to brighten my face. Painting on a clown's smile. Time to be the girl Sebastian wants me to be, not the girl I am.

I stayed in my room until Sebastian arrived. I couldn't look at the photos outside my room in the eye. Instead, I silently moved past them as if my family history didn't exist. Like nothing existed.

Now I'm in Corfu town by the Venetian walls waiting for the action to happen. Holy Saturday is always marked here by the old custom of *botides*. Large clay jugs filled with water are thrown from balconies, smashing onto the streets below. Sebastian's caught up in the Easter energy, buzzing to get in the thick of it all. As jugs and pots begin to be thrown out of windows, I'm hit with thoughts I don't want to have. It's as though shards from each pot are landing on my skin, cutting and bruising it. Why can't life be simple again? I used to love watching the pots fall to the ground each year, and the noise of the crowd's excited roar rumbling through my chest. The shattering pots are meant to sound like an earthquake, representing the one that struck after the resurrection of Jesus. It was so exciting back when I was younger. Baba would hoist me onto his shoulders, and I'd point out every pot as soon as I saw one on a balcony ready to go. Streaks of colour whoosh through the air — blues, whites, reds. Some of the pots are intricately decorated, some are bigger than a child, all pushed to their doom, freefalling without any control.

Sebastian shouts in my ear that he wants to move closer to the front, but my phone is vibrating in my pocket.

'Hold on, my phone is ringing.' I turn away from him and try to step away from it all. There's nowhere in town to hide from people today, but the crowd thins out a little further back from the action. The numbers are still lower than normal too, since this is the first year back in full swing after the pandemic.

'*Yassou*, Mama. Are you alright?'

The phone crackles and I can just about hear her in the distance if I press the phone as hard as I can to my ear. After a moment, I feel confident that she's called me by mistake. I hang up and push the phone into my back pocket. When I look up, I'm faced with the last person I expected to see.

Melodie.

She's just how I remember her – all innocent doe eyes and wavy hazel hair – but with one obvious difference. A protruding round pregnancy belly rests under her hand. She's with two young girls who look nothing like her. Both catch sight of me and wrinkle their noses in confusion.

I can't handle any of this. My lungs tighten, and my eyes and nose sting with the pain of a loss that I can't explain or rationalise. I was holding it all together, but the sight of her has tipped me over the edge like I'm one of the falling pots. I'd tried to forget about her existence and the part she has played in the anguish I've felt in these last months. Then here she is right in front of me, here to pull at the very last threads of me until there's nothing left.

Sebastian's arm hooks around my neck, and he's laughing so loudly in my ear I can't help but wince. As he follows my eyeline, his arm goes tense.

'*Gamoto,* who the fuck is that? She looks just like you!' How can he seem angry at this? He does, of course. There's a spiteful note in his voice that's impossible to miss and his arm seems even heavier than usual, weighing down my neck.

One of the girls says something to Melodie in English, but I only catch 'Who is that?'

Why is it that I spent so much time wishing I would bump into her and she was nowhere to be found, and now she's here, when I least expected it?

I need to get as far away from this situation as I can, as fast as I can. My heart is climbing up in my chest again and making its way towards my head like a volcano readying itself for an explosion.

I turn to escape, but Sebastian's arm hasn't moved with me. As I twist, I'm strangled as my throat presses into his arm. I claw at him trying to get out of his grasp. Thrusting his arm away from me, I do my best to dissolve into the crowd. He grabs my hand and hurls abuse and questions like he's throwing a blanket of hate over me. It's a hot day and it's warmer as we press deeper into the crowds of festive onlookers. All I have is pushing forwards. Focusing on finding a way to get as far away as I possibly can.

Another voice, a woman's voice, shouts over his bitter words and over the hum of the people around me.

'Theadora! I'm sorry! Please hear me out!'

The air slices with the smash of an enormous blue-and-white striped pot crashing to the ground. The sound cuts through my ears and feels like it has pierced my heart that's now hiding where my brain once was. Pumping so hard inside me, my eardrums throb with the sound of it beating.

I turn back to see Melodie next to Sebastian. I shake my head at the sight of her. I have the urge to scream, *You shut the door in my face when I needed someone to help me!*, but I don't; I can't. My throat feels like I've swallowed all the salt in the sea. She ruined the idea of having a sister to talk to. It's all I wanted, all I needed. I wanted help, guidance, anything! I still need it with so much out of my control, but now it's too late. Now, the last thing I need is someone else to complicate my life and destroy what little hope I have left in people.

A wave of excitement rolls around the crowd at the smashing of another pot. People dart to grab some broken pieces for luck, before pushing their way back into the crowd for safety before the next one drops.

Melodie's face crumples, and she throws her head forwards. She's curling herself over, grabbing her bump.

Something's wrong.

My bones turn to cottonwool and I can hardly stand looking at her. My heart abruptly sinks back down to my chest from where it feels like it's been beating in my head. Everything shifts.

'Let's go. You can explain this shit in the car.' Sebastian hisses so close to my ear I can feel the damp of his breath.

Without a thought, I push past him and reach for Melodie's cheek. I need to see her face, to check on her.

Her dilated eyes are laced in tears, and I can see a vein in her forehead throbbing under her skin. Something about the sheen over her face makes her look like a wax doll. I can't leave her here, not like this. Not alone.

'Move now!' I scream at those around me. 'Can't you see this woman is pregnant and in pain? Move!'

People do their best to cram together and create a narrow path. I lead Melodie away from the thick of the crowd. She's walking slowly and still hunched over her stomach, although not as much as before. That's something. We haven't made it far before her husband appears by her side, looking every bit the giant man I'd seen towering over her in photos, but without the laughing eyes. Now his emerald eyes darken as he sees Melodie's face. He sees exactly what I saw. Pain and fear. He reflects it back at her like a mirror.

Without a word, he scoops her up in his arms and follows me as I clear a path for them. What's his name? What's his name? Anton! That's it. I remember it from the newspaper. Anton.

Looking back, I realise he isn't alone. Another tall man, who looks like he could be Anton's brother, follows on until Anton turns and calls something to him. This makes him stop before he pushes back to go in the opposite direction and away from us.

I can't see Sebastian. Good. That's one less thing to worry about. Or, at least, something I can push to the back of my mind and worry about later.

I burst into the closest restaurant and pull out a chair for Melodie to sit on.

Involuntary tears have fallen across my cheeks. I do my best to wipe them away with the back of my hand while maintaining as much dignity as I can muster. I think about Mama, and how she has taught me to carry myself with my chin up no matter how I'm feeling on the inside. I'm grateful for so much she has given me, but even that causes more tears to swell behind my eyes as I think of Dinos and his words only a matter of hours ago. *I'm glad they did too, otherwise we wouldn't know each other.*

'Do you need a doctor?' I blurt out in English before anyone can ask how I might be feeling. Not that they would, I'm sure.

'I'm not sure.' Melodie looks from her bump to me to Anton.

'Tell me about the pain.' My logic takes over. It's the only control over anything I have now.

'It's like cramps, and my belly keeps feeling tense.'

'I was there when my *theía* went into labour.' This isn't true. Apparently, I'm becoming so accustomed to lying, it's easier for me than telling the truth. It's becoming a shorthand for stories I don't want to bother with. It was actually Phoebe's *theía,* not mine.

'I'm only around thirty weeks, though.'

'Who the fuck are these people, Theadora? You clearly know these English morons. Who the fuck are they? Why does that woman have your face?'

I didn't even realise Sebastian had come in behind me. I turn to face him. His arms are knotted across his chest and he's wearing a scowl that reminds me of that day at the hotel when I should've been saying goodbye to my best friend, and instead ended up crying in front of Dinos because Sebastian had terrified me.

'Watch your mouth, child,' Anton growls in Greek from the floor next to Melodie.

Sebastian clearly didn't think either of them spoke Greek. All he could hear was English and the sound of his own questions in his head, instead of worrying about anyone else.

Sebastian exhales like a sulky idiot before storming out of the restaurant.

I can feel my cheeks burn. He reflects badly on me. If I marry him, he'll reflect badly on me for the rest of my life. Everyone will think that I think this behaviour is acceptable.

I turn back to Melodie trying to forget what Sebastian has said, although I avoid Anton's sharp eyes.

'How do you feel now?'

For the first time, Melodie smiles for me. I know it's for me, not just in my direction. There's a softness in it, the way a parent looks at a child when they've done something sweet. It leaves me feeling itchy with confusion.

'A bit better, actually. The pains aren't as strong.'

'Are they regular? Is it contractions?' Anton asks, before kissing her hand.

'I think it's maybe those practice ones. I don't remember the name.' She rubs at her head with her other hand before turning back to me.

'Thank you. I don't know what I would have done without you.'

I shake my head. I didn't do anything anyone else wouldn't have done. I couldn't leave her there drowning in a sea of people.

It strikes me that Sebastian could have. He would have left her. How can I stay with a man like him? But it's that same thought that makes me know I *have* to stay. There's no other choice, because knowing someone's that cold, means knowing they're capable of anything, and I'm too afraid to know what that could be.

'I should go. I hope you and your baby are well. Good luck, Melodie.'

'No, please. I'm sorry about what happened before. I was in shock. Please, I want to get to know you. Please?' She tries to stand, but her legs give way. She slaps back down into the chair.

I take one final look at my sister. The woman with my face, my round eyes and the same hollows of my cheeks.

'I decided I have parents I love, a boyfriend, and a happy life. I wasn't looking to hurt anyone. I'm sorry.' Most of the statements are true. Enough to hold my head up high and leave.

'Please...' Her voice sounds strangled. It hurts me to hear it, a tone so similar to my own, that I bite hard on my lip at the sound. 'Tomorrow, if you want, we are having a big family gathering at our house. Bring your family if you like. We can all meet.'

Sebastian appears in the doorway. I glance from him to Melodie. I know what I have to do.

'I can't. I'm sorry.'

And for the second time, I walk away from her. Only this time, it's *my* choice.

Chapter 47

Sebastian tugs me away from the restaurant and the last of the smashing pots. His fingers dig into my hand, crushing the bones together. Our path is interrupted by someone he knows, and we briefly stop for a chat. He maintains the crushing grip on my hand, and by some miracle, I smile blankly the whole time, unable to pinpoint who this person is and whether I'm meant to know them. All I can think about is the searing pain between my bones.

As soon as we step away, I can't even remember their face and it's as though it didn't even happen at all. It's as if nothing is real and I'm being dragged down to hell for Sebastian to feast on my soul. The thought makes a giggle rise out of me. I was named

Keres at birth after the goddesses of violent death, the ones who would feast on the dead on a battlefield. How serendipitous that I should fall into the hands of someone who reminds me of something so similar. The hysteria bubbles up to the point of gulping laughter. It loudly echoes in my chest and my knees feel as stable as wet sand.

'What the hell are you laughing at?' Sebastian turns and presses his nose to mine. 'None of this has been funny to me. You're making a fool of yourself. A fool of *me*.'

He then presses his lips hard against mine, grabbing the back of my head to press me against him. Maybe he didn't want people to see the real reason he was so close to my face. Everything about him is for show. Every little bit.

The kiss sobers me up out of my laughter. There is the taste of smoke on his lips and the smell of stale weed on his clothing. His eyes are quietly red and searching mine with the aggression of a viper.

He pulls me in the direction of where he left his car out of town just enough to be able to escape the crowd. It's a nice walk, normally. The thick ash-grey walls of the Venetian fortress impose on the landscape unmissably as it watches over everything that goes on in the town. Sebastian dragging me about is nothing compared to the things it's seen on these cobbled streets over the centuries. My tripping over my feet to keep up with Sebastian and wishing he would let go of my hand is insignificant.

I'm sure my hand is starting to swell. It's sticky with sweat and surely I could almost escape him if I wiggled it just right. But then what? Then what would I do? Run? I can't outrun whatever shit he has to throw at me and the ones I love. No matter what my parents may or may not have done, or how many secrets they have kept from me, I know Dinos is right. They love me and without them I wouldn't know him even if I can't have him for myself. There's a high chance that in my parents' heads these secrets were necessary to protect me. Even if I don't think certain things should have happened the way they have.

I can't take any more, I have to say something. 'My fingers feel broken,' I squeal. 'Please let me go.'

No response. It's as though I haven't spoken as Sebastian continues on, moving around others walking along the path. I bite my cheek to distract from the white-hot pain in my hand. It's only when we get to the car and Sebastian opens the passenger door for me, that he lets go. The blood rushes back making my hand tingle and sting as I shake it, only to yelp. That was a bad idea. A really bad idea. I don't want to make a fuss. I want to go home.

He looms to make sure I get in properly before slamming me shut into my prison.

I slip on my belt without a word. We're meant to spend the afternoon with his yiayia and pappoús. Right now, I can't imagine a worse fate. Trying not to process everything that's happening while playing the part of the sweet girlfriend to a man I now loathe.

'Who in the hell was that bitch?'

'Don't call her that.'

As I rub my bruised hand, I watch a couple stop and kiss under a tree. They're perhaps my age. It's hard to tell age when someone is an adult. They could be nineteen, they could be thirty-nine. It doesn't matter, they look content in each other's arms, and relaxed in the shade of the tree on the cobbled street. I can't imagine ever feeling that way again with Sebastian. Once we had that, or something like it. Now that childish dream has turned into a dreadful nightmare.

'I'll call her, and *you*, what I like. Now talk.'

I exhale, closing my eyes. Why couldn't Dinos have worked out he loved me five years ago? I wonder where I would be now if he had? If he had had the guts to tell me how he felt when we were kids? Would I be at the pots bumping into Melodie with Dinos on my arm? Would I be somewhere else completely?

'Well?' Sebastian demands. His hand smacks down on his steering wheel.

'How did we come to this?'

'Because you never answer my questions!' I can almost hear his eyes rolling back in his head.

'She's my sister.'

'Don't be fucking stupid. You're adopted.'

Under my eyelids, my eyes roll in return, before I open them to look at Sebastian's burning red face. His right hand grips the steering wheel as hard as he gripped my fingers. I contract and open my hand to try to get the blood moving again, but the fingers don't move properly.

'She's my biological sister. I only found out about her this year and–'

'And you didn't think to mention it to me?'

'She wasn't interested in knowing me, so it didn't seem important. I don't tell you everything.'

'Is that right?' A sinister note ripples over his voice, 'What else have you been hiding from me?'

'That's not what I meant.'

'Perhaps I should keep a better eye on you. I can't have you humiliating me again. Today was bad enough. We were having a good time, and then I find out you've been hiding *this* from me.' He waves his hand towards the car window in the direction of where we watched the pots fall. 'I don't want to hear about her again. Do you understand me? Ever. She doesn't exist. I don't need this sort of complication.'

I know I'm going to see Melodie again, because however much I might want to protect my family, I'm not going to let Sebastian decide who exactly my family is. I just have to hide it from him for as long as possible.

Chapter 48

By the time we've finished a delightful meal with Sebastian's grandparents, during which I struggled to cut the food with my left hand, and after watching brass bands parade the streets in their village, I've missed most of my family's Easter Saturday traditions.

When Sebastian drops me off, he tells me I did good with his grandparents, before leaning across the car for a casual kiss. As soon as we were with them it was like he switched over into the man I thought he was at the start. I'm almost impressed at how easily deceitful he can be. It's deeply ugly, but still strangely impressive. There was no more mention of Melodie. He's told me his demands and I guess to him, that's it. I must obey.

As soon as I'm alone in my empty home, the door firmly closed at my back, I sprint up the stairs, past the photos and throw myself onto my bed with such force that I almost bounce right back off again.

My hand's purple and still throbbing. It has been for hours now. When Kalista asked what I'd done, Sebastian told her someone stamped on it when I tried to pick up a piece of pot from the ground. She accepted the idea with complete ease.

I roll from my stomach to my back. I haven't bothered turning the lights on, and suddenly the whole room looks like it's on fire in an instant. Golden then green.

The fireworks have started. Mama and Baba are probably wondering where I am and when I'll arrive. I wonder where Dinos is, if he's out on the boat or wandering the streets.

The vision of him in his fresh Easter clothes is enough to get me off the bed. I strip off my Sebastian clothes that smell of the sickly cherry air freshener in his car. Standing in my underwear, I pull open the chest of draws next to my mirror and claw through my clothes. The contents spill out until I find a simple polka dot dress I've had for years. I slip it over my head and don't even check the mirror before running back out of the house.

I skim the pavement as the cloudless night sky continues to fill with bursts of colour, and even at this distance from the harbour, I can already hear the festivities in full swing, and getting louder as I run towards the spectacle. People meander around but most will have accumulated at the harbour. As I get nearer, I slow my pace and catch my breath.

People holding simple white candles watch the sky. It's set alight at regular intervals with booming sounds as if the cannons have been fired after years of silence.

Everyone's fixated on the glittering lights above. Even Dinos, standing with his sister in silence only a matter of metres away from me. I'm in two minds about joining them. It's a busy place, nothing to report back to Sebastian even for Konstantinos, surely?

I step towards Dinos and he turns. Everyone else stays glued to the sky like they've been hypnotised, but he turns.

Seeing me, he whispers something to Anna before turning back and splitting the distance between us.

'Hi.'

'Hi.'

I say, 'Can I stand next to you?'

'Forever.'

I say hello to Anna, briefly kissing her cheek and exchanging Easter greetings. She beams at me from under her oversized denim jacket. She's bleached her hair, and it's pulled in a ponytail to one side. I'd seen a picture of it online but not in person. I haven't seen her in the flesh in such a long time. She hides her illness well, but her cheekbones are more prominent than when I last saw her. I can only imagine she's trying to keep up with people she sees online. She's a pretty girl, unique. She shouldn't try to change herself for anyone.

A tug of emotion pulls at me — it's the thought that I shouldn't change who I am and my life for someone else. The throb in my hand tells me that. But I'm trapped; Anna is free to be whoever she wants to be.

In our own bubble of silence surrounded by music and the final explosions, the three of us stand shoulder to shoulder with me in the middle. The back of Dinos's hand skims mine. I want to squeak with pain as his thumb runs along the bruise, but if I do, I will have to tell him the truth. I promised him that if I was hurt again, I would tell him — and I will tell him, one day. I only said I'd tell him, not *when* I'd tell him.

I scrunch my eyes closed to stop the tears that are gathering behind my eyelids. As the fireworks come to a climactic end, I turn to Anna and Dinos.

'I've got to find my parents. I'll hopefully catch you both later. It was nice to see you, Anna.' I gently squeeze her arm with my good hand. Even under the weight of the denim I can tell she's tiny. I'm so proud of Dinos for finding a way to help her. I'm glad he came to me about it, even if it has made it harder to leave him behind — now that I know how he really feels about me.

'Your parents went in that direction.' Anna points towards the right-hand curve of the harbour. Hundreds of people are spread in that direction and all across the town. 'It was nice to see you too. It's been too long.'

I nod and smile before turning briefly to Dinos.

'*Kalinikta*.' One word of goodnight is all I can manage.

'I hope to see you soon, Dora.'

My lips press together, and I force a thin smile. 'Me too.'

I turn and walk further into the horde of people with their candles. The fireworks marked the arrival of midnight, and the day of the resurrection of Jesus. Mama and Papa will be socialising with our neighbours and friends now. They will have found a little pocket of people and will be chatting and celebrating for some time.

I smile and send good wishes to many people I know as I pass them. Zander being one of them. He's avoided talking to me ever since the evening I spend on the boat with Dinos. I can't say I blame him. He probably thinks I'm a dreadful friend. There's no way he ever believed Sebastian's lies.

Maybe I should head home. I don't feel much like celebrating tonight.

'Theadora! When did you get here?' Mama springs in front of me from my left, grabbing my cheeks and kissing them.

'Marios! Marios! She made it at last. We've missed seeing you today. I suppose we'll need to get used to sharing you more when you're married.' Mama sighs as Baba turns away from a crowd to welcome me back home. It's as though I've been gone a month instead of a day.

'I need to tell you both something.' If I don't get it out now, I might never get to say it. I need tomorrow not to be about this. Tomorrow there are more important things to be said. 'I saw my sister today, Melodie, in town. She's pregnant and, well... she asked to see me again. For me to visit her tomorrow.'

They both look as though I've told them I did a hit-and-run earlier in the day and I'm not sure if the victim has lived.

'You won't see her though, will you? Not after what she did?' Baba musters.

'I don't know. It was different, she seemed different. She seemed sorry.'

People excuse themselves as shoulders bump and rub together. The crowd moves like the currents of the sea. We are stones and everyone is slipping around us.

'We can't talk about this here.' Mama shakes her head and her eyes shine with tears.

'Zeta,' Baba soothes.

'No, not here, not now.'

With that shut down, I'm ushered over to talk to our neighbours and friends. Mama and Baba's reaction doesn't exactly fill me with confidence to tell them anything in the future.

Chapter 49

I'm at home, standing in front of the family photos. I needed to look at them deeply again, to check how much faith I have in all these people from the past.

I woke up this morning with a pain in my neck. By the time I managed to fall asleep, I think I'd done so in the strangest position, contorted by the events of the day.

I'm not sure what was worse, running into Melodie, Sebastian nearly breaking the bones in my hand, spending a few hours with his grandparents smiling, telling Mama and Baba about Melodie or being up half the night worrying again.

I nearly messaged Dinos so many times. I wanted to tell him about Melodie, about my hand, and just to say *I miss you already*.

I even typed out a message only to delete it. At least typing it meant I could feel out the words I would say to him. There was something nice about that, like I've started the conversation and I'm just waiting for him to get back to me. I wonder if he'll ever message me, or when I'll next see him around the village, hopping into his fishing boat with his pa, or out for drinks with friends.

These aren't questions for today. These aren't questions I should let myself ask ever.

Today I need to pull strength from deep down inside me and face my family head on. I need to get the words out of my mouth. The right words, at the right time.

'What are you doing?' Baba's voice from the stairs sends a shockwave through my spine and I physically jolt.

'You frightened me!'

'Sorry,' he chortles.

'You don't sound sorry.'

'Well then, I suppose I'm not sorry enough. Why are you standing there like a lost chicken?'

'I'm saying good morning to the past.'

Lately, I've been avoiding my ritual of looking at the photos, but today I felt like this needed to be done. Some days it's only in passing I give them my nod, then there's a day like today when I hover and stare at the details of the background as well as the smiles on the lips of people posing for the shots. I like to take in the way the garden looked before it was finished, with bare patches and overgrown grass, or the private look between Mama and Baba captured by someone, likely Agatha, for us all to see a slice of their relationship there in print.

'Does the past ever say good morning back?' The playful expression on his face at his comment is enough to make my lips slide into a comfortable smile, one I've missed.

I shake my head. 'No. Not one that I can hear.'

Baba moves around the banister to stand by my side.

'Good morning past.' He bumps me with his elbow before waving his hand at the wall, which makes me think of Dinos and his playful manner. Sadness rolls over me at the loss of him, as though he has died, and I've been told in no uncertain terms I'm not allowed to mourn. The thought stings in the back of my throat and nose.

'Do you miss it?'

'What?' My voice is strangled and tight. For a moment, I think he means Dinos, then I cotton on to his meaning. 'The past?' I inhale a deep soothing breath before puffing it out. 'Every day. You?'

My eyes stay locked on the photos but from the corner of my eye I see Baba snatch a look at me.

'Really?' There's no playful tone now. It's exploded away in his shock at my answer. 'But you're young with everything ahead of you. You have a strong man who will be able to run your house...' My mouth burns with acid at this thought. I don't want any man to run my house. He continues, '... and a good home on a beautiful island, and parents who would give their lives to see you smile.'

My eyes drop to the floor away from the innocents of the past. I want to believe him, and I do. I hope I do. I hope I'm right to trust them all.

Baba pulls me round and holds my shoulders so that we are eye to eye.

'I know this sister of yours has got you confused and hurting. You have the same blood and that can mean something, but it doesn't have to. We are all people, we all make mistakes and not one of us is all evil or all good. Not one. We can be fools one minute and Plato the next. It's up to you how you judge someone, but I like my gut for these things.' He removes his right hand from my shoulder and slaps his stomach. 'It's never let me down. Take your time and think. But at the end of the day, your instincts should never be ignored.'

Letting go of my shoulders, he picks up my hands and squeezes them. An involuntary noise like a yelp from a dog being stepped on squeaks out of me. I snatch my hands away and grip the one that Sebastian crushed to my chest.

'What's wrong?' Baba looks as hurt as my hand, his face folding into deep wrinkles of concern.

'Nothing. I, I hurt my hand yesterday in town.'

'What happened?'

'Someone... stepped on it.' Another lie; even I don't trust me anymore. I'm regurgitating Sebastian's lies now. How could I trust my gut when the words that come out of my mouth aren't trustworthy? Who knows what decisions I could make without a thought.

'Stepped on it? How on earth–?'

'I was picking up a piece of the pot for good luck. Someone stepped back on my hand. It was silly, embarrassing. I'm sure it'll be fine.'

'Marios! What's taking so long?' Mama's voice bellows from under our feet.

'Come on, Theadora mou.' Baba lays his hands softly on my shoulders and I lower my chin for him to kiss my forehead. 'Theía Agatha and Theía Ria will be here soon.'

'I'll be down in a bit.'

Baba presses his lips into a smile but his eyebrows are still low over his eyes. He does as I ask though, and turns to go down the stairs.

I narrow my eyes on Agatha and Ria on the wall. One from an Easter when I was perhaps nine or ten years old. It must be so hard to be in love, be next to each other and never show the world the affection you feel for one another.

Mama and Baba are holding hands. Ria and Agatha aren't even touching each other. I remember being the one to put the camera on a timer. I was so excited to do it. I thought I was so grown up.

Agatha called me when Mama told her I knew about their relationship. She said sorry so many times for not telling me. They've been afraid they would be fired from their jobs at the Children's Community Home. It was only in 2005 that discrimination against sexual orientation was banned in the work place, and a same sex relationship with someone at work... Even now, they're both too worried about it to be open. It's probably not helped by how Mama and Theía Agatha's parents were about it. Even now, debate has been going on about same sex marriage being legalised.

'Would you marry Ria, if you could?' I asked.

She went quiet on the other end of the line. 'I can't imagine anything better than telling the whole world about us, and for them to accept us. Maybe when we retire we'll be brave enough.'

Outside of that she spent more time checking I was okay with their relationship. Their love for me gives me hope for today.

Leaning closer, I study the photo.

It's not the same, but hiding how I feel from Dinos is hard enough. I'd hate to have to wait until retirement to be with him in public. Then it hits me like a punch in the stomach... I might never get to be with him, in private or in public.

Chapter 50

In the barbecue shed outside, the lamb sizzles over the coals as it slowly rotates round and round on its shaky metal stand. The smell fills the garden and the gardens beyond. Or perhaps it's that so many are making this very same dish, and the aromas have converged into a delicious cloud over our homes.

Baba likes to have ours rubbed in salt, pepper, olive oil and not a thing more. He likes the lamb to *speak for itself*. They're his words not mine. Although he often adds that the lamb shouldn't be so raw that it'll stand up and *baa* halfway through the meal.

With each rotation of the lamb, the dinner hour comes one step closer.

Agatha and Ria look happy. They allow themselves to hold hands, something I haven't seen before. This is the first time seeing them together through fresh eyes, with the truth about their relationship out in the open.

When we spoke about it on the phone, Agatha spent more time asking how *I* felt, if *I* was okay. She sounded truly worried about it all. I suppose, if your parents can't accept who you are to the point they would cut you out of their lives, it must leave a deep scar.

She must have trust issues. Being left at birth has left a mark on me, and I never loved my biological family. They didn't raise me or comfort me when I was hurt, and yet the burden of their loss still hangs over me. It must be so much worse for Theía Agatha, believing she was loved unconditionally, only to find there was a condition to the love, and she had broken it.

My biggest problem with it all, if I'm honest, is how easily they've been able to lie to me about who they fundamentally. It's left me with a bigger knot of fear as to what else they are capable of hiding. They only thing to counteract it is the relief from Agatha at my acceptance.

We sit outside in the sun as it streams down around us. The big umbrella is already open over the table. Mama and I bring out the avgolemono, the traditional egg and lemon soup. Baba always says how this is all they used to have on Easter Sunday in his house growing up, but now many roast a leg of lamb on the same day, although each house has its own take on traditions.

Avgolemono can be a thick, heavy soup that easily can fill someone for a week let alone a day. This is our starter.

The meat has already been pulled from the lamb ready for our main meal. Soon it'll be pulled from the bones of the family too if I'm not careful with my words.

With each creamy, tangy mouthful of soup, I'm a step closer. Ria and Agatha tell stories of the children they look after as though they belong to them; they miss them when they leave them behind. They sound like they wish they could've brought them to dinner today. Apparently one or the other would love this soup, and another would love to look at the flowers blooming pink and yellow in the garden that my parents keep so very neat.

I put down my spoon and take them all in, appreciating this moment of their warm smiles and being a part of this day before I go ahead and ruin it.

'So, what about you, Theodora?' Ria places her spoon down. 'After your dramatic story about this sister of yours, will you give her a second chance?'

'It's a lot to think about. I still don't know what to do. I think I might. She asked me to go there today.'

Mama's jaw tenses at this reminder of the invite. 'Not today, you're here with us today. Give yourself some time.' She scrapes her bowl and licks the last drips of the smooth soup from her spoon. 'Please excuse me. I'll be back in a moment.'

'Do you need help?' I push my chair back to stand.

'No, no. It's all prepared now. I'm just going to get the salads.'

I tuck my chair back in and notice that Ria is still watching me with her coal-black eyes. She dips her chin towards her chest as if to say, *please continue.*

'I think maybe Mama is right. Everything needs time. Maybe I'll friend her on social media. It's a simple step, maybe it might be the right one. I haven't thought about it much. I guess I'll go with my gut.' I send a smile towards Baba. His gentle eyes light up at this small recognition.

It's partly true, I haven't thought about how I'll go about seeing Melodie. I only know I will, because Sebastian forbade me to. He doesn't run my house yet. He can't decide who I can and can't see. Apart from Dinos. It's easier to fight for seeing Melodie than Dinos, because ultimately, I know deep down that Sebastian is right. I do want Dinos to be more than just a friend. With Melodie, he's only irritated because he was caught off guard, that's all.

'Good to go with your gut. Your mama may say you should think about things, but she gave no thought to adopting you. Not one logical thought, anyway. She looked at you, and that was that. There was nothing that could change her mind.' Baba links his fingers together on the table and sits back in his chair, tilting his head into the warmth of the sun.

I cast my mind back to the conversation I had with Mama last year at the fortress, with us looking out to sea while she told me the harrowing story of her lost baby and how it brought her to finding me. The baby she had been dreaming about. That's what she *said* really happened. Surely it has to be truth. No one would lie about that sort of loss at least. The pain in her voice seemed real, the sorrow at the back of her eyes and the catch in her voice.

'What's wrong, Theodora? You've gone so pale.' Theía Agatha reaches across and curls her fingers softly into mine. 'Your hands are cold.' She rubs the back of my hand with her thumb and I wince at the sensation.

'What's happened to your hand?'

I snatch it away. 'It's a bruise. It was a silly accident.

Mama returns with two large bowls of salads bursting with peppers and feta.

'Marios, fetch the lamb you carved. Now, please. I'll get the potatoes.' She collects up the empty bowls of soup and makes her way back to the kitchen.

'Do you need anything while I'm up?' Baba lowers his eyebrows in my direction.

'No, I'm fine.'

'Anyone else?'

Ria and Agatha shake their heads and give him glancing smiles before turning their attention back to me, as if they're shining the light of the sun on my skin. It's already beginning to sting and burn.

'We work with troubled children every day.' Ria lays her dark hands flat on the table. I wonder if this is how she talks to the teens at the children's home.

'And we know when something's wrong,' Agatha adds. Quite the double act.

'It must be a lot to take in, having a new sister and not knowing where you stand. We all know you must be wondering what she will have to say about your biological mother, and whether you'll be meeting her if you do decide to see Melodie again.'

'It's not that.'

I can't start now, not without everyone at the table. I need to gauge their reaction as a group with nothing to hide behind. *Why do I have a birth certificate that says I'm my parents' real daughter? What really happened when I was born?* I can feel my chest labouring over each breath, just a touch, as though I need more air than I'm receiving to function, even though nothing has changed in the past minute. My emotions are running at a sprint, and I feel like I need more air to stop myself from suffocating.

All at once Baba and Mama march to the table and place the rest of the food down. I pinch out a smile for Agatha. She sucks in her full bottom lip in thought then wraps her baby-blue blouse around her as she sits back in her chair. Baba's right hand holds a plate heaped with juicy lamb and his other balances the plates for the table. Mama puts down the potatoes, takes the plates from him and passes one to each person. As she does so, she seems to cotton on to something not being quite right. A frown deepens with each plate that she passes out.

'Have I missed something?'

I wish she'd sit down.

'No, no. Happy Easter!' I lift my glass, but my hand is shaking enough that I'm sure it's not only me who can see it.

'Theadora? What on earth is the matter?' Mama narrows her eyes on me.

It's now. It has to be now. I have to tell them everything I know, and they have to tell me everything I don't know, or I'll be leaving and never coming back.

Chapter 51

I look down at my empty plate to catch my breath. The plate is a decorative circle that my Easter dinner has been served on since I was old enough to be trusted with the good china. It's white with a decorative dark blue pattern of flowers, leaves and tiny dots. I've studied these plates enough over the years that I can count the leaves in my head with my eyes closed. These people have kept me fed and safe and warm. No matter what happens next, I have to hold onto that.

'I found my birth certificate. It says that you are my birth parents, which I know can't be true.'

I look up from the plate and see Mama thumping her bottom down in her chair, Agatha's eyes as wide as the plate I was just studying and Ria and Baba as still and quiet as cypress trees.

No one speaks. No one can think of a lie quick enough.

'We cannot discuss this here.' Mama shakes her hand towards the fences that pen us in away from our neighbours. 'This is not the time. This is the time to celebrate Christ and to eat food, and be together. It is not the time for this conversation.'

'Zeta...' Agatha begins.

'No! This is not the time!' Mama hisses through her teeth like an angry serpent, her chin thrusting out with her words before recoiling and calmly saying, 'Ria, help yourself to some lamb, please.'

Anger boils inside me. She won't even do me the decency to respond, or even look at me. My hands sweat and my breathing spikes as I bite my cheeks.

'She may once have been yours, Zeta, but she is a grown woman, and without us you would never have had her,' Agatha says in a low voice only just audible above the gentle creak of a nearby olive tree. 'She needs the whole truth, not a slice of it. Even if for no other reason than to protect us.'

Protect them?

'After we eat. Then we will discuss the matter indoors.' Mama almost growls the word *indoors* through bared teeth.

'If that's acceptable to you, Theadora. If you want answers now, I'll take you indoors now and answer anything you want to know.' Agatha's voice is very matter of fact. It's as though she's said, *I can be the one to get the napkins.*

It's tempting. It's not as though I feel able to stomach anything else right now. My stomach feels like the acidity from the lemon soup earlier wants to burn back out of my throat. But I need them all together, so that one of them can't tell lies that the others can go along with. I need to be there to see their faces all at once.

'Thank you, but no. We can talk after. It was my plan all along, to talk after dinner. I didn't mean to ask between courses... I just...'

'We pushed you too hard. We could see something was bothering you, and we pushed it out of you. It's our fault not yours.' Ria's voice is as soft as a cushion compared to Mama and Theía Agatha.

'Thank you,' I whisper.

Food is piled onto plates amid strained pleasantries — *Doesn't this smell delicious? Thank you, Zeta, for all this wonderful food* — from everyone, apart from me. I place a minimal amount of food on my plate because I'm afraid that if I eat too much, I'll bring it all up again.

I focus on each mouthful while holding in tears. The lamb is so succulent, so tender, that I don't even have to chew more than twice before I can swallow it. Mama and Baba have outdone themselves. The salad is divine, crisp and bright, and the potatoes, roasted in garden herbs and garlic, are beautiful. I'm the problem. Without me the day would be perfect.

As everyone around me falls into the silence of eating, there's an awkward air that rolls in like the mist from the sea.

I am a grown woman, and as such, I need to behave like one. Not like a child who hasn't got her own way. With the next mouthful I swallow my emotions as much as I can and say, 'I'm sorry I've caused an atmosphere. This is exactly what I didn't want. What are the children eating today? Lamb? Or will they save it for tomorrow?'

I actually know the answer. It's the same each year, but this is a start. The metaphorical olive branch and it had to come from me.

Ria beams and tells us about the children having their traditional soup, and all the things they'll be doing while she and Agatha are not there. It does the trick, and everyone at our table slips into conversation.

That doesn't stop me from being the first to place my cutlery on my plate.

'Thank you, Mama, Baba. That was truly delicious.'

'You're welcome, Theadora mou.' Baba smiles across at me, but I get the distinct feeling Mama's finding it hard to even glance in my direction.

I wait patiently as time ticks past me, with the beating of birds' wings and the tickle of my hair in the breeze. It's like the slowest countdown from four.

Four: Ria finishes her meal and places her hands on the table, giving me a subtle nod.

Three: Baba doesn't take seconds when Mama thrusts the plate of meat in his direction.

Two: Agatha joins them in placing her cutlery down.

Mama talks and pushes her last potato around her plate for an age. Everyone watches, laughs in the right places, tuts in the right places. Eyes follow the potato being pushed from side to side.

'Is no one going round for seconds?' She looks around at us all. 'No? No, I thought not. Perhaps later then. Marios, bring the food in and put it away.' Then she looks at me and cocks her head towards the house in one sharp motion. 'Come.'

I guess that's *One* then, the countdown is done. Mama thrusts back her chair and marches off towards the house.

I gather up the plates, empty save for one potato and take them to the kitchen.

Ria and Agatha help Baba to save on time and we all make our way to the living room. Not a word is spoken until every door and window in the house is closed.

All eyes are on Mama, who's sitting straight in her chair, so straight it looks like a board has been pinned to her back. Her face looks more weathered today, like I've worn her down to a toothpick already.

She turns to me and says abruptly, 'We stole you from the Children's Community Home. It was my fault. I refused to give you up. I told you as much. The only difference to the story is, it would've taken years to adopt you back then. Most of your life, if we were lucky! As soon as I saw you, I wouldn't let you out of my sight. I would barely let you out of my arms. This is all my fault, but I don't regret a moment of it. I will always be grateful for everything Agatha and Ria have done for us, but if anyone found out we all stole you...'

'But the birth certificate?'

'That was my idea,' Ria pipes up. 'I thought that Zeta should take you and register you as her own. I told her not to take Marios, because you were so pale and already had tufts of white hair. We got him to sign that you were his but he was too busy with work to go along to the appointment. There was no reason not to question any of this. We knew what would be asked and what to say. It would be the only way to have paperwork for you to apply for things when you came of age, because there was no way we could get you adopted.'

'But that didn't help with explaining your disappearance from the Children's Community Home...' Baba groans.

'No,' Ria shakes her head and presses her lips into a thin line.

'For that, I had to go with your parents to Athens. That was during the time Zeta and Marios would come to say they were in Romania adopting you. Instead, I filled in the paperwork to say we couldn't house you in Corfu. That having a newborn baby here wasn't appropriate with the ages of the other children. As far as the charity was concerned, I took you to another facility for abandoned children on the mainland.'

'We wanted to say you were ours,' Mama muses, 'but you look nothing like us.'

'The problem is, has always been, your colouring,' Agatha weighs in again. 'No one would believe you were their daughter by birth. No one! The narrative had to be adoption, even with your mother's pregnancy to hide behind... It just wouldn't work. Couldn't work.' Agatha's eyes lack focus like she's still trying to work this puzzle out almost twenty years on.

More lies and blank spaces being filled. Why couldn't they have told me all of this when the DNA test threw it all up, the way the sea vomits seaweed onto the sand. Confusion and anger pinch my nerves. They took me to the mainland to pretend they left me there? That's what the Children's Community Home charity think? That I've grown up somewhere else entirely.

'Is there anything else I should know? Anything else you're not telling me?' I'm so numb my words mumble out like my lips have been frozen.

'You know everything now.' Mama's voice is firm, but it wobbles in the middle. Baba shuffles on the sofa and moves towards her to wrap his arm around her shoulder. 'Do you understand now why we were so reluctant to tell you, and certainly couldn't when you were a girl? We broke the law. All of us.'

I suck my lips in on themselves and nod. It's only now that it hits me, what I've done. I've emailed that woman, Maria Karagiannis, the chair of the charity board, the woman who, is probably on the hire-and-fire board. She isn't part of the day-to-day lives of the children, but she's at the top of the hierarchy, and I've fed her more information than I should've.

All the blood in my body turns to ice, and if someone so much as flicked me, I'd break into a thousand pieces.

'I'm so sorry, Theadora mou, I wanted to tell you up at the castle that day.' Mama's eyes swell with tears. 'I wanted to tell you everything. But I couldn't. Not without Ria and Agatha. They put their lives at risk for nothing, only to help us and help you. We gained a daughter, we should bare the judgement. When we all came together to discuss telling you, time had passed, and you've been through so much... it seemed silly to tell you things that didn't matter. You had your ID Card, you had the truth of being found here. Our crimes are not yours, and we didn't want to burden you with them.'

My heart breaks from the contorted expression on Mama's face. The pain she's feeling looks more physical than emotional. It hurts me, but my heart is breaking from the fear of what I've done too.

'Who else knows all this?' I stutter, hoping Maria Karagiannis already knows and that's why she hasn't returned my email.

'No one else. No one else knows the *whole* truth behind what we did.'

Not Maria then. She isn't on the trusted list.

'What would happen if anyone did find out?' My pulse races along as I do my best to look inquisitive instead of terrified. These people gifted me a life in a good family house, with a normal upbringing. Foolishly we've filled ourselves with distrust. They were too frightened of their crimes to tell me the truth and I didn't trust them enough to talk to them before going behind their backs and now I've put them all in danger. Why couldn't they have trusted me sooner? If they had, none of this would've happened!

'I don't know what they would do. Arrest us? Put us in prison? I dread to think!' Agatha splutters.

'But it's been such a long time—' I protest.

'True,' Ria joins in. 'We removed all the red tape and regulations and sold you to the highest bidder as far as anyone is concerned. They might see it as akin to child trafficking. Time might be on our side. It's been over fifteen years, they might not be able to prosecute.'

Agatha cuts across her. 'At best we both lose our jobs.'

'At worst...' Ria shrugs.

I snatch a breath, it's now or never. 'I sent an email to Maria Karagiannis, the head of the Children's Community Home charity board—'

'We know who she is. What did you say to her?' Agatha cuts over my words like a knife.

'I asked to see my adoption file.' I blurt it out, because they need to know the truth in the same way I need it from them. Only, I wish I'd been brave enough to confront them sooner. And I wish they'd been brave enough to tell me their truth sooner too.

Chapter 52

I burst out of the house and sprint to my car. All I want to do is drive to Dinos, but I can't and there's only one other place I can think of to hide... Melodie's.

I drive towards the lowering sun. As both the sun and I move further west, I'm hit with flashbacks of the moments before I left.

'Christ!' Mama crossed herself, something she rarely does. 'Instead of opening your mouth and asking, you've made things so hard. You, you, you drown in a spoonful of water! Making life too difficult!'

'I didn't mean to make this difficult. I didn't feel I could talk to you. You've been hiding so much that I didn't feel safe anymore. If you had trusted me, none of this would've happened! If you had trusted me, I would've known what I was looking at! You've shut me out of my own life, my own history!'

'Don't be hard on each other.' Ria's voice was calming like the mellow waves of the sea. 'You've both had a lot to process in a short space of time.'

That didn't stop the torrent of tears and screaming from mama. 'We're all going to prison now! What have you done? Was our love not enough? You want the family that left you so much that you do this to us?'

I blink as hard as I can to push it all away, to push away the vision of Mama collapsing into Baba's arms and sinking down like a puddle.

The road winds around like my thoughts, and the sun hangs heavy in the sky, ready for its final glorious ending.

Eventually I pass Taste Me, the place where Dinos and I had a drink and some cake. I can't even look at it as I pass. Instead, I focus on the row of shops at the end of the road. I remember the way so easily. I've only been here once but it's engrained in my memory even if it was six months or more ago.

I arrive at Melodie and Anton's home, and find there's a woman in the driveway carrying a child. She slams a car door, and lights flash to show it's locked. Most driveways couldn't fit this many parked cars, let alone have space for more. I stop my car next to hers and get out. She's very fair, but the child has a mass of wild dark hair.

'Theadora, I hope?' Her pale eyes search my face, and she wrinkles her pointed nose.

The boy looks up from a toy laptop in his arms; he's maybe four or five. He takes one look at me and frowns. 'That woman looks like Auntie Melodie,' he loudly whispers so close to his mother's ear that she winces.

I let out an awkward laugh, and tuck a strand of hair that keeps blowing into my face behind my ear.

'I guess you'd better come with me, then.' The fair woman hoists her son higher on her hip. He wriggles to get a better look at his toy. She puts him down and takes one of his hands instead before manoeuvring him through the open front door.

As we step inside, she turns back and looks me over again, pressing her lips together. 'Maybe, wait here.' She calls out, 'Athena? Athena, could you get Melodie, please? There's someone here.' She puts a strange emphasis in her voice on the word *someone*, a subtle signal to the woman she's calling on.

As Athena comes into sight, I recognise her as the woman who opened the door just after Melodie when I was here last. The one to threatened to call the police. As she lays eyes on me, her mouth opens and she backs away towards an enormous wooden dining table. 'Yes, yes, I'll get her.' She rushes backwards, almost knocking into one of the tall dining chairs on her way.

The house is incredible. Last time I didn't really see inside; there was a wall of big men blocking the view, and I had other things on my mind. Now I'm presented with a place that has almost as much space as one of Sebastian's hotels. There's a giant staircase in the centre in line with the front door, and the whole downstairs area is one massive room by the looks of it. I can't help but let my eyes trail like a slug sticking to every surface. There are thick brown leather sofas, a sweeping kitchen at the back that feels like it's a kilometre away on the left and–

'Melodie!' the woman next to me calls out.

She comes into view on the right of the stairs, inline with an enormous wooden dining table with tall chairs: Melodie. It's Melodie. She's wearing chic statement jewellery in a bright fuchsia and her lipstick, although faded, matches it perfectly. I wonder if she's ever not well put together. My simple dress and stud earrings seem a bit boring compared to her.

She rushes over to me with one hand curved on her swollen belly, the other outstretched towards me. 'Come in, come in! Thank you for coming. We've had dinner, but there will be cake soon.' She hasn't even said hello and she's offering me cake. She must be Greek at heart, the same as me.

The thought brings joy to my face, but I politely decline the offer. I still don't feel like eating. I came here to hide, to rebel, to find some different answers, a new narrative while my family at home work out how to undo the mistakes I've made, because they chose to hide my past from me for so long. I hadn't been trusted with the secrets that belong to the beginning of my own story, and now those secrets might be the undoing of everything.

I follow Melodie as she tells me everyone else is in the garden enjoying the last of the sun. It's been a perfect Easter Sunday, at least in terms of the weather.

Everyone greets me with polite nods, and Melodie does her best to put a name to each face. This isn't a normal Greek welcome into a family. No one kisses me or holds my hands or face. If anything, it's as though I've brought a bad smell into the place and no one wants to stand too close to me.

Lastly, Melodie points at the little boy from outside who is trailing behind us with his mother, Louise. 'And that is Angelos, Louise and Dimi's son.'

The boy looks up from the toy laptop and squints at me again. He says, 'Mummy, who *is* the woman who looks like Auntie Melodie?'

Everyone laughs and his mother squats down next to him to explain that I'm her sister.

'I have two sisters,' he tells me in a very confident voice. His says it like he is better than me, because he has two, as though family members are a competition of sorts.

'You are a lucky boy, I'm sure.' I smile. The atmosphere only breaks for a moment, then everyone is back to quiet tones and odd glances while Melodie has a big smile plastered onto her painted lips. 'Maybe I should go,' I whisper to her.

'No. Stay, please. I invited you here, stay.' Her hand moves towards me like she might take it, but I move it away. I can't have someone else grab my hand and hurt it all over again.

'Maybe we could go for a walk.' I've come this far after all. Maybe if we could just take a moment away from the crowd of people.

I indicate the side gate that leads past the house and back towards the cars at the front.

'No!' her husband, Anton, bellows. 'I mean, yes, but why not go for a walk around the garden? This part looks small, but we own far into the trees and beyond.'

Adrenaline spikes inside me at his strange reaction, making me want to run as far away as I can from this place. I don't. I'm not being chased away from my sister because yet another man doesn't want me to know her.

'I am happy to walk around the garden, if this is alright with you?'

Melodie nods enthusiastically and we begin to move away from the tall men and their much shorter women. Melodie and I are both much taller than the other women present.

We weave through lemon and olive trees. It's nothing like my garden at home. The first part here is quite neat, a little more like ours, I suppose, with flowers and grass and a patio, then they have a few trees for shelter and behind them, enough space for a swimming pool with a lawn around it that slopes up to swinging seats, and beyond that what looks like an entire olive grove.

We make our way towards the seat at the back of this section of their land. 'Your home is lovely,' I say. 'I like your pink door and frames.'

'Thank you. I think Gaia picked this house just for those.'

'Is that your daughter?'

'Sort of. She's my stepdaughter. Anton and I only got married last year.' She takes a breath and hisses it out between her teeth. 'I have a lot to tell you if you want to know about me and the people you're related to. But if you don't mind, I'd like to ask you a couple of things first.'

Chapter 53

As the sun begins to set, lights spring on around the garden, in the trees and edging the lawn. It looks magical, like a place made for fairies and elves to live.

I twist myself in the swinging seat to face Melodie. It's a little awkward being so close to her elbow. I wish I could sit opposite her and see her face full on, to absorb as much information as I possibly can from this conversation. It's better than nothing I suppose. It's a start.

I nod to encourage her to ask anything she likes. A pain shoots through my bruised hand. I don't want to draw attention to it, so I carefully clasp it within the other for a little extra warmth on the joints.

'What's your date of birth?'

This is an interesting question, since no one really knows the answer. No one I know anyway. Maybe Melodie knows it. All I know is, it's very likely I was found the same day I was born; no one can tell me for sure.

I pout my lips as I think how to word my answer. It's always easier to find the right words in Greek. I'm glad my English is strong.

'I do not know my real birthday. They had to guess that I was maybe one or two days old when I was found. I was what you call in English a foundling. I was left with a nasty note. They think my parents are English because the note was in English. Now I know it, of course, thanks to the DNA test and meeting you.'

Melodie exhales and her shoulders relax enough for her to sit a little more comfortably in the seat next to me. She obviously wanted to check I was who I said I was. Can't she see in my face I'm her sister? Her nephew was vocal enough about how similar we look. I'm the blonde, younger version of her. It's so obvious.

'Why did you want to find me?'

Another question I'd rather not go into in much detail. 'I only wanted to know where I came from.' It's true, that's how all this began, with the desire to know about my heritage. It's not my fault I'd been lied to about it, and I thought my family would be hundreds of miles from Corfu when I believed I was from Romania. I didn't expect to find any direct relations, even if part of me hoped for a sibling. The reality is, I thought I was at a safe enough distance that it would be like reading about them in a magazine. 'I love my family very much. But with no understanding why I was abandoned, I wanted to know. My parents told me from a young age that family is who you love and not who gave birth to you. I know this. But, I just wanted to know who I would have been or where I came from. I don't look very Greek.' I sweep my hand over my bright blonde hair, thinking how brightly it seems to shine so that everyone knows I'm not from around here.

'You look a lot like our mother,' Melodie says, 'and our grandmama, and me. You are blonde like Mum... like she was. She actually lightened her hair.'

'Was?'

Melodie takes a deep breath and exhales through her teeth. 'This is going to be a lot to take in, and I know it's going to sound...' She waves her hands in small circles. '...crazy. But it's all true. As true as I've been told and to the best of what I know. It might be hard to hear at times too, so if you want me to stop, then tell me, okay?'

I nod and swallow a lump that's formed in my throat. Melodie shuffles a little, as though settling in for a big story. I wish she would hurry up and spit it all out.

'When my, *our*, mother was sixteen, she had a boyfriend. An older boyfriend. One that took her to fancy places, and treated her nicely. His name was Adam. He's our father. The thing is, he wasn't that nice, and back then getting pregnant and not wanting to tell Grandmama and Grandpapa who the father was... Well, it caused a lot of problems. They knew nothing about her secret boyfriend. They were older parents themselves. Anyway, she was pregnant and they weren't happy about it, as you can imagine.' I can, easily. Mama would be burning with anger if I came home pregnant by a secret boyfriend. 'They grounded her, but by then she already knew Adam was no good.' Melodie frowns for a moment and looks down at her black dress ruffled over her knees. 'Wait, did she? Yes,' Melodie answers her own question, 'he had been very forceful at this point. Sorry, I don't want to muddle it all. Anyway, she gave birth to me and then as far as Grandmama and Grandpapa were concerned, she disappeared. Upped and left me, with a note posted through the door. Runaway. That was that. They tried to find her but as there was a note and she was sixteen, no authorities were that bothered, and they had to put their energy into looking after me. So...' Melodie looks up at the sky, and I follow her gaze. The moon is starting to show its face in the dimming light. 'God, this is such a lot,' she says. 'Okay, this bit does link in, so bear with me. We'd always holidayed in Greece, on different islands and different parts of Corfu. My, *our*, grandparents used to bring my mum, sorry... I did it again, *our* mum, here when she was younger too. They both passed away at the start of the pandemic. It broke me to lose them after not being able to see them for so long beforehand, or have a proper funeral. Sorry, that's not part of this story... anyway, I ended up coming here to Agios Stefanos as a way to connect to them again. That's when I had the pleasure of meeting Anton and Gaia. Here's where it gets...' she tilts her head from side to side in thought. 'Serendipitous. Thing is, Anton and Gaia used to live near this woman, Liliana. Gaia was sure she knew me from somewhere and had seen my face before. Then she realised that I looked like Liliana. You can imagine, I was so shocked. I literally fainted when she said the name Liliana! Anton had to scoop me up off the floor.' Melodie laughs a little at the memory before her expression turns thoughtful again.

'Seriously?'

'Seriously. You saw me yesterday. I don't think I deal well with surprises.'

'If it makes you feel better, when I saw our mother on the DNA website, I had a panic attack and couldn't breathe.'

'Well, you're dealing well with all this information now.'

'I suppose. I've had a lot of new information lately. I think I'm learning to deal with more and more.' Before Melodie can quiz me about this, and by the look on her face she wants to, I jump in.

'Am I getting this right, Liliana, our mother, went missing after you were born and you found her here? Many years later?'

'Pretty much.'

'So, what happened next?'

'Next? Oh, well, I went and found her. She looked like a short version of you. Look, I'll get a picture up.'

Melodie picks her phone up from next to her on the swinging seat and scrolls her images. 'Here.' She passes me the phone.

Two faces smile at me. One is Melodie and the other is Liliana, our mother. Her hair is very light, a white blonde to cover the grey at a guess. She has rosy tanned skin, like me. She does look a lot like me, like Melodie.

Something about seeing her face closes up my throat. Maybe I'm not as good at dealing with all of this as I thought. I can't let it in.

Melodie continues as I study the round eyes of the woman in the photo. 'She didn't want to tell me why she left me all those years ago, but eventually I got it out of her. He, Adam, had abducted her from our house in Cambridgeshire. He used to...' Melodie pauses, and even her hands fall still. She glances at me then back towards the twinkling lights in the garden. The lights make it look like a perfect place for children to play and hide with fairies and elves. I wish I could hide away, because the story Melodie is telling me is a nightmare. I always knew my past had to be ugly. I wasn't brought into this world with love. That was clear from the start. Or at least from finding out I was born in Corfu not Romania. I look back at the gentle woman on the screen. Zooming in, I can see a scar running from her eyebrow into her white-blonde hair that's tied back from her face.

'He used to hurt her, and... force himself on her. If you know what I mean.'

I nod. I understand well enough even if English isn't my first language. I wonder if he gave her that scar. Anger rushes through me and the back of my nose stings with the threat of tears. I lock the phone screen and pass it back.

A mixture of emotions and thoughts surges up inside me — sadness for my mother and what she must have gone through. I can tell that Melodie is holding back, not wanting to reveal the harsh reality of what she knows. I think of Sebastian. How I thought he was one thing only to find that he was something else. He's never forced himself on me, which I'm grateful for, quite the opposite in fact. Keeping me as his pure princess. But that's not to say he wouldn't. I never thought he would do or say some of the things he has done. I have no idea what he is really capable of. Perhaps we never really know who people are and who they can be.

'Then, she got pregnant with you. She told me that she managed to hide it from him for a long time. I think she tried to keep herself slim, and wear baggy clothing. Anyway, when he found out, when it was impossible to hide anymore—' Melodie pinches the bridge of her nose. 'I'm sorry. This must be really hard for you to hear. Bloody hell, it's hard for me to say.' Her voice cracks and my chest aches at the sound of it. Her tone softens as though this might help with the harsh words. 'He beat her half to death to try and get rid of you. She was in and out of consciousness and when she eventually did come round, he said you had died, that you were a boy and that he had buried you at the bottom of the garden.'

My ears begin to ring and I'm glad I'm sitting down. The gentle movement of the swing chair suddenly makes me nauseous. I knew I couldn't have come from anything good, not with the note that was left, but this? This is unthinkable. This is a gut-wrenching car crash of a start to my life.

'I'm so sorry. I think he wanted her all to himself. There wasn't room for anything or anyone else. That's all I can imagine anyway. He was possessive with her. I guess Mum was further along than she had thought because here you are!' She exhales with a strained smile on her lips and tears reflecting the fairy lights of the garden and the crimson of the sunset.

'Thank you for telling me.' I can barely recognise the words as my own, not just because I'm speaking English but because my voice is twisted into knots.

'I will do my best to answer your questions, but I only met our mum a handful of times before she died.'

'How did she die?'

'Oh bloody hell, that was really what you asked at the start wasn't it? Sorry. It's like I had to get everything out to get here. She had a brain tumour. It was very sudden. She'd been looking for you after finding clues you might not have died after all. I found it a bit hard going to understand it all at times. Some of the things she told me were very different to what she had written down. I think she had days that were worse than others. She didn't tell me about the tumour. She didn't tell me the truth about looking for you either. She only told me Adam's version of the truth, that you were a boy and had passed away. She really was looking for you when she did that DNA test. It's all written in her diaries. She'd have done anything to see you.' A single tear falls from Melodie's hazel eyes, quickly followed by another.

'How did they end up in Corfu if she was abducted in England?'

'He travelled for work, and because she holidayed here as a girl, she persuaded him it would be a good place to settle. She always hoped that by magic she would see her mum and dad here on holiday. She waited over twenty years and it didn't happen. But eventually, I found her because she was here. So maybe not serendipity after all. She'd been waiting long enough to be found.'

'And what of our father? Adam? Is he still alive?'

Melodie shakes her head. 'No. He died a few years before Mum.'

I don't ask to see a photo of him. She might not even have one. If she does, I don't want to see it. He's better off a faceless ghost than putting an image in my head I'll have to live with. One day maybe I'll be able to look at a picture, but not today. I've already had the longest day of my life. My muscles ache and my hand throbs. Adrenaline and lack of sleep are wearing me down quicker than the sea can wear down chalk.

'Liliana. It's good to have her name at least.' I recall her face in my mind's eye instead of thinking about his. 'It only says "LP" on the website.' I pick at my nail to avoid looking at Melodie for fear I'll crack and break and maybe never be able to put the pieces back together. 'When Liliana came up as my DNA mother, I was in shock to find her so easily. As though she had been there waiting for me. I contacted her, but she never answered. With only "LP" to go on I could not find her. She could have been anywhere in the whole world. I thought she must really not want me.'

I don't know what feels worse: to know she would have kept me, but that I was taken away by my evil father, or feeling completely dejected for over a year because I thought she didn't want me. No. This is worse. Knowing she died before I could show her that I was alright. I can't imagine how that must have felt.

'Then you appeared,' I continue, 'my sister. You at least registered with a full name, and I found you on social media right away. The last pictures were here in Corfu. Greenwood is not a common name on the island, so you were easy to find.'

I smile, a deep genuine smile because I have the truth in my hands and a sister who seems like she might be normal after all. 'I am sad Liliana passed before I could meet her.' Sad is an understatement, but if I pull at that thread of emotions now, it'll soon unravel me. 'Do I sound bad to say I'm pleased she was not just ignoring me?' This is the only positive I can find in all this. That at least she hadn't ignored me after all.

'No, I know what you mean. She really did only sign up to the DNA site in the hope of finding you.' Melodie hesitates, shuffling her weight on the chair, making it rock back and forth. 'I need to explain why I closed the door on you.'

'It's not a problem. I should never have turned up without hearing from you first. Afterwards, I realised your husband had been missing. It must have been too much. I see that.'

'I wish that's all it was.' Melodie rests her hands on her belly. 'We have a sister. A half-sister, named Evangelina.'

A choked laugh splutters out of me. 'Wow.'

'She is our father's daughter. He had an affair with someone near Athens. That's a story for a different day. It's very complicated... When I met her, she was squatting in their old house.'

Squatting... I search my mind to understand this word. Melodie must have read my thoughts because she rephrases. 'She was living there when she shouldn't have been. She broke into Liliana's house and stayed there. She told me so many lies. She let me believe her name was Keres.'

'That was the name they gave me on the note left with me.'

She nods. 'Well, all she really wanted was to divide and conquer. To take any inheritance money she could from my mother and from my grandparents. Sorry–, *our* mother, *our* grandparents. I promise I'll try to get that right! Evangelina was pretending to be you and poisoning Gaia. She even pushed Anton down a mountain near Old Perithia. That's why he was missing. She is crazy, and if you ever meet her, run away. She is much too much like our father.'

I can't find any words. Not one. How can this be what I come from? I've had so many peaceful loving years. What if Liliana and Adam had kept me? Would he have beaten me too? He really did try to kill me after all. It could've all been so different. I never knew how lucky I truly was until today.

The silence of thought is only filled by birdsong, the chirping of insects and the rustling of the olive trees in the breeze.

'I can understand why you did not want to see me now. You were afraid I might be like her.'

A white feather floats down between us, defying the natural laws by ignoring the breeze that's moving my hair and the leaves. It falls completely straight. We both look up to see if there's a bird overhead. Nothing. It's as though it appeared for us to see it. Pure and white.

'Theadora, I hope we can at least be friends.'

I look at her and as I speak, I can't believe my own words. 'Call me Dora.' No one calls me Dora, only Dinos. 'Would you send me that image of you with our mother?'

'Of course, you'll need to give me your number first, though.'

Chapter 54

I didn't stay much after the explanation of my beginnings. I need time to take it all in, to formulate new questions. But we have promised to see each other again soon, and Melodie sent me the photo of her and Liliana.

I know I shouldn't have gone there, shouldn't have removed myself from all that was happening at home. It certainly wasn't the sort of distraction I was expecting. Not in the least. My brain and body tingle like I've been crushed under a dreadful weight, leaving me with a dreadful sensation of pins and needles.

The closer I get to home, the slower I go. I now have all of this information to share with my family. More dirty truths we could do without. I'm not hiding it though. I'm not hiding anything anymore, except for the truth about Sebastian; that's wholly different though. I don't think it would be fair to lay out my pathetic love life for them on top of everything else.

I pull in through our gates and into the drive. Agatha and Ria's car is still there. Every time I close my eyes, I can hear my mum screaming, 'Don't you dare leave!' But I did. I left. I ran. It's always my stupid compulsion, to disappear and process it all alone. Or to find someone to distract me.

When I enter the house, the gentle hum of conversation in the living room halts.

'Thank goodness you're home.' Mama throws a blanket off her knees and charges towards me with open hands. Grabbing my face, she holds me close enough that I'm confronted by her tear-stained cheeks and bloodshot eyes.

Before I left, I'd been hit with so many questions I couldn't pick one out. There was only the sound of anger and hurt. I layered apologies over them all and an attempt at an explanation. All they wanted to know was what I'd said, and they were so devastated at the answers, I pushed past Ria and left my mother collapsed on the floor.

'Where have you been? You left us and we have all been so worried.'

'For me or for yourselves?' That was too harsh. It came out too harsh. There's too much trauma jumping around in my head, making my body course with adrenaline, and all I want to do is run away again. As soon as the words pass my lips, I wish I could bite them back. But it's too late now.

Mama's hands drop from my face and her lip trembles until she bites it, shaking her head.

'For you, Theadora mou.' She walks back to the couch, and I put my keys away.

I turn back to face everyone in the room. I linger close to the door. Agatha is to my right sitting in the armchair, Ria is kneeling in front of the piano on a thick cushion and Mama and Baba are on the couch. Except for the expressions on their faces, it would be easy to believe that they are having a nice chat late on Easter Sunday. Enjoying the spoils and festivities of the day. But the tension in their mouths and foreheads tells of people deep in anguish.

'I've been—' A lie nearly falls out of me like a blunt and ghastly stone on the floor, but I stop myself and start again. No more lies. 'I've been to see Melodie.' Side glances pass like a wave around the room. 'She told me about how I came to be on the island and how she did.'

Emotions smack me in the face all at once. I choke and splutter, pressing my hands to my face to hide them. It's impossible. My shoulders slump and my chest trembles. I kept it together so well with Melodie, but now I'm with my people it all floods out of me.

Forgetting that I left them to pick up the pieces of my stupidity, of our collective stupidity, my family lead me to the armchair in front of the window and carefully sit me down. They stroke my hair, and words of comfort and questions rattle around under my heaving sobs. We are a family born in love, not blood.

It's Mama that I can hear over it all. 'Come on, my child, we are here. We will always be here for you.'

That's the truth. That's more important than all the lies, half-truths and secrets I've been drowning myself in. There is love here.

'Here.' Theía Agatha waves tissues over my lap for me to see with my head angled at my lap.

I gladly take them and do my best to calm my breathing. In my head I think of Dinos telling me to focus on him, to breathe and to think about the stars that are always up there, unchanged. He is out there, but there's no way he is unchanged. He's changed me. Made me better... made me worse.

'What happened?'

'My–' I falter. I don't want to say *mother*. She wasn't my mother, even if that wasn't her fault. My mother is here, in our comfy living room with our photos and nick-nacks. The woman who spent hours brushing my hair, brushing my teeth, feeding me up, pushing me to be better at school – she is my mother, and no one else ever could be. 'Liliana, the woman who gave birth to me. Melodie told me her story, the overview at least. It was...' I swallow on a dry throat as words escape me. Which one do I pick? 'It was worse than I could've expected.'

I look away from my knees for the first time in minutes. Baba is standing to the left with Ria while Mama and Agatha have both dropped to their knees like bookends. Mama hates getting down on the floor, always groaning, *it's not the getting down, it's the getting up again,* but she'd do anything to be there for me.

'I'm sorry, Theadora.' Theía Agatha grips my knee.

I do my best to retell the things Melodie told me. She was young, Liliana, although I can't remember how old Melodie said she was, and her boyfriend abducted her leaving Melodie's biological grandparents to bring her up.' I begin to doubt myself, rubbing at my throbbing temples.

'He did try to kill me. Tried to make her miscarry, but I lived. Melodie seemed to think she wasn't conscious, and he told her I died at birth.'

It's the micro movements in a situation like this that tell everything a person is thinking. It's in the way Agatha looks away, and Mama's nostrils flare. The way Baba's hands curl into fists and Ria shakes her head.

'All the children we lost,' Mama's voice is as thick and spitting as burning damp wood, 'and he tries to force that poor woman to lose her child. And then, when you are strong and you live, he throws you away. Where is he now?' She growls as though if I know his location she will leave and take the axe from the shed and hunt him down herself.

'Dead,' I quickly snap. 'They've both passed away. That's why my–, Liliana never replied to my message. She died before reading it, according to Melodie.'

Then there's a void of speech, a void of life, because everyone has to process this information just as I have.

'I'm sorry I left when you all needed me here. I felt so guilty for sending that email. I'd do anything to undo it. Anything.' Tears begin to gather in my eyelashes again.

'We know,' Ria soothes. 'We think we can sort this out somehow. We'll find a way. Do you think we could look at the email you sent?'

'Sure, I put my phone on the side near the keys when I came in. This dress doesn't have pockets.' I smooth my hands over the lemon cotton dress with mild disappointment.

Ria retrieves my phone from the shelf by the stairs, and it doesn't take me long to find the email. I don't send many emails.

Dear Ms Karagiannis
Thank you for the message you left me. I'm sorry it's taken me so long to return the email. I am the "Keres" baby that was found in 2003. I would like to know any details you may have of my adoption.Thank you,Theadora Makris

'I thought it would be worse,' Ria muses.

'How can it be worse?' I look up at her as she paces the floor.

'It could be a joke, or a dare.' Ria stops and points at me with only her index finger before waggling it. 'There's no evidence.'

'You must know Maria,' I direct at Agatha. 'Will she follow this up?'

'I don't know.' Agatha's shoulders rise and fall. 'We're not exactly close. We only come together for board meetings and it's all very standard.'

'We need Theadora to apologise,' Ria continues. 'For an inappropriate prank on her theía's place of work.'

'I don't suppose this is a good time to tell you, but I've invited Melodie and her husband to lunch next week. She knows I'm the Keres baby. She knows the truth. Even if I lie to the charity board, by telling them my email was a prank, and even if they believe it, what's to stop someone somewhere telling them the truth? Either on purpose or by accident?'

'How can they prove otherwise? How could they prove you're the Keres baby? You might've read about her somewhere and known it was me who retrieved her.' Agatha's voice is pleading, as though we have some kind of say over what people believe.

'It could make them look at the paperwork we falsified in Athens. The paperwork is... questionable. Things were very different back then. Things have changed a lot in the past twenty years.' Theía Agatha stands up from the floor and helps Mama up too. Mama dusts herself off to recapture her dignity, where Agatha doesn't care. She works with the kids on the farm. She tells me all about it, how she's always up about in the dirt and running from place to place. I'm sure kneeling on our tiles is nothing to her.

'Maybe you could misplace it? It's been twenty years.' Baba leans his hand on my chair.

Agatha and Ria look at each other, and they have an entire conversation in complete silence. How could I not see them as a couple sooner? It's so obvious. Only people who have been together intimately can do this, the ones who've spent time studying each other's face until they know every word that's being said behind their eyes.

Agatha says, 'Maybe. Let's hope it doesn't come to that. Let's hope they accept this apology Theadora is going to write. What do you think, little one?'

'Let's get it sent.'

Maybe. Maybe a plan is forming to undo some of the mess I've caused.

Chapter 55

A week sitting in the shop is my punishment, which isn't too different to usual. An unnoticeable punishment for going behind their backs. There are worse fates. No one has frozen me out. In fact, quite the opposite. Once Theía Agatha and Ria left, Mama and Baba came up to my room to play *tsougrisma*, the game of hitting together eggs dyed a shiny red to see whose will break first. Usually, we would have played it much earlier on Easter Sunday, but the eggs had been forgotten with everything that had happened.

We played in my room, tapping one egg onto the other to see which one would withstand the blow. I won. It was nice, strangely normal and we all settled into smiles. Mama and Baba had kissed my head and reassured me that no matter what happens, it's not my fault. I was born into this mess. They couldn't be more sorry about it all.

Sebastian crashed his car on Tuesday, so I haven't seen him since he nearly broke my hand. No one was hurt in his accident, not even his pride, I'm sure. Apparently Xristina was there; I think she must have been with Konstantinos. Sebastian called me ranting about the car, and how it has to go to the garage and how he has to pay for the damage out of his own money this time. I couldn't care less.

Today our shop will be closed all day so that we can get ready for Melodie and Anton, and receive them for lunch. I thought about telling Sebastian about it, but he went on and on so much that I didn't bother to. I let him rant while I got on with things about the house. We continue to message each morning to check in on each other. Enough to know we are still alive but not all that much more. I wish he would be done with me already.

Mama and I spend the morning in the kitchen waltzing around each other to make every possible dish we can fit on the table outside.

'We must make them welcome,' Mama says every so often. It's not really to me, if anything, it sounds like she's talking to the food as though it has to know the part it will play in making the day special. Melodie and Anton know everything; they knew about me before I knew about me. Well, they knew about baby me. *Keres* me. Now we will have to find the right time to ask them for silence should anyone start questioning who I am. We can't have anyone connecting me to baby me, to *Keres* me.

We all agreed it was a priority to make Melodie and Anton feel welcome in our home. To welcome them as family, which we always do with guests, but this is as though royalty is visiting.

Baba comes in from tidying the garden to wash his hands. 'Theadora mou, they'll be here soon enough. Do you think we will be able to ask about your other sister today? She must know the truth too if she was pretending to be you.'

Mama slams the oven door shut and drops a hot tray of freshly cooked fish on the hob.

'Why had we not thought of this sooner? This isn't going to work. It's a mess. It's all a mess. This other sister, she could come along and ruin it all.' Mama almost throws off the oven gloves before pacing the tiles.

'Zeta mou, that's enough. One step at a time. Theadora says these are good people. They won't turn us in.'

'But the other sister—' Mama is cut off by the doorbell chiming around the house. From our faces, anyone would think it was a death knell being rung.

Mama dusts her hands on her apron before removing it and putting on a bold smile.

'We are Greek, we will feed them until they love us. Now, *káni ti pápia.*' *To do like the duck* — a typical Greek phrase that Mama rarely uses. It's more one of Baba's. He would say it when I was little. If we made a big mess with toys, he would joke that we must be quiet so that we weren't blamed for it. He would tell me to act innocent by saying *káni ti pápia. To do like the duck*. As a child I always wondered what ducks were hiding behind those sleek feathers.

As soon as Melodie and Anton appear with a bunch of flowers for Mama and compliments for our home, everything seems to fizzle away – all the fear, all the urgent pains in my stomach. I know everything will be alright. There's something in Melodie's face, and not just that it looks so much like mine; she's open. Open, and easy to read. If she's upset or happy I doubt she could hide anything from anyone. This thought warms me until it doesn't, and I'm left with the fear that this openness might mean she would not be able to hold in a secret after all.

I truly hope I'm wrong.

Chapter 56

The table is more stuffed than a plate of dolmades, which, incidentally, also feature on the menu. Mama loves stuffed vine leaves and uses her herbs differently to anyone else on the island, so she has always told me. There's also the fish, bright salads picked from the garden and Mama's special beetroot dip in the centre of the table; the purple is so bright it's almost pink. The only thing we didn't have time to make was the bread, but Baba was under strict instructions to get the best bread from the bakers early this morning.

Conversation runs smoothly. There's only a brief mention of Liliana. Mama handles it perfectly and elegantly, saying I'd relayed what Melodie had told me and she is sorry for our mother. Melodie seems to appreciate this genuine sorrow, but we keep the conversation moving. Today isn't the day for sorrow over the past. It's a day for building trust in these two strangers.

We don't know each other. All we have in common is a history, an ancestor, we don't even share in memory. What I do enjoy is hearing about Melodie's childhood with our grandparents and their holidays in Corfu.

Both Melodie and Anton seem to want to get to know who I am, and what I do. They constantly bring the conversation back to my ideas or feelings. They're well meaning, both of them listening to my answers with bright smiles, but I can't help but feel like I don't know who I am or what I'm doing. I'm taking an online English course, because with everything that's happened, I still haven't applied for my passport, let alone made any other travel arrangements. Although, I'm still hopeful.

Melodie is just about to finish her food when the doorbell rings in the distance. My mind scrambles with thoughts as to who it might be. Then it hits me like an electric shock. It's Sebastian. I look at my watch. It is. It's him. I haven't even told him about seeing Melodie again. Knocking echoes from the depths of the house.

'I am so sorry. I forgot to remind Sebastian that I couldn't drive him today. I must go and tell him.' My chair scrapes along the floor and I catch a twitch from Melodie out of the corner of my eye before I sprint into the kitchen.

When he crashed his car, I agreed to take him to one of the hotels for work today. With everything going on, I completely forgot to tell him I couldn't.

As I reach the door my hands tremble, and my mouth is as dry as sand.

I pull the door open and begin to apologise before even saying hello.

'Wait, wait.' He smiles at me like he used to, with softly turned-up lips. 'What's wrong?' His tone is sickly-sweet.

I step back, letting him into the living room, and I snatch a breath to calm my raging pulse. It's all okay. He takes my hands and kisses them, cooing to calm me.

'Theadora mou, what's happened? Where are your parents?'

'Outside... My, my sister, Melodie, is here. I'm so sorry. I forgot to tell you I can't take you to work today. Is there someone else who can do it? I'm so sorry!'

'Outside?' Sebastian lowers his voice. 'With that woman and her husband? I thought I said I didn't want them in our lives. Now what should I do? Konstantinos dropped me off here on his way to work. There's no one else to take me.'

'I'll find someone. I can message Xristina. She's not working today.'

Sebastian's grip tightens on my hand. I snatch it away, but his hand jumps higher and tugs on my wrist. I gasp through my teeth at the strength of his fingers on my fragile arm.

'Please! I'm sorry!' I squeak into his ear as he groans and swears under his breath. His fingers bite down harder. 'Sorry, sorry, sorry!'

The sound of movement in the kitchen is enough for him to unclamp me and turn to leave, slamming the door behind him.

Without even thinking, I pull down my sleeve over the hot patch on my wrist. It's already red and I can't risk it being seen.

'Are you alright?'

I physically jump at the clarity of Melodie's voice. Even though I'd heard some movement, a small part of me didn't believe someone was actually there.

I turn and smile to reassure her. Please say she didn't see what happened. I can't risk there being any problems between us. My whole family depends on me creating a strong bond with her, and her agreeing to keep our secrets. I don't want her to think anything bad of me or this dreadful situation.

'I'm fine.' A thin laugh passes my lips. I sound pathetic. I feel pathetic. 'How long were you standing there for?'

'Not long.'

Relief rolls over my spine and down to my toes.

'Sorry. Sebastian had forgotten that you would be here. He isn't sure how he will get to work now. It's my fault. I should have been more clear.' He forgot because I didn't tell him. None of this was actually his fault. I've probably just added to the trouble he'll be in with his parents and grandparents after crashing the car they gifted him. I snap out of my thoughts. 'Were you looking for me?'

'Oh, no. The baby is on my bladder again.' Melodie rubs her protruding bump, and a soft smile spreads across her face.

She's too easy to read. There is an unease that wasn't there before. Maybe she did see more than she said.

Returning her smile, I pass her and head towards my parents.

I wish I could say something to them, but obviously I can't. Firstly, Anton is out there with them, and secondly, I don't want them to worry for me. Sebastian is mostly kind and caring, in his own way. He's just got a childish streak, that's all. When he doesn't get his own way, he stamps his feet and doesn't care about the toys that get crushed. I just wish I wasn't his biggest plaything.

'Is everything well?' Mama is back speaking in Greek now that Melodie has left the table.

'Yes, sorry. I was meant to take Sebastian to work as his car is being fixed. I forgot, and he's gone to find someone else to take him.'

'What is it you do again, Anton? Melodie has told us about her work in social media, although I'm still not sure I understand it. I think I'm too old for all that.' Mama tilts her head at Anton. Everything about her is poised and elegant. No one could read that she might have any residual fear underneath her calm manner.

Anton exhales and stretches himself out before apologising for stepping on my father under the table with his incredibly long legs.

'I used to buy and renovate houses with my first wife then rent them out or sell them. When she passed away, I stopped the renovations and kept a few to rent. I like to help people out if they need me. People often call me up when everyone else is too busy to help. It's a hobby, doing odd jobs or picking things up with my van. It's nice to be useful.'

'Does Gaia like to be involved?' Baba takes Mama's hand in his and for a split second I'm envious. When I was a child, I could sit between them and be comforted. My wrist is tingling with the imprint of Sebastian's fingers lingering there. I could burst with the urge to cry. I've finally got a sister, something I've always wanted, and I can't relax and get to know her as I'd like, because everything has got me in a stranglehold, ripping at my emotions.

'No, no. Gaia works in a restaurant called Greek Secret for her best friend's family. She likes to be independent and earn her own money. She knows her own mind.'

'It would be lovely to meet her. It's wonderful to have you both here. I know it means so much to our Theadora mou. Finding she has a sister, and putting together her story, it's part of a very challenging journey. But hopefully we are finding a happy ending here.' Mama glances away towards the house. Melodie walks through the double doors and back to the table, moving cautiously with her bump.

Mama returns to English now Melodie is back. Snatching her hand from Baba's, she presses it to her heart. 'Melodie, we are saying how lovely it is to have you both here. We must meet Gaia next time.'

'That would be lovely. It would be nice to officially be introduced to Sebastian, too.' His name is enough to bring acid to the back of my throat and for my wrist to throb.

Please don't bring him into it.

My hand is a lot better now. It must've been sprained by him and not broken, but it still isn't right yet.

Mama, please don't agree to him being a part of this! Please! I stare at her, hoping my words will end up in her mind.

'Mmm, yes. That would be nice. Sebastian is from a good family.' Mama rests her chin on her hand, and returns her other hand to Baba's on the table. She clearly didn't hear my cry for help, or, if she did, she chose to ignore me.

'That's nice to hear. I don't know anything about him. How old is he?' This is an interrogation. Melodie might have the sweetest smile, and her soft light brown eyes might be innocently glittering in the sun, but I can see through it. Who asks a person's age like that? No one. He is a grown man; she doesn't need to know more.

'He's twenty-eight,' I say, and hide behind my water, sipping at it. I don't want to add that soon he'll be twenty-nine.

'Was he the one in Corfu Town?' Anton nods at me before picking up a piece of baklava and placing it onto his plate.

I smile and nod, trying to embody enthusiasm and bashfulness for the man I love. God, I pray I'm pulling this off. Am I as open as Melodie? Surely not. Phoebe and Dinos can both tell by my nose when I lie. That's different though. They've known me forever. And anyway, with Melodie, it's not that there's a tell. There's a shift in her whole body, something I can't place my finger on. It's almost akin to poor acting. Almost as though, now she has something else on her mind, her body has become stiff and unnatural.

'How long have you been together?'

Melodie mimics Anton and places some baklava on her plate. She presses her lips together as she looks it over. I'm sure she doesn't even want it, not from the look on her face. It's something to hide behind. Please let me be overthinking! Perhaps worry has sent me mad. I'm so out of touch with reality I have no idea about anything anymore. I'm probably wrong, and these questions are surely the result of wanting to get to know me better.

'A couple of years now.' I scan the dishes on the table, looking for something to choose. It's like trying to settle on one of the thoughts in my head, and all of it is making me dizzy.

'Melodie mou, are you okay?' Anton leans towards Melodie.

Her skin has turned sour, almost yellow, and her breathing has become visible in her chest, puffing in and out.

'I think I've eaten too much. The baby's kicking. It's giving me heartburn. I'm so sorry, but I think we should be going.' She slides back her chair and it's like nails on a blackboard.

'We must do this again soon, though, yes? I know Dora is very excited to have a sister,' Mama says as she leads the way to the house. Melodie smiles behind her, but she's clinging to Anton like she's not sure of her steps. 'Next time we will invite Sebastian and Gaia.'

'I would very much like that,' Melodie beams before we all kiss cheeks to say goodbye.

Now I'm left with the dread of telling Sebastian that not only have I invited *that woman* into my life, but he has to be a part of it now too.

Chapter 57

The door closes with Mama's hand lingering on it as though she has to stay there to hold it closed for fear that Melodie and Anton might come back. The sound of their car moving out of the driveway is the signal that all is clear.

'They seem nice.' She turns to face us. 'They were trying hard, I like that. Beautiful flowers too.'

A large bunch of flowers the colours of a sunrise are now pride of place on the kitchen table. An effort was made. They tried to make polite conversation, and answered questions.

'How much money does he have that he works to pass the time?' Baba walks back towards the kitchen. 'Anyone want a glass of water?'

'Oh, a lot! Of money I mean, not water. Although, actually, yes please, I would like a glass.' I stop in my tracks and add, 'You should see their house. It must be at least three times the size of ours.'

'Yes, please, Marios mou. No, in fact, I think I'll have another glass of wine.'

Baba opens the fridge to get the wine then hovers at the fridge door waving the bottle slightly. 'And that car. Did you see that car? Bright yellow convertible. It was a Mustang, wasn't it?'

'It's garish,' Mama sneers, propping herself up on the counter.

'At least they aren't those people who talk about what they have all day long. They aren't those look-at-me types.' I think about Sebastian. He's a look-at-me type.

'No, that's very true,' Mama nods. 'They seemed to ask a lot of questions.'

'Too many questions?' Baba pulls a fresh glass from the overhead cupboard, his fingers lingering on the silver handle.

'No.' My face crumples into a frown. 'I don't think so, do you?'

Mama and Baba shake their heads to reassure each other.

'No, no. Not too many. They were more interested in Theodora, don't you think? Theodora, will you help me bring in the plates and leftovers?'

'Sure.'

I follow Mama out into the blinding sun again as we continue discussing the Greenwoods, while we collect the plates.

'You two look so much alike. You're prettier, of course. You even have some mannerisms alike. Given that you didn't grow up together I find that most surprising. I mean, look at Agatha and me. We look nothing alike! Do you like how similar you look? Or does it bother you to look at someone and see so much of yourself?'

I scrape leftovers off a plate more slowly as I ponder whether or not I am bothered by it. I guess I can't be, otherwise I'd be able to answer straight away.

'I hadn't thought of it like that. I knew right away when I saw her photo that we looked alike, but no. I like it. I like the idea of having a sister.'

We carry empty plates and glasses to the house before all settling round the table indoors.

'I think we can trust them.' I sit tall, flicking my hair off my shoulder, and announce this with the confidence of someone armed with facts that I don't possess. I falter. 'What do you think?'

'We have little choice,' Mama says into her wine.

'There's always a choice, but I think Theadora has made it for us. You like Melodie and you want to keep seeing her. Getting to know her.' Baba raises an eyebrow as if to say, *I'm right, right*?

'That's why we have no choice.' Mama raises her wine glass to him. 'If you didn't like her, we could call her a liar if she didn't do as we asked. As it is, we are lucky. I think we have found people we can trust.'

I nod a little too enthusiastically. I want us to be able to trust them. I want an older sister I can chat to about things — maybe about Dinos and Sebastian. I adore my family, but having more people to love and welcome into my life can only be a good thing. I've felt so far away from everyone lately. With Phoebe gone and Xristina off with god knows who, I feel so disconnected. The only person I've felt I could talk to who wasn't my parents is Dinos, and now I can't even see him anymore.

I still have other friends, people I talk to when we are out in groups, but it's not the same as people my own age I can connect with. Melodie isn't my age, I think she's in her early thirties, but that's thirty years younger than Mama and Baba.

Sitting here, in the kitchen I've sat in my whole life, with only the occasional change of tiles and doors, it strikes me how lonely I've become at a time when I thought I would be surrounded by people and new friends.

University or not, I need to go and see the world this winter. Once we have sorted all of this... mess, I'm going to do something, anything, with my life.

Chapter 58

Melodie messaged me to invite us all to a meal in a couple of days. The invitation has been extended to Sebastian. Every time I think about it, I feel a little ill. Mama quizzed me about how much Sebastian knows. I couldn't exactly say *less than Dinos*. We've decided to make sure conversations at this meeting are kept simple. If anyone tries to talk too much in any direction, we must divert it, and once this meeting is over, I need to speak to Melodie and trust her with the secret of my adoption, or lack of adoption. It's the only way we can move forward safely.

Late last night, after talking about Melodie and Anton at length, I needed water. I crept out of my bedroom and paused, as always, at the photos. Mama and Baba's door was open a crack.

It's not like I was trying to listen in, but I heard Mama suggest we could move to a different island and start again if it turns out we can't trust them. Even she's wanting to run away. I wanted to burst in and ask whether we could take Dinos with us. Baba started to talk her down, even saying I have a life to lead with Sebastian as a reason not to leave. If only they knew.

As I eventually lay back in bed, I felt the warmth of gratitude for my parents. Even now, they would change their entire life, their business, everything, for me. Baba might have talked Mama out of it, but he didn't disagree with the idea as a worst case. He just reassured her that it wouldn't come to that.

I feel lucky to have them as my parents, but also lucky to have a sister. I don't know her well enough yet, only well enough to know I want to know her more.

It's strange, because I can tell people I have a sister, but to do that, I want to mention I was born here in Corfu. Then I feel I need to explain how it is she lives here too. Coincidence? Well... sort of. Corfu was a place she had holidayed with her, *our*, grandparents. It's also a place they took Liliana, our mother, on holiday, I think. Yes, that's what she said, I'm sure. It's so complicated I'm not sure I've got it right, late at night when I replay it in my mind. I'm sure I've got it wrong. It feels like all I have are dreams and restless nights while my brain tries to work through this gigantic puzzle.

I stifle a yawn just thinking about last night's dreams and lack of sleep before I shiver against the warmth of the evening. Did our "real" father bring our "real" mother here? Or did she ask him to? Was it luck? Was it judgement? There's so much to take in. I feel so trapped by the web of lies stemming from my own abduction that it's hard to keep track of Liliana's much more traumatic one.

Mine at least was a welcome abduction. But people could see it as an abduction none the less if they find out. I was stolen, after all. I've never been adopted, and on paper, I was born to my parents. They broke the law. It's my face and my genetics that tell the truth.

Phoebe came home for Easter, but with all her family obligations, this is the first time I'll be seeing her. I march towards the harbour where we are meeting. I'm set to be early, but I can't wait to feel normal again, with the three of us back together at last. Things haven't been the same without her here. I didn't realise how much she gelled Xristina and me together until she wasn't there anymore. I have so much to tell them, and so much I'm not allowed to.

As I walk past all the familiar bustling shops and bars lining my way, a sense of calm layers over my skin. Mama, Baba and Melodie have all agreed I can tell people she's my sister, only Melodie doesn't know how blurry I need to keep the lines of the truth.

I pass palm trees and twisted olive trees dotted in front of whitewashed walls that line the smooth grey slabs of the road. As I turn towards the Old School Taverna, Dinos and his pa step out in front of me.

'Theadora! How are you?' Manolis booms out. 'I hope you're keeping well. How are your parents? You need to remind your father he owes me a game of *tavli*!'

'They're very well, thank you. I'll make sure to tell him.' My eyes are locked onto Manolis to stop myself from consuming the sight of Dinos. He's in faded shorts and a tatty linen shirt. His short curly hair is a dreadful mess. I wish it mattered. I wish I hated this grubby version of him, straight from work, but I don't. If anything, I want him more. It's the real him, the wild unkempt him. I want to kiss his mouth and beg him to run away with me again. It's only been eleven days since we were last together. Eleven. Two hundred and sixty four hours... ish.

'And you, are you well?' he continues.

'I am, thank you. I hope you are well, and Maria and Anna.'

'Yes, yes. They're both very well.'

'I've actually found I have a sister.'

'What?! A sister? Your parents are a bit old to still be adopting, no?'

I begin to laugh but before I can explain Dinos cuts in. 'What? What the hell has happened? Are you okay?' Dinos was hiding behind his father's shoulder, hanging back politely. Now he's almost pushing him out of the way to get to me.

'I'm fine. I'll have to explain another time.' I turn to his pa. 'She's not adopted. I found her through a DNA test. It's a long and complicated story, but it turns out I have a British sister. She seems really nice.'

Dinos's black eyebrows have shifted into high arches and his mouth is twisted into complete confusion.

'Why don't you tell Dinos all about it? I'll just be next door to discuss some prices. We've had a very good catch today — some octopus and bream. Nice to see you, Theadora.'

Dinos and I stand looking at each other in silence as Manolis walks towards the tavernas. People move around us on the street.

'I'm meeting Phoebe and Xristina.'

'I'm surprised you weren't out with them last night. I was hoping you would show up. Sebastian was there.'

I feel a stab of jealousy in my chest. Not that Sebastian was out without me, but that my girls were. 'Where?'

'It doesn't matter. You're here now. What happened with Melodie?'

'Theadora?' Phoebe's voice cuts over us from a distance.

'Can we meet, please?' I look up at Dinos as he pushes his fingers through his black curls.

'Are you still with Sebastian?' His voice is low and cutting.

I don't answer. We hold each other's gaze longer than we should.

I turn towards Phoebe and the boats bobbing on the sea. I glance to check for cars before sprinting towards the middle of the roundabout and the stumpy palm tree, then check again and run towards her.

I sprint across the road and wrap her up in my arms. '*Yassas*!'

As we spin round laughing, I catch sight of Dinos looking at us from the other side of the roundabout before turning back in the direction his father disappeared in.

I ask Phoebe a deluge of questions, although mostly I already know the answers. We message and keep up to date, so I know she loves what she's doing and is happy, but I ask again about her theatre course all the same. It's different face to face.

'We might as well go. Xristina isn't coming.' Phoebe purses her lips.

'What? Why?' My hands lock to my hips. I feel like stamping my foot in protest.

'She says she's not well. But it's okay. I'm looking forward to us seeing each other. The last time was cut short.'

'I know. I wish I could explain. I guess I can now a little.'

We walk towards the double bay for a stroll and I tell her all about Melodie, or as much as I can. When she begins to ask questions, I realise I either can't answer them because I don't know the answers myself, or, if I do answer them, we'll have a whole host of other problems to worry about.

It keeps coming back to, 'I don't know much. I've only met her once or twice.'

Half a dozen times Phoebe echoes the same thing. 'What a coincidence she lives here! Corfu of all places. You need to find out how this came to be!'

I could explain a lot of it, but the truth is a strange line that I keep falling off. I still can't tell her I was found here, so it's not that much of a coincidence after all.

Chapter 59

We meet Melodie and half of Anton's family at The Waves Taverna. Last week I had to own up to my previous visit there, when Melodie asked how I had found out where she lived. It was an awkward revelation, but nice not to lie for a change. She knew exactly the couple I described, saying her grandparents would often spend their holiday avoiding them, because once they got talking, they never stopped. Which I can imagine is true from the amount I got from them in such a short time.

That's one less secret to weigh me down.

We got lost on our way to Waves. Well, my parents did. I tried to tell them the way, but Baba was being stubborn and Sebastian was weighing in. I didn't want him to know all about my last visit here, so I kept my mouth shut and let them get on with it.

The taverna is exactly as I remember it from last year. The deep-blue sun loungers are scattered about as people angle themselves to follow the turning of the sun. It's still early in the season, but people are napping under books or walking down to the sea to feel the tingle of the salt on their skin. I need that. To take a moment to find some peace in the sea. Soon. Not today, though, that's for sure.

We make polite introductions to Anton's family before we take up our menus.

'Are we having starters?' Anton's nephew, Tom, asks. I remember him from Easter. He's maybe my age. Handsome with a strong jaw.

'Yes!' Melodie and I say in unison.

Everyone looks up from their menus with furtive glances.

Melodie narrows her eyes at me, but the twitch of her lips looks like she might giggle. She says, 'The courgette balls–'

'Yes!' I reply, 'They're so good!'

'My favourite!'

'Mine too.'

We grin at each other for a moment before Tom cuts in. 'Oh yeah, you had them at the wedding. They were mint. Totally having those!'

Sebastian grips my hand. He came here under sufferance. Not for my sake, but to save face with my parents. I told him he was personally invited by them. I added that Melodie and Anton were desperate to meet him again too, as I've told them so many wonderful things about him. This helped, of course. The most important things to Sebastian are being adored and his cars.

Two of Anton's brothers are here with him, Akis and Marty. Tom is Marty's son.

As we order and starters arrive, I catch Tom looking at me several times. Perhaps he's wondering how I can look so much like his auntie. My intuition tells me it's more than that, and if Sebastian weren't glued to my hand, Tom might like to strike up more of a conversation with me.

Sebastian's actually being very helpful. He keeps telling stories about his cars or the strange people he meets at work. His stories are all in Greek, because he's not very good with languages. He always says, *that's what the staff are for*. But I think he struggles, so he refuses to try. For someone who works in hospitality, this is almost unheard of. So many people speak many languages, but not him. He can afford for it to be someone else's problem. The stories are a good distraction though, keeping the subject matter light and slowing conversation with translating.

Gaia, Anton's daughter, seems to be an interesting character. I'd like to find out more about her. She's shot Sebastian some looks that make me think she's about as keen on him as Melodie, who's been doing a terrible job of hiding the fact she's trying to work out every word he has to say. Watching her watch him has made bubbles of laughter rise up inside me a few times. I've had to play it off as laughter at whatever current story has been underway. I hope I'm not so obvious as Melodie. She's as see-through as the air around us.

Now it's Gaia's turn to talk. She speaks perfectly in English, leaving me to quietly translate for Sebastian, who tells me he understands even when I'm sure he doesn't.

'Did Melodie tell you how she found your mother?' Gaia pushes some feta around her plate.

This is not a topic I want to stay on. Thankfully, it's in English, which Sebastian won't admit he doesn't understand. I don't think he can anyway. I can't be sure. His head is angled like he's taking it all in, but his face isn't screaming shock, more a polite interest.

'She did. You have a great memory for faces.'

'You all look so alike. In some ways you look more like Liliana than Melodie, with your colouring.' She points a finger at her own hair set on the top of her head in a messy bun. I think if I had seen you first, I would have realised right away.'

'Do you know where the toilets are?' I have to change the subject before I run into a problem and Sebastian asks me to translate. Gaia points me in the right direction.

Sebastian smiles up at me and releases me from his grasp. Only now I feel I can breathe. Sweat is beginning to form under the weight of my hair on my back.

Tom stands, and says, 'Too much of this Corfu cider.' He grins at me. 'Nice though.' He follows on behind me towards the toilets. 'I've only tried lemon. What's the orange one like?' He walks with what the English call *swagger*. There's something about the way his shoulders move under his polo shirt.

'I'm not sure. I have never had the orange drink. Do you like the lemon?'

'Yeah. I like it.' Tom's accent is heavy, not as much as the accent of his grandfather, Chris, but heavy enough for me to have to concentrate on his words. The Greenwood men are from the county of Essex, in England. Anton's mother is Greek. They told us how they met here many years ago. The men talk with a brash twang and sometimes quite quickly. It's interesting. I like hearing the different accents. Essex is a county near London, I think. Anton is the only one who speaks English with a soft Greek accent, but he is also the only one who lives here.

The bathrooms are unisex. I don't normally feel awkward about this, but something about the way Tom tries to keep up a lively conversation leaves me feeling strangely shy. Once I'm out of the bathroom and washing my hands, he looks at me in the mirror and tells me I have a problem.

'A problem?'

'Yeah.' He turns on the tap. 'Big one, too.'

Carefully I dry my hands at the dryer.

Tom raises his voice over the hum, 'You seem to have some loo roll on your heel.'

My face screws up in thought. *Loo roll... heel?* It hits me. I lift my long black skirt and look at my foot. A white tail grows from the back of my foot.

We share laughter about it, and compare mildly embarrassing stories as we make our way back to the table. He goes on to tell me he's thinking of moving to Corfu.

'Would you recommend it? Living here?'

'How can I? I've never lived anywhere else.'

'Yeah, but would you want to?' He leans in with a cheeky tone to his voice as we move towards the table. My nerves prickle as Sebastian looks up at us.

'No.' It's true that I want to travel and see the world, but this is my home.

As I sit down next to Sebastian, he pulls me in for a lingering kiss. His hand grips mine tighter than before, and a crushing sensation brings heat to my cheeks. My hand still hasn't fully recovered.

When I look up, Anton's mother, Athena, and my mama are putting the world to rights while people tuck into their meals all around me. The medley of fresh thyme and garlic reminds me of childhood feasts. It's strangely soothing. I wish Agatha and Ria could be here with us. I scan the faces; everyone looks calm and happy, all except Melodie. She looks like someone has spent the past half an hour pinching her cheeks. Her nose is wrinkled, and her breath is measured as she takes the smallest bite from her mixed grill.

Anton has noticed too, as I see his mouth move at her ear. 'Are you okay, Melodie mou?'

She nods and smiles, but I'm sure something's not right. She presses her phone to light up the screen before letting it fall dark again as she takes another small bite of food.

I do my best to engage in one of the many conversations around me, until Melodie excuses herself to use the toilet.

After less than a minute, I excuse myself too, and follow her. As I slip through the saloon-style doors to the toilets, I call to see whether she's okay.

'Melodie? Are you okay? I am sorry to follow you in here, but you were looking a bit red in the face, and I was worrying for you.'

'Yes, I'm fine.' Her voice squeaks from behind a door.

The door unlocks and she smiles as she passes me to wash her hands. For a moment we look at ourselves in the mirror to replace the awkwardness of staring at each other. Or, at least, that's why I'm looking in the mirror.

Melodie's dress is clinging to her more than before. The flowers that are scattered over the fabric are getting watered from sweat.

'Are you okay, Dora? I see you were getting on with Tom.'

I let out a delighted exhale. It's hard to deny that the attention of a handsome man isn't appealing, even if it does make me miss Dinos more. It would be nice to have another friend. It's not as though I can tell her about Dinos. I tuck a strand of hair behind my ear as I think of him. I think he would get on well with Tom.

'He is a nice man. I had toilet paper on my shoe. He saved me from embarrassing myself.'

'How do you think Sebastian is finding us all? I hope bringing everyone wasn't too off-putting?'

'No, of course not! I love big family celebrations.'

'And Sebastian?'

'Yes. He is Greek. He loves family.' I turn the tap on to wash my hands. There's no need to, other than the desire to wash my hands of Sebastian perhaps.

'Marty is thinking of moving back here. I know Tom is thinking about it, too. If he does, maybe you could show him around Corfu Town or something. It would be nice for him to know people his own age.'

Melodie suddenly grips the sink and hisses through her teeth. The image of her doubled over at Easter flashes past my eyes. This is worse though. I can see her stomach tighten under her dress.

'Melodie, these are contractions. We must get you to hospital.'

I shake my hands to dry them, then wipe them on my skirt. There's no time to stand at a dryer now.

'I'm fine. I'm fine now.'

'No, you're not. Here, take my hand.'

As we make our way back to the table, Melodie grips my left shoulder and my left hand with her left hand. I don't let on how much this hurts still. She's not holding that tight after all. Just enough to make me want to wince.

Anton jumps up, leaving his chair to drop to the floor like a stone as soon as he sees her.

Suddenly it's all movement, picking things up to put them down again. Meals are abandoned and people are talking over one another about cars and keys. Anton takes Melodie from me and I barely have a chance to say good luck before she's gone.

I know the next time I see her, everything will be different. She'll have a baby to think of. I just hope I'll be able to see her again soon.

Chapter 60

I am a theía. I never thought I would be a theía, unless it was by marriage. Why would I, without siblings?

Now, I've gained a sister and a niece. I suppose I'm a step-theía to Gaia too. I hadn't thought about that until Lily was born. That's my niece's name. I haven't met her yet. Lily. Named in honour of Liliana, our mother. I've seen a photo of a tiny round face and tuft of hair. Her eyes were closed, and she was wrapped in a blanket.

In the shop we sell some elegant dreamcatchers with white feathers and a bright blue evil eye at the centre. I asked for them to be stocked and they've been popular each season since. I pick one out and pay for it before putting it in a bag to one side for baby Lily.

A smiling family come in, and storm around the shop. The buzz of summer is edging in nicely. If only I didn't have everything hanging over me. I can't exactly ask to be next in line to see Lily, and even if I did, I can't now drop everything on Melodie and ask her to keep my fake adoption a secret. She's a new mother, she'll have enough to deal with.

My phone buzzes just as a young couple come up to the counter in matching black shorts and concert T-shirts. They place down a handful of items, mostly crisps, and add a packet of hemp flowers. The couple look giddy. I don't bother to point out the hemp is low in THC and unlikely to get anyone stoned. It's still not legal to sell the heavy stuff, but so many tourists get excited seeing this next to the counter still. I can't bear the smell even before it's lit.

My phone buzzes again, then three times more. A queue begins to form at the counter. I carry on with my work, ignoring the jiggle of my phone. I offer a bag, scan, take the payment, and repeat, as my phone carries on its merry little dance in my jeans pocket.

Eventually the shop falls quiet again and I look at my phone. There're messages from almost everyone, Mama, Baba, Agatha, Ria in one group chat, then separately Melodie. It's Melodie's message I gravitate to first.

Hi! How's things? I'd really love to introduce you to Lily soon, if you're free. It would be easier if you could come to ours, but we can meet somewhere else if you'd prefer. Xx

Even with a new baby in her arms, she's still thinking about me and what I might prefer. I'm confident she'll be alright keeping our secret, and as long as no one questions her face to face, I think it'll be fine. I'm not convinced she could lie even if she wants to.

She might say the lie, but surely no one would believe her. Her expressive face could tell a story without her so much as opening her mouth.

Before replying to Melodie, I open the stream of messages in the family group chat and scroll back to the first one from Theía Agatha.

I've had an email from Maria Karagiannis asking for a meeting about the Keres baby and the breach of trust with Theadora.

From there it's a barrage of questions resulting in a screenshot of the email and a decision that's hingeing on me being available tonight for a family meeting. Quickly I let everyone know that I'll be there. Maria never replied to my email, but clearly she had received it. We thought maybe they'd all gone to junk, and we had got away with it.

A film of sweat gathers on my top lip and around my hairline. What have I done? What if Agatha and Ria get found out? I'm an adult now, surely it shouldn't matter. I'm not held captive. I shake my head and hiss out at my phone.

'Kalomina!' A bright voice calls before disappearing between shelves.

'Kalomina!' I call to the faceless voice as the customer rustles around the shop.

I look back at my phone and return to my message from Melodie.

I would love to meet Lily. I'm not working tomorrow. If you are free? X

A reply comes within minutes telling me she'd love to see me, and I should come when I like. I'm a theía now just like Agatha, and I wonder how it felt for her when I came into her life. Not the same as this. Mama stole me and caused stress and paperwork. Becoming a theía for her was probably more traumatic than anything else she's done out of choice. It was a situation she was forced into, though, Ria too. Mama wouldn't let me go, so she told me up at the castle. My very existence has held them against a wall at knifepoint for almost twenty years.

I hope I can be as kind to Lily, and Gaia too, as they have been to me. Agatha and Ria didn't need a blood connection to look after me, nor did Mama and Baba. And now it's the same for Gaia and Lily. I walk away from the counter, something I try not to do when I know someone will soon need to be served, but I look at the dreamcatchers again. I pick out a similar one in white and beige for Gaia. She is just as important to me as Lily.

Chapter 61

Over and over, we churn through the three lines of the email. A meeting has been booked with Maria to see Agatha in her office at the Children's Community Home and farm next week.

It's a bit like whirling on a spinning top until it makes you want to vomit. One person says, 'What do you think she'll say?' Agatha or Ria go through the possibilities or say they don't know, then each possibility is scrutinised. *How was the paperwork filled in all those years ago? Could it have been lost in digitising? Why would she look into this? Is she just upset that Agatha told the story of one child to her niece?* Round and round we go to the smell of warm oregano and melting cheese as a moussaka heats up in the oven.

'I have some other news,' I announce. I have to because I can't stand hearing these details one more time and watching the wide eyes of my mother and her sister as they share in a duet of blind panic. 'Melodie has asked me to meet Lily tomorrow. I've decided that if we can find a moment to talk, I will tell her about the birth certificate. We need to know we can trust her, she knows who I *really* am. She might be telling people without knowing the harm it could cause. I can't keep holding everything in. If we know she won't tell people I was born in Corfu and that I am the found *Keres* baby, we all have one less thing to worry about.'

Silent glances circle the room now. An alarm sounds making everyone inhale in unison. Mama's phone is on full volume and she'd set a timer so that she wouldn't forget the dinner.

'I trust you, Theadora, and Melodie and Anton, they seem like good people.' Mama turns off her phone and disappears into the kitchen.

'I think this is the right choice too.' Baba studies my face. 'Would you go back and do the DNA test again, knowing all that's happened?'

I know what the answer is without thinking. Taking a moment, I scratch at the back of my neck. I don't want them to see how easy it is for me to answer this. It's a yes. I want it to all work out, but I want to keep my sister now I have her.

'I think so. Knowing that at least one of my parents didn't choose to throw me away like a dead cat, and gaining a sister... I don't want any of this pain for us, but I'm sure we will get through it. It would be impossible for the charity that runs the community home to prove I am the Keres baby now anyway, wouldn't it? I'm an adult. I don't have to share anything with them.' I lick my lips to prepare myself. 'I know it's dreadful, but I've been thinking something.'

When I'd paid for my second dreamcatcher in the shop, other than the one person in there, I didn't have another customer for almost thirty minutes. It gave me time to think in a new direction. It's a direction I know Mama and Baba won't like and I'm reluctant to suggest it.

I thought of Gaia, and how I thought she was Melodie's child when she wasn't; that started me off. As always, my mind had drifted towards Dinos when it shouldn't have. I thought about how Dinos looks nothing like his mother, and a lot like his father. It's the same with his sister too. They have the same colouring. She's attractive but still distinctly looks like their father.

'My birth certificate say I am yours. Both of yours. What if Mama had an affair with Melodie's father, so we have the same father but different mothers?'

Mama rests on the doorframe to the kitchen, holding a tea towel in her hands.

'You said I was adopted because of the shame of the affair, even thought I wasn't adopted. The charity could never prove anything else; there's no DNA that they have access to.' I turn to Agatha. 'Can't you blame someone in Athens? If paperwork is missing or wrong, it doesn't mean it was your fault? You may have got some paperwork wrong, but it was so long ago you hardly remember, even if you remember taking me to Athens.'

'I remember most of the children.' Agatha shrugs, looking at the floor, talking to her feet more than to me. 'But this could work. I spend more time thinking about what's good for the kids than the paperwork I have to do. What do you think?' She scans the others in the room for reassurance.

'It's brilliant. I don't know why we didn't think of it sooner.' Ria's serious face doesn't match her words.

'We've all been too focused on being caught out.' Baba folds his arms over his chest.

'I was raped.' Mama says this with such authority I almost fear she's telling the truth. It takes me a moment of looking at her to see she means this is her sticking point on the story. 'It will only work if it was rape. No one would believe it was an affair. Dinner's ready now. We have time to work out the details. Well done, Theadora mou.' With that she turns towards the kitchen and without another word we follow on like lemmings.

I didn't want to say to her that I've spent so much of the past year or so hiding things from people that it's no wonder *I'm* the one to come up with a plausible lie.

Chapter 62

Another night in my childhood room unable to sleep. For a time I silently play the keyboard under my window, with only the clicking of the keys for company. I could put on headphones, but I rarely do when I feel this way. It would be too much to hear it instead of hearing it in my mind.

It has been decided. If Melodie agrees, the new story is that Mama was raped by Adam, my biological father. We won't be putting it in newspapers or stopping people in the street for them to hear about it. I will tell some of my friends, knowing they will tell friends and parents until everyone knows the secret but never relays it to us. It can become unspoken knowledge, just as my adoption has always been. People never bring it up; it has just been fact. It can be the case that my parents believed it kinder to let me think I was adopted than brought into the world with such sorrow. That will be the official narrative for now.

Other than that, Agatha will prepare for her meeting as best she can and play dumb as best she can.

I exhale hard and roll to my side. The cold corner of the pillow presses to my cheek and is some relief on this warm night. My birthday is round the corner. I haven't told Melodie yet. Turning twenty now seems so insignificant.

Tugging at my sheets, I roll the other way, hoping that side will be cool now too. It's not. I sit up and flip the pillow before flopping down again.

Creaks echo in the empty landing then I hear the click of a light coming on in the bathroom. I'm not the only one unable to sleep tonight. I swing my feet over the side of the bed and tiptoe towards the door, waiting to hear the toilet flush. Eventually I hear it, soon followed by the door creaking open.

I peep around my door to see Mama about to switch off the light.

'Mama?' I whisper.

Mama's shoulder jolts upwards and her hands slap to her chest.

'Theadora, you terrified me. What are you doing awake at this ungodly hour?'

'Can't sleep.'

Mama wraps herself in her white cotton nightgown a little tighter before stretching her arms out to me.

Without even a glance at the photos I rush to meet her embrace.

'Shh, shh. It's all fine. We have each other. You have been worth every moment of worry and much more, Theadora mou. Much more.'

'Sure?'

'There's no doubt.'

She unravels me and holds me at arm's length, gripping my shoulders to look up at me. The light from the bathroom pours in from the half-closed door, leaving her in a strange shadow. My eyes have already adjusted to the blinding light from the darkness I came from. She squeezes my arms as she smiles at me.

'I'm proud of you, Theadora. I understand you needed to know where you came from. If you see the past, it can help you to see the future you want, and sometimes the one you don't want. We all need this. It's why I had to leave my parents in my past, for Agatha. I have the strongest feeling we'll all look back on this time and laugh about it over a bottle of retsina.' She stretches up and taps my left cheek. 'Get some sleep now. Tomorrow will be a long day.'

I stoop to kiss her cheek before she disappears towards the gentle sound of Baba's snoring.

I move into the bathroom. The day I took the test pops into my head. Almost two years ago now. If only I'd known what I was going to find.

Clutching the cold bowl of the sink, I lean close to the mirror, twisting my face this way and that. I wonder if Melodie and I are as alike on the inside as we are on the outside. I don't think so. I think she's a much better person than I could ever be. I suppose, at least, I could be worse. My father and my other sister have done things I could never do. At least that's something.

Now all I can do is hope for sleep and kindness from Melodie in the morning.

Chapter 63

In the shade of a lemon tree, Melodie sits in a chair holding a little bundle dressed in colours to match the fruit hanging over her head. Her wavy hair ruffles to one side and her long dress softly moves around her ankles as a breeze rolls past.

Gaia opened the door and showed me the way here to Melodie and Lily, explaining that her father was out getting food.

I don't know how she does it, but Melodie looks radiant even only a few days after giving birth. Her hair might be slightly messier than I've seen it, and she hasn't got the same amount of makeup as she usually does, but there's a graceful element that can't be denied, a serenity. A calming smile glows on her face in the dappled light beneath the tree. I hope I can be like her one day, although, as long as I'm with Sebastian, I won't have children. I push the thought away. I'll find a way to get away from him somehow. Dinos's face as I run from him replays over and over in my nightmare. His sadness is a knife to my throat.

I shake the thought away and focus on what's in front of me. I wonder what my mama looked like bringing me home. Was she terrified, or was she happy? Probably both.

There are some photos from very early on, perhaps when they took me away to pretend that I had been adopted abroad. I was only very small. Mama's eyes were always on me, never looking at the camera taking the pictures.

Gaia's a doting sister, it's obvious. As soon as we reach Melodie, she asks if she can help or if anything is needed before gently coaxing away the two fluffy cats whose names I can't remember. I think one's Morty. I'm not sure about the other.

'I'm so pleased you're here. Sorry I didn't answer the door. Lily was feeding. As you can see, she's sleeping again now.'

'That's all she's done,' Gaia adds. 'That and poo.' She pulls her mouth into a wide grimace and shakes her head making her dark hair flow over her shoulders.

'Come, sit.' Melodie indicates a chair beside her with a tip of her head.

A small cluster of metal chairs have been moved from around the table on the mosaic patio to the shade of the lemon tree. Other than the occasional wasp buzzing past, it's the perfect place to sit on a warm day in May.

I clutch my bag under my arm like a shield against the swell of emotions threatening to burst out of me. Only when I sit, and stare at the tiny round face of Lily, do I remember the real reason I'm clutching the big bag.

'Oh! I have gifts. This is for you, Melodie, and this is for Lily.' Melodie manages to balance Lily in the crook of her elbow, and opens the small box that I've passed her, wrapped in blue tissue paper – luxury olive oil body wash and moisturiser – and the dreamcatcher wrapped in white tissue paper. 'And Gaia, this is for you.' I pass her the gift, wrapped the same as Lily's to keep things fair.

'For me?' Gaia's jade eyes narrow and dart from Melodie to me. 'What have I done?'

'I have gained two nieces, not just one.'

A rose glaze brushes Gaia's cheeks.

'How thoughtful.' Melodie's eyes gloss with tears. She catches one as it rolls down her cheek. 'I'm so sorry. The slightest thing sets me off.'

They unwrap their gifts and gush about them. They're tokens, nothing more, but it's as though I've brought gold, frankincense and myrrh.

'Would you like to hold her, now you're settled?'

'Yes please.' I can't remember if I've ever held a newborn baby. I've held babies before, younger siblings of friends at school. But Lily, Lily is *so* young. Only a few days old. Her face is pink and her skin looks delicate and paper-thin. I haven't even seen her open her eyes yet. It's as though Melodie has been balancing a doll in her arms this whole time, whose eyes will remain closed as long as she's lying down.

Carefully Melodie stands to ease Lily into my arms.

She's so light, it doesn't even feel like holding a bag of flour, let alone a child. Lily squirms against me, stretching her body to its full length before curling back up and snuggling against me even more.

'She's beautiful, isn't she?' Still clutching her dreamcatcher, Gaia tiptoes to look at the baby's face in my arms.

'She's like an angel,' I agree, without taking my eyes off her to look up at Gaia. I'm transfixed by Lily's blushing skin and thick stubby black eyelashes. Her lips pout before she yawns, her mouth forming a tiny oval.

'I haven't even got you anything to drink yet!' Melodie thrusts her hands onto her hips and shakes her head. 'I'm not thinking straight.'

'It's okay.' I look up at her, smiling. 'How could you get me a drink? You've been holding Lily, and I've only been here five minutes.'

'I've sent Anton to get us all something nice to eat. It won't be anything homemade. I haven't had the time, and to be honest, I'm not the best baker. I should have tried to do something. Sorry about that.'

'You've just had a baby! Look at you! I cannot believe anyone could look so glamorous after having a baby.'

'I don't feel glamorous in the slightest. I have the biggest knickers on,' she whispers to us, then blushes. 'I wouldn't have even managed to wash my hair if it wasn't for Gaia and Anton. Ah! We have fresh lemonade. Anton put some in the fridge. Would you like some?'

Even if I didn't, which luckily I do, I wouldn't be able to say no. Melodie's face has lifted at the thought of being able to offer me something wholesome and homemade. It would be impossible to crush her relief.

'That would be lovely.'

Melodie leaves me with my two nieces. Gaia's still smiling as she pulls round one of the chairs to watch over us. She must be about fifteen, closer to my age than Melodie.

'What's it like to have a stepmother?' I flick my eyes towards Gaia.

She slumps back and crosses one leg over the other.

'I don't think I'd like to say for everyone. We are all so different. But I suppose if everyone had a stepmother like Melodie, they would probably be pleased with the idea. She's the mother I never got to have. Not that it's my mother's fault that she passed away. But I do feel lucky to have Melodie. She makes my dad happy, and I know she'd do anything for me. And now I've got a gorgeous baby sister. How can I complain?'

'Was it strange at first?'

'Yes and no. I didn't know she was going to start seeing my dad when I met her, and I liked her. When I realised they were dating, I guess that made it easier. I had already made my judgment on her and thought she was a nice person, so I guess it made sense that Dad thought she was a nice person too.'

Melodie reappears, balancing a tray with a jug of lemonade topped with ice, along with three glasses, and she remarks on the fact that Gaia and I haven't switched to speaking Greek in her absence. I hadn't even given it a thought. She puts the tray down on the patio table and fills each glass. When she returns, she places my drink on a chair next to me. There's no way I can risk taking a drink while holding Lily. I'm too frightened of dropping it on her, or worse, dropping *her*.

Gaia jumps up and announces she needs to put the dreamcatcher away before someone spills sticky lemonade on it. There's a distinct look of accusation in Melodie's direction that seems to go completely unnoticed, before Gaia jogs towards the house.

This is my chance, and I don't know how long I have. At least their house is big. Hopefully Gaia will take her time going up to her room.

'Melodie, I need to tell you something, and I'm afraid of what you might think.'

Clutching her glass, she slowly sits on the chair Gaia had been sitting on, so she's facing me directly. Her face crumples like a tissue.

'Okay.' She says this word as though it's a kilometre long. 'It's about who I am, about my past.'

Chapter 64

Gaia bounds towards us, scoops up the drink Melodie left for her and gulps it down before wiping her mouth with her thumb. It's only then that she takes us in. I'm confident I'm not giving much away, as I've redirected my focus to Lily, who's beginning to squirm in my arms. It's Melodie who can't contain her face.

'What's happened?' Gaia's tone is dark and defensive.

'Nothing, nothing.' Melodie's tone is too light, too breezy. Too obvious.

Lily squirms, her eyes briefly open before she makes a sound like a hungry cat. She stretches out and another sound vibrates. This one's much lower and leaves her nappy a lot warmer on my arm than before.

'Theadora, do you want to help me change Lily?'

No. Surely no one wants to help change a baby?

Melodie's eyes are narrowed on me, and Gaia's too. I feel as though I've been turned on, and now I'm beginning to doubt my ability to tell the truth. If they're angry when I haven't said anything yet, how will they feel when I ask them to lie for me?

'Gaia,' Melodie continues, 'can you set some plates out ready for when your dad's home with the food?'

Gaia nods and turns on her heels, glass still in hand, to skulk off towards the kitchen.

Melodie moves towards me to wriggle her fingers under Lily's armpits. She places the baby on her shoulder while making noises and saying comforting words in a high-pitched voice. It makes no difference. Lily's mouth stretches into the biggest O it can form and wails about the tragedy of filling her nappy in public.

'We can talk in Lily's room,' Melodie says, as I snatch up my drink and take a few deep gulps. My throat's dry and scratchy as though I've forgotten to drink for weeks. It's only a short glass, so I quickly finish it and follow Melodie towards the house. We skirt the kitchen where Gaia is emptying a dishwasher and putting out plates in a pile. We pass the long wooden dining table and come to the stairs at the front of the house.

'You'll like Lily's room. Won't she? Hey? Dora will like your room, won't she?' Melodie bounces up each step to soothe the now very red-faced Lily.

As we get to the top, a large sepia photo of a woman and Anton holding a child comes into view. It must be Gaia's mother; they have a similar mouth. I wonder how Melodie must feel with her watching over everything she does each day. It's nice for Gaia though, to be able to see her there, assuming my guess about it being her mother is right.

As we step into the baby's room, my mouth opens and a small gasp comes out.

'I know. Tom painted it while he was here. The house seems so empty without everyone here. Although, Athena and Chris will be back in a couple of weeks. They're getting everything ready to buy a house they've seen.'

Melodie's still talking and Lily's still squawking, but everything's muted compared to the mural on the wall. A rainbow like no other has been spread across the sky and into the sea. The remaining walls are a simple clean, buttery yellow to frame the cot.

'I recognise this place.' I point at the mural as Melodie lays Lily on a pale lemon and white changing table.

'It's Agios Stefanos.'

'Of course, it is. Tom did this? Marty's son, Tom?'

'Uh huh. Talented, isn't he?'

'Very talented.'

His use of colour and lines has left the rainbow and the sea with a dreamlike quality. I've never seen anything like it.

'What did you want to tell me?'

Melodie straps a small lion rattle wristband onto Lily and it's enough to confuse her into a lesser cry. Lily's arms move as if someone else is controlling her and she has no idea what might happen next.

'I need to ask you a favour, one I pray you'll agree too.'

I shake my fingers out. They tingle, as though the blood passing through them is full of itchy feathers.

Melodie's eyes flick from me to the dirty diaper she's dealing with. 'You can ask.'

I lick my lips and hope I get these words right. 'My parents didn't adopt me. It would have been impossible. It's a very long story, but they took me when they were not allowed. If anyone finds out who I really am, my family could be destroyed.'

This is the first time since meeting her that I can't tell what Melodie's thinking. She stutters over some words then asks me to hold one moment while she quickly finishes up with Lily. She gives nothing away. After the briefest furrowing of her brows, she set her face to neutral and it hasn't budged since. Maybe she could keep a secret if she really wanted to.

Anton announces his arrival downstairs just as Lily is fully dressed again.

'Wait here.' Melodie points at the floor where I'm standing as though I'm a puppy being trained. She clutches Lily to her chest with the other hand.

Melodie leaves the room and the wooden stairs creak as she descends. My heart is pounding. I'm frightened to move from the spot she so clearly pointed at. Our fate is in her hands now. My whole life, my family's lives, could fall between her fingers.

Footsteps rush back up the stairs and towards the door. Melodie comes back into the room, her hands free of Lily, and closes the door.

'Sit down and start again.' There's a big squishy-looking cream armchair in the corner of the room with a rainbow cushion on it. Doing as instructed, I take a seat. It's even softer than it looks. Like being cuddled by a cloud. Melodie hitches up her flowing dress and carefully kneels on the floor in front of me.

'Dora, if you want something from me, I need one simple thing from you. The truth. All of it.'

So, I give it to her. I go over it all and in much more detail. As much as I can manage while finding the right English words. I tell her about Mama and the miscarriages and her dreams about me, then not being able to let go when I was there in her arms. I tell her about how they hatched a plan so Mama and Baba could keep me. That Mama registered me as her own and how they all went together to the mainland to hide two lies. The first that I had been left with another facility for abandoned babies, and the second that Mama and Baba were adopting me in Romania. Then of course there is the fact I didn't know the truth. Not until recently, not until the DNA test turned my peaceful life on its head. Then little by little my family had to share it all with me. Or at least I hope this is all of it. I even tell her about my stupidity in calling the Children's Community Home about it, all because I was worried about my parents lying to me. Everything spews out of me like mushroom spores that linger unseen in the room as I fall silent waiting for her response.

'That's not what I expected.' She inhales a deep breath before puffing it out. 'But Anton has said a few times how he was surprised your parents managed to adopt you so easily. He's like a dog with a bone when things don't add up.' She shakes her head before running her fingers through the ends of her long wavy hair. 'He's very perceptive. I also think he's on edge about sisters who lie to me.'

'I've wanted to tell you the truth, and this is something that can only hurt me, not you.'

'True, but you haven't met Evangelina. If you had been subjected to what she's capable of you might understand why he's so cautious. Why we all are. I'll tell you more about her one of these days.'

'What I really need is to change my story. Would you agree to a lie about me? One that could keep my family safe?'

She presses her fingertips into the centre of her forehead as though she's pressing something to it.

'Yes, with two conditions.'

'Anything!'

'Firstly, we all have to agree to the lie. That includes all of Anton's family. I can't answer on behalf of them. It's unlikely they will ever need to tell the lie, but still.' She flips her hands up and presses her lips together.

'And the second of the conditions?'

'If I ask you a question, you promise to tell the truth.'

Relief is so brilliant it's like the sun has come out after a storm to cleanse my skin. I nod in agreement. This is the best possible outcome.

But the question she asks in a soft voice is not what I expected.

'Dora,' she says, 'has Sebastian ever hurt you?'

Chapter 65

I stutter and my body reacts, twitching to hold in the truth that has to come out. It only delays the inevitable. Melodie wants the truth, and I've promised it. But how do I word it? After a few more glottal stops, a word brings itself to the forefront. The only one I can possibly say.

'Yes.' The three-letter word does its best to hide itself and shelter in a whisper, but it's out none the less.

Melodie slaps her thigh with a hard, clapping sound. Her eyebrows lower over her eyes, making them dark slits.

'I knew it. I'll kill him!' She grits her teeth, her mouth twisting. Her fingers twitch like they're ready to claw him to death.

'No, you can't! Please! You ask for the truth, and I'll give it to you from now until I die if I have to, but, but—' My English leaves me as my brain can't keep up with the scramble for words. 'You don't have the right to interfere with all of my life. Please! I'm begging for help. You know the truth about me being the Keres baby. If you don't help and you are happy to tell people the truth about me, I understand. But you will destroy us! And if you hurt Sebastian, *he* will destroy us.'

Melodie falls still. Her hands flop on her legs and her eyes soften. Her face, which had been racked with anger, now alters as her head shakes.

'W–what?'

I swallow and suck in a measured breath before I can find the words in the language required.

'I am his. He says he will hurt my family if I hurt him. With everything my mama and baba have done for me, I can't let this happen. I can't.'

Tears swell and cloud my eyes and Melodie makes a shushing sound like she might to Lily. I press my hand over my face to cover myself, to hide from everything that's been sitting under the surface for so long.

The weight of Melodie's arms coiling around me is enough to make my heart jump.

'We'll figure it all out. He won't hurt you anymore,' she whispers, as I crumple into her kindness. 'I know I'm not Greek, but I really think I should feed you now.'

I laugh so hard I dribble on Melodie's shoulder.

'*Sygnómi*! Sorry!' I pull away from our embrace and wipe first her shoulder and then my face. She opens a cupboard door under the changing table and pulls out a box of tissues, passing them over to me.

'God, don't worry about it. Have you seen this dress? Look.' She pulls her hair to one side then twists. 'Lily spat up on my shoulder and it looks like a bird pooed all down me. I'm worse than a pirate with a parrot.' Her eyes roll. 'Honestly, Lily likes to do much worse!'

We laugh together while I blow my nose and wipe my eyes. Her reassurance is what I need. She's my sister, but it wasn't until right then, for the very first time, that I really felt like she was my sister. Not a woman with a face that makes us look like bookends, but my real sister. Someone who doesn't care if I accidently spit on them, someone who will help me out. After the rollercoaster of the past two years, finally I can see a light at the end of it all.

To say I feel welcomed into Melodie's home is far below an understatement. Melodie, Anton and Gaia lay out enough food to rival Mama and Baba's table. We all sit at the long dining table. Anton and Gaia aren't blind; they can see my puffy eyes and they've been sheepish while setting out dips and cakes.

Melodie says, 'This is now a family meeting. Dora needs our help. Instead of keeping a problem secret, she's come forward and asked for our help and I would like for you both to listen to what she has to say and to decide what we should do.'

I go over it all again, and this time Melodie asks me to add in the lie they think people will believe if they ever come asking for the truth. I explain: the lie is that my mother was raped by our father, Adam, making us half-sisters.

'I suppose it's believable, with Evangelina out there. He might have other children.'

'I can't get my head around why our mother wasn't allowed to keep me, or you, but Evangelina he accepted.'

Anton shakes his head. 'The problem is, people like us can't understand the inner workings of someone like that. We all try to rationalise, but it never works. Look at Evangelina. Melodie did everything to make her welcome, but all she wanted was Melodie's money at any cost. I could never understand this.'

'I guess you're right,' I sigh. How could I be related to such unhinged people?

'Right.' Melodie sits straight in the chair. 'Before our younger daughter needs feeding again, Anton, Gaia, what do you think? Can you support Theadora's idea and protect her family's secret?'

'I don't like lies, but there are lies and there are lies. This seems more like a bulletproof vest. You put it on and hope no one shoots you.' Anton rolls up the sleeves of his shirt and tilts his head.

'Should I take that as a yes?'

'Yes,' he chortles.

'Gaia?'

Gaia looks me over, her eyes narrow like a beam.

'Why did you take the DNA test in the first place? You were left for dead, why would you want to know the parents who did that to you?'

'Gaia!' Anton taps his fork twice on the side of his plate to gain her attention.

'It's alright. I can easily answer. When I first bought the test, I thought I had been left in an orphanage in Romania. When I found out that wasn't the case, it didn't stop me from wanting to know my heritage. In fact, it made me want to know more. I was born in Corfu, what if I was part Greek? I had no idea where

I was from. I've always felt so... disjointed. I thought knowing where my blood line came from might help me.'

Gaia purses her lips. 'Okay. Well, I think the lie is good enough. If anyone asks me, I can tell it if I need to.'

Anton nods over a mouthful of cake.

'Good! That settles it,' Melodie announces. 'I'm confident the other Greenwoods will understand too. I'll speak to Athena and Chris when they're back. Something like this is better face to face. I think we need to tell them the other problem now.' Melodie links her hands together on the table, but before we can start, Lily begins to cry.

Chapter 66

After spending time listening to me and reassuring me, and stuffing me with food, we are now all sitting on thick brown leather sofas drinking strong coffee, and I have a cat purring at my side.

This is a house much like my own, one built in love and support. Somewhere along the way I've stopped seeing it in my own home. The love and support my parents have brought me over the years. Not that it's stopped me wanting to protect them as much as they've wanted to protect me. They hid things from me thinking they could protect me, and I've been doing the same stupid thing to them about Sebastian. Being here and talking to Melodie has made me see this for myself. I know how much damage their secret has caused; I don't want my secrets about Sebastian to cause damage too.

After pausing to feed Lily, Melodie comes back with a rectangle of paper in one hand, and Lily curled in the other arm.

'Take a look at this.' She passes the paper to me, 'It's not much, but it's what I have.'

'What is it?' As soon take it I recognise the smiling face and the bright blonde hair. 'That's our mum and dad.'

Gaia reaches her arms out towards Melodie, stretching and scrunching her fingers open and closed until Melodie slips Lily into her arms.

Carefully, Melodie settles next to me on the sofa.

'They look happy,' I muse.

It's true, they do. Sitting at a table in a restaurant with wine and smiling faces. Liliana's hair was closer to Melodie's colour back then. Adam, our father, had my blonde hair. I don't know what I imagined, but this wasn't it. He was handsome and unassuming. Sort of jolly looking.

'Yeah. Looks can be deceiving, can't they? That angelic looking man stole that young girl from her family, and left you for dead. Come to think of it, he left me crying in a pram alone in a house. Thing is Theadora, I don't want you to be her. Smiling to the world but afraid. Your parents don't want that either. They've come this far for you to be happy, not for you to give your life away to someone who doesn't see how wonderful you are. You should be cherished. We will defend whatever truth keeps you and your family safe.'

'Of course,' Anton pipes up from the armchair.

'It's your life, and if you choose Sebastian, we will be here for you. Blimey, this isn't what I expected for today. Doesn't matter though. Family is family.'

'Thank you. I'm so sorry I've put this on you all.' I press my lips together not wanting to say what I need to next. 'And Evangelina... Do I need to worry about her?'

'We all need to worry about her,' Gaia mutters under her breath.

Melodie shoots her a look, her eyes narrowing to a point. Gaia ignores her, keeping her eyes on her baby sister instead.

'What Gaia means is,' Anton leans forward, his elbow resting on his knees, 'she is dangerous. I know Melodie has shared this much with you. She drugged Gaia, ran me off the road before tricking me and rolling me off down a hill... that's without all the lies. But,' Anton lowers one eyebrow, 'this is the one time this is helpful.'

'Helpful?' Melodie turns her pointed look on him now.

'Yes, Melodie mou. Think. She's a liar. Everyone knows she is all lies. Even if she turned up today telling the truth, why would people believe her over us?'

Melodie's eyebrows shoot up and she turns to me waggling her finger. 'He has a point. And to be honest, I don't see her coming back any time soon. She has too much to lose. If she showed up tomorrow, we'd send the police after her for attempted murder. We've done our best to avoid thinking about it all since it happened. With Lily on the way we didn't really want all the negativity, but I'm pretty sure she's on some wanted list.'

The cat next to me stretches and swivels onto its back to present its soft tummy, waiting to be tickled.

'So, this is it then? You'll keep my family secret, and Evangelina is not to be trusted. Now I need to hope my Theía Agatha isn't already in trouble because of my stupidity. Then I have to figure out what to do with Sebastian.'

'I know it really isn't my place, but seeing as I've spent half the day dishing out advice whether you like it or not, I may as well continue.' Melodie twists in the seat to face me head on. 'I *really* think you need to tell your parents about Sebastian. I wish I still had Grandmama and Grandpapa to talk to. Don't let him be the thing that fractures your family after all you've already been through. You're their responsibility, not the other way around. If he is threatening them as well as you, I think they have a right to know, and you can decide as a family what to do about him.'

'I think you're right. Thank you. Thank you for everything. I suppose I best, what is it the English say? Face the music?'

This brings a smile to Melodie's mouth, but a sadness in the depths of her eyes.

'You sound like Grandpapa, that's what he would've said. Before you go, there's one more thing I need to talk to you about.'
**

After saying my goodbyes, I had every intention of going straight home. Straight to find out what has happened with Agatha and to tell Mama and Baba all about today, and maybe all about Sebastian too — about how unhappy I am when I'm with him and how he has threatened the family, and the business.

Instead, I've stopped at Taste Me to sit with a coffee and admire the view. The perfect V carved into the land frames the sea beyond. The breeze tosses my hair over my face leaving golden strands in my eyes. I push it back as the air falls still again.

I try to replay Melodie's face, with the expressions she gives to the world, unable to hide a thing. Although, as I found out, not everything. I haven't asked how old she is. I must. I would guess her early thirties, but there's a strange delicate innocence that makes her seem much younger. In some ways I feel like I've hardened over the past two years. I've lost some of my shine, some of my innocence. Meeting Melodie has changed my life in more ways than I could've dreamed. Good and bad. I think of the last thing she said to me, even though I want to push it away. I shake my head and focus on what I need to do instead. There's no point dealing with that quite yet.

I pick up the cup and hold it under my nose as I inhale the bittersweet liquid and watch a flock of birds fly past. They're free from the strange worries and dynamics that only humans can invent. We seem to be able to find new and interesting ways to hurt each other all the time, and even when we love each other deeply, we still manage to fall at hurdles that shouldn't even exist.

I think of Mama and Baba. All they ever wanted to do was adopt me and look after me. I'm so glad the laws have changed now and it's an accessible option for many children and parents, but back then... I sip the hot liquid and close my eyes to try to stop the stinging in them. I pray to god, my foolishness hasn't hurt this family.

Please, god, if you are there, let everything be okay with Theía Agatha. If it is, then I'll never keep anything important from my parents again. I'll speak to them about anything important. I open my eyes to catch a bright lime Cleopatra butterfly opening and closing its wings on the rail in front of me.

If I'm not going to keep secrets, that means I have to tell them about my dislike of Sebastian, and why. If all is fine with Agatha, I'm going to tell him it's over. Today. We will stand up to him as a family. No matter what he might throw at us.

Chapter 67

By the time I'm outside my front door, it's the middle of the afternoon. Melodie and Anton put out such a wonderful spread of food for the *elevenses*, as Melodie called it, that lunch wasn't required. I'm not sure if people would normally eat both, but I don't think they should. Not if it's normally so large.

Konstantinos passes me in his car heading towards the sea. Sebastian must be meeting him there. In his good morning message, he told me he would be meeting Konstantinos in the village to drive round together. He knew I was going to see Melodie and spend time with my family today.

Ria's car is in the drive. Usually they come in Agatha's car, not Ria's. My fingers tingle on my steering wheel as fear touches my extremities.

Why is Agatha not here?

I park carefully next to Ria's car and jump out. Each step I take pounds as hard as my heart in my chest as I reach our bright yellow door. Its sunshine colour is too happy. Garish compared to how I feel.

I push the door open, expecting there to be a wall of sound. Crying and wailing, moans of sadness. There's nothing. Not a cicada in the room to fill it with sound.

'*Kalispera*. Mama? Baba? Ria?'

A door creaks upstairs. 'Theadora?'

'Theía Agatha?'

'Theadora!' Agatha bounds down the stairs towards me, feet hitting the floor like roaring thunder before grabbing me and pulling me into a tight embrace that makes my eyes feel like they might bulge out of my head.

'You're here? I thought something bad might have happened. You never bring Ria's car.'

'I was too shaky to drive. Come, everyone's outside.'

She steps away but I catch her arm.

'No, I need to know what happened. I need you to tell me.' My voice catches in my throat.

Agatha nods, and her features soften. 'I think Maria knows the truth, or, she doesn't believe our story. Doesn't believe your email was a prank.' There's a coil in my stomach like a tape worm that wants to eat me alive at this thought. 'But she nodded along like it was true before leaning in towards me,' Agatha leans forward, acting it out, 'and quietly saying, I trust you, Agatha. I always have. What I know is that you would do anything to give these children the best life they can have. At any cost. Then she sort of pressed her lips together in this knowing look. And that was it. No mention of action, only compliments for my good work over the years and how we must celebrate twenty-five years soon enough.' Agatha giggles then blows out a breath like she's blowing up a balloon. 'Now you, how did it go with Melodie?'

'They will keep our secret. They will tell any story we need them to. Any at all, but they think the lie that Adam raped Mama would be believable.'

'Then we are free again?'

'Almost...' I think of Sebastian. I can't be free until I'm away from him. An urgency itches at my feet like the desperate urge to run. 'I need to do something. I won't be long. Tell everyone it went well, and I'll explain more when I'm back.' I kiss Theía Agatha's soft cheek.

'Are you okay?' She holds onto my arm.

'I will be.'

Chapter 68

I run. Faster than I've ever run. My feet hitting the pavement in bounds, I bolt towards the sea.

Sebastian said he would be with Konstantinos, and I saw his car coming this way. Without Sebastian's car being race-ready yet, they've spent the past few days driving up and down together in one car. I think Konstantinos has been trying to impress girls since things never worked out with Xristina.

My thumb hits hard on my phone, as hard as my feet on the ground, to call Sebastian. It rings and rings, but there's no answer. I have to do this while I'm feeling brave enough. After what Melodie told me, I don't feel like Sebastian could hurt us the same.

Lots of Melodie's words flood past my eyes as I pass shops with people spilling out into the road in front of me.

Don't let your story be like our mother's. You do have a choice, and hopefully this will help you make that choice...

I try again and again to call him to find out exactly where he is. Nothing.

My lungs burn as I pass shops and tavernas and finally reach sight of the harbour with its row of multicoloured boats. I stop outside the Old School Taverna, hands on knees as I heave in hard breaths, each one more painful than the last. The recognisable drone of a sports engine, with one of those fancy oversized exhausts, begins to vibrate in my chest along with the juddered breath. Konstantinos, it has to be.

I stride into the road next to the roundabout, and toward his car, waving my arms. His tyres screech to a stop. Along here, he can't be going fast, there's too many people. Besides, what would be the point? Then no one would see him posing in his car.

He stops and I skirt round the car and thrust my head in the tinted window, expecting to find Sebastian, but he's not there.

'Where is Sebastian?'

'*Kalispera*, Theodora. Can you get your head out of my car?'

'Where is he?'

Konstantinos shifts in his seat and shrugs. 'He's your boyfriend. Why don't you know?'

'He said he was with you.'

'Yeah, well, he's not.'

'Where is he then?'

'I don't know, and I don't care.' He glances from me to the road and bites his lip. 'Why don't you try your favourite spot? Don't you both like hanging about down there?' He nods towards the curve of the bay and the rocks. 'Now get out of my car,' he barks.

Was he like this at school? Or just since hanging out with Sebastian? I don't remember him always being so mean.

I stagger back, my chest still unsettled from the running. Sweat drips down my spine in the afternoon heat. Without another thought, I set off running again, this time in the road to avoid people on the footpath where it narrows. It's not too far, but it's an incline and one I'm not used to running. As I reach the stairs down to the sea, I pause to catch my breath.

I need to be calm. I need to get this right.

My hands are clammy and I can only imagine how red my face must be. I wipe my hands on my top. Another green Cleopatra butterfly dances past me and lands on a bush by my side. It's now. It has to be now.

Slowly, I move down through the trees and past a frozen lizard, towards the cactus where Sebastian had tried too hard to carve our names, and instead carved his hand. I round the corner, and there he is looking out to sea on the rocks. He lies down, and I freeze. Shock twists into laughter that tickles and twists on its way out, a manic sound piercing the air like an arrow heading towards him.

Towards them.

They both look round in shock at my crazed laughter. It's hard to contain myself. I try to calm myself as I move out of the shadows of the trees and towards them, but it feels impossible.

'So, this is why you've been avoiding me,' I call out.

Xristina staggers to her feet. Her hair is messy and her lips look a little raw.

'Theadora, it's not what it looks like. We were...' She struggles for words as she adjusts her top to make sure it looks presentable. All she's done is pull the already low neck even lower. Sebastian, outside of the initial shock, calmly turns to face me. He hops down from the rock as Xristina scrambles to pick up her things and continues to tidy herself. I want to tell her she's welcome to him, but I wouldn't want to inflict him on anyone, even a friend who's just stabbed me in the back.

Sebastian steps forward and cups my face in his hand.

'I'm sorry, my pure princess, this won't happen again. A man has needs, you know. And I can't save myself for you forever. Once we are married, it will be different.' His mouth is so close to my face that I can smell Xristina's perfume on his skin and his breath burns my already hot face.

'You're right about one thing. It won't happen again. We're finished.' The words hold such clarity it's as though I've cut a rotten umbilical cord with a hard crunch. 'Oh,' I lower my voice, 'and I was never your pure princess. I've had boyfriends before you, you know.' I pull my face from his hands and step back. A smugness at winding him up makes me feel like I'm glowing. 'You're welcome to him, Xristina. You've done me a favour. Although,' I call over my shoulder as I turn to walk away, 'I think you could do a lot better, Xristina.'

Pain shoots through my arm as Sebastian yanks me back. As he whips me round, I raise my hand and slap him across the face as hard as I can.

'If you ever touch me again', the words throb out of me as he clutches his face in shock, 'you will live to regret it!' Then I lean in and spit the words, 'If you live at all', under my breath.

'I'm more than happy to make sure your family business is destroyed for this. Your reputation too.' The smug tone in his voice is enough to make me stop.

'*My* reputation? Mine? I'm more than happy to share the story of my sprained fingers, or how you've treated me and the threats you've made. There's nothing you can do to hurt my family. We are strong. If you care about your reputation, you best leave us alone. You can go back to your hotels with their beautiful views across the real life here in the villages. Sit in your tower on your hill, ideally as far away from me as possible. Try to destroy us and you'll only make yourself look more of a fool than you already are. Xristina is my witness to your behaviour, and it's her reputation in the balance now, and yours, so leave me alone. I tell you what, you can go ahead and tell everyone this ended amicably. That is my gift to you both for disappearing from my life. I pity the girl foolish enough to marry you.'

I move on. Physically and mentally.

'You're not worth it anyway, whore.'

As I walk away, I'm surprised my legs can hold my weight. Everything has turned to jelly. I have to make it home. If I make it home, everything will be okay.

Chapter 69

I walk home a lot slower than I came into the village. Everything around me feels different. A cool breeze eases my skin and people nod and say, *Yassou*. It's like the world has opened up again, the same way I felt each time we came out of lockdown. Hope rises up and enriches the world. I hope it can last.

I quicken my pace, excited to tell my family everything that's happened. At last, I can leave the burden of lies behind. I hope I can. I hope I can let them go. Seeing the photo of Liliana and Adam in that restaurant was a warning about my life, a much more extreme one, but Melodie is right, I don't want my life to go that way, not even slightly. Who really knows how Liliana's and Adam's relationship went sour; was it something as apparently small as him grabbing her hand too hard? Was it the little things before it was the big things? What threats did he make? Liliana told Melodie that Adam said her family never wanted her anyway and didn't even look for her. She began to believe all the poison he fed her. Liliana never told her family about Adam. If she had, if she had even said his name out loud to them, maybe they could've found her, and done something to rescue her. It makes me realise just how bad it is to hide things from the ones we love the most. If I stayed with Sebastian, would he have done that to me? Stopped me from seeing my family? It was bad enough the lies that began to gnaw at the roots of our tree. Never again. That much I've learnt. Ask questions and don't hide the truth. It might be painful, but it's worth it.

As I arrive at the sunshine yellow of our front door, I can already hear them out in the garden laughing, celebrating Theía Agatha's good news.

I slip in the unlocked door and into the home I've always known with the worn terracotta sofa and the squishy cushions. I pass through the kitchen with the table where we've celebrated every Christmas.

There's a single glass there with a bottle of open retsina next to it, condensation pooling around the bottom. I pick the bottle up, still icy from the fridge, and press it to my cheeks for some relief before glugging some into the glass.

As I appear through the double doors, glass in hand, everyone cheers and lifts their glasses.

'*Yamas*!' they cry in a crescendo and glasses slosh wine and the air fills with laughter.

Mama puts her glass in Baba's hand and rushes towards me, tears in her eyes. She pulls me in almost knocking the wine from my hand.

'My girl, Theadora mou! Thank goodness, we are saved!' She releases me and I switch the wine to my other hand and shake out my fingers. 'Agatha, Ria, saved! Agatha says Melodie agrees too. If it did come to anyone asking questions,' she whispers this part, 'she will hide what we did for us.'

Baba moves forward, kisses my cheeks and lightly pinches one before giving me a wink.

'She did,' I say. 'She agreed.'

Ria and Agatha embrace me too as they all buzz and squeal with delight.

'There were conditions though.'

The buzz dies down, heads tilt and arms fold across chests.

'She said Anton and Gaia had to agree too, which they have. She also made me agree to promise to tell the truth whenever she asked me a question.' I sip at the sharp liquid a little too quickly.

'And what did she ask?' Ria leans forward before joining me in a sip.

I snatch another, deeper sip to brace myself.

'She asked... she asked if Sebastian had ever hurt me.'

I stare into my glass.

'And?' Baba's voice is demanding, like he wants to stamp his foot alongside it.

'You can tell us.' Ria uses the voice she must use on the children at the home. It's her normal voice but with the edges sanded down.

I look up into her deep eyes, dark as a black hole you could fall into.

'I said, yes.'

Baba erupts and storms towards the kitchen announcing that he will kill him, rip his tiny little head off, no one hurts his daughter! Mama grabs at his arms and wine drops to the ground.

'Stop!' I actually do stamp my foot. 'Stop!'

'It's over. I've broken up with him. Melodie made me see I should talk to you all about it, and here I am, so don't leave me now.' I turn away and place my glass down on the table under its parasol.

I don't want to cry again today. I nip my teeth on the end of my tongue in an attempt to hold it all back.

'When did he hurt you?' Agatha slides into a chair at the table as everyone, including Baba, crowds round me.

'Easter, my hand. That was the worst of it.'

'The hand someone stood on? He stood on it?' Baba growls.

'No. He, sort of crushed it in anger at meeting Melodie.'

'Why didn't you break it off sooner? Why would you stay with a man like that?' Mama lifts the glasses off her face and puts them in her hair before rubbing the bridge of her nose.

'Because I had to. He said if I left him, he would hurt our family, and we've all heard the rumour about George, his father. How he burned down that man's restaurant.' I glare across all their faces. I know they all know this rumour, everyone does. 'What if Sebastian did that to the shop? I couldn't let it happen. I've caused enough problems for this family, I couldn't cause another. It's only because I found out about Liliana and I didn't want to end up like her that I finally knew I had to end it. And Melodie gave me the confidence to do it, and to talk to you all. I don't want there to be any more lies.'

'Theadora,' Baba's thick grey eyebrows ruffle together, 'I can replace the shop. There's insurance for that. I can't replace you.' He pulls me in, and even though our height is a close match, I still feel like I'm a child again in his soft embrace. 'No more hiding things. We work everything out as a family.'

I nod into his shoulder before pressing my cheek to it.

'I want to be honest,' Baba says. 'I still want to kill him.'

I begin to laugh as I pull away and wipe a stray tear away from my eye.

'There's no point, it's over. I did slap him though,' I grin.

Baba pinches my chin. 'That's my girl.'

I slump down into the nearest chair.

'There's more I need to tell you all, something else Melodie said.'

Ria, Mama and Baba all find chairs around the table.

'When my grandparents in England died, they left Melodie a lot of money, and so did Liliana. She wants to gift me over £100,000.'

Choked laughter spills out of everyone, followed by raised glasses. At that, the celebration starts up all over again.

I feel as light and as bright as glitter sparkling in the sun. There's only one other person I want to see now. One other person who can make everything better than it already is.

Chapter 70

‖‖‖‖‖‖‖‖‖‖‖‖‖‖‖‖‖‖‖‖‖‖‖‖‖‖‖‖‖‖‖‖

It's a calm morning, one that promises to be warmer than a normal day in May. In a week I'll be twenty. For the first time, I'm actually excited about my birthday. Excited to start a new decade. I've asked for a small party, and Melodie said I could hold it in their garden if I wanted to. I haven't decided yet. Everything hinges on what happens now.

I love the peace of being up here again, with the sun on my cheek as it rises higher into the sky and the view across the trees rolling below. I could stay here forever. There's only one thing missing, but hopefully he'll be here soon.

The gate squeaks its familiar moan. I don't look up, because part of me can't even believe this meeting is real. Every nerve in my body is electric and the hairs on my arms stand on end.

Footsteps hit the dirt, slow and steady, until they reach me, and Dinos sits next to me on the wall.

'Seen any tortoises today?'

'None yet.'

We sit in a comfortable silence while I gather up words in my head like they're olives being harvested.

'I broke it off with Sebastian yesterday.'

'So, it's not just a rumour then?'

'You heard already? And you didn't say anything?' I nudge his arm.

'Your message to meet was all the confirmation I needed. That or you were bringing me here to tell me he hurt you again and I have to bury him.'

'No. I did slap him though.'

'Good.'

Our eyes meet for the first time. It's all I can do not to reach up and kiss him. I hold it back, instead enjoying seeing his face, his pale hazel eyes against his black lashes, and the mop of hair that needs a trim

'I've missed you,' he exhales.

'I've missed you too.'

I launch myself towards him, wrapping my arms around his neck, pressing my lips to his. I've caught him off guard, and we topple from the stone wall. Dinos manages to put out one arm and rolls me on top of him in one smooth movement as we hit the ground. His hands slip along my spine as our mouths meet for the first time.

My fingers move over his smooth cheek and weave into the silky springs of his hair. I want to inhale every part of him and never leave this moment. This feels so natural and it's never felt more ridiculous that we haven't spent our time doing this for years.

I pull back to look at him and smooth my hand over his face to check that he's real.

'However much I wanted this to be what happened today, I never imagined I could be right... or that you would knock me off the wall.'

I giggle and press my forehead to his. 'Yeah, I guess we should get up.'

Before we do, Dinos kisses me slowly, softly, his warm, velvet lips pressing into mine before letting me go. My heart aches for more and my entire body pulses with an energy like no other.

I stand and chuckle at the heap Dinos has ended up in. He sits up and points out our audience. 'Look, there's two of them.'

My gaze follows his, and I see two wild tortoises off on their own adventure in Corfu.

'Before we run off together,' Dinos chuckles as I pull him up, 'there's something important I need to talk to you about,' I lick my lips, readying myself to tell him everything.

'Oh yeah?'

He begins to brush the dust off his shorts, and I help, brushing my hand over his firm back and buttocks.

'Any excuse, Dora. Can't keep your hands off me now.'

'Shh!' I can feel myself blush, even though I know he's right. 'There's a lot I need to tell you. Come on, let's walk.'

Dinos's fingers naturally wind around mine. I look up at him, his messy hair and hazel eyes glistening in the dappled light of the trees.

'I went to see my sister again. She's actually really nice. It's pretty complicated, but I now understand why she shut the door in my face.'

Dinos grunts like he isn't sure.

'I know, I know, but hear me out. She wants to give me a gift.'

'I should think so after shutting a door in your face when you needed her.'

'A gift of over £100,000.'

'Bloody hell, does she want to shut a door in *my* face? Are you serious?'

'Yeah. It's sort of an inheritance from my English grandparents. Melodie insists I have something.'

'I'm happy for you.' He stops walking and pulls me close to him. 'I just want to hold you and never let go.'

I pull away and put my hands firmly on my hips. 'There's one big problem with that.'

Dinos narrows his eyes.

'How long do we wait to tell everyone without it looking like we've been together behind Sebastian's back?'

Dinos chuckles and pulls me in again. 'As long as I can see you, I can wait forever.'

'God, not that long, I hope. I *might've* already told my mama and baba.'

'I *might've* already told mine.'

'You haven't!' I look up at him and gently thump his chest.

'No, but I felt left out. Anna knows I like you. She's known for a long time though. She used to tease me about it.'

I don't know why, but this thought tickles me. It fills my chest with warmth that he couldn't hide the way he felt in the quiet safety of his home.

'What did they say?'

'Who?'

Dinos rolls his eyes. 'Your parents.'

'Oh! Well, it turns out they've always liked you, and never liked Sebastian very much. Apparently always saying that Sebastian comes from a good family was because they couldn't think of much else good to say about him. And there I was worried how they would feel if I dropped someone who, in their eyes, was such a good match.'

Dinos begins to laugh as I rest my ear to the top of his chest so that I can hear the rhythm of his body as it presses to mine. I close my eyes. Everything's falling into place.

'I know what I want for my birthday.'

'Oh yeah?'

'For us to be together.'

'That, I can do.'

I tilt my head back and Dinos gathers me up, pressing his mouth to mine. I could stand here forever with the delicate taste of mint from Dinos's tongue in my mouth. Dinos might be able to wait forever for me, but I don't think I could wait forever for him. I want to make him mine as soon as possible.

Epilogue

I'd never dated a friend before Dinos. I was so excited to be with him, I didn't think about what I could lose if we had got it wrong. If we jumped into one another's arms and it all fell apart. Today is the day we have decided to say goodbye.

I think back to my birthday, we held hands in public at my party in Melodie's garden. Dinos spoilt me with gifts that day, not in the way Sebastian used to – all money and no thought – but gifts whose detail was based on things he knows about me. Like, he got me a massage voucher, knowing how sitting at the counter in the shop all day hurts my shoulders.

At the end of the party, when it was all over and it was just Melodie's family and mine, she took me to one side and told me she had put the money into my bank account. A birthday gift. Apparently, she'd asked Mama for the account details.

That was months ago now, and so far, I haven't touched a penny of it.

Another good outcome from everything that's happened, is Sebastian is rarely seen in the village now. Even Konstantinos never mentions him. His threats ended as quickly as they started. I heard he's moved on to some poor girl even younger than me. I pity her.

Weeks after catching Xristina with him, she came up to me and told me he didn't want her anyway, not as a wife. I feel sorry for her, but we don't talk any more. She might've done me a favour, but she didn't help me on purpose. Being with someone of status was more important to her than to me, and if he had kept her around, that's exactly where she would've stayed. I don't need someone like that in my life.

Then there's Dinos and I. Even though everyone knows about us, we've still been meeting in our secret place regularly. Enjoying the peace, until now.

Today, we arrive together, in the same car. We're here again, high above Kassiopi, for our goodbye. We creak through the gate together and wander from place to place under the trees and past the gravestones. Our voices mirror each other in sadness. The dull tones of quiet loss.

Looking out over the carpet of green leading to the sea is a comfort. Somethings never seem to change, even if everything else has to. Looking back at the past few years, I barely recognise the girl I was when I started going out with Sebastian.

However much my heart throbs with loss today, I'm grateful for everything that's brought me to this point in my life. I'm stronger for everything that's passed. I'm better equipped to handle what happens next. The stars are always there, hiding behind the blue sky. They don't change. Only the way we see them changes and what we do with that information. There's some information I need to share today, and it might change everything, even the way we see the stars.

The sun isn't as high in the sky as it was in the summer months. Those long days gave me a lot of time to think, and now I need to find out what Dinos thinks of everything I've been storing in my head.

Conversation has flowed from the moment he picked me up this morning. We pass through every subject to avoid the inevitable. Our feet meander as much as the conversation as we pass lizards scuttling along the wall beside us and birds of prey circle higher into the sky.

Eventually I pluck up the courage to begin a conversation I've wanted to have for days. The problem is, I don't know where it will take us, and with *goodbye* around the corner, I guess it's now or never.

'I need to talk to you about something.'

'Oh yeah?' Dinos releases my hand and weaves his arms around my waist so we are standing gently pressed together, but with enough space to see each others faces. My hands automatically make their way around the back of his neck. My fingers gently trace the line of his hair, letting the short curls twist over my fingers.

'You know that money Melodie gave me?'

Dinos acknowledges this with an agreeable sound in the back of his throat.

'I know how I want to spend it now.' I snatch a breath and the words rush out of me with the air in my lungs. 'I want to travel. I need to see the world.'

Dinos's chin drops down before he turns his face away from me and looks out towards the sea in the distance.

'Good for you, Dora. You deserve it.' He smiles down at me with half his mouth, stopping to hold me. 'You really only deserve good things.'

'Is that right?'

I know he means it, but there's more overwhelming sadness in his voice than before, one I suppose I expected.

'Yeah, I'll miss you though.' He drags his eyes back from the sea and meets mine again. 'But I'll still be here, when I get back from conscription and you get back from your adventures.'

Dinos had his conscription delayed due to the pandemic, but there's no getting around it now. I want to stay here with him forever, in our place away from everyone else. Holding him and taking him in. Everything from his crumpled shirt, to the way his hazel eyes glitter almost amber in the sun.

'That's the thing,' I try to keep my voice level, 'I want you to come with me.'

His eyes widen and his eyebrows rise. 'Seriously?'

'Yeah, why? Don't you want to see the world with me?'

'More than you can imagine. I just don't think I can afford it, and I don't want you to pay for everything. I'm saving up for the new boat, for the new business.'

'Yeah, about that. Any chance you would go into business with me? I was thinking, I'm pretty good at English...' Dinos snorts at my faux modesty. 'Maybe you could oversee the fishing, and I could, I don't know... host?' I wrap my hands tighter around his neck, pulling him closer. 'Make the picnics? Make sure no one gets heatstroke? We could go halves on the boat. What do you think? Do you think you could do a little travelling when your conscriptions over? Call it a business trip while we plan for the future?'

Dinos curves to lean his forehead against mine, so I can see every detail of his smooth skin in minute detail.

'I love you, Dora.' His lips briefly find me. 'I love you. You're all I want. The idea of being with you every day, getting to work with you...' He kisses me again, his tongue briefly finding mine. Then he says into my mouth as we kiss, 'You're everything I could want.'

It might be goodbye, but not for long. Then soon, we have everything to look forward to.

FOUND IN CORFU

Thank you for reading 'Found in Corfu'

Thank you for reading Found in Corfu. I truly hope you have enjoyed Theadora's story. It is completely fictional but inspired by real places and history in Greece. I'd love to hear what you thought! Feel free to message me on socials or leave a review – I read them all!

Although my book is completely fictional, and the Children's Community Home is fictional, I like to make sure everything "could" be possible. There is a children's charity in Corfu that inspired the "what if" of this book. I have made a donation to the charity, if you would like to join me in supporting them, here is a link to their website:

https://www.hamogelo.gr/gr/en/houses/to-agroktima-mas-stin-kerkira/#:~:text=Our%20community%20home%20in%20Corfu,Smile%20of%20the%20Child%20®

(link was live when last checked in 2024)

About the author

FRANCESCA CATLOW loves to travel. Born and raised in the heart of Suffolk, Catlow has travelled extensively in Europe with her French husband and, more recently, their two young children. Of all the places she's been, it is the Greek islands that have captured her heart. She now splits her time between England and her home in France, where she spends her days writing and her evenings poring over books with her family of bookworms.

The Little Blue Door was Catlow's first novel – written during the lockdown of 2020 while feeding her newborn in the early hours. To stay up to date please visit www.francescacatlow.co.uk.

T: @francescacatlow
F: @francescacatlowofficial
I: @francescacatlowofficial
TikTok: @francescacatlow

For trigger warnings visit: francescacatlow.co.uk/triggerwarnings/

Also by

Printed in Great Britain
by Amazon